The Aleph and Other Stories
1933–1969

"As sharp as the knives brandished by outlaws. The violence that saturates the tales has a peculiar purity, as if it existed apart from the will of man.

"In a story called *The Meeting,* two youths start quarreling over cards. They are drawn to a cabinet containing the knives of famous duelists of the past. They fight, one is killed, the other breaks down in tears over his senseless deed . . . the knives, not their tools, the men—knew how to fight.

"In *The Challenge,* one gaucho slashes another, then refrains from the fatal thrust. 'I'm letting you live,' he tells his antagonist, 'so you'll come back looking for me again.' Life cannot be lived without the dignity of danger [and] there can hardly be a more powerful intimation of union through suffering than Borges' fiercely compressed parable *The Maker* . . . This 1958 work suggests Borges' own fate by invoking the life of the blind Homer."—**Time**

The
Aleph
and
Other
Stories
1933-1969

Together with
Commentaries and an
Autobiographical Essay

Edited
and translated
by NORMAN THOMAS
DI GIOVANNI
in collaboration
with the author.

A NATIONAL GENERAL COMPANY

THE ALEPH AND OTHER STORIES 1933-1969
*A Bantam Book / published by arrangement with
E. P. Dutton & Co., Inc.*

PRINTING HISTORY
E. P. Dutton edition published November 1970
2nd printing ..... January 1971
*Certain of the translations in this volume first appeared in the
following periodicals:*
BUENOS AIRES HERALD: *"The Intruder," "The Life of Tadeo
Isidoro Cruz (1829-1874)," "The Dead Man," "The Circular Ruins,"
"The Captive," "The Makers," "Borges and Myself."*
MUNDUD ARTIUM: *"Streetcorner Man," "Rosendo's Tale."*
The NEW YORKER: *"The Other Death," "The Immortals," "The
Man on the Threshold," "Ibn Hakkan al-Bokhari, Dead in His
Labyrinth," "The Two Kings and Their Two Labyrinths," "The
Challenge," "The Meeting."*
THE NEW YORK REVIEW OF BOOKS: *"Pedro Salvadores."*
The *"Autobiographical Essay"* first appeared as a NEW YORKER
profile.

Bantam edition published November 1971

*Grateful acknowledgment is made to Grove Press, publishers of
FICCIONES, for permission to make new translations of "The
Circular Ruins" and "Death and the Compass," and to the
University of Texas Press, publishers of DREAMTIGERS, for permis-
sion to retranslate "The Captive," "Borges and Myself," and "The
Maker."*

*Assistance for the translation of this volume was given by the
Ingram Merrill Foundation.*

Contents

Preface

Since my fame rests on my short stories, it is only natural that we should want to include a selection of them among the several volumes of my writings we are translating for E. P. Dutton. At the same time, one of our aims here has been to make available in English all my previously untranslated older stories, as well as to offer a sampling from my latest work in this form.

Perhaps the chief justification of this book is the translation itself, which we have undertaken in what may be a new way. Working closely together in daily sessions, we have tried to make these stories read as though they had been written in English. We do not consider English and Spanish as compounded of sets of easily interchangeable synonyms; they are two quite different ways of looking at the world, each with a nature of its own. English, for example, is far more physical than Spanish. We have therefore shunned the dictionary as much as possible and done our best to rethink every sentence in English words. This venture does not necessarily mean that we have willfully tampered with the original, though in certain cases we have supplied the American reader with those things—geographical, topographical, and historical—taken for granted by any Argentine.

We would have preferred a broader selection that might have included such stories as "Tlön, Uqbar, Orbis Tertius," "El jardín de senderos que se bifurcan," "Funes el memorioso," "La secta del Fénix," and "El Sur" from *Ficciones*, and "Los teólogos," "Deutsches Requiem," "La busca de Averroes," and "El Zahir" from *El Aleph*. However, rights to make our own translations of these stories were denied us, despite the unselfish and unswerving efforts of Dr. Donald Yates on our behalf.

The autobiographical essay and commentaries, prepared especially for this volume, were written directly in English.

J.L.B.

N.T. di G.

Buenos Aires, August 12, 1970

The
Aleph
and
Other
Stories
1933-1969

The Aleph

To Estela Canto
(1945)

O God! I could be bounded in a nutshell, and count myself
a King of infinite space. . . .

Hamlet, II, 2

But they will teach us that Eternity is the Standing still of the
Present Time, a *Nunc-stans* (as the Schools call it); which
neither they, nor any else understand, no more than they
would a *Hic-stans* for an Infinite greatness of Place.

Leviathan, IV, 46

On the burning February morning Beatriz Viterbo died,
after braving an agony that never for a single moment gave
way to self-pity or fear, I noticed that the sidewalk bill-
boards around Constitution Plaza were advertising some
new brand or other of American cigarettes. The fact pained
me, for I realized that the wide and ceaseless universe was
already slipping away from her and that this slight change
was the first of an endless series. The universe may change
but not me, I thought with a certain sad vanity. I knew
that at times my fruitless devotion had annoyed her; now
that she was dead, I could devote myself to her memory,
without hope but also without humiliation. I recalled that
the thirtieth of April was her birthday; on that day to visit
her house on Garay Street and pay my respects to her
father and to Carlos Argentino Daneri, her first cousin,
would be an irreproachable and perhaps unavoidable act of
politeness. Once again I would wait in the twilight of the

Jorge Luis Borges

small, cluttered drawing room, once again I would study
the details of her many photographs: Beatriz Viterbo in
profile and in full color; Beatriz wearing a mask, during
the Carnival of 1921; Beatriz at her First Communion;
Beatriz on the day of her wedding to Roberto Alessandri;
Beatriz soon after her divorce, at a luncheon at the Turf
Club; Beatriz at a seaside resort in Quilmes with Delia San
Marco Porcel and Carlos Argentino; Beatriz with the Pe-
kinese lapdog given her by Villegas Haedo; Beatriz, front
and three-quarter views, smiling, hand on her chin. . . . I
would not be forced, as in the past, to justify my presence
with modest offerings of books—books whose pages I finally
learned to cut beforehand, so as not to find out, months
later, that they lay around unopened.

Beatriz Viterbo died in 1929. From that time on, I
never let a thirtieth of April go by without a visit to her
house. I used to make my appearance at seven-fifteen sharp
and stay on for some twenty-five minutes. Each year, I
arrived a little later and stayed a little longer. In 1933, a
torrential downpour coming to my aid, they were obliged to
ask me to dinner. Naturally, I took advantage of that lucky
precedent. In 1934, I arrived, just after eight, with one of
those large Santa Fe sugared cakes, and quite matter-of-
factly I stayed to dinner. It was in this way, on these
melancholy and vainly erotic anniversaries, that I came
into the gradual confidences of Carlos Argentino Daneri.

Beatriz had been tall, frail, slightly stooped; in her walk
there was (if the oxymoron may be allowed) a kind of
uncertain grace, a hint of expectancy. Carlos Argentino was
pink-faced, overweight, gray-haired, fine-featured. He held
a minor position in an unreadable library out on the edge
of the Southside of Buenos Aires. He was authoritarian but
also unimpressive. Until only recently, he took advantage
of his nights and holidays to stay at home. At a remove of
two generations, the Italian "S" and demonstrative Italian
gestures still survived in him. His mental activity was
continuous, deeply felt, far-reaching, and—all in all—
meaningless. He dealt in pointless analogies and in trivial

4

scruples. He had (as did Beatriz) large, beautiful, finely shaped hands. For several months he seemed to be obsessed with Paul Fort—less with his ballads than with the idea of a towering reputation. "He is the Prince of poets," Daneri would repeat fatuously. "You will belittle him in vain—but no, not even the most venomous of your shafts will graze him."

On the thirtieth of April, 1941, along with the sugared cake I allowed myself to add a bottle of Argentine cognac. Carlos Argentino tasted it, pronounced it "interesting," and, after a few drinks, launched into a glorification of modern man.

"I view him," he said with a certain unaccountable excitement, "in his inner sanctum, as though in his castle tower, supplied with telephones, telegraphs, phonographs, wireless sets, motion-picture screens, slide projectors, glossaries, timetables, handbooks, bulletins. . . ."

He remarked that for a man so equipped, actual travel was superfluous. Our twentieth century had inverted the story of Mohammed and the mountain; nowadays, the mountain came to the modern Mohammed.

So foolish did his ideas seem to me, so pompous and so drawn out his exposition, that I linked them at once to literature and asked him why he didn't write them down. As might be foreseen, he answered that he had already done so—that these ideas, and others no less striking, had found their place in the Proem, or Augural Canto, or, more simply, the Prologue Canto of the poem on which he had been working for many years now, alone, without publicity, without fanfare, supported only by those twin staffs universally known as work and solitude. First, he said, he opened the floodgates of his fancy; then, taking up hand tools, he resorted to the file. The poem was entitled *The Earth*; it consisted of a description of the planet, and, of course, lacked no amount of picturesque digressions and bold apostrophes.

I asked him to read me a passage, if only a short one. He opened a drawer of his writing table, drew out a thick stack of papers—sheets of a large pad imprinted with the letter-head of the Juan Crisóstomo Lafinur Library—and, with ringing satisfaction, declaimed:

> Mine eyes, as did the Greek's, have known men's towns
>   and fame,
> The works, the days in light that fades to amber;
> I do not change a fact or falsify a name—
> The *voyage* I set down is . . . *autour de ma chambre*.

"From any angle, a greatly interesting stanza," he said, giving his verdict. "The opening line wins the applause of the professor, the academician, and the Hellenist—to say nothing of the would-be scholar, a considerable sector of the public. The second flows from Homer to Hesiod (generous homage, at the very outset, to the father of didactic poetry), not without rejuvenating a process whose roots go back to Scripture—enumeration, congeries, conglomeration. The third—baroque? decadent? example of the cult of pure form?—consists of two equal hemistichs. The fourth, frankly bilingual, assures me the unstinted backing of all minds sensitive to the pleasures of sheer fun. I should, in all fairness, speak of the novel rhyme in lines two and four, and of the erudition that allows me—without a hint of pedantry!—to cram into four lines three learned allusions covering thirty centuries packed with literature—first to the *Odyssey*, second to *Works and Days*, and third to the immortal bagatelle bequeathed us by the frolicking pen of the Savoyard, Xavier de Maistre. Once more I've come to realize that modern art demands the balm of laughter, the scherzo. Decidedly, Goldoni holds the stage!"

He read me many other stanzas, each of which also won his own approval and elicited his lengthy explications. There was nothing remarkable about them. I did not even find them any worse than the first one. Application, resignation, and chance had gone into the writing; I saw, however, that Daneri's real work lay not in the poetry but in his invention of reasons why the poetry should be admired. Of course, this second phase of his effort modified the writing in his eyes, though not in the eyes of others. Daneri's style of delivery was extravagant, but the deadly drone of his metric regularity tended to tone down and to dull that extravagance.*

Only once in my life have I had occasion to look into the fifteen thousand alexandrines of the *Polyolbion*, that topographical epic in which Michael Drayton recorded the flora, fauna, hydrography, orography, military and monastic history of England. I am sure, however, that this limited but bulky production is less boring than Carlos Argentino's similar vast undertaking. Daneri had in mind to set to verse the entire face of the planet, and, by 1941, had already displaced a number of acres of the State of Queensland, nearly a mile of the course run by the River Ob, a gasworks to the north of Veracruz, the leading shops in the Buenos Aires parish of Concepción, the villa of Mariana Cambaceres de Alvear in the Belgrano section of the Argentine capital, and a Turkish baths establishment not far from the well-known Brighton Aquarium. He read me certain long-winded passages from his Australian section, and at one point praised a word of his own coining, the color "celestewhite," which he felt "actually *suggests* the sky, an element of utmost importance in the landscape of the continent Down Under." But these sprawling, lifeless hexameters lacked even the relative excitement of the so-called Augural Canto. Along about midnight, I left.

Two Sundays later, Daneri rang me up—perhaps for the first time in his life. He suggested we get together at four o'clock "for cocktails in the salon-bar next door, which the forward-looking Zunino and Zungri—my landlords, as you

---

* Among my memories are also some lines of a satire in which he lashed out unsparingly at bad poets. After accusing them of dressing their poems in the warlike armor of erudition, and of flapping in vain their unavailing wings, he concluded with this verse:

But they forget, alas, one foremost fact—BEAUTY!

Only the fear of creating an army of implacable and powerful enemies dissuaded him (he told me) from fearlessly publishing this poem.

doubtless recall—are throwing open to the public. It's a place you'll really want to get to know."

More in resignation than in pleasure, I accepted. Once there, it was hard to find a table. The "salon-bar," ruthlessly modern, was only barely less ugly than what I had expected; at the nearby tables, the excited customers spoke breathlessly of the sums Zunino and Zungri had invested in furnishings without a second thought to cost. Carlos Argentino pretended to be astonished by some feature or other of the lighting arrangement (with which, I felt, he was already familiar), and he said to me with a certain severity, "Grudgingly, you'll have to admit to the fact that these premises hold their own with many others far more in the public eye."

He then reread me four or five different fragments of the poem. He had revised them following his pet principle of verbal ostentation: where at first "blue" had been good enough, he now wallowed in "azures," "ceruleans," and "ultramarines." The word "milky" was too easy for him; in the course of an impassioned description of a shed where wool was washed, he chose such words as "lacteal," "lactescent," and even made one up—"lactinacious." After that, straight out, he condemned our modern mania for having books prefaced, "a practice already held up to scorn by the Prince of Wits in his own graceful preface to the *Quixote*." He admitted, however, that for the opening of his new work an attention-getting foreword might prove valuable—"an accolade signed by a literary hand of renown." He next went on to say that he considered publishing the initial cantos of his poem. I then began to understand the unexpected telephone call; Daneri was going to ask me to contribute a foreword to his pedantic hodgepodge. My fear turned out unfounded; Carlos Argentino remarked, with admiration and envy, that surely he could not be far wrong in qualifying with the epithet "solid" the prestige enjoyed in every circle by Álvaro Melián Lafinur, a man of letters, who would, if I insisted on it, be only too glad to dash off some charming opening words to the poem. In order to avoid

ignominy and failure, he suggested I make myself spokes-
man for two of the book's undeniable virtues—formal perfection and scientific rigor—"inasmuch as this wide garden
of metaphors, of figures of speech, of elegances, is inhospi-
table to the least detail not strictly upholding of truth." He
added that Beatriz had always been taken with Álvaro.

I agreed—agreed profusely—and explained for the sake
of credibility that I would not speak to Álvaro the next day,
Monday, but would wait until Thursday, when we got
together for the informal dinner that follows every meeting
of the Writers' Club. (No such dinners are ever held, but it
is an established fact that the meetings do take place on
Thursdays, a point which Carlos Argentino Daneri could
verify in the daily papers, and which lent a certain reality
to my promise.) Half in prophecy, half in cunning, I said
that before taking up the question of a preface I would
outline the unusual plan of the work. We then said goodbye.

Turning the corner of Bernardo de Irigoyen, I reviewed
as impartially as possible the alternatives before me. They
were: *a*) to speak to Álvaro, telling him this first cousin of
Beatriz' (the explanatory euphemism would allow me to
mention her name) had concocted a poem that seemed to
draw out into infinity the possibilities of cacophony and
chaos: *b*) not to say a word to Álvaro. I clearly foresaw that
my indolence would opt for *b*.

But first thing Friday morning, I began worrying about
the telephone. It offended me that that device, which had
once produced the irrecoverable voice of Beatriz, could now
sink so low as to become a mere receptacle for the futile
and perhaps angry remonstrances of that deluded Carlos
Argentino Daneri. Luckily, nothing happened—except the
inevitable spite touched off in me by this man, who had
asked me to fulfill a delicate mission for him and then had
let me drop.

Gradually, the phone came to lose its terrors, but one
day toward the end of October it rang, and Carlos Argentino was on the line. He was deeply disturbed, so much so

that at the outset I did not recognize his voice. Sadly but angrily he stammered that the now unrestrainable Zunino and Zungri, under the pretext of enlarging their already outsized "salon-bar," were about to take over and tear down his house.

"My home, my ancestral home, my old and inveterate Garay Street home!" he kept repeating, seeming to forget his woe in the music of his words.

It was not hard for me to share his distress. After the age of fifty, all change becomes a hateful symbol of the passing of time. Besides, the scheme concerned a house that for me would always stand for Beatriz. I tried explaining this delicate scruple of regret, but Daneri seemed not to hear me. He said that if Zunino and Zungri persisted in this outrage, Doctor Zunni, his lawyer, would sue *ipso facto* and make them pay some fifty thousand dollars in damages.

Zunni's name impressed me; his firm, although at the unlikely address of Caseros and Tacuarí, was nonetheless known as an old and reliable one. I asked him whether Zunni had already been hired for the case. Daneri said he would phone him that very afternoon. He hesitated, then with that level, impersonal voice we reserve for confiding something intimate, he said that to finish the poem he could not get along without the house because down in the cellar there was an Aleph. He explained that an Aleph is one of the points in space that contains all other points.

"It's in the cellar under the dining room," he went on, so overcome by his worries now that he forgot to be pompous. "It's mine—mine. I discovered it when I was a child, all by myself. The cellar stairway is so steep that my aunt and uncle forbade my using it, but I'd heard someone say there was a world down there. I found out later they meant an old-fashioned globe of the world, but at the time I thought they were referring to the world itself. One day when no one was home I started down in secret, but I stumbled and fell. When I opened my eyes, I saw the Aleph."

"The Aleph?" I repeated.

"Yes, the only place on earth where all places are—seen

from every angle, each standing clear, without any confusion or blending. I kept the discovery to myself and went back every chance I got. As a child, I did not foresee that this privilege was granted me so that later I could write the poem. Zunino and Zungri will not strip me of what's mine—no, and a thousand times no! Legal code in hand, Doctor Zunni will prove that my Aleph is inalienable."

I tried to reason with him. "But isn't the cellar very dark?" I said.

"Truth cannot penetrate a closed mind. If all places in the universe are in the Aleph, then all stars, all lamps, all sources of light are in it, too."

"You wait there. I'll be right over to see it."

I hung up before he could say no. The full knowledge of a fact sometimes enables you to see all at once many supporting but previously unsuspected things. It amazed me not to have suspected until that moment that Carlos Argentino was a madman. As were all the Viterbos, when you came down to it. Beatriz (I myself often say it) was a woman, a child, with almost uncanny powers of clairvoyance, but forgetfulness, distractions, contempt, and a streak of cruelty were also in her, and perhaps these called for a pathological explanation. Carlos Argentino's madness filled me with spiteful elation. Deep down, we had always detested each other.

On Garay Street, the maid asked me kindly to wait. The master was, as usual, in the cellar developing pictures. On the unplayed piano, beside a large vase that held no flowers, smiled (more timeless than belonging to the past) the large photograph of Beatriz, in gaudy colors. Nobody could see us; in a seizure of tenderness, I drew close to the portrait and said to it, "Beatriz, Beatriz Elena, Beatriz Elena Viterbo, darling Beatriz, Beatriz now gone forever, it's me, it's Borges."

Moments later, Carlos came in. He spoke drily. I could see he was thinking of nothing else but the loss of the Aleph.

"First a glass of pseudo-cognac," he ordered, "and then

down you dive into the cellar. Let me warn you, you'll have to lie flat on your back. Total darkness, total immobility, and a certain ocular adjustment will also be necessary. From the floor, you must focus your eyes on the nineteenth step. Once I leave you, I'll lower the trapdoor and you'll be quite alone. You needn't fear the rodents very much—though I know you will. In a minute or two, you'll see the Aleph—the microcosm of the alchemists and Kabbalists, our true proverbial friend, the *multum in parvo!*"

Once we were in the dining room, he added, "Of course, if you don't see it, your incapacity will not invalidate what I have experienced. Now, down you go. In a short while you can babble with *all* of Beatriz' images."

Tired of his inane words, I quickly made my way. The cellar, barely wider than the stairway itself, was something of a pit. My eyes searched the dark, looking in vain for the globe Carlos Argentino had spoken of. Some cases of empty bottles and some canvas sacks cluttered one corner. Carlos picked up a sack, folded it in two, and at a fixed spot spread it out.

"As a pillow," he said, "this is quite threadbare, but if it's padded even a half-inch higher, you won't see a thing, and there you'll lie, feeling ashamed and ridiculous. All right now, sprawl that hulk of yours there on the floor and count off nineteen steps."

I went through with his absurd requirements, and at last he went away. The trapdoor was carefully shut. The blackness, in spite of a chink that I later made out, seemed to me absolute. For the first time, I realized the danger I was in: I'd let myself be locked in a cellar by a lunatic, after gulping down a glassful of poison! I knew that back of Carlos' transparent boasting lay a deep fear that I might not see the promised wonder. To keep his madness undetected, to keep from admitting that he was mad, *Carlos had to kill me.* I felt a shock of panic, which I tried to pin to my uncomfortable position and not to the effect of a drug. I shut my eyes—I opened them. Then I saw the Aleph.

I arrive now at the ineffable core of my story. And here

begins my despair as a writer. All language is a set of symbols whose use among its speakers assumes a shared past. How, then, can I translate into words the limitless Aleph, which my floundering mind can scarcely encompass? Mystics, faced with the same problem, fall back on symbols: to signify the godhead, one Persian speaks of a bird that somehow is all birds; Alanus de Insulis, of a sphere whose center is everywhere and circumference is nowhere; Ezekiel, of a four-faced angel who at one and the same time moves east and west, north and south. (Not in vain do I recall these inconceivable analogies; they bear some relation to the Aleph.) Perhaps the gods might grant me a similar metaphor, but then this account would become contaminated by literature, by fiction. Really, what I want to do is impossible, for any listing of an endless series is doomed to be infinitesimal. In that single gigantic instant I saw millions of acts both delightful and awful; not one of them amazed me more than the fact that all of them occupied the same point in space, without overlapping or transparency. What my eyes beheld was simultaneous, but what I shall now write down will be successive, because language is successive. Nonetheless, I'll try to recollect what I can.

On the back part of the step, toward the right, I saw a small iridescent sphere of almost unbearable brilliance. At first I thought it was revolving; then I realized that this movement was an illusion created by the dizzying world it bounded. The Aleph's diameter was probably little more than an inch, but all space was there, actual and undiminished. Each thing (a mirror's face, let us say) was infinite things, since I distinctly saw it from every angle of the universe. I saw the teeming sea; I saw daybreak and nightfall; I saw the multitudes of America; I saw a silvery cobweb in the center of a black pyramid; I saw a splintered labyrinth (it was London); I saw, close up, unending eyes watching themselves in me as in a mirror; I saw all the mirrors on earth and none of them reflected me; I saw in a backyard of Soler Street the same tiles that thirty years before I'd seen in the entrance of a house in Fray Bentos; I saw bunches of grapes, snow, tobacco, lodes of metal, steam; I saw convex equatorial deserts and each one of their grains of sand; I saw a woman in Inverness whom I shall never forget; I saw her tangled hair, her tall figure, I saw the cancer in her breast; I saw a ring of baked mud in a sidewalk, where before there had been a tree; I saw a summer house in Adrogué and a copy of the first English translation of Pliny—Philemon Holland's—and all at the same time saw each letter on each page (as a boy, I used to marvel that the letters in a closed book did not get scrambled and lost overnight); I saw a sunset in Querétaro that seemed to reflect the color of a rose in Bengal; I saw my empty bedroom; I saw in a closet in Alkmaar a terrestrial globe between two mirrors that multiplied it endlessly; I saw horses with flowing manes on a shore of the Caspian Sea at dawn; I saw the delicate bone structure of a hand; I saw the survivors of a battle sending out picture postcards; I saw in a showcase in Mirzapur a pack of Spanish playing cards; I saw the slanting shadows of ferns on a greenhouse floor; I saw tigers, pistons, bison, tides, and armies; I saw all the ants on the planet; I saw a Persian astrolabe; I saw in the drawer of a writing table (and the handwriting made me tremble) unbelievable, obscene, detailed letters, which Beatriz had written to Carlos Argentino; I saw a monument I worshiped in the Chacarita cemetery; I saw the rotted dust and bones that had once deliciously been Beatriz Viterbo; I saw the circulation of my own dark blood; I saw the coupling of love and the modification of death; I saw the Aleph from every point and angle, and in the Aleph I saw the earth and in the earth the Aleph and in the Aleph the earth; I saw my own face and my own bowels; I saw your face; and I felt dizzy and wept, for my eyes had seen that secret and conjectured object whose name is common to all men but which no man has looked upon—the unimaginable universe.

I felt infinite wonder, infinite pity.

"Feeling pretty cockeyed, are you, after so much spying into places where you have no business?" said a hated and jovial voice. "Even if you were to rack your brains, you couldn't pay me back in a hundred years for this revelation. One hell of an observatory, eh, Borges?"

Carlos Argentino's feet were planted on the topmost step. In the sudden dim light, I managed to pick myself up and utter, "One hell of a—yes, one hell of a."

The matter-of-factness of my voice surprised me. Anxiously, Carlos Argentino went on.

"Did you see everything—really clear, in colors?"

At that very moment I found my revenge. Kindly, openly pitying him, distraught, evasive, I thanked Carlos Argentino Daneri for the hospitality of his cellar and urged him to make the most of the demolition to get away from the pernicious metropolis, which spares no one—believe me, I told him, no one! Quietly and forcefully, I refused to discuss the Aleph. On saying goodbye, I embraced him and repeated that the country, that fresh air and quiet were the great physicians.

Out on the street, going down the stairways inside Constitution Station, riding the subway, every one of the faces seemed familiar to me. I was afraid that not a single thing on earth would ever again surprise me; I was afraid I would never again be free of all I had seen. Happily, after a few sleepless nights, I was visited once more by oblivion.

Postscript of March first, 1943—Some six months after the pulling down of a certain building on Garay Street, Procrustes & Co., the publishers, not put off by the considerable length of Daneri's poem, brought out a selection of its "Argentine sections." It is redundant now to repeat what happened. Carlos Argentino Daneri won the Second National Prize for Literature.* First Prize went to Dr. Aita; Third Prize, to Dr. Mario Bonfanti. Unbelievably, my own book *The Sharper's Cards* did not get a single vote. Once

---

* "I received your pained congratulations," he wrote me. "You rage, my poor friend, with envy, but you must confess—even if it chokes you!—that this time I have crowned my cap with the reddest of feathers; my turban with the most *caliph* of rubies."

again dullness and envy had their triumph! It's been some time now that I've been trying to see Daneri; the gossip is that a second selection of the poem is about to be published. His felicitous pen (no longer cluttered by the Aleph) has now set itself the task of writing an epic on our national hero, General San Martín.

I want to add two final observations: one, on the nature of the Aleph; the other, on its name. As is well known, the Aleph is the first letter of the Hebrew alphabet. Its use for the strange sphere in my story may not be accidental. For the Kabbalah, that letter stands for the *En Soph*, the pure and boundless godhead; it is also said that it takes the shape of a man pointing to both heaven and earth, in order to show that the lower world is the map and mirror of the higher; for Cantor's *Mengenlehre*, it is the symbol of transfinite numbers, of which any part is as great as the whole. I would like to know whether Carlos Argentino chose that name or whether he read it—applied to another point where all points converge—in one of the numberless texts that the Aleph in his cellar revealed to him. Incredible as it may seem, I believe that the Aleph of Garay Street was a false Aleph.

Here are my reasons. Around 1867, Captain Burton held the post of British Consul in Brazil. In July, 1942, Pedro Henríquez Ureña came across a manuscript of Burton's, in a library at Santos, dealing with the mirror which the Oriental world attributes to Iskander Zu al-Karnayn, or Alexander Bicornis of Macedonia. In its crystal the whole world was reflected. Burton mentions other similar devices—the sevenfold cup of Kai Kosru; the mirror that Tariq ibn-Ziyad found in a tower (*Thousand and One Nights,* 272); the mirror that Lucian of Samosata examined on the moon (*True History,* I, 26); the mirrorlike spear that the first book of Capella's *Satyricon* attributes to Jupiter; Merlin's universal mirror, which was "round and hollow . . . and seem'd a world of glas" (*The Faerie Queene,* III, 2, 19)— and adds this curious statement: "But the aforesaid objects (besides the disadvantage of not existing) are mere optical instruments. The Faithful who gather at the mosque of Amr, in Cairo, are acquainted with the fact that the entire universe lies inside one of the stone pillars that ring its central court. . . . No one, of course, can actually see it, but those who lay an ear against the surface tell that after some short while they perceive its busy hum. . . . The mosque dates from the seventh century; the pillars come from other temples of pre-Islamic religions, since, as ibn-Khaldun has written: 'In nations founded by nomads, the aid of foreigners is essential in all concerning masonry.' "

Does this Aleph exist in the heart of a stone? Did I see it there in the cellar when I saw all things, and have I now forgotten it? Our minds are porous and forgetfulness seeps in; I myself am distorting and losing, under the wearing away of the years, the face of Beatriz.

Streetcorner Man

To Enrique Amorim
(1933)

Fancy your coming out and asking me, of all people, about the late Francisco Real. Sure, I knew him, even though he wasn't from around here. He was a big shot on the North-side—that whole stretch from the Guadalupe pond to the old Artillery Barracks. I never laid eyes on the guy above three times and these three times were all the same night. But nights like that you don't forget. It was when La Lujanera got it in her head to come around to my shack and bed down with me, and Rosendo Juárez took off from the Maldonado for good. Of course, you're not the kind that name would mean much to. But around Villa Santa Rita, Rosendo Juárez—the Slasher we called him—had a reputation for being pretty tough. He was one of don Nicolás Paredes' boys, the same as Paredes was one of Morel's gang, and he'd earned respect for the way he handled a knife. Sharp dresser too. Always rode up to the whorehouse on a dark horse, his riding gear decked out with silver. There wasn't a man or dog around didn't hold him in regard—and that goes

18

for the women as well. Everybody knew he had at least a couple of killings to his name. He'd have on one of those soft hats with a narrow brim and tall crown, and it would sit there kind of cocky on his long thick hair he wore slicked straight back. Lady luck smiled on him, like they say, and around Villa all us younger guys used to ape him even to the way he spit. But then one night we got a good look at what this Rosendo was made of.

All this might seem made-up, but the story of what happened that particular night starts when this flashy red-wheeled buggy—jamful of men—comes barreling its way down those hard-packed dirt roads out between the brick kilns and the empty lots. Two guys in black were making a big racket twanging away on guitars, and the driver kept cracking his whip at the stray dogs snapping at the legs of the horse. Sitting all quiet in the middle was one guy wrapped in a poncho. This was the famous Butcher—he'd picked that name up working in the stockyards—and he was out for a good fight and maybe a killing. The night was cool and welcome. A couple of them sat up on the folded hood just like they were parading along some downtown avenue in Carnival. A lot more things happened that night, but it was only later on we got wind of this first part. Our gang was there at Julia's pretty early. This dance hall of hers, between the Gauna road and the river, was really just a big shed made out of sheets of corrugated iron. You could spot the place from two or three blocks off either by the red lamp hanging out front or by the rumpus. Julia, even though she was a darkie, took trouble to run things right—there was always plenty of fiddlers and good booze and dancing partners ready to go all night. But La Lujanera—she was Rosendo's woman—had the others all beat by a mile. She's dead now, and I can tell you years go by when I don't give her a thought anymore. But in her day you ought to have seen her—what eyes she had! One look at her was enough to make a man lose sleep.

The rum, the music, the women, Rosendo with that rough talk pouring out of his mouth and a slap on the back for each of us that I tried to take for a sign of real friendship—the thing is, I was happy as they come. I was lucky too. I had me a partner who could follow my steps just like she knew ahead of time which way I was going to turn. The tango took hold of us, driving us along and then splitting us up and then bringing us back together again. There we were in the middle of all this fun, like in some kind of dream, when all of a sudden I feel the music sort of getting louder. Turns out it was those two guitar pickers riding in the buggy, coming closer and closer, their music getting mixed up with ours. Then the breeze shifted, you couldn't hear them anymore, and my mind went back to my own steps and my partner's, and to the ins and outs of the dance. A good half hour later there was this pounding on the door and a big voice calling out like it could have been the cops. Everything went silent. Then somebody out there starts shouldering the door and the next thing we know a guy busts in. Funny thing is he looked exactly like his voice.

To us he wasn't Francisco Real—not yet—but just some big hefty guy. He was all in black from head to toe, except for this reddish-brown scarf draped over one shoulder. I remember his face. There was something Indian and kind of angular about it.

When the door come flying in it smacked right into me. Before I even knew what I was doing I was on top of the guy, throwing him a left square in the teeth while my right goes inside my vest for my knife. But I never got a chance. Steadying himself, he puts his arms out and shoves me aside like he's brushing something out of the way. There I was down on my ass—back of him now—my hand still inside the jacket grabbing for the knife. And him wading forward like nothing happened. Just wading forward, a whole head taller than all these guys he's pushing his way through—and acting like he never even saw them. The first of our guys—bunch of gaping wops—just back out of his way, scared as hell. But only the first. In the next bunch the Redhead was waiting for him, and before the newcomer could lay a hand on his shoulder, Red's knife was out and he let him have one across the face with the flat of the blade. Soon as they saw that they all jumped the guy. The hall was pretty long, maybe more than nine or ten yards, and they drove him from one end almost to the other—like Christ in one of the Stations—roughing him up, hooting at him, spitting all over him. First they let him have it with their fists, then, seeing he didn't bother shielding the blows, they started slapping him openhanded and flicking the fringes of their scarves at him, mocking him. At the same time they were saving him for Rosendo, who all this time was standing with his back against the far wall and not moving a muscle, not saying a word. All he did was puff on his cigarette, a little worried-looking, like he already knew what came clear to the rest of us only later on. The Butcher, who was hanging on but was beginning to bleed here and there—that whole hooting pack behind him—got pushed closer and closer to Rosendo. Laughed at, lashed at, spit on, he only started talking when the two of them came face to face. Then he looked at Rosendo and, wiping his face on his sleeve, said something like this:

"I'm Francisco Real and I come from the Northside. People call me the Butcher. I let all these punks lay their hands on me just now because what I'm looking for is a man. Word's going around there's someone out in these lousy mudflats supposed to be pretty good with a knife. They call him the Slasher and they say he's pretty tough. I'd like to meet up with the guy. Maybe he can teach a nobody like me how a man with guts handles himself."

He had his say looking straight at Rosendo, and all at once this big knife he must have had up his sleeve was flashing in his hand. Instead of pressing in, now everyone starts opening up space for a fight—at the same time staring at the two of them in dead silence. Even the thick lips of the blind nigger playing the fiddle were turned that way.

Right then I hear this commotion behind me and in the frame of the door I get me a glimpse of six or seven men who must have been the Butcher's gang. The oldest, a leathery-faced guy with a big gray moustache, who looked like a hick, comes in a few steps and, going all goggle-eyed at the women and the lights, takes off his hat, respectful. The rest of them kept their eyes peeled, ready to swing into action if anything underhanded went on.

What was the matter with Rosendo all this time, not bouncing that loudmouth the hell out? He was still keeping quiet, not even raising his eyes. I don't know if he spit his cigarette out or if it fell from his mouth. Finally he manages to come up with a couple of words, but so low the rest of us at the other end of the dance floor didn't get what he said. Francisco Real challenged him again, and again Rosendo refused. At this point, the youngest of the newcomers lets out a whistle. La Lujanera gave the guy a look that went right through him. Then, her hair swinging down over her shoulders, she wedged her way through the crowd and, going up to her man, slips his knife out and hands it to him.

"Rosendo," she says to him, "I think you're going to need this."

Way up under the roof was this kind of long window that opened out over the river. Rosendo took the knife in his two hands and turned it over like he never laid eyes on it before. Then all of a sudden he raises his arms up over his head and flips the knife behind him out the window into the Maldonado. I felt a chill go through me.

"The only reason I don't carve you up is cause you sicken me," the Butcher says then, making to let Rosendo have it. That split second La Lujanera threw her arms around the Butcher's neck, giving him one of those looks of hers, and says to him, mad as hell, "Let the bastard alone— making us think he was a man."

For a minute Francisco Real couldn't figure it out. Then wrapping his arms around her like it was forever, he calls to the musicians to play loud and strong and orders the rest of us to dance. The music went like wildfire from one end of the hall to the other. Real danced sort of stiff but held his partner up tight, and in nothing flat he had her charmed. When they got near the door he shouted, "Make way, boys,

22

she's all mine now!" and out they went, cheek to cheek, like the tango was floating them off.

I must have turned a little red with shame. I took a couple of turns with some woman, then dropped her cold. On account of the heat and the jam, I told her, then edged my way around the room toward the door. It was a nice night out—but for who? There was their buggy at the corner of the alley with two guitars standing straight up on the seat like men. Boy, it galled me seeing that—it was as much as saying we weren't even good enough to clip a lousy guitar. The thought that we were a bunch of nobodys really had me burned up, and I snatched the carnation from behind my ear and threw it in a puddle. I stood there a while staring at it, trying to take my mind off things. I wished it was already tomorrow—I wished that night were over. Then the next thing I knew there's this elbow shoving me aside and it almost came like a relief. It was Rosendo—all by himself, slinking off.

"You're always getting in the way, kid," he says to me half snarling. I couldn't tell if he was just getting something off his chest or what. He disappeared in the dark toward the Maldonado. I never laid eyes on him again.

I stood there looking at the things I'd seen all my life—the big wide sky, the river going on down there in its own blind way, a horse half asleep, the dirt roads, the kilns—and it came to me that in the middle of this ragweed and all these dump heaps and this whole stinking place, I'd grown up just another weed myself. What else was going to come out of this crap but us—lots of lip but soft inside, all talk but no standing up to anyone? Then I thought no, the worse the neighborhood the tougher it had to be. Crap? Back toward the dance hall the music was still going strong, and on the breeze came a smell of honeysuckle. Nice night, but so what? There were so many stars, some right on top of others, it made you dizzy just looking at them. I tried hard to tell myself that what happened meant nothing to me, but I just couldn't get over Rosendo's yellow streak and the newcomer's plain guts. Real even managed to

23

get hold of a woman for the night—for that night and a lot
of nights and maybe forever, I thought, because La Lujanera
was really something. God knows which way they headed.
They couldn't have wandered very far. By then the two of
them were probably going at it in some ditch.

When I got back, the dance was in full swing. I slipped
into the crowd, quiet as I could, noticing that some of our
boys had taken off and that the Northside bunch were
dancing along with everyone else. There was no shoving, no
rough stuff. Everybody was watching out and on good
behavior. The music sounded sleepy, and the girls tangoing
away with the outsiders didn't have much to say.

I was on the lookout for something, but not for what
happened. Outside there were sounds of a woman crying
and then that voice we all knew by then—but real low,
almost too low, like somehow it didn't belong to anyone
anymore.

"Go on in, you slut," it was telling her—then more tears.
After that the voice sounded desperate.

"Open the door, you understand me? Open it, you lousy
tramp. Open it, bitch."

At that point the shaky door opens and in comes La
Lujanera, all alone. Just like someone's herding her.

"Must be a ghost out there behind her," said the Redhead.

"A dead man, friend." It was the Butcher, and he stag-
gers in, his face like a drunk's, and in the space we opened
up for him he takes a couple of reeling steps—tall, hardly
seeing—then all at once goes down like a log. One of his
friends rolled him over and fixed him a pillow with his
scarf, but all this fussing only got him smeared with blood.
We could see there was a big gash in his chest. The blood
was welling up and blackening a bright red neckerchief I
hadn't noticed before because his scarf covered it. For first
aid one of the women brought rum and some scorched rags.
The man was in no shape to explain. La Lujanera looked at
him in a daze, her arms hanging by her sides. There was
one question on everyone's face and finally she got out an

answer. She said after leaving with the Butcher they went
to a little field and at that point someone she didn't know
turned up and challenged him to fight and then gave him
this stab. She swore she didn't know who it was, but that it
wasn't Rosendo. Was anyone going to believe that?

The man at our feet was dying. It looked to me like the
hand that done the job done it well. Just the same, the man
hung on. When he knocked that second time Julia was
brewing some matés. The cup went clear around the circle
and back to me before he died. When the end came, he said
in a low voice, "Cover my face." All he had left was pride
and he didn't want us gaping at him while his face went
through its agony. Someone put his hat over him and that's
how he died—without a sound—under that high black crown.
It was only when his chest stopped heaving they dared
uncover him. He had that worn-out look dead men have. In
his day, from the Artillery Barracks all the way to the
Southside, he was one of the scrappiest men around. When
I knew he was dead and couldn't talk, I stopped hating
him.

"All it takes to die is being alive," says one of the girls in
the crowd. And in the same way another one says, "A man's
so full of pride and now look—all he's good for is gathering
flies."

Right then the Northside gang starts talking to each
other in low voices. Then two of them come out together
saying, "The woman killed him." After that, in a real loud
voice, one of them threw the accusation in her face, and
they all swarmed in around her. Forgetting I had to be
careful, I was on them like a light. I don't know what kept
me from reaching for my knife. There were a lot of eyes
watching—maybe everybody's—and I said, putting them
down, "Look at this woman's hands. How could she get the
strength of the nerve to knife a man?"

Then, kind of offhand, I added, "Whoever would have
dreamed the deceased, who—like they say—was a pretty
tough guy in his own neck of the woods, would end up this
way? And in a place sleepy as this, where nothing ever

happens till some outsider comes around trying to show us a little fun and for all his pains only gets himself spit on?"

Nobody offered his hide for a whipping.

Right then, in the dead silence, you could make out the approach of riders. It was the law. Everybody—some more, some less—had his own good reason for staying clear of the police. The best thing was to dump the body in the Maldonado. You remember that long window the knife went flying out of? Well, that's where the man in black went. A bunch of guys lifted him up. There were hands stripping him of every cent and trinket he had, and someone even hacked off one of his fingers to steal his ring. They helped themselves, all right—real daring bunch with a poor defenseless stiff once a better guy already straightened him out. One good heave and the current did the rest. To keep him from floating, they maybe even tore out his guts. I don't know—I didn't want to look. The old-timer with the gray moustache never took his eyes off me. Making the best of all the commotion, La Lujanera slipped away.

When the lawmen came in for a look, the dance was going good again. That blind fiddler could really scrape some lively numbers on that violin of his—the kind of thing you never hear anymore. It was beginning to get light outside. The fence posts on a nearby slope seemed to stand alone, the strands of wire still invisible in the early dawn.

Nice and easy, I walked the two or three blocks back to my shack. A candle was burning in the window, then all at once went out. Let me tell you, I hurried when I saw that. Then, Borges, I put my hand inside my vest—here by the left armpit where I always carry it—and took my knife out again. I turned the blade over, real slow. It was as good as new, innocent-looking, and you couldn't see the slightest trace of blood on it.

The Approach to al-Mu'tasim

(1935)

Philip Guedalla informs us that the novel *The Approach to al-Mu'tasim* by the Bombay barrister Mir Bahadur Ali "is a rather uneasy combination of those Islamic allegories which never fail to impress their own translators, and of that brand of detective stories which inevitably outdoes even Dr. Watson and heightens the horror of human life as it is found in the most respectable boardinghouses of Brighton." Before him, Mr. Cecil Roberts had blasted Bahadur's book for "its unaccountable double influence of Wilkie Collins and of the famed twelfth-century Persian, Ferid Eddin Attar"—a simple enough observation which Guedalla merely parrots, though in a more angry jargon. Essentially, both reviewers are in agreement, pointing out the book's detective-story mechanism and its undercurrent of mysticism. This hybridization may lead us to suspect a certain kinship with Chesterton; we shall presently find out, however, that no such affinity exists.

The first edition of *The Approach to al-Mu'tasim* appeared in Bombay toward the end of 1932. The paper on which the volume was issued, I am told, was almost newsprint; the jacket announced to the purchaser that the book was the first detective novel to be written by a native of Bombay City. Within a few months, four printings of a thousand copies each were sold out. The *Bombay Quarterly Review,* the *Bombay Gazette,* the *Calcutta Review,* the *Hindustani Review* (of Allahabad), and the *Calcutta Englishman* all sang its praises. Bahadur then brought out an illustrated edition, which he retitled *The Conversation with the Man Called al-Mu'tasim* and rather beautifully subtitled *A Game with Shifting Mirrors.* This is the edition which Victor Gollancz has just reissued in London, with a foreword by Dorothy L. Sayers and the omission—perhaps merciful—of the illustrations. It is this edition that I have at hand; I have not been able to obtain a copy of the earlier one, which I surmise may be a better book. I am led to this suspicion by an appendix summarizing the differences between the 1932 and the 1934 editions. Before attempting a discussion of the novel, it might be well to give some idea of the general plot.

Its central figure—whose name we are never told—is a law student in Bombay. Blasphemously, he disbelieves in the Islamic faith of his fathers, but on the tenth night of the moon of Muharram, he finds himself in the midst of a civil disorder between Muslims and Hindus. It is a night of drums and prayers. Among the mob of the heathen, the great paper canopies of the Muslim procession force their way. A hail of Hindu bricks flies down from a roof terrace. A knife is sunk into a belly. Someone—Muslim? Hindu?—dies and is trampled on. Three thousand men are fighting—stick against revolver, obscenity against curse, God the Indivisible against the many Gods. Instinctively, the student freethinker joins in the fighting. With his bare hands, he kills (or thinks he has killed) a Hindu. The Government police—mounted, thunderous, and barely awake—intervene, dealing impartial whiplashes. The student flees, almost under the legs of the horses, heading for the farthest ends of

28

town. He crosses two sets of railroad tracks, or the same tracks twice. He scales the wall of an unkempt garden at one corner of which rises a circular tower. "A lean and evil mob of mooncoloured hounds" lunges at him from the black rosebushes. Pursued, he seeks refuge in the tower. He climbs an iron ladder—two or three rungs are missing—and on the flat roof, which has a blackish pit in the middle, comes upon a squalid man in a squatting position, urinating vigorously by the light of the moon. The man confides to him that his profession is stealing gold teeth from the white-shrouded corpses that the Parsis leave on the roof of the tower. He says a number of other vile things and mentions, in passing, that fourteen nights have lapsed since he last cleansed himself with buffalo dung. He speaks with obvious anger of a band of horse thieves from Gujarat, "eaters of dogs and lizards—men, in short, as abominable as the two of us." Day is dawning. In the air there is a low flight of well-fed vultures. The student, in utter exhaustion, lies down to sleep. When he wakes up, the sun is high overhead and the thief is gone. Gone also are a couple of Trichinopoly cigars and a few silver rupees. Threatened by the events of the night before, the student decides to lose himself somewhere within the bounds of India. He knows he has shown himself capable of killing an infidel, but not of knowing with certainty whether the Muslim is more justified in his beliefs than the infidel. The name of Gujarat haunts him, and also the name of a *malka-sansi* (a woman belonging to a caste of thieves) from Palanpur, many times favored by the curses and hatred of the despoiler of corpses. He reasons that the anger of a man so thoroughly vile is in itself a kind of praise. He resolves—though rather hopelessly—to find her. He prays and sets out slowly and deliberately on his long journey. So ends the novel's second chapter.

It is hardly possible to outline here the involved adventures that befall him in the remaining nineteen. There is a baffling pullulation of dramatis personae, to say nothing of a biography that seems to exhaust the range of the human spirit (running from infamy to mathematical speculation) or of a pilgrimage that covers the vast geography of India. The story begun in Bombay moves on into the lowlands of Palanpur, lingers for an evening and a night before the stone gates of Bikaner, tells of the death of a blind astrologer in a sewer of Benares; the hero takes part in a conspiracy in a mazelike palace in Katmandu, prays and fornicates in the pestilential stench of the Machua Bazaar in Calcutta, sees the day born out of the sea from a law office in Madras, sees evenings die in the sea from a balcony in the state of Travancore, falters and kills in Indapur. The adventure closes its orbit of miles and years back in Bombay itself, only steps away from the garden of the "mooncoloured hounds." The underlying plot is this: a man, the fugitive student freethinker we already know, falls among the lowest class of people and, in a kind of contest of evildoing, takes up their ways. All at once, with the wonder and terror of Robinson Crusoe upon discovering the footprint of a man in the sand, he becomes aware of a brief and sudden change in that world of ruthlessness—a certain tenderness, a moment of happiness, a forgiving silence in one of his loathsome companions. "It was as though a stranger, a third and more subtle person, had entered into the conversation." The hero knows that the scoundrel with whom he is talking is quite incapable of this sudden turn; from this, he guesses that the man is echoing someone else, a friend, or the friend of a friend. Rethinking the problem, he arrives at the mysterious conclusion that "somewhere on the face of the earth is a man from whom this light has emanated; somewhere on the face of the earth there exists a man who is equal to this light." The student decides to spend his life in search of him.

The story's outline is now plain: the untiring search for a human soul through the barely perceptible reflections cast by this soul in others—in the beginning, the faint trace of a smile or a single word; in the end, the differing and branching splendors of reason, of the imagination, and of righteousness. The nearer to al-Mu'tasim the men he examines are, the greater is their share of the divine, though it is understood that they are but mirrors. A mathematical analogy may be helpful here. Bahadur's populous novel is an ascendant progression whose last term is the foreshadowed "man called al-Mu'tasim." Al-Mu'tasim's immediate predecessor is a Persian bookseller of striking happiness and politeness; the man before the bookseller, a saint. Finally, after many years, the student comes to a corridor "at whose end is a door and a cheap beaded curtain, and behind the curtain a shining light." The student claps his hands once or twice and asks for al-Mu'tasim. A man's voice—the unimaginable voice of al-Mu'tasim—prays him to enter. The student parts the curtain and steps forward. At this point the novel comes to its end.

If I am not mistaken, the proper handling of such a plot places the writer under two obligations. One, to abound richly in prophetic touches; the other, to make us feel that the person foreshadowed by these touches is more than a mere convention or phantom. Bahadur fulfills the first; how far he achieves the second, I wonder. In other words, the unheard and unseen al-Mu'tasim should leave us with the impression of a real character, not of a clutter of insipid superlatives. In the 1932 version, there are but few supernatural traces; "the man called al-Mu'tasim" is obviously a symbol, though certain personal traits are not lacking. Unfortunately, this literary good conduct did not last. In the 1934 version—the one I have read—the novel declines into allegory. Al-Mu'tasim is God and the hero's various wanderings are in some way the journey of a soul on its ascending steps toward the divine union. There are a few regrettable details: a black Jew from Cochin speaks of al-Mu'tasim as having dark skin; a Christian describes him standing on a height with his arms spread open; a Red lama recalls him seated "like that image of yak butter that I modeled and worshiped in the monastery of Tachilhunpo." These statements seem to suggest a single God who reconciles himself to the many varieties of mankind. In my opinion, the idea is not greatly exciting. I will not say the same of another idea—the hint that the Almighty is also in search of Someone, and that Someone of Someone above him (or Someone simply indispensable and equal), and so on to the End (or rather, Endlessness) of Time, or perhaps cyclically. Al-Mu'tasim (the name of that eighth Abbasid caliph who was victorious in eight battles, fathered eight sons and eight daughters, left eight thousand slaves, and ruled for a period of eight years, eight moons, and eight days) means etymologically "The Seeker after Help." In the 1932 version, the fact that the object of the pilgrimage was himself a pilgrim justified well enough the difficulty of finding him. The later version gives way to the quaint theology I have just spoken of. In the twentieth chapter, words attributed by the Persian bookseller to al-Mu'tasim are, perhaps, the mere heightening of others spoken by the hero; this and other hidden analogies may stand for the identity of the Seeker with the Sought. They may also stand for an influence of Man on the Divinity. Another chapter hints that al-Mu'tasim is the Hindu the student believes he has killed. Mir Bahadur Ali, as we have seen, cannot refrain from the grossest temptation of art—that of being a genius.

On reading over these pages, I fear I have not called sufficient attention to the book's many virtues. It includes a number of fine distinctions. For example, a conversation in chapter nineteen in which one of the speakers, who is a friend of al-Mu'tasim, avoids pointing out the other man's sophisms "in order not to be obviously in the right."

It is considered admirable nowadays for a modern book to have its roots in an ancient one, since nobody (as Dr. Johnson said) likes owing anything to his contemporaries. The many but superficial contacts between Joyce's *Ulysses* and Homer's *Odyssey* go on receiving—I shall never know why—the harebrained admiration of critics. The points of contact between Bahadur's novel and the celebrated *Parliament of Birds* by Farid ud-Din Attar, have awakened the no less mysterious approval of London, and even of Allahabad and Calcutta. As far as I can judge, the points of contact between the two works are not many. Other sources are present. Some inquisitor has listed certain analogies between the novel's opening scene and Kipling's story "On the City Wall." Bahadur admits this, but argues that it would be highly abnormal if two descriptions of the tenth night of Muharram were quite unlike each other. Eliot, more to the point, is reminded of the seventy cantos of the unfinished allegory *The Faerie Queene*, in which the heroine, Gloriana, does not appear even once—a fault previously noted by Richard William Church (*Spenser*, 1879). With due humility, I suggest a distant and possible forerunner, the Jerusalem Kabbalist Isaac Luria, who in the sixteenth century advanced the notion that the soul of an ancestor or a master may, in order to comfort or instruct him, enter into the soul of someone who has suffered misfortune. *Ibbür* is the name given to this variety of metempsychosis.*

---

* In the course of this review, I have referred to the *Mantiq ut-Tair* (Parliament of Birds) by the Persian mystic Farid al-Din Abu Talib Mohammad ibn-Ibraham Attar, who was killed by the soldiers of Tului, one of Genghis Khan's sons, during the sack of Nishapur. Perhaps it would be useful to summarize the poem. The distant king of birds, the Simurgh, drops one of his splendid feathers somewhere in the middle of China; on learning of this, the other birds, tired of their age-old anarchy, decide to seek him. They know that the king's name means "thirty birds"; they know that his castle lies in the Kaf, the range of mountains that ring the earth. Setting out on the almost endless adventure, they cross seven valleys or seas, the next to last bearing the name Bewilderment, the last, the name Annihilation. Many of the pilgrims desert; the journey takes its toll among the rest. Thirty, made pure by their sufferings, reach the great peak of the Simurgh. At last they behold him; they realize that they are the Simurgh and that the Simurgh is each of them and all of them. (Plotinus [*Enneads*, V, 8, 4] also states a divine extension of the principle of identity: "All things in the intelligible heavens are in all places. Any one thing is all other things. The sun is all the stars, and each star is all the other stars and the sun.") The *Mantiq ut-Tair* has been translated into French by Garcin de Tassy; parts of it into English by Edward FitzGerald. For this footnote, I have consulted the tenth volume of Burton's *Arabian Nights* and Margaret Smith's study *The Persian Mystics: Attar* (1932).

The Circular Ruins

(1940)

And if he left off dreaming about you. . . .
Through the Looking-Glass, IV

Nobody saw him come ashore in the encompassing night, nobody saw the bamboo craft run aground in the sacred mud, but within a few days everyone knew that the quiet man had come from the south and that his home was among the numberless villages upstream on the steep slopes of the mountain, where the Zend language is barely tainted by Greek and where lepers are rare. The fact is that the gray man pressed his lips to the mud, scrambled up the bank without parting (perhaps without feeling) the brushy thorns that tore his flesh, and dragged himself, faint and bleeding, to the circular opening watched over by a stone tiger, or horse, which once was the color of fire and is now the color of ash. This opening is a temple which was destroyed ages ago by flames, which the swampy wilderness later desecrated, and whose god no longer receives the reverence of men. The stranger laid himself down at the foot of the image.

Wakened by the sun high overhead, he noticed—somehow

without amazement—that his wounds had healed. He shut his pale eyes and slept again, not because of weariness but because he willed it. He knew that this temple was the place he needed for his unswerving purpose; he knew that downstream the encroaching trees had also failed to choke the ruins of another auspicious temple with its own fire-ravaged, dead gods; he knew that his first duty was to sleep. Along about midnight, he was awakened by the forlorn call of a bird. Footprints, some figs, and a water jug told him that men who lived nearby had looked on his sleep with a kind of awe and either sought his protection or else were in dread of his witchcraft. He felt the chill of fear and searched the crumbling walls for a burial niche, where he covered himself over with leaves he had never seen before.

His guiding purpose, though it was supernatural, was not impossible. He wanted to dream a man; he wanted to dream him down to the last detail and project him into the world of reality. This mystical aim had taxed the whole range of his mind. Had anyone asked him his own name or anything about his life before then, he would not have known what to answer. This forsaken, broken temple suited him because it held few visible things, and also because the neighboring villagers would look after his frugal needs. The rice and fruit of their offerings were nourishment enough for his body, whose one task was to sleep and to dream.

At the outset, his dreams were chaotic; later on, they were of a dialectic nature. The stranger dreamed himself at the center of a circular amphitheater which in some way was also the burnt-out temple. Crowds of silent disciples exhausted the tiers of seats; the faces of the farthest of them hung centuries away from him and at a height of the stars, but their features were clear and exact. The man lectured on anatomy, cosmography, and witchcraft. The faces listened, bright and eager, and did their best to answer sensibly, as if they felt the importance of his questions, which would raise one of them out of an existence as a shadow and place him in the real world. Whether asleep or awake, the man pondered the answers of his phantoms

35

and, not letting himself be misled by impostors, divined in certain of their quandaries a growing intelligence. He was in search of a soul worthy of taking a place in the world.

After nine or ten nights he realized, feeling bitter over it, that nothing could be expected from those pupils who passively accepted his teaching, but that he might, however, hold hopes for those who from time to time hazarded reasonable doubts about what he taught. The former, although they deserved love and affection, could never become real; the latter, in their dim way, were already real. One evening (now his evenings were also given over to sleeping, now he was only awake for an hour or two at dawn) he dismissed his vast dream-school forever and kept a single disciple. He was a quiet, sallow, and at times rebellious young man with sharp features akin to those of his dreamer. The sudden disappearance of his fellow pupils did not disturb him for very long, and his progress, at the end of a few private lessons, amazed his teacher. Nonetheless, a catastrophe intervened. One morning, the man emerged from his sleep as from a sticky wasteland, glanced up at the faint evening light, which at first he confused with the dawn, and realized that he had not been dreaming. All that night and the next day, the hideous lucidity of insomnia weighed down on him. To tire himself out he tried to explore the surrounding forest, but all he managed, there in a thicket of hemlocks, were some snatches of broken sleep, fleetingly tinged with visions of a crude and worthless nature. He tried to reassemble his school, and barely had he uttered a few brief words of counsel when the whole class went awry and vanished. In his almost endless wakefulness, tears of anger stung his old eyes.

He realized that, though he may penetrate all the riddles of the higher and lower orders, the task of shaping the senseless and dizzying stuff of dreams is the hardest that a man can attempt—much harder than weaving a rope of sand or of coining the faceless wind. He realized that an initial failure was to be expected. He then swore he would forget the populous vision which in the beginning had led him astray, and he sought another method. Before attempting it, he spent a month rebuilding the strength his fever had consumed. He gave up all thoughts of dreaming and almost at once managed to sleep a reasonable part of the day. The few times he dreamed during this period he did not dwell on his dreams. Before taking up his task again, he waited until the moon was a perfect circle. Then, in the evening, he cleansed himself in the waters of the river, worshiped the gods of the planets, uttered the prescribed syllables of an all-powerful name, and slept. Almost at once, he had a dream of a beating heart.

He dreamed it throbbing, warm, secret. It was the size of a closed fist, a darkish red in the dimness of a human body still without a face or sex. With anxious love he dreamed it for fourteen lucid nights. Each night he perceived it more clearly. He did not touch it, but limited himself to witnessing it, to observing it, to correcting it now and then with a look. He felt it, he lived it from different distances and from many angles. On the fourteenth night he touched the pulmonary artery with a finger and then the whole heart, inside and out. The examination satisfied him. For one night he deliberately did not dream; after that he went back to the heart again, invoked the name of a planet, and set out to envision another of the principal organs. Before a year was over he came to the skeleton, the eyelids. The countless strands of hair were perhaps the hardest task of all. He dreamed a whole man, a young man, but the young man could not stand up or speak, nor could he open his eyes. Night after night, the man dreamed him asleep.

In the cosmogonies of the Gnostics, the demiurges mold a red Adam who is unable to stand on his feet; as clumsy and crude and elementary as that Adam of dust was the Adam of dreams wrought by the nights of the magician. One evening the man was at the point of destroying all his handiwork (it would have been better for him had he done so), but in the end he restrained himself. Having exhausted his prayers to the gods of the earth and river, he threw himself down at the feet of the stone image that may have been a tiger or a stallion, and asked for its blind aid. That same evening he dreamed of the image. He dreamed it alive, quivering; it was no unnatural cross between tiger and stallion but at one and the same time both these violent creatures and also a bull, a rose, a thunderstorm. This manifold god revealed to him that its earthly name was Fire, that there in the circular temple (and in others like it) sacrifices had once been made to it, that it had been worshiped, and that through its magic the phantom of the man's dreams would be wakened to life in such a way that—except for Fire itself and the dreamer—every being in the world would accept him as a man of flesh and blood. The god ordered that, once instructed in the rites, the disciple should be sent downstream to the other ruined temple, whose pyramids still survived, so that in that abandoned place some human voice might exalt him. In the dreamer's dream, the dreamed one awoke.

The magician carried out these orders. He devoted a period of time (which finally spanned two years) to initiating his principle into the riddles of the universe and the worship of Fire. Deep inside, it pained him to say goodbye to his creature. Under the pretext of teaching him more fully, each day he drew out the hours set aside for sleep. Also, he reshaped the somewhat faulty right shoulder. From time to time, he was troubled by the feeling that all this had already happened, but for the most part his days were happy. On closing his eyes he would think, "Now I will be with my son." Or, less frequently, "The son I have begotten awaits me and he will not exist if I do not go to him."

Little by little, he was training the young man for reality. On one occasion he commanded him to set up a flag on a distant peak. The next day, there on the peak, a fiery pennant shone. He tried other, similar exercises, each bolder than the one before. He realized with a certain bitterness that his son was ready—and perhaps impatient—to be born. That night he kissed him for the first time and sent him down the river to the other temple, whose whitened ruins were still to be glimpsed over miles and miles of impenetrable forest and swamp. At the very end (so that the boy would never know he was a phantom, so that he would think himself a man like all men), the magician imbued his disciple with total oblivion of his long years of apprenticeship.

His triumph and his peace were blemished by a touch of weariness. In the morning and evening dusk, he prostrated himself before the stone idol, perhaps imagining that his unreal son was performing the same rites farther down the river in other circular ruins. At night he no longer dreamed, or else he dreamed the way all men dream. He now perceived with a certain vagueness the sounds and shapes of the world, for his absent son was taking nourishment from the magician's decreasing consciousness. His life's purpose was fulfilled; the man lived on in a kind of ecstasy. After a length of time that certain tellers of the story count in years and others in half-decades, he was awakened one midnight by two rowers. He could not see their faces, but they spoke to him about a magic man in a temple up north who walked on fire without being burned. The magician suddenly remembered the god's words. He remembered that of all the creatures in the world, Fire was the only one who knew his son was a phantom. This recollection, comforting at first, ended by tormenting him. He feared that his son might wonder at this strange privilege and in some way discover his condition as a mere appearance. Not to be a man but to be the projection of another man's dreams—what an unparalleled humiliation, how bewildering! Every father cares for the child he has begotten—he has allowed—in some moment of confusion or happiness. It is understandable, then, that the magician should fear for the future of a son thought out organ by organ and feature by feature over the course of a thousand and one secret nights.

The end of these anxieties came suddenly, but certain signs foretold it. First (after a long drought), a far-off cloud on a hilltop, as light as a bird; next, toward the south, the sky, which took on the rosy hue of a leopard's gums; then, the pillars of smoke that turned the metal of the nights to rust; finally, the headlong panic of the forest animals. For what had happened many centuries ago was happening again. The ruins of the fire god's shrine were destroyed by fire. In a birdless dawn the magician saw the circling sheets of flame closing in on him. For a moment, he thought of taking refuge in the river, but then he realized that death was coming to crown his years and to release him from his labors. He walked into the leaping pennants of flame. They did not bite into his flesh, but caressed him and flooded him without heat or burning. In relief, in humiliation, in terror, he understood that he, too, was an appearance, that someone else was dreaming him.

Death and the Compass

To Mandie Molina Vedia
(1942)

Of the many problems ever to tax Erik Lönnrot's rash mind, none was so strange—so methodically strange, let us say—as the intermittent series of murders which came to a culmination amid the incessant odor of eucalyptus trees at the villa Triste-le-Roy. It is true that Lönnrot failed to prevent the last of the murders, but it is undeniable that he foresaw it. Neither did he guess the identity of Yarmolinsky's ill-starred killer, but he did guess the secret shape of the evil series of events and the possible role played in those events by Red Scharlach, also nicknamed Scharlach the Dandy. The gangster (like so many others of his ilk) had sworn on his honor to get Erik Lönnrot, but Lönnrot was not intimidated. Lönnrot thought of himself as a pure logician, a kind of Auguste Dupin, but there was also a streak of the adventurer and even of the gambler in him.

The first murder took place in the Hôtel du Nord—that tall prism which overlooks the estuary whose broad waters are the color of sand. To that tower (which, as everyone

41

knows, brings together the hateful blank white walls of a hospital, the numbered chambers of a cell block, and the overall appearance of a brothel) there arrived on the third of December Rabbi Marcel Yarmolinsky, a gray-bearded, gray-eyed man, who was a delegate from Podolsk to the Third Talmudic Congress. We shall never know whether the Hôtel du Nord actually pleased him or not, since he accepted it with the ageless resignation that had made it possible for him to survive three years of war in the Carpathians and three thousand years of oppression and pogroms. He was given a room on floor R, across from the suite occupied—not without splendor—by the Tetrarch of Galilee.

Yarmolinsky had dinner, put off until the next day a tour of the unfamiliar city, arranged in a closet his many books and his few suits of clothes, and before midnight turned off his bed lamp. (So said the Tetrarch's chauffeur, who slept in the room next door.) On the fourth of December, at three minutes past eleven in the morning, an editor of the *Jüdische Zeitung* called him by telephone. Rabbi Yarmolinsky did not answer; soon after, he was found in his room, his face already discolored, almost naked under a great old-fashioned cape. He lay not far from the hall door. A deep knife wound had opened his chest. A couple of hours later, in the same room, in the throng of reporters, photographers, and policemen, Inspector Treviranus and Lönnrot quietly discussed the case.

"We needn't lose any time here looking for three-legged cats," Treviranus said, brandishing an imperious cigar. "Everyone knows the Tetrarch of Galilee owns the world's finest sapphires. Somebody out to steal them probably found his way in here by mistake. Yarmolinsky woke up and the thief was forced to kill him. What do you make of it?"

"Possible, but not very interesting," Lönnrot answered. "You'll say reality is under no obligation to be interesting. To which I'd reply that reality may disregard the obligation but that we may not. In your hypothesis, chance plays a large part. Here's a dead rabbi. I'd much prefer a purely rabbinical explanation, not the imagined mistakes of an imagined jewel thief."

"I'm not interested in rabbinical explanations," Treviranus replied in bad humor; "I'm interested in apprehending the man who murdered this unknown party."

"Not so unknown," corrected Lönnrot. "There are his complete works." He pointed to a row of tall books on a shelf in the closet. There were a *Vindication of the Kabbalah,* a *Study of the Philosophy of Robert Fludd,* a literal translation of the *Sefer Yeçirah,* a *Biography of the Baal Shem,* a *History of the Hasidic Sect,* a treatise (in German) on the Tetragrammaton, and another on the names of God in the Pentateuch. The Inspector stared at them in fear, almost in disgust. Then he burst into laughter.

"I'm only a poor Christian," he said. "You may cart off every last tome if you feel like it. I have no time to waste on Jewish superstitions."

"Maybe this crime belongs to the history of Jewish superstitions," Lönnrot grumbled.

"Like Christianity," the editor from the *Jüdische Zeitung* made bold to add. He was nearsighted, an atheist, and very shy.

Nobody took any notice of him. One of the police detectives had found in Yarmolinsky's small typewriter a sheet of paper on which these cryptic words were written:

The first letter of the Name has been uttered

Lönnrot restrained himself from smiling. Suddenly turning bibliophile and Hebraic scholar, he ordered a package made of the dead man's books and he brought them to his apartment. There, with complete disregard for the police investigation, he began studying them. One royal-octavo volume revealed to him the teachings of Israel Baal Shem Tobh, founder of the sect of the Pious; another, the magic and the terror of the Tetragrammaton, which is God's unspeakable name; a third, the doctrine that God has a secret name in which (as in the crystal sphere that the

Persians attribute to Alexander of Macedonia) His ninth attribute, Eternity, may be found—that is to say, the immediate knowledge of everything under the sun that will be, that is, and that was. Tradition lists ninety-nine names of God; Hebrew scholars explain that imperfect cipher by a mystic fear of even numbers; the Hasidim argue that the missing term stands for a hundredth name—the Absolute Name.

It was out of this bookworming that Lönnrot was distracted a few days later by the appearance of the editor from the *Jüdische Zeitung*, who wanted to speak about the murder. Lönnrot, however, chose to speak of the many names of the Lord. The following day, in three columns, the journalist stated that Chief Detective Erik Lönnrot had taken up the study of the names of God in order to find out the name of the murderer. Lönnrot, familiar with the simplifications of journalism, was not surprised. It also seemed that one of those tradesmen who have discovered that any man is willing to buy any book was peddling a cheap edition of Yarmolinsky's *History of the Hasidic Sect*.

The second murder took place on the night of January third out in the most forsaken and empty of the city's western reaches. Along about daybreak, one of the police who patrol this lonely area on horseback noticed on the doorstep of a dilapidated paint and hardware store a man in a poncho laid out flat. A deep knife wound had ripped open his chest, and his hard features looked as though they were masked in blood. On the wall, on the shop's conventional red and yellow diamond shapes, were some words scrawled in chalk. The policeman read them letter by letter. That evening, Treviranus and Lönnrot made their way across town to the remote scene of the crime. To the left and right of their car the city fell away in shambles; the sky grew wider and houses were of much less account than brick kilns or an occasional poplar. They reached their forlorn destination, an unpaved back alley with rose-colored walls that in some way seemed to reflect the garish sunset. The dead man had already been identified. He turned out to be Daniel Simon Azevedo, a man with a fair reputation in the old northern outskirts of town who had risen from teamster to electioneering thug and later degenerated into a thief and an informer. (The unusual manner of his death seemed to them fitting, for Azevedo was the last example of a generation of criminals who knew how to handle a knife but not a revolver.) The words chalked up on the wall were these:

The second letter of the Name has been uttered

The third murder took place on the night of February third. A little before one o'clock, the telephone rang in the office of Inspector Treviranus. With pointed secrecy, a man speaking in a guttural voice said his name was Ginzberg (or Ginsburg) and that he was ready—for a reasonable consideration—to shed light on the facts surrounding the double sacrifice of Azevedo and Yarmolinsky. A racket of whistles and tin horns drowned out the informer's voice. Then the line went dead. Without discounting the possibility of a practical joke (they were, after all, at the height of Carnival), Treviranus checked and found that he had been phoned from a sailors' tavern called Liverpool House on the Rue de Toulon—that arcaded waterfront street in which we find side by side the wax museum and the dairy bar, the brothel and the Bible seller. Treviranus called the owner back. The man (Black Finnegan by name, a reformed Irish criminal concerned about and almost weighed down by respectability) told him that the last person to have used the telephone was one of his roomers, a certain Gryphius, who had only minutes before gone out with some friends. At once Treviranus set out for Liverpool House. There the owner told him the following story:

Eight days earlier, Gryphius had taken a small room above the bar. He was a sharp-featured man with a misty gray beard, shabbily dressed in black. Finnegan (who used that room for a purpose Treviranus immediately guessed) had asked the roomer for a rent that was obviously steep, and Gryphius paid the stipulated sum on the spot. Hardly

45

ever going out, he took lunch and supper in his room; in fact, his face was hardly known in the bar. That night he had come down to use the telephone in Finnegan's office. A coupé had drawn up outside. The coachman had stayed on his seat; some customers recalled that he wore the mask of a bear. Two harlequins got out of the carriage. They were very short men and nobody could help noticing that they were very drunk. Bleating their horns, they burst into Finnegan's office, throwing their arms around Gryphius, who seemed to know them but who did not warm to their company. The three exchanged a few words in Yiddish—he in a low, guttural voice, they in a piping falsetto—and they climbed the stairs up to his room. In a quarter of an hour they came down again, very happy. Gryphius, staggering, seemed as drunk as the others. He walked in the middle, tall and dizzy, between the two masked harlequins. (One of the women in the bar remembered their costumes of red, green, and yellow lozenges.) Twice he stumbled; twice the harlequins held him up. Then the trio climbed into the coupé and, heading for the nearby docks (which enclosed a string of rectangular bodies of water), were soon out of sight. Out front, from the running board, the last harlequin had scrawled an obscene drawing and certain words on one of the market slates hung from a pillar of the arcade.

Treviranus stepped outside for a look. Almost predictably, the phrase read:

The last letter of the Name has been uttered

He next examined Gryphius-Ginzberg's tiny room. On the floor was a star-shaped spatter of blood; in the corners, cigarette butts of a Hungarian brand; in the wardrobe, a book in Latin—a 1739 edition of Leusden's *Philologus Hebraeo-Graecus*—with a number of annotations written in by hand. Treviranus gave it an indignant look and sent for Lönnrot. While the Inspector questioned the contradictory witnesses to the possible kidnapping, Lönnrot, not even bothering to take off his hat, began reading. At four o'clock they left. In the twisted Rue de Toulon, as they were stepping over last night's tangle of streamers and confetti, Treviranus remarked, "And if tonight's events were a put-up job?"

Erik Lönnrot smiled and read to him with perfect gravity an underlined passage from the thirty-third chapter of the *Philologus*: " '*Dies Judaeorum incipit a solis occasu usque ad solis occasum diei sequentis.*' Meaning," he added, " 'the Jewish day begins at sundown and ends the following sundown.' "

The other man attempted a bit of irony. "Is that the most valuable clue you've picked up tonight?" he said.

"No. Far more valuable is one of the words Ginzberg used to you on the phone."

The evening papers made a great deal of these recurrent disappearances. *La Croix de l'Épée* contrasted the present acts of violence with the admirable discipline and order observed by the last Congress of Hermits. Ernst Palast, in *The Martyr,* condemned "the unbearable pace of this unauthorized and stinting pogrom, which has required three months for the liquidation of three Jews." The *Jüdische Zeitung* rejected the ominous suggestion of an anti-Semitic plot, "despite the fact that many penetrating minds admit of no other solution to the threefold mystery." The leading gunman of the city's Southside, Dandy Red Scharlach, swore that in his part of town crimes of that sort would never happen, and he accused Inspector Franz Treviranus of criminal negligence.

On the night of March first, Inspector Treviranus received a great sealed envelope. Opening it, he found it contained a letter signed by one "Baruch Spinoza" and, evidently torn out of a Baedeker, a detailed plan of the city. The letter predicted that on the third of March there would not be a fourth crime because the paint and hardware store on the Westside, the Rue de Toulon tavern, and the Hôtel du Nord formed "the perfect sides of an equilateral and mystical triangle." In red ink the map demonstrated that the three sides of the figure were exactly the same length. Treviranus read this Euclidean reasoning

47

with a certain weariness and sent the letter and map to Erik Lönnrot—the man, beyond dispute, most deserving of such cranky notions.

Lönnrot studied them. The three points were, in fact, equidistant. There was symmetry in time (December third, January third, February third); now there was symmetry in space as well. All at once he felt he was on the verge of solving the riddle. A pair of dividers and a compass completed his sudden intuition. He smiled, pronounced the word Tetragrammaton (of recent acquisition) and called the Inspector on the phone.

"Thanks for the equilateral triangle you sent me last night," he told him. "It has helped me unravel our mystery. Tomorrow, Friday, the murderers will be safely behind bars; we can rest quite easy."

"Then they aren't planning a fourth crime?"

"Precisely because they *are* planning a fourth crime we can rest quite easy."

Lönnrot hung up the receiver. An hour later, he was traveling on a car of the Southern Railways on his way to the deserted villa Triste-le-Roy. To the south of the city of my story flows a dark muddy river, polluted by the waste of tanneries and sewers. On the opposite bank is a factory suburb where, under the patronage of a notorious political boss, many gunmen thrive. Lönnrot smiled to himself, thinking that the best-known of them—Red Scharlach—would have given anything to know about this sudden excursion of his. Azevedo had been a henchman of Scharlach's. Lönnrot considered the remote possibility that the fourth victim might be Scharlach himself. Then he dismissed it. He had practically solved the puzzle; the mere circumstances—reality (names, arrests, faces, legal and criminal proceedings)—barely held his interest now. He wanted to get away, to relax after three months of desk work and of snail-pace investigation. He reflected that the solution of the killings lay in an anonymously sent triangle and in a dusty Greek word. The mystery seemed almost crystal clear. He felt ashamed for having spent close to a hundred days on it.

The train came to a stop at a deserted loading platform. Lönnrot got off. It was one of those forlorn evenings that seem as empty as dawn. The air off the darkening prairies was damp and cold. Lönnrot struck out across the fields. He saw dogs, he saw a flatcar on a siding, he saw the line of the horizon, he saw a pale horse drinking stagnant water out of a ditch. Night was falling when he saw the rectangular mirador of the villa Triste-le-Roy, almost as tall as the surrounding black eucalyptus trees. He thought that only one more dawn and one more dusk (an ancient light in the east and another in the west) were all that separated him from the hour appointed by the seekers of the Name.

A rusted iron fence bounded the villa's irregular perimeter. The main gate was shut. Lönnrot, without much hope of getting in, walked completely around the place. Before the barred gate once again, he stuck a hand through the palings—almost mechanically—and found the bolt. The squeal of rusted iron surprised him. With clumsy obedience, the whole gate swung open.

Lönnrot moved forward among the eucalyptus trees, stepping on the layered generations of fallen leaves. Seen from up close, the house was a clutter of meaningless symmetries and almost insane repetitions: one icy Diana in a gloomy niche matched another Diana in a second niche; one balcony appeared to reflect another; double outer staircases crossed at each landing. A two-faced Hermes cast a monstrous shadow. Lönnrot made his way around the house as he had made his way around the grounds. He went over every detail; below the level of the terrace he noticed a narrow shutter.

He pushed it open. A few marble steps went down into a cellar. Lönnrot, who by now anticipated the architect's whims, guessed that in the opposite wall he would find a similar sets of steps. He did. Climbing them, he lifted his hands and raised a trapdoor.

A stain of light led him to a window. He opened it. A round yellow moon outlined two clogged fountains in the unkempt garden. Lönnrot explored the house. Through serv-

49

ing pantries and along corridors he came to identical court-yards and several times to the same courtyard. He climbed dusty stairways to circular anterooms, where he was multi-plied to infinity in facing mirrors. He grew weary of opening or of peeping through windows that revealed, out-side, the same desolate garden seen from various heights and various angles; and indoors he grew weary of the rooms of furniture, each draped in yellowing slipcovers, and the crystal chandeliers wrapped in tarlatan. A bedroom caught his attention—in it, a single flower in a porcelain vase. At a touch, the ancient petals crumbled to dust. On the third floor, the last floor, the house seemed endless and growing. The house is not so large, he thought. This dim light, the sameness, the mirrors, the many years, my unfamiliarity, the loneliness are what make it large.

By a winding staircase he reached the mirador. That eve-ning's moon streamed in through the diamond-shaped panes; they were red, green, and yellow. He was stopped by an awesome, dizzying recollection.

Two short men, brutal and stocky, threw themselves on him and disarmed him: another, very tall, greeted him solemnly and told him, "You are very kind. You've saved us a night and a day."

It was Red Scharlach. The men bound Lönnrot's wrists. After some seconds, Lönnrot at last heard himself saying, "Scharlach, are you after the Secret Name?"

Scharlach remained standing, aloof. He had taken no part in the brief struggle and had barely held out his hand for Lönnrot's revolver. He spoke. Lönnrot heard in his voice the weariness of final triumph, a hatred the size of the universe, a sadness as great as that hatred.

"No," said Scharlach. "I'm after something more ephem-eral, more frail. I'm after Erik Lönnrot. Three years ago, in a gambling dive on the Rue de Toulon, you yourself arrested my brother and got him put away. My men man-aged to get me into a coupé before the shooting was over, but I had a cop's bullet in my guts. Nine days and nine nights I went through hell, here in this deserted villa, racked with fever. The hateful two-faced Janus that looks on the sunsets and the dawns filled both my sleep and my wakefulness with its horror. I came to loathe my body, I came to feel that two eyes, two hands, two lungs, are as monstrous as two faces. An Irishman, trying to convert me to the faith of Jesus, kept repeating to me the saying of the *goyim*—All roads lead to Rome. At night, my fever fed on that metaphor. I felt the world was a maze from which escape was impossible since all roads, though they seemed to be leading north or south, were really leading to Rome, which at the same time was the square cell where my brother lay dying and also this villa, Triste-le-Roy. During those nights, I swore by the god who looks with two faces and by all the gods of fever and of mirrors that I would weave a maze around the man who sent my brother to prison. Well, I have woven it and it's tight. Its materials are a dead rabbi, a compass, an eighteenth-century sect, a Greek word, a dagger, and the diamond-shaped patterns on a paint-store wall."

Lönnrot was in a chair now, with the two short men at his side.

"The first term of the series came to me by pure chance," Scharlach went on. "With some associates of mine—among them Daniel Azevedo—I'd planned the theft of the Tetrarch's sapphires. Azevedo betrayed us. He got drunk on the money we advanced him and tried to pull the job a day earlier. But there in the hotel he got mixed up and around two in the morning blundered into Yarmolinsky's room. The rabbi, unable to sleep, had decided to do some writing. In all likelihood, he was preparing notes or a paper on the Name of God and had already typed out the words 'The first letter of the Name has been uttered.' Azevedo warned him not to move. Yarmolinsky reached his hand toward the buzzer that would have wakened all the hotel staff; Azevedo struck him a single blow with his knife. It was probably a reflex action. Fifty years of violence had taught him that the easiest and surest way is to kill. Ten days later, I found out through the *Jüdische*

51

Zeitung that you were looking for the key to Yarmolinsky's death in his writings. I read his *History of the Hasidic Sect*. I learned that the holy fear of uttering God's Name had given rise to the idea that that Name is secret and all-powerful. I learned that some of the Hasidim, in search of that secret Name, had gone as far as to commit human sacrifices. The minute I realized you were guessing that the Hasidim had sacrificed the rabbi, I did my best to justify that guess. Yarmolinsky died the night of December third. For the second 'sacrifice' I chose the night of January third. The rabbi had died on the Northside; for the second 'sacrifice' we wanted a spot on the Westside. Daniel Azevedo was the victim we needed. He deserved death—he was impulsive, a traitor. If he'd been picked up, it would have wiped out our whole plan. One of my men stabbed him; in order to link his corpse with the previous one, I scrawled on the diamonds of the paint-store wall 'The second letter of the Name has been uttered.' "

Scharlach looked his victim straight in the face, then continued. "The third 'crime' was staged on the third of February. It was, as Treviranus guessed, only a plant. Gryphius-Ginzberg-Ginsburg was me. I spent an interminable week (rigged up in a false beard) in that flea-ridden cubicle on the Rue de Toulon until my friends came to kidnap me. From the running board of the carriage, one of them wrote on the pillar, 'The last letter of the Name has been uttered.' That message suggested that the series of crimes was *threefold*. That was how the public understood it. I, however, threw in repeated clues so that you, Erik Lönnrot the reasoner, might puzzle out that the crime was *fourfold*. A murder in the north, others in the east and west, demanded a fourth murder in the south. The Tetragrammaton—the Name of God, JHVH—is made up of *four* letters; the harlequins and the symbol on the paint store also suggest *four* terms. I underlined a certain passage in Leusden's handbook. That passage makes it clear that the Jews reckoned the day from sunset to sunset; that passage makes it understood that the deaths occurred on the *fourth* of each month. I was the one who sent the triangle to Treviranus, knowing in advance that you would supply the missing point—the point that determines the perfect rhombus, the point that fixes the spot where death is expecting you. I planned the whole thing, Erik Lönnrot, so as to lure you to the loneliness of Triste-le-Roy."

Lönnrot avoided Scharlach's eyes. He looked off at the trees and the sky broken into dark diamonds of red, green, and yellow. He felt a chill and an impersonal, almost anonymous sadness. It was night now; from down in the abandoned garden came the unavailing cry of a bird. Lönnrot, for one last time, reflected on the problem of the patterned, intermittent deaths.

"In your maze there are three lines too many," he said at last. "I know of a Greek maze that is a single straight line. Along this line so many thinkers have lost their way that a mere detective may very well lose his way. Scharlach, when in another incarnation you hunt me down, stage (or commit) a murder at A, then a second murder at B, eight miles from A, then a third murder at C, four miles from A and B, halfway between the two. Lay in wait for me then at D, two miles from A and C, again halfway between them. Kill me at D, the way you are going to kill me here at Triste-le-Roy."

"The next time I kill you," said Scharlach, "I promise you such a maze, which is made up of a single straight line and which is invisible and unending."

He moved back a few steps. Then, taking careful aim, he fired.

The Life of Tadeo Isidoro Cruz (1829–1874)

(1944)

> I'm looking for the face I had
> Before the world was made.
> Yeats, *A Woman Young and Old*

On the sixth of February, 1829, a troop of gaucho militia, harried all day by Lavalle on their march north to join the army under the command of López, made a halt some nine or ten miles from Pergamino at a ranch whose name they did not know. Along about dawn, one of the men had a haunting nightmare and, in the dim shadows of a shed where he lay sleeping, his confused outcry woke the woman who shared his bed. Nobody ever knew what he dreamed, for around four o'clock that afternoon the gauchos were routed by a detachment of Suárez' cavalry in a chase that went on for over twenty miles and ended, in thickening twilight, in tall swamp grasses, where the man died in a ditch, his skull split by a saber that had seen service in the Peruvian and Brazilian wars. The woman's name was Isidora Cruz. The son born to her was given the name Tadeo Isidoro.

My aim here is not to recount his whole personal history. Of the many days and nights that make up his life, only a single night concerns me; as to the rest, I shall tell only what is necessary to that night's full understanding. The episode belongs to a famous poem—that is to say, to a poem which has come to mean "all things to all men" (I Corinthians 9:22), since almost endless variations, versions, and perversions have been read into its pages. Those who have theorized about Tadeo Isidoro's story—and they are many—lay stress upon the influence of the wide-open plains on his character, but gauchos exactly like him were born and died along the wooded banks of the Paraná and in the hilly back country of Uruguay. He lived, it must be admitted, in a world of unrelieved barbarism. When he died, in 1874, in an outbreak of smallpox, he had never laid eyes on a mountain or a gas jet or a windmill pump. Nor on a city. In 1849, he went to Buenos Aires on a cattle drive from the ranch of Francisco Xavier Acevedo. The other drovers went into town on a spending spree; Cruz, somewhat wary, did not stray far from a shabby inn in the neighborhood of the stockyards. There he spent several days, by himself, sleeping on the ground, brewing his maté, getting up at daybreak, and going to bed at dusk. He realized (beyond words and even beyond understanding) that he could not cope with the city. One of the drovers, having drunk too much, began poking fun at him. Cruz ignored him, but several times on the way home, at night around the campfire, the other man kept on with his gibes, and Cruz (who up till then had shown neither anger nor annoyance) laid him out with his knife.

On the run, Cruz was forced to hide out in a marshy thicket. A few nights later, the cries of a startled plover warned him he had been ringed in by the police. He tested his knife in a thick clump of grass and, to keep from entangling his feet, took off his spurs. Choosing to fight it out rather than be taken, he got himself wounded in the forearm, in the shoulder, and in the left hand. When he felt the blood dripping between his fingers, he fought harder than ever, badly wounding the toughest members of the search party. Toward daybreak, weak with loss of blood, he was disarmed. The army in those days acted as a kind of penal institution; Cruz was sent off to serve in an outpost on the northern frontier. As a common soldier, he took part in the civil wars, sometimes fighting for the province of his birth, sometimes against. On the twenty-third of January, 1856, in the Cardoso marshes, he was one of thirty white men who, led by Sergeant Major Eusebio Laprida, fought against two hundred Indians. In this action he was wounded by a spear.

The dim and hardy story of his life is full of gaps. Around 1868, we hear of him once more in Pergamino, married or living with a woman, father of a son, and owner of a small holding of land. In 1869, he was appointed sergeant of the local police. He had made up for his past and, in those days, may have thought of himself as a happy man, though deep down he wasn't. (What lay in wait for him, hidden in the future, was a night of stark illumination—the night in which at last he glimpsed his own face, the night in which at last he heard his name. Fully understood, that night exhausts his story; or rather, one moment in that night, one deed, since deeds are our symbols.) Any life, no matter how long or complex it may be, is made up essentially *of a single moment*—the moment in which a man finds out, once and for all, who he is. It has been said that Alexander the Great saw his iron future in the fabled story of Achilles, and Charles XII of Sweden, his in the story of Alexander. To Tadeo Isidoro Cruz, who did not know how to read, this revelation was not given by a book; it was in a manhunt and in the man he was hunting that he learned who he was. The thing happened in this way:

During the last days of the month of June, 1870, he received orders to capture an outlaw who had killed two men. The man was a deserter from the forces of Colonel Benito Machado on the southern frontier; he had killed a Negro in a drunken brawl in a whorehouse and, in another brawl, a man from the district of Rojas. The report added that he had last been seen near the Laguna Colorada. This was the same place where the troop of gaucho militia had gathered, some forty years earlier, before starting out on the misadventure that gave their flesh to the vultures and dogs. Out of this spot had come Manuel Mesa, who was later made to stand before a firing squad in the central square of Buenos Aires while the drums rolled in order to drown out his last words; out of this spot had come the unknown man who fathered Cruz and died in a ditch, his skull split by a saber that had seen action on the battlefields of Peru and Brazil. Cruz had forgotten the name of the place. Now, after a vague and puzzling uneasiness, it came to him.

Pursued by the soldiers and shuttling back and forth on horseback, the hunted man had woven a long maze, but nonetheless, on the night of July twelfth, the troops tracked him down. He had taken shelter in a growth of tall reeds. The darkness was nearly impenetrable; Cruz and his men, stealthily and on foot, advanced toward the clumps in whose swaying center the hidden man lay in wait or asleep. A startled plover let out a cry. Tadeo Isidoro Cruz had the feeling of having lived this moment before. The hunted man came out of his hiding place to fight them in the open. Cruz made out the hideous figure—his overgrown hair and gray beard seemed to eat away his face. An obvious reason keeps me from describing the fight that followed. Let me simply point out that the deserter badly wounded or killed several of Cruz's men. Cruz, while he fought in the dark (while his body fought in the dark), began to understand. He understood that one destiny is no better than another, but that every man must obey what is within him. He understood that his shoulder braid and his uniform were now in his way. He understood that his real destiny was as a lone wolf, not a gregarious dog. He understood that the other man was himself. Day dawned over the boundless plain. Cruz threw down his kepi, called out that he would not be party to the crime of killing a brave man, and began fighting against his own soldiers, shoulder to shoulder with Martín Fierro, the deserter.

The Two Kings and Their Two Labyrinths

(1946)

[This is the story the Reverend Allaby tells from the pulpit in "Ibn Hakkan al-Bokhari, Dead in His Labyrinth."

See page 77]

Chroniclers worthy of trust have recorded (but only Allah is All-Knowing) that in former times there was a king of the isles of Babylon who called together his architects and his wizards and set them to build him a labyrinth so intricate that no wise man would dare enter inside, and so subtle that those who did would lose their way. This undertaking was a blasphemy, for confusion and marvels belong to God alone and not to man. With the passage of time there came to his court a king of the Arabs, and the king of Babylon (wishing to mock his guest's simplicity) allowed him to set foot in his labyrinth, where he wandered in humiliation and bewilderment until the coming of night. It was then that the second king implored the help of God and soon after came upon the door. He suffered his lips to utter no complaint, but he told the king of Babylon that he, too, had a labyrinth in his land and that, God willing, he would one day take pleasure in showing it to his host. Then he returned to Arabia, gathered his captains and his armies, and overran the realms of Babylon with so fair a fortune that he ravaged its castles, broke its peoples, and took captive the king himself. He bound him onto a swift camel and brought him into the desert. Three days they rode, and then the captor said, "O king of time and crown of the century! In Babylon you lured me into a labyrinth of brass cluttered with many stairways, doors, and walls; now the Almighty has brought it to pass that I show you mine, which has no stairways to climb, nor doors to force, nor unending galleries to wear one down, nor walls to block one's way."

He then loosened the bonds of the first king and left him in the heart of the desert to die of thirst and hunger. Glory be to the Living, who dieth not.

The Dead Man
(1946)

That a man from the outlying slums of a city like Buenos
Aires, that a sorry hoodlum with little else to his credit
than a passion for recklessness, should find his way into
that wild stretch of horse country between Brazil and
Uruguay and become the leader of a band of smugglers,
seems on the face of it unbelievable. To those who think so,
I'd like to give an account of what happened to Benjamín
Otálora, of whom perhaps not a single memory lingers in
the neighborhood where he grew up, and who died a fitting
death, struck down by a bullet, somewhere on the border of
Río Grande do Sul. Of the details of his adventures I know
little; should I ever be given the facts, I shall correct and
expand these pages. For the time being, this outline may
prove of some use.

Benjamín Otálora, along about 1891, is a strapping
young man of nineteen. He has a low forehead, candid blue
eyes, and that country-boy appearance that goes with
Basque ancestry. A lucky blow with a knife has made clear

to him that he is also brave; his opponent's death causes him no concern, nor does his need to flee the country. The political boss of the district gives him a letter of introduction to a certain Azevedo Bandeira, in Uruguay. Otálora books passage; the crossing is stormy and the ship pitches and creaks. The next day, he wanders the length and breadth of Montevideo, with unacknowledged or perhaps unsuspected homesickness. He does not find Azevedo Bandeira. Getting on toward midnight, in a small saloon out on the northern edge of town, he witnesses a brawl between some cattle drovers. A knife flashes. Otálora has no idea who is in the right or wrong, but the sheer taste of danger lures him, just as cards or music lure other men. In the confusion, he blocks a lunging knife thrust that one of the gauchos aims at a man wearing a rough countryman's poncho and, oddly, the dark derby of a townsman. The man turns out to be Azevedo Bandeira. (As soon as he finds this out, Otálora destroys the letter, preferring to be under no one's obligation.) Azevedo Bandeira, though of stocky build, gives the unaccountable impression of being somehow misshapen. In his large face, which seems always to be too close, are the Jew, the Negro, and the Indian; in his bearing, the tiger and the ape. The scar that cuts across his cheek is one ornament more, like his bristling black moustache.

A fantasy or a mistake born of drunkenness, the fight ends as quickly as it broke out. Otálora takes a drink with the drovers and then goes along with them to an all-night party and after that—the sun high in the sky by now—to a rambling house in the Old Town. Inside, on the bare ground of the last patio, the men lay out their sheepskin saddle blankets to sleep. Dimly, Otálora compares this past night with the night before; here he is, on solid ground now, among friends. A pang of remorse for not missing his Buenos Aires nags at him, however. He sleeps until nightfall, when he is wakened by the same gaucho who, blind drunk, had tried to knife Bandeira. (Otálora recalls that the man has shared the high-spirited night with the rest of them, and that Bandeira had seated him at his right hand and forced him to go on drinking.) The man says the boss has sent for him. In a kind of office opening into the entrance passage (Otálora has never before seen an entrance with doors opening into it from the sides), Azevedo Bandeira, in the company of an aloof and showy red-haired woman, is waiting for him. Bandeira praises him up and down, offers him a shot of rum, tells him he has the makings of a man of guts, suggests that he go up north with the others to bring back a large cattle herd. Otálora agrees; toward dawn they are on the road, heading for Tacuarembó.

For Otálora a new kind of life opens up, a life of far-flung sunrises and long days in the saddle, reeking of horses. It is an untried and at times unbearable life, but it's already in his blood, for just as the men of certain countries worship and feel the call of the sea, we Argentines in turn (including the man who weaves these symbols) yearn for the boundless plains that ring under a horse's hooves. Otálora has grown up in a neighborhood of teamsters and liverymen. In under a year, he makes himself into a gaucho. He learns to handle a horse, to round up and slaughter cattle, to throw a rope for holding an animal fast or bolas for bringing it down, to fight off sleep, to weather storms and frosts and sun, to drive a herd with whistles and hoots. Only once during this whole apprenticeship does he set eyes on Azevedo Bandeira, but he has him always in mind because to be one of Bandeira's men is to be looked up to and feared, and because after any feat or hard job the gauchos always say Bandeira does it better. Somebody has it that Bandeira was born on the Brazilian side of the Cuareim, in Rio Grande do Sul; this, which should lower him in Otálora's eyes, somehow—with its suggestion of dense forests and of marshes and of inextricable and almost endless distances—only adds to him. Little by little, Otálora comes to realize that Bandeira's interests are many and that chief among them is smuggling. To be a cattle drover is to be a servant; Otálora decides to work himself up to the level of smuggler. One night, as two of his companions are about to go over the border to bring back a consignment of rum, Otálora picks a fight with one of them, wounds him, and takes his place. He is driven by ambition and also by a dim sense of loyalty. The man (he thinks) will come to find out that I'm worth more than all his Uruguayans put together.

Another year goes by before Otálora sees Montevideo again. They come riding through the outskirts and into the city (which to Otálora now seems enormous); reaching the boss's house, the men prepare to bed down in the last patio. The days pass, and Otálora still has not laid eyes on Bandeira. It is said, in fear, that he is ailing; every afternoon a Negro goes up to Bandeira's room with a kettle and maté. One evening, the job is assigned to Otálora. He feels vaguely humiliated, but at the same time gratified.

The bedroom is bare and dark. There's a balcony that faces the sunset, there's a long table with a shining disarray of riding crops, bullwhips, cartridge belts, firearms, and knives. On the far wall there's a mirror and the glass is faded. Bandeira lies face up, dreaming and muttering in his sleep; the sun's last rays outline his features. The big white bed seems to make him smaller, darker. Otálora notes his graying hair, his exhaustion, his weakness, the deep wrinkles of his years. It angers him being mastered by this old man. He thinks that a single blow would be enough to finish him. At this moment, he glimpses in the mirror that someone has come in. It's the woman with the red hair; she is barefoot and only half-dressed, and looks at him with cold curiosity. Bandeira sits up in bed; while he speaks of business affairs of the past two years and drinks maté after maté, his fingers toy with the woman's braided hair. In the end, he gives Otálora permission to leave.

A few days later, they get orders to head north again. There, in a place that might be anywhere on the face of the endless plains, they come to a forlorn ranch. Not a single tree or a brook. The sun's first and last rays beat down on it. There are stone fences for the lean longhorn cattle. This rundown set of buildings is called "The Last Sigh."

Sitting around the fire with the ranch hands, Otálora hears that Bandeira will soon be on his way from Montevideo. He asks what for, and someone explains that there's an outsider turned gaucho among them who's giving too many orders. Otálora takes this as a friendly joke and is flattered that the joke can be made. Later on, he finds out that Bandeira has had a falling out with one of the political bosses, who has withdrawn his support. Otálora likes this bit of news.

Crates of rifles arrive; a pitcher and washbasin, both of silver, arrive for the woman's bedroom; intricately figured damask draperies arrive; one morning, from out of the hills, a horseman arrives—a sullen man with a full beard and a poncho. His name is Ulpiano Suárez and he is Azevedo Bandeira's strong-arm man, or bodyguard. He speaks very little and with a thick Brazilian accent. Otálora does not know whether to put down his reserve to unfriendliness, or to contempt, or to mere backwoods manners. He realizes, however, that to carry out the scheme he is hatching he must win the other man's friendship.

Next into Benjamín Otálora's story comes a black-legged bay horse that Azevedo Bandeira brings from the south, and that carries a fine saddle worked with silver and a saddle blanket trimmed with a jaguar skin. This spirited horse is a token of Bandeira's authority and for this reason is coveted by the young man, who comes also—with a desire bordering on spite—to hunger for the woman with the shining hair. The woman, the saddle, and the big bay are attributes or trappings of a man he aspires to bring down.

At this point the story takes another turn. Azevedo Bandeira is skilled in the art of slow intimidation, in the diabolical trickery of leading a man on, step by step, shifting from sincerity to mockery. Otálora decides to apply this ambiguous method to the hard task before him. He decides to replace Azevedo Bandeira, but to take his time over it. During days of shared danger, he gains Suárez' friendship. He confides his plan to him; Suárez pledges to help. Then a number of things begin happening of which I know only a few. Otálora disobeys Bandeira's orders; he takes to overlooking them, changing them, defying them. The whole world seems to conspire with him, hastening events. One noontime, somewhere around Tacuarembó, there is an exchange of gunfire with a gang from Brazil; Otálora takes Bandeira's place and shouts out orders to the Uruguayans. A bullet hits him in the shoulder, but that afternoon Otálora rides back to "The Last Sigh" on the boss's horse, and that evening some drops of his blood stain the jaguar skin, and that night he sleeps with the woman with the shining hair. Other accounts change the order of these events, denying they happened all in the same day.

Bandeira, nevertheless, remains nominally the boss. He goes on giving orders which are not carried out. Benjamín Otálora leaves him alone, out of mixed reasons of habit and pity.

The closing scene of the story coincides with the commotion of the closing night of the year 1894. On this night, the men of "The Last Sigh" eat freshly slaughtered meat and fall into quarreling over their liquor; someone picks out on the guitar, over and over again, a *milonga* that gives him a lot of trouble. At the head of the table, Otálora, feeling his drink, piles exultation upon exultation, boast upon boast; this dizzying tower is a symbol of his irresistible destiny. Bandeira, silent amid the shouting, lets the night flow noisily on. When the clock strikes twelve, he gets up like a man just remembering he has something to do. He gets up and softly knocks at the woman's door. She opens at once, as though waiting to be called. She steps out barefoot and half-dressed. In an almost feminine, soft-spoken drawl, Bandeira gives her an order.

"Since you and the Argentine care so much for each other," he says, "you're going to kiss him right now in front of everyone."

He adds an obscene detail. The woman tries to resist, but two men have taken her by the arms and fling her upon

Otálora. Brought to tears, she kisses his face and chest. Ulpiano Suárez has his revolver out. Otálora realizes, before dying, that he has been betrayed from the start, that he has been sentenced to death—that love and command and triumph have been accorded him because his companions already thought of him as a dead man, because to Bandeira he already was a dead man.

Suárez, almost in contempt, fires the shot.

The Other Death

(1948)

I have mislaid the letter, but a couple of years or so ago
Gannon wrote me from his ranch up in Gualeguaychú
saying he would send me a translation, perhaps the very
first into Spanish, of Ralph Waldo Emerson's poem "The
Past," and adding in a P.S. that don Pedro Damián, whom
I might recall, had died of a lung ailment a few nights
earlier. The man (Gannon went on), wasted by fever, had
in his delirium relived the long ordeal of the battle of
Masoller. It seemed to me there was nothing unreasonable
or out of the ordinary about this news since don Pedro,
when he was nineteen or twenty, had been a follower of the
banners of Aparicio Saravia. Pedro Damián had been working as a hand up north on a ranch in Río Negro or
Paysandú when the 1904 revolution broke out. Although
he was from Gualeguaychú, in the province of Entre Ríos,
he went along with his friends and, being as cocky and
ignorant as they were, joined the rebel army. He fought in
one or two skirmishes and in the final battle. Returned

home in 1905, Damián, with a kind of humble stubbornness, once more took up his work as a cowhand. For all I know, he never left his native province again. He spent his last thirty years living in a small lonely cabin eight or ten miles from Ñancay. It was in that out-of-the-way place that I spoke with him one evening (that I tried to speak with him one evening) back around 1942; he was a man of few words, and not very bright. Masoller, it turned out, was the whole of his personal history. And so I was not surprised to find out that he had lived the sound and fury of that battle over again at the hour of his death. When I knew I would never see Damián another time, I wanted to remember him, but so poor is my memory for faces that all I could recall was the snapshot Gannon had taken of him. There is nothing unusual in this fact, considering that I saw the man only once at the beginning of 1942, but had looked at his picture many times. Gannon sent me the photograph and it, too, has been misplaced. I think now that if I were to come across it, I would feel afraid.

The second episode took place in Montevideo, months later. Don Pedro's fever and his agony gave me the idea for a tale of fantasy based on the defeat at Masoller; Emir Rodríguez Monegal, to whom I had told the plot, wrote me an introduction to Colonel Dionisio Tabares, who had fought in that campaign. The Colonel received me one evening after dinner. From a rocking chair out in the side yard, he recalled the old days with great feeling but at the same time with a faulty sense of chronology. He spoke of ammunition that never reached him and of reserves of horses that arrived worn out, of sleepy dust-covered men weaving labyrinths of marches, of Saravia, who might have ridden into Montevideo but who passed it by "because the gaucho has a fear of towns," of throats hacked from ear to ear, of a civil war that seemed to me less a military operation than the dream of a cattle thief or an outlaw. Names of battles kept coming up: Illescas, Tupambaé, Masoller. The Colonel's pauses were so effective and his manner so vivid that I realized he had told and retold these same things many times before, and I feared that behind his words almost no true memories remained. When he stopped for a breath, I managed to get in Damián's name.

"Damián? Pedro Damián?" said the Colonel. "He served with me. A little half-breed. I remember the boys used to call him Daymán—after the river." The Colonel let out a burst of loud laughter, then cut it off all at once. I could not tell whether his discomfort was real or put on.

In another voice, he stated that war, like women, served as a test of men, and that nobody knew who he really was until he had been under fire. A man might think himself a coward and actually be brave. And the other way around, too, as had happened to that poor Damián, who bragged his way in and out of saloons with his white ribbon marking him as a Blanco, and later on lost his nerve at Masoller. In one exchange of gunfire with the regulars, he handled himself like a man, but then it was something else again when the two armies met face to face and the artillery began pounding away and every man felt as though there were five thousand other men out there grouping to kill him. That poor kid. He'd spent his life on a farm dipping sheep, and then all of a sudden he gets himself dragged along and mixed up in the grim reality of war. . . .

For some absurd reason Tabares' version of the story made me uncomfortable. I would have preferred things to have happened differently. Without being aware of it, I had made a kind of idol out of old Damián—a man I had seen only once on a single evening many years earlier. Tabares' story destroyed everything. Suddenly the reasons for Damián's aloofness and his stubborn insistence on keeping to himself were clear to me. They had not sprung from modesty but from shame. In vain, I told myself that a man pursued by an act of cowardice is more complex and more interesting than one who is merely courageous. The gaucho Martín Fierro, I thought, is less memorable than Lord Jim or Razumov. Yes, but Damián, as a gaucho, should have been Martín Fierro—especially in the presence of Uruguayan gauchos. In what Tabares left unsaid, I felt his assumption (perhaps undeniable) that Uruguay is more primitive than Argentina and therefore physically braver. I remember we said goodbye to each other that night with a cordiality that was a bit marked.

During the winter, the need of one or two details for my story (which somehow was slow in taking shape) sent me back to Colonel Tabares again. I found him with another man of his own age, a Dr. Juan Francisco Amaro from Paysandú, who had also fought in Saravia's revolution. They spoke, naturally, of Masoller.

Amaro told a few anecdotes, then slowly added, in the manner of someone who is thinking aloud, "We camped for the night at Santa Irene, I recall, and some of the men from around there joined us. Among them a French veterinarian, who died the night before the battle, and a boy, a sheepshearer from Entre Ríos. Pedro Damián was his name."

I cut him off sharply. "Yes, I know," I said. "The Argentine who couldn't face the bullets."

I stopped. The two of them were looking at me, puzzled.

"You are mistaken, sir," Amaro said after a while. "Pedro Damián died as any man might wish to die. It was about four o'clock in the afternoon. The regular troops had dug themselves in on the top of a hill and our men charged them with lances. Damián rode at the head, shouting, and a bullet struck him square in the chest. He stood up in his stirrups, finished his shout, and then rolled to the ground, where he lay under the horses' hooves. He was dead, and the whole last charge of Masoller trampled over him. So fearless, and barely twenty."

He was speaking, doubtless, of another Damián, but something made me ask what it was the boy had shouted.

"Filth," said the Colonel. "That's what men shout in action."

"Maybe," said Amaro, "but he also cried out, 'Long live Urquiza!'"

We were silent. Finally the Colonel murmured, "Not as if we were fighting at Masoller, but at Cagancha or India

Muerta a hundred years ago." He added, genuinely bewildered, "I commanded those troops, and I could swear it's the first time I've ever heard of this Damián."

We had no luck in getting the Colonel to remember him.

Back in Buenos Aires, the amazement that his forgetfulness produced in me repeated itself. Browsing through the eleven pleasurable volumes of Emerson's works in the basement of Mitchell's, the English bookstore, I met Patricio Gannon one afternoon. I asked him for his translation of "The Past." He told me that he had no translation of it in mind, and that, besides, Spanish literature was so boring it made Emerson quite superfluous. I reminded him that he had promised me the translation in the same letter in which he wrote me of Damián's death. He asked me who was Damián. I told him in vain. With rising terror, I noticed that he was listening to me very strangely, and I took refuge in a literary discussion on the detractors of Emerson, a poet far more complex, far more skilled, and truly more extraordinary than the unfortunate Poe.

I must put down some additional facts. In April, I had a letter from Colonel Dionisio Tabares; his mind was no longer vague and now he remembered quite well the boy from Entre Ríos who spearheaded the charge at Masoller and whom his men buried that night in a grave at the foot of the hill. In July, I passed through Gualeguaychú; I did not come across Damián's cabin, and nobody there seemed to remember him now. I wanted to question the foreman Diego Abaroa, who saw Damián die, but Abaroa had passed away himself at the beginning of the winter. I tried to call to mind Damián's features; months later, leafing through some old albums, I found that the dark face I had attempted to evoke really belonged to the famous tenor Tamberlik, playing the role of Othello.

Now I move on to conjectures. The easiest, but at the same time the least satisfactory, assumes two Damiáns: the coward who died in Entre Ríos around 1946, and the man of courage who died at Masoller in 1904. But this falls apart in its inability to explain what are really the puzzles:

the strange fluctuations of Colonel Tabares' memory, for one, and the general forgetfulness, which in so short a time could blot out the image and even the name of the man who came back. (I cannot accept, I do not want to accept, a simpler possibility—that of my having dreamed the first man.) Stranger still is the supernatural conjecture thought up by Ulrike von Kühlmann. Pedro Damián, said Ulrike, was killed in the battle and at the hour of his death asked God to carry him back to Entre Ríos. God hesitated a moment before granting the request, but by then the man was already dead and had been seen by others to have fallen. God, who cannot unmake the past but can affect its images, altered the image of Damián's violent death into one of falling into a faint. And so it was the boy's ghost that came back to his native province. Came back, but we must not forget that it did so as a ghost. It lived in isolation without a woman and without friends; it loved and possessed everything, but from a distance, as from the other side of a mirror; ultimately it "died" and its frail image just disappeared, like water in water. This conjecture is faulty, but it may have been responsible for pointing out to me the true one (the one I now believe to be true), which is at the same time simpler and more unprecedented. In a mysterious way I discovered it in the treatise *De Omnipotentia* by Pier Damiani, after having been referred to him by two lines in Canto XXI of the *Paradiso,* in which the problem of Damiani's identity is brought up. In the fifth chapter of that treatise, Pier Damiani asserts—against Aristotle and against Fredegarius de Tours—that it is within God's power to make what once was into something that has never been. Reading those old theological discussions, I began to understand don Pedro Damián's tragic story.

This is my solution. Damián handled himself like a coward on the battlefield at Masoller and spent the rest of his life setting right that shameful weakness. He returned to Entre Ríos; he never lifted a hand against another man, he never cut anyone up, he never sought fame as a man of

courage. Instead, living out there in the hill country of
Ñancay and struggling with the backwoods and with wild
cattle, he made himself tough, hard. Probably without realizing it, he was preparing the way for the miracle. He
thought from his innermost self, If destiny brings me another battle, I'll be ready for it. For forty years he waited
and waited, with an inarticulate hope, and then, in the end,
at the hour of his death, fate brought him his battle. It
came in the form of delirium, for, as the Greeks knew, we
are all shadows of a dream. In his final agony he lived his
battle over again, conducted himself as a man, and in
heading the last charge he was struck by a bullet in the
middle of the chest. And so, in 1946, through the working
out of a long, slow-burning passion, Pedro Damián died in
the defeat at Masoller, which took place between winter
and spring in 1904.

In the *Summa Theologiae*, it is denied that God can
unmake the past, but nothing is said of the complicated
concatenation of causes and effects which is so vast and so
intimate that perhaps it might prove impossible to annul a
single remote fact, insignificant as it may seem, without
invalidating the present. To modify the past is not to
modify a single fact; it is to annul the consequences of that
fact, which tend to be infinite. In other words, it involves
the creation of two universal histories. In the first, let us
say, Pedro Damián died in Entre Ríos in 1946; in the
second, at Masoller in 1904. It is this second history that
we are living now, but the suppression of the first was not
immediate and produced the odd contradictions that I have
related. It was in Colonel Dionisio Tabares that the different stages took place. At first, he remembered that Damián
acted as a coward; next, he forgot him entirely; then he
remembered Damián's fearless death. No less illuminating
is the case of the foreman Abaroa; he had to die, as I
understand it, because he held too many memories of don
Pedro Damián.

As for myself, I do not think I am running a similar risk.
I have guessed at and set down a process beyond man's

understanding, a kind of exposure of reason; but there are certain circumstances that lessen the dangers of this privilege of mine. For the present, I am not sure of having always written the truth. I suspect that in my story there are a few false memories. It is my suspicion that Pedro Damián (if he ever existed) was not called Pedro Damián and that I remember him by that name so as to believe someday that the whole story was suggested to me by Pier Damiani's thesis. Something similar happens with the poem I mentioned in the first paragraph, which centers around the irrevocability of the past. A few years from now, I shall believe I made up a fantastic tale, and I will actually have recorded an event that was real, just as some two thousand years ago in all innocence Virgil believed he was setting down the birth of a man and foretold the birth of Christ.

Poor Damián! Death carried him off at the age of twenty in a local battle of a sad and little-known war, but in the end he got what he longed for in his heart, and he was a long time getting it, and perhaps there is no greater happiness.

Ibn Hakkan al-Bokhari, Dead in His Labyrinth

(1949)

> . . . like the spider, which
> builds itself a feeble house.
> The Koran, xxix, 40

"This," said Dunraven with a sweeping gesture that did not fail to embrace the misty stars while it took in the bleak moor, the sea, the dunes, and an imposing, tumbledown building that somehow suggested a stable long since fallen into disrepair, "this is the land of my forebears."

Unwin, his companion, drew the pipe out of his mouth and made some faint sounds of approval. It was the first summer evening of 1914; weary of a world that lacked the dignity of danger, the two friends set great value on these far reaches of Cornwall. Dunraven cultivated a dark beard and thought of himself as the author of a substantial epic, which his contemporaries would barely be able to scan and whose subject had not yet been revealed to him; Unwin had published a paper on the theory supposed to have been written by Fermat in the margin of a page of Diophantus. Both men—need it be said?—were young, dreamy, and passionate.

"It's about a quarter of a century ago now," said Dunraven, "that Ibn Hakkan al-Bokhari, chief or king of I don't know what Nilotic tribe, died in the central room of this house at the hands of his cousin Zaid. After all these years, the facts surrounding his death are still unclear."

Unwin, as was expected of him, asked why.

"For several reasons," was the answer. "In the first place, this house is a labyrinth. In the second place, it was watched over by a slave and a lion. In the third place, a hidden treasure vanished. In the fourth place, the murderer was dead when the murder happened. In the fifth place—"

Tired out, Unwin stopped him.

"Don't go on multiplying the mysteries," he said. "They should be kept simple. Bear in mind Poe's purloined letter, bear in mind Zangwill's locked room."

"Or made complex," replied Dunraven. "Bear in mind the universe."

Climbing the steep dunes, they had reached the labyrinth. It seemed to them, up close, a straight and almost endless wall of unplastered brick, barely higher than a man's head. Dunraven said that the building had the shape of a circle, but so wide was this circle that its curve was almost invisible. Unwin recollected Nicholas of Cusa, to whom a straight line was the arc of an infinite circle. They walked on and on, and along about midnight discovered a narrow opening that led into a blind, unsafe passage. Dunraven said that inside the house were many branching ways but that, by turning always to the left, they would reach the very center of the network in little more than an hour. Unwin assented. Their cautious footsteps resounded off the stone-paved floor; the corridor branched into other, narrower corridors. The roof was very low, making the house seem to want to imprison them, and they had to walk one behind the other through the complex dark. Unwin went ahead, forced to slacken the pace because of the rough masonry and the many turns. The unseen wall flowed on by his hand, endlessly. Unwin, slow in the blackness, heard from his friend's lips the tale of the death of Ibn Hakkan.

"Perhaps the oldest of my memories," Dunraven said, "is

the one of Ibn Hakkan al-Bokhari in the port of Pentreath. At his heels followed a black man with a lion—unquestionably they were the first black man and the first lion my eyes had ever seen, outside of engravings from the Bible. I was a boy then, but the beast the color of the sun and the man the color of night impressed me less than Ibn Hakkan himself. To me, he seemed very tall; he was a man with sallow skin, half-shut black eyes, an insolent nose, fleshy lips, a saffron-colored beard, a powerful chest, and a way of walking that was self-assured and silent. At home, I said, 'A king has come on a ship.' Later, when the bricklayers were at work here, I broadened his title and dubbed him King of Babel.

"The news that this stranger would settle in Pentreath was received with welcome, but the scale and shape of his house aroused disapproval and bewilderment. It was not right that a house should consist of a single room and of miles and miles of corridors. 'Among foreigners such houses might be common,' people said, 'but hardly here in England.' Our rector, Mr. Allaby, a man with out-of-the-way reading habits, exhumed an Eastern story of a king whom the Divinity had punished for having built a labyrinth, and he told this story from the pulpit. The very next day, Ibn Hakkan paid a visit to the rectory; the circumstances of the brief interview were not known at the time, but no further sermon alluded to the sin of pride, and the Moor was able to go on contracting masons. Years afterward, when Ibn Hakkan was dead, Allaby stated to the authorities the substance of their conversation.

"Ibn Hakkan, refusing a chair, had told him these or similar words: 'No man can place judgment upon what I am doing now. My sins are such that were I to invoke for hundreds upon hundreds of years the Ultimate Name of God, this would be powerless to set aside the least of my torments; my sins are such that were I to kill you, Reverend Allaby, with these very hands, my act would not increase even slightly the torments that Infinite Justice holds in store for me. There is no land on earth where my name is unknown. I am Ibn Hakkan al-Bokhari, and in my day I ruled over the tribes of the desert with a rod of iron. For years and years, with the help of my cousin Zaid, I trampled them underfoot until God heard their outcry and suffered them to rebel against me. My armies were broken and put to the sword; I succeeded in escaping with the wealth I had accumulated during my reign of plunder. Zaid led me to the tomb of a holy man, at the foot of a stone hill. I ordered my slave to watch the face of the desert. Zaid and I went inside with our chest of gold coins and slept, utterly worn out. That night, I believed that a tangle of snakes had trapped me. I woke up in horror. By my side, in the dawn, Zaid lay asleep; a spider web against my flesh had made me dream that dream. It pained me that Zaid, who was a coward, should be sleeping so restfully. I reflected that the wealth was not infinite and that Zaid might wish to claim part of it for himself. In my belt was my silver-handled dagger; I slipped it from its sheath and pierced his throat with it. In his agony, he muttered words I could not make out. I looked at him. He was dead, but, fearing that he might rise up, I ordered my slave to obliterate the dead man's face with a heavy rock. Then we wandered under the sun, and one day we spied a sea. Very tall ships plowed a course through it. I thought that a dead man would be unable to make his way over such waters, and I decided to seek other lands. The first night after we sailed, I dreamed that I killed Zaid. Everything was exactly the same, but this time I understood his words. He said: "As you now kill me, I shall one day kill you, wherever you may hide." I have sworn to avert that threat. I shall bury myself in the heart of a labyrinth so that Zaid's ghost will lose its way.'

"After having said this, he went away. Allaby did his best to think that the Moor was mad and that his absurd labyrinth was a symbol and a clear mark of his madness. Then he reflected that this explanation agreed with the extravagant building and with the extravagant story but not with the strong impression left by the man Ibn Hakkan.

Who knew whether such tales might not be common in the sand wastes of Egypt, who knew whether such queer things corresponded (like Pliny's dragons) less to a person than to a culture? On a visit to London, Allaby combed back numbers of the *Times;* he verified the fact of the uprising and of the subsequent downfall of al-Bokhari and of his vizier, whose cowardice was well known.

"Al-Bokhari, as soon as the bricklayers had finished, installed himself in the center of the labyrinth. He was not seen again in the town; at times, Allaby feared that Zaid had caught up with the king and killed him. At night, the wind carried to us the growling of the lion, and the sheep in their pens pressed together with an ancient fear.

"It was customary for ships from Eastern ports, bound for Cardiff or Bristol, to anchor in the little bay. The slave used to go down from the labyrinth (which at that time, I remember, was not its present rose color but was crimson) and exchanged guttural-sounding words with the ships' crews, and he seemed to be looking among the men for the vizier's ghost. It was no secret that these vessels carried cargoes of contraband, and if of alcohol or of forbidden ivories, why not of dead men as well?

"Some three years after the house was finished, the *Rose of Sharon* anchored one October morning just under the bluffs. I was not among those who saw this sailing ship, and perhaps the image of it I hold in my mind is influenced by forgotten prints of Aboukir or of Trafalgar, but I believe it was among that class of ships so minutely detailed that they seem less the work of a shipbuilder than of a carpenter, and less of a carpenter than of a cabinetmaker. It was (if not in reality, at least in my dreams) polished, dark, fast, and silent, and its crew was made up of Arabs and Malayans.

"It anchored at dawn, and in the late afternoon of that same day Ibn Hakkan burst into the rectory to see Allaby. He was dominated—completely dominated—by a passion of fear, and was scarcely able to make it clear that Zaid had entered the labyrinth and that his slave and his lion had

79

already been killed. He asked in all seriousness whether the authorities might be able to help him. Before Allaby could say a word, al-Bokhari was gone—as if torn away by the same terror that had brought him for the second and last time to the rectory. Alone in his library, Allaby reflected in amazement that this fear-ridden man had kept down Sudanese tribes by the knife, knew what a battle was, and knew what it was to kill. Allaby found out the next day that the boat had already set sail (bound for the Red Sea port of Suakin, he later learned). Feeling it was his duty to verify the death of the slave, he made his way up to the labyrinth. Al-Bokhari's breathless tale seemed to him utterly fantastic, but at one turn of the corridor he came upon the lion, and the lion was dead, and at another turn there was the slave, who was also dead, and in the central room he found al-Bokhari—with his face obliterated. At the man's feet was a small chest inlaid with mother-of-pearl; the lock had been forced, and not a single coin was left."

Dunraven's final sentences, underlined by rhetorical pauses, were meant to be impressive; Unwin guessed that his friend had gone over them many times before, always with the same confidence—and with the same flatness of effect. He asked, in order to feign interest, "How were the lion and the slave killed?"

The relentless voice went on with a kind of gloomy satisfaction, "Their faces were also bashed in."

A muffled sound of rain was now added to the sound of the men's steps. Unwin realized that they would have to spend the night in the labyrinth, in the central chamber, but that in time this uncomfortable experience could be looked back on as an adventure. He kept silent. Dunraven could not restrain himself, and asked, in the manner of one who wants to squeeze the last drop, "Can this story be explained?"

Unwin answered, as though thinking aloud, "I have no idea whether it can be explained or not. I only know it's a lie."

Dunraven broke out in a torrent of strongly flavored

language and said that all the population of Pentreath could bear witness to the truth of what he had told and that if he had to make up a story, he was a writer after all and could easily have invented a far better one. No less astonished than Dunraven, Unwin apologized. Time in the darkness seemed more drawn out; both men began to fear they had gone astray, and were feeling their tiredness when a faint gleam of light from overhead revealed the lower steps of a narrow staircase. They climbed up and came to a round room that lay in ruin. Two things were left that attested to the fear of the ill-starred king: a slit of a window that looked out onto the moors and the sea, and a trapdoor in the floor that opened above the curve of the stairway. The room, though spacious, had about it something of a prison cell.

Less because of the rain than because of a wish to have a ready anecdote for friends, the two men spent the night in the labyrinth. The mathematician slept soundly; not so the poet, who was hounded by verses that his judgment knew to be worthless:

> Faceless the sultry and overpowering lion,
> Faceless the stricken slave, faceless the king.

Unwin felt that the story of al-Bokhari's death had left him indifferent, but he woke up with the conviction of having unraveled it. All that day, he was preoccupied and unsociable, trying to fit the pieces of the puzzle together, and two nights later he met Dunraven in a pub back in London and said to him these or similar words: "In Cornwall, I said your story was a lie. The *facts* were true, or could be thought of as true, but told the way you told them they were obviously lies. I will begin with the greatest lie of all—with the unbelievable labyrinth. A fugitive does not hide himself in a maze. He does not build himself a labyrinth on a bluff overlooking the sea, a crimson labyrinth that can be sighted from afar by any ship's crew. He has no need to erect a labyrinth when the whole world already is one.

81

For anyone who really wants to hide away, London is a better labyrinth than a lookout tower to which all the corridors of a building lead. The simple observation I have just propounded to you came to me the night before last while we were listening to the rain on the roof and were waiting for sleep to fall upon us. Under its influence, I chose to put aside your absurdities and to think about something sensible."

"About the theory of series, say, or about a fourth dimension of space?" asked Dunraven.

"No," said Unwin, serious. "I thought about the labyrinth of Crete. The labyrinth whose center was a man with the head of a bull."

Dunraven, steeped in detective stories, thought that the solution of a mystery is always less impressive than the mystery itself. Mystery has something of the supernatural about it, and even of the divine; its solution, however, is always tainted by sleight of hand. He said, to put off the inevitable, "On coins and in sculpture the Minotaur has a bull's head. Dante imagined it as having the body of a bull and a man's head."

"That version also fits my solution," Unwin agreed. "What matters is that both the dwelling and the dweller be monstrous. The Minotaur amply justifies its maze. The same can hardly be said of a threat uttered in a dream. The Minotaur's image once evoked (unavoidably, of course, in a mystery in which there is a labyrinth), the problem was virtually solved. Nonetheless, I confess I did not fully understand that this ancient image held the key, but in your story I found a detail I could use—the spider web."

"The spider web?" repeated Dunraven, baffled.

"Yes. It wouldn't surprise me at all if the spider web (the Platonic spider web—let's keep this straight) may have suggested to the murderer (for there is a murderer) his crime. You remember that al-Bokhari, in the tomb, dreamed about a tangle of snakes, and upon waking found that a spider web had prompted his dream. Let us go back to that night in which al-Bokhari had that dream. The defeated king and the vizier and the slave are escaping over the desert with treasure. They take shelter for the night in a tomb. The vizier, whom we know to be a coward, sleeps; the king, whom we know to be a brave man, does not sleep. In order not to share the treasure, the king knifes the vizier. Several nights later, the vizier's ghost threatens the king in a dream. All this is unconvincing. To my understanding, the events took place in another way. That night, the king, the brave man, slept, and Zaid, the coward, lay awake. To sleep is to forget all things, and this particular forgetfulness is not easy when you know you are being hunted down with drawn swords. Zaid, greedy, bent over the sleeping figure of his king. He thought about killing him (maybe he even played with his dagger), but he did not dare. He woke the napping slave, they buried part of the treasure in the tomb, and they fled to Suakin and to England. Not to hide themselves from al-Bokhari but to lure him and to kill him, they built—like the spider its web—the crimson labyrinth on the high dunes in sight of the sea. The vizier knew that ships would carry to Nubian ports the tale of the red-bearded man, of the slave, and of the lion, and that sooner or later al-Bokhari would come in search of them in their labyrinth. In the last passageway of the maze, the trap lay waiting. Al-Bokhari had always underrated Zaid, and now did not lower himself to take the slightest precaution. At last, the wished-for day came; Ibn Hakkan landed in England, went directly to the door of the maze, made his way into its blind corridors, and perhaps had already set foot on the first steps when his vizier killed him—I don't know whether with a bullet—from the trapdoor in the ceiling. The slave would finish off the lion and another bullet would finish off the slave. Then Zaid crushed the three faces with a rock. He had to do it that way; one dead man with his face bashed in would have suggested a problem of identity, but the beast, the black man, and the king formed a series, and, given the first two terms, the last one would seem natural. It is not to be wondered at that he was driven by fear when he spoke to Allaby; he had just finished his awful job and was about to flee England and unearth the treasure."

A thoughtful silence, or disbelief, followed Unwin's words. Dunraven asked for another tankard before giving his judgment.

"I admit," he said, "that my Ibn Hakkan could have been Zaid. Such metamorphoses are classic rules of the game, are accepted *conventions* demanded by the reader. What I am unwilling to admit is your conjecture that a part of the treasure remained in the Sudan. Remember that Zaid fled from the king and from the king's enemies both; it is easier to picture him stealing the whole hoard than taking the time to bury a portion of it. At the very end, perhaps no coins were found in the chest because no coins were left. The bricklayers would have eaten up a fortune that, unlike the red gold of the Nibelungs, was not inexhaustible. And so we have Ibn Hakkan crossing the seas in order to recover a treasure already squandered."

"I shouldn't say squandered," Unwin said. "The vizier invested it, putting together on an island of infidels a great circular trap made of brick and destined not only to lure a king but to be his grave. Zaid, if your guess is correct, acted out of hate and fear, and not out of greed. He stole the treasure, and only later found that he was really after something else. He really wanted to see Ibn Hakkan dead. He pretended to be Ibn Hakkan, he killed Ibn Hakkan, and in the end he *became* Ibn Hakkan."

"Yes," agreed Dunraven. "He was a good-for-nothing who, before becoming a nobody in death, wanted one day to look back on having been a king or having been taken for a king."

The Man
on the Threshold
(1952)

Bioy-Casares brought back with him from London a strange
dagger with a triangular blade and a hilt in the shape of an
H; a friend of ours, Christopher Dewey of the British
Council, told us that such weapons were commonly used in
India. This statement prompted him to mention that he
had held a job in that country between the two wars.
(*"Ultra Auroram et Gangen,"* I recall his saying in Latin,
misquoting a line from Juvenal.) Of the stories he enter-
tained us with that night, I venture to set down the one
that follows. My account will be faithful; may Allah deliver
me from the temptation of adding any circumstantial details or of weighing down the tale's Oriental character with
interpolations from Kipling. It should be remarked that the
story has a certain ancient simplicity that it would be a
pity to lose—something perhaps straight out of the *Arabian
Nights.*

The precise geography [Dewey said] of the events I am
going to relate is of little importance. Besides, what would

the names of Amritsar or Oudh mean in Buenos Aires? Let me only say, then, that in those years there were disturbances in a Muslim city and that the central government sent out one of their best people to restore order. He was a Scotsman from an illustrious clan of warriors, and in his blood he bore a tradition of violence. Only once did I lay eyes on him, but I shall not forget his deep black hair, the prominent cheekbones, the somehow avid nose and mouth, the broad shoulders, the powerful set of a Viking. David Alexander Glencairn is what he'll be called in my story tonight; the names are fitting, since they belonged to kings who ruled with an iron scepter. David Alexander Glencairn (as I shall have to get used to calling him) was, I suspect, a man who was feared; the mere news of his coming was enough to quell the city. This did not deter him from putting into effect a number of forceful measures. A few years passed. The city and the outlying district were at peace; Sikhs and Muslims had laid aside their ancient enmities, and suddenly Glencairn disappeared. Naturally enough, there was no lack of rumors that he had been kidnapped or murdered.

These things I learned from my superior, for the censorship was strict and the newspapers made no comment on (nor did they even record, for all I recall) Glencairn's disappearance. There's a saying that India is larger than the world; Glencairn, who may have been all powerful in the city to which he was destined by a signature scrawled across the bottom of some document, was no more than a cog in the administration of Empire. The inquiries of the local police turned up nothing; my superior felt that a civilian might rouse less suspicion and achieve greater results. Three or four days later (distances in India are generous), I was appointed to my mission and was working my way without hope of success through the streets of the commonplace city that had somehow whisked away a man.

I felt, almost at once, the invisible presence of a conspiracy to keep Glencairn's fate hidden. There's not a soul in this city (I suspected) who is not in on the secret and who is not sworn to keep it. Upon being questioned, most people professed an unbounded ignorance; they did not know who Glencairn was, had never seen him, had never heard anyone speak of him. Others, instead, had caught a glimpse of him only a quarter of an hour before talking to So-and-So, and they even accompanied me to the house the two had entered and in which nothing was known of them, or which they had just that moment left. Some of those meticulous liars I went so far as to knock down. Witnesses approved my outbursts, and made up other lies. I did not believe them, but neither did I dare ignore them. One afternoon, I was handed an envelope containing a slip of paper on which there was an address.

The sun had gone down when I got there. The quarter was poor but not rowdy; the house was quite low; from the street I caught a glimpse of a succession of unpaved inner courtyards, and somewhere at the far end an opening. There, some kind of Muslim ceremony was being held; a blind man entered with a lute made of a reddish wood.

At my feet, motionless as an object, an old, old man squatted on the threshold. I'll tell what he was like, for he is an essential part of the story. His many years had worn him down and polished him as smooth as water polishes a stone, or as the generations of men polish a sentence. Long rags covered him, or so it seemed to me, and the cloth he wore wound around his head was one rag more. In the dusk, he lifted a dark face and a white beard. I began speaking to him without preamble, for by now I had given up all hope of ever finding David Alexander Glencairn. The old man did not understand me (perhaps he did not hear me), and I had to explain that Glencairn was a judge and that I was looking for him. I felt, on speaking these words, the pointlessness of questioning this old man for whom the present was hardly more than a dim rumor. This man might give me news of the Mutiny or of Akbar (I thought) but not of Glencairn. What he told me confirmed this suspicion.

"A judge!" he cried with weak surprise. "A judge who

has got himself lost and is being searched for. That happened when I was a boy. I have no memory for dates, but Nikal Seyn (Nicholson) had not yet been killed before the wall of Delhi. Time that has passed stays on in memory; I may be able to summon back what happened then. God, in his wrath, had allowed people to fall into corruption; the mouths of men were full of blasphemy and of deceit and of fraud. Yet not all were evil, and when it was known that the queen was about to send a man who would carry out in this land the law of England, those who were less evil were cheered, for they felt that law is better than disorder. The Christian came to us, but it was not long before he too was deceiving and oppressing us, concealing abominable crimes, and selling decisions. We did not blame him in the beginning; the English justice he administered was not familiar to anyone, and the apparent excesses of the new judge may have obeyed certain valid arcane reasoning. Everything must have a justification in his book, we wished to think, but his kinship with all evil judges the world over was too obvious to be overlooked, and at last we were forced to admit that he was simply a wicked man. He turned out to be a tyrant, and the unfortunate people (in order to avenge themselves for the false hopes they had once placed in him) began to toy with the idea of kidnapping him and submitting him to judgment. To talk was not enough; from plans they had to move to action. Nobody, perhaps, save the very foolish or the very young, believed that that rash scheme could be carried out, but thousands of Sikhs and Muslims kept their word and one day they executed—incredulous—what to each of them had seemed impossible. They sequestered the judge and held him prisoner in a farmhouse beyond the outskirts of the town. Then they called together all those who had been wronged by him, or, in some cases, orphans and widows, for during those years the executioner's sword had not rested. In the end—this was perhaps the most difficult— they sought and named a judge to judge the judge."

At this point, the old man was interrupted by some

women who were entering the house. Then he went on, slowly.

"It is well known that there is no generation that does not include in it four upright men who are the secret pillars of the world and who justify it before the Lord: one of these men would have made the perfect judge. But where are they to be found if they themselves wander the world lost and nameless, and do not know each other when they meet, and are unaware of the high destiny that is theirs? Someone then reasoned that if fate forbade us wise men, we should seek out the witless. This opinion prevailed. Students of the Koran, doctors of law, Sikhs who bear the name of lions and who worship one God, Hindus who worship a multitude of gods, Mahavira monks who teach that the shape of the universe is that of a man with his legs spread apart, worshipers of fire, and black Jews made up the court, but the final ruling was entrusted to a madman."

Here he was interrupted by people who were leaving the ceremony.

"To a madman," he repeated, "so that God's wisdom might speak through his mouth and shame human pride. His name has been forgotten, or was never known, but he went naked through the streets, or was clothed in rags, counting his fingers with a thumb and mocking at the trees."

My common sense rebelled. I said that to hand over the verdict to a madman was to nullify the trial.

"The defendant accepted the judge," was his answer, "seeing, perhaps, that because of the risk the conspirators would run if they set him free, only from a man who was mad might he not expect a sentence of death. I heard that he laughed when he was told who the judge was. The trial lasted many days and nights, drawn out by the swelling of the number of witnesses."

The old man stopped. Something was troubling him. In order to bridge the lapse, I asked him how many days.

"At least nineteen," he replied.

People who were leaving the ceremony interrupted him

again; wine is forbidden to Muslims, but the faces and voices were those of drunkards. One, on passing, shouted something to the old man.

"Nineteen days—exactly," he said, setting matters straight. "The faithless dog heard sentence passed, and the knife feasted on his throat."

He had spoken fiercely, joyfully. With a different voice now he brought the story to an end. "He died without fear; in the most vile of men there is some virtue."

"Where did all this happen?" I asked him. "In a farmhouse?"

For the first time, he looked into my eyes. Then he made things clear, slowly, measuring his words. "I said that he had been confined in a farmhouse, not that he was tried there. He was tried in this city, in a house like any other, like this one. One house differs little from another; what is important to know is whether the house is built in hell or in heaven."

I asked him about the fate of the conspirators.

"I don't know," he told me patiently. "These things took place and were forgotten many years ago now. Maybe what they did was condemned by men, but not by the Lord."

Having said this, he got up. I felt his words as a dismissal, and from that moment I no longer existed for him. Men and women from all the corners of the Punjab swarmed over us, praying and intoning, and nearly swept us away. I wondered how, from courtyards so narrow they were little more than long passageways, so many persons could be pouring out. Others were coming from the neighboring houses; it seems they had leaped over the walls. By shoving and cursing, I forced my way inside. At the heart of the innermost courtyard I came upon a naked man, crowned with yellow flowers, whom everyone kissed and caressed, with a sword in his hand. The sword was stained, for it had dealt Glencairn his death. I found his mutilated body in the stables out back.

The Challenge
(1952)

All over the Argentine runs a story that may belong to legend or to history or (which may be just another way of saying it belongs to legend) to both things at once. Its best recorded versions are to be found in the unjustly forgotten novels about outlaws and desperadoes written in the last century by Eduardo Gutiérrez; among its oral versions, the first one I heard came from a neighborhood of Buenos Aires bounded by a penitentiary, a river, and a cemetery, and nicknamed Tierra del Fuego. The hero of this version was Juan Muraña, a wagon driver and knife fighter to whom are attributed all the stories of daring that still survive in what were once the outskirts of the city's Northside. That first version was quite simple. A man from the Stockyards or from Barracas, knowing about Muraña's reputation (but never having laid eyes on him), sets out all the way across town from the Southside to take him on. He picks the fight in a corner saloon, and the two move into the street to have

91

it out. Each is wounded, but in the end Muraña slashes the other man's face and tells him, "I'm letting you live so you'll come back looking for me again."

What impressed itself in my mind about the duel was that it had no ulterior motive. In conversation thereafter (my friends know this only too well), I grew fond of retelling the anecdote. Around 1927, I wrote it down, giving it the deliberately laconic title "Men Fought." Years later, this same anecdote helped me work out a lucky story—though hardly a good one—called "Streetcorner Man." Then, in 1950, Adolfo Bioy-Casares and I made use of it again to plot a film script that the producers turned down and that would have been called *On the Outer Edge*. It was about hard-bitten men like Muraña who lived on the outskirts of Buenos Aires before the turn of the century. I thought, after such extensive labors, that I had said farewell to the story of the disinterested duel. Then, this year, out in Chivilcoy, I came across a far better version. I hope this is the true one, although since fate seems to take pleasure in a thing's happening many times over, both may very well be authentic. Two quite bad stories and a script that I still think of as good came out of the poorer first version; out of the second, which is complete and perfect, nothing can come. Without working in metaphors or details of local color, I shall tell it now as it was told to me. The story took place to the west, in the district of Chivilcoy, sometime back in the 1870's.

The hero's name is Wenceslao Suárez. He earns his wages braiding ropes and making harnesses, and lives in a small adobe hut. Forty or fifty years old, he's a man who has won a reputation for courage, and it is quite likely (given the facts of the story) that he has a killing or two to his credit. But these killings, because they were in fair fights, neither trouble his conscience nor tarnish his good name. One evening, something out of the ordinary happens in the routine life of this man: at a crossroads saloon, he is told that a letter has come for him. Don Wenceslao does not know how to read; the saloonkeeper puzzles out word by word an epistle certainly not written by the man who sent it. In the name of certain friends, who value dexterity and true composure, an unknown correspondent sends his compliments to don Wenceslao, whose renown has crossed over the Arroyo del Medio into the Province of Santa Fe, and extends him the hospitality of his humble home in a town of the said province. Wenceslao Suárez dictates a reply to the saloonkeeper. Thanking the other man for his expression of friendship, and explaining that he dare not leave his mother—who is well along in years—alone, he invites the other man to his own place in Chivilcoy, where a barbecue and a bottle or so of wine may be looked forward to. The months drag by, and one day a man riding a horse harnessed and saddled in a style unknown in the area inquires at the saloon for the way to Suárez' house. Suárez, who has come to the saloon to buy meat, overhears the question and tells the man who he is. The stranger reminds him of the letters they exchanged some time back. Suárez shows his pleasure that the other man has gone to the trouble of making the journey; then the two of them go off into a nearby field and Suárez prepares the barbecue. They eat and drink and talk at length. About what? I suspect about subjects involving blood and cruelty—but with each man on his guard, wary.

They have eaten, and the oppressive afternoon heat weighs over the land when the stranger invites don Wenceslao to join in a bit of harmless knife play. To say no would dishonor the host. They fence, and at first they only play at fighting, but it's not long before Wenceslao feels that the stranger is out to kill him. Realizing at last what lay behind the ceremonious letter, Wenceslao regrets having eaten and drunk so much. He knows he will tire before the other man, on whom he has a good nine or ten years. Out of scorn or politeness, the stranger offers him a short rest. Don Wenceslao agrees and, as soon as they take up their dueling again, he allows the other man to wound him on the left

hand, in which he holds his rolled poncho.* The knife slices
through his wrist, the hand dangles loose. Suárez, springing
back, lays the bleeding hand on the ground, clamps it down
under his boot, tears it off, feints a thrust at the amazed
stranger's chest, then rips open his belly with a solid stab.
So the story ends, except that, according to one teller, the
man from Santa Fe is left lifeless, while to another (who
withholds from him the dignity of death) he rides back to
his own province. In this latter version, Suárez gives him
first aid with the rum remaining from their lunch.

In this feat of Manco (One Hand) Wenceslao—as Suárez
is now known to fame—certain touches of mildness or politeness (his trade as harness and rope maker, his qualms
about leaving his mother alone, the exchange of flowery
letters, the two men's leisurely conversation, the lunch)
happily tone down and make the barbarous tale more effective. These touches lend it an epic and even chivalrous
quality that we hardly find, for example—unless we have
made up our minds to do so—in the drunken brawls of
Martín Fierro or in the closely related but poorer story of
Juan Muraña and the man from the Southside. A trait
common to the two may, perhaps, be significant. In both of
them, the challenger is defeated. This may be due to the
mere and unfortunate necessity for the local champion to
triumph, but also (and this is preferable) to a tacit disapproval of aggression, or (which would be best of all) to the
dark and tragic suspicion that man is the worker of his own
downfall, like Ulysses in Canto XXVI of the *Inferno* or
like that other doomed captain in *Moby Dick*.

---

* Montaigne (*Essays*, I, 49) says that this manner of fighting with cloak
and dagger is very old, and quotes Caesar's finding, *"Sinistras sagis invol-
vunt, gladiosque distringunt"*—"They wrapped their cloaks around their left
arms and drew their swords" (*Civil War*, I, 75). Lugones, in *El payador*
(1916), quotes these verses from a sixteenth-century *romance* of Bernardo
del Carpio:

> Revolviendo el manto al brazo,
> la espada fuera a sacar.

[Wrapping the cape round his arm, he drew his sword.]

Something fundamental in the brutal story just told saves it from falling into unalloyed barbarousness—an episode out of *La Terre* or Hemingway. I speak of a religious core. "His beliefs," said the poet Lugones of the gaucho, "could be reduced to a few superstitions, which had no great bearing on his everyday life." He then adds, "The one thing he respected was courage, which he cultivated with a chivalrous passion." I would say that the gaucho, without realizing it, forged a religion—the hard and blind religion of courage—and that this faith (like all others) had its ethic, its mythology, and its martyrs. On the plains and out on the raw edges of the city, men who led extremely elementary lives—herders, stockyard workers, drovers, outlaws, and pimps—rediscovered in their own way the age-old cult of the gods of iron. In a thirteenth-century saga, we read:

"Tell me, what do you believe in?" said the earl.
"I believe in my own strength," said Sigmund.

Wenceslao Suárez and his nameless antagonist, and many others whom myth has forgotten or has absorbed in these two, doubtless held this manly faith, and in all likelihood it was no mere form of vanity but rather an awareness that God may be found in any man.

The Captive

(1956)

This story is told out in one of the old frontier towns—either Junín or Tapalquén. A boy was missing after an Indian raid; it was said that the marauders had carried him away. The boy's parents searched for him without any luck; years later, a soldier just back from Indian territory told them about a blue-eyed savage who may have been their son. At long last they traced him (the circumstances of the search have not come down to us and I dare not invent what I don't know) and they thought they recognized him. The man, marked by the wilderness and by primitive life, no longer understood the words of the language he spoke in childhood, but he let himself be led, uncurious and willing, to his old house. There he stopped—maybe because the others stopped. He stared at the door as though not understanding what it was. All of a sudden, ducking his head, he let out a cry, cut through the entranceway and the two long patios on the run, and burst into the kitchen. Without a second's pause, he buried his arm in the soot-blackened oven chimney and drew out the small knife with the horn handle that he had hidden there as a boy. His eyes lit up with joy and his parents wept because they had found their lost child.

Maybe other memories followed upon this one, but the Indian could not live indoors and one day he left to go back to his open spaces. I would like to know what he felt in that first bewildering moment in which past and present merged; I would like to know whether in that dizzying instant the lost son was born again and died, or whether he managed to recognize, as a child or a dog might, his people and his home.

Borges and Myself

(1956)

It's to the other man, to Borges, that things happen. I walk along the streets of Buenos Aires, stopping now and then—perhaps out of habit—to look at the arch of an old entrance-way or a grillwork gate; of Borges I get news through the mail and glimpse his name among a committee of professors or in a dictionary of biography. I have a taste for hourglasses, maps, eighteenth-century typography, the roots of words, the smell of coffee, and Stevenson's prose; the other man shares these likes, but in a showy way that turns them into stagy mannerisms. It would be an exaggeration to say that we are on bad terms; I live, I let myself live, so that Borges can weave his tales and poems, and those tales and poems are my justification. It is not hard for me to admit that he has managed to write a few worthwhile pages, but these pages cannot save me, perhaps because what is good no longer belongs to anyone—not even the other man—but rather to speech or tradition. In any case, I am fated to become lost once and for all, and only some moment of myself will survive in the other man. Little by little, I have been surrendering everything to him, even though I have evidence of his stubborn habit of falsification and exaggerating. Spinoza held that all things try to keep on being themselves; a stone wants to be a stone and the tiger, a tiger. I shall remain in Borges, not in myself (if it is so that I am someone), but I recognize myself less in his books than in those of others or than in the laborious tuning of a guitar. Years ago, I tried ridding myself of him and I went from myths of the outlying slums of the city to games with time and infinity, but those games are now part of Borges and I will have to turn to other things. And so, my life is a running away, and I lose everything and everything is left to oblivion or to the other man.

Which of us is writing this page I don't know.

Until then, he had never dwelled on the pleasures of memory. Impressions had always washed over him, fleeting and vivid. A potter's design in vermilion; the vault of heaven clustered with stars that were also gods; the moon, from which a lion had fallen; the smoothness of marble under one's lingering fingertips; the taste of boar meat, which he liked to strip with quick flashing bites; a Phoenician word; the black shadow cast by a spear on yellow sand; the nearness of the sea or of women; the heavy wine whose roughness he cut with honey—any of these could wholly encompass the range of his mind. He was acquainted with fear as well as with anger and courage, and once he was the first to scale an enemy wall. Eager, curious, unquestioning, following no other law than to enjoy things and forget them, he wandered over many lands and, on one side or the other of the sea, looked on the cities of men and their palaces. In bustling marketplaces or at the foot of a mountain whose hidden peak may have sheltered satyrs, he had heard entangled stories, which he accepted as he accepted reality, without attempting to find out whether they were true or imaginary.

Little by little, the beautiful world began to leave him; a persistent mist erased the lines of his hand, the night lost its multitude of stars, the ground became uncertain beneath his steps. Everything grew distant and blurred. When he knew he was going blind, he cried out; stoic fortitude had not yet been invented, and Hector could flee from Achilles without dishonor. I shall no longer look upon the sky and its mythological dread (he felt), nor this face which the years will transform. Days and nights passed over these fears of his body, but one morning he awoke, looked (without astonishment now) at the dim things around him, and unexplainably felt—the way one recognizes a strain of music or a voice—that all this had already happened to him and that he had faced it with fear, but also with joy, hope, and curiosity. Then he went deep into his past, which seemed to him bottomless, and managed to draw out of that dizzying descent the lost memory that now shone like a coin under the rain, maybe because he had never recalled it before except in some dream.

This was the memory. Another boy had wronged him and he had gone to his father and told him the story. His father, letting him speak, appeared not to listen or understand, and took down from the wall a bronze dagger, beautiful and charged with power, which in secret the boy had coveted. Now it lay in his hands and the suddenness of possession wiped out the injury he had suffered, but his father's voice was telling him, "Let them know you're a man," and in that voice was a command. Night blinded the paths. Clasping the dagger, in which he felt a magic power, he scrambled down the steep hillside that surrounded the house and ran to the edge of the sea, thinking of himself as Ajax and Perseus, and peopling with wounds and battles the dark salt air. The exact taste of that moment was what he now sought. The rest mattered little to him—the insults leading to the challenge, the clumsy fight, the way home with the blade dripping blood.

Another memory, also involving night and an expectation of adventure, sprang out of that one. A woman, the first to be given him by the gods, had waited for him in the shadow of a crypt until he reached her through galleries that were like nets of stone and down slopes that sank into darkness. Why did these memories come back to him and why without bitterness, as if foretelling of things about to happen?

With slow amazement he understood. In this nighttime of his mortal eyes into which he was now descending, love and danger were also in wait for him—Ares and Aphrodite— because he already divined (because he was already ringed in by) a rumor of hexameters and glory, a rumor of men defending a shrine which the gods would not save and of black ships roaming the seas in search of a loved island, the rumor of the Odysseys and the Iliads it was his destiny to sing and to leave resounding forever in mankind's hollow memory. These things we know, but not what he felt when he went down into his final darkness.

The Intruder
(1966)

> . . . passing the love of women.
> 2 Samuel 1:26

People say (but this is unlikely) that the story was first told by Eduardo, the younger of the Nelsons, at the wake of his elder brother Cristián, who died in his sleep sometime back in the nineties out in the district of Morón. The fact is that someone got it from someone else during the course of that drawn-out and now dim night, between one sip of maté and the next, and told it to Santiago Dabove, from whom I heard it. Years later, in Turdera, where the story had taken place, I heard it again. The second and more elaborate version closely followed the one Santiago told, with the usual minor variations and discrepancies. I set down the story now because I see in it, if I'm not mistaken, a brief and tragic mirror of the character of those hard-bitten men living on the edge of Buenos Aires before the turn of the century. I hope to do this in a straightforward way, but I see in advance that I shall give in to the writer's temptation of emphasizing or adding certain details.

In Turdera, where they lived, they were called the Nilsens. The priest there told me that his predecessor remembered having seen in the house of these people— somewhat in amazement—a worn Bible with a dark binding and black-letter type; on the back flyleaf he caught a glimpse of names and dates written in by hand. It was the only book in the house—the roaming chronicle of the Nilsens, lost as one day all things will be lost. The rambling old house, which no longer stands, was of unplastered brick; through the arched entranceway you could make out a patio paved with red tiles and beyond it a second one of hard-packed earth. Few people, at any rate, ever set foot inside; the Nilsens kept to themselves. In their almost bare rooms they slept on cots. Their extravagances were horses, silver-trimmed riding gear, the short-bladed dagger, and getting dressed up on Saturday nights, when they blew their money freely and got themselves into boozy brawls. They were both tall, I know, and wore their red hair long. Denmark or Ireland, which they probably never heard of, ran in the blood of these two Argentine brothers. The neighborhood feared the Redheads; it is likely that one of them, at least, had killed his man. Once, shoulder to shoulder, they tangled with the police. It is said that the younger brother was in a fight with Juan Iberra in which he didn't do too badly, and that, according to those in the know, is saying something. They were drovers, teamsters, horse thieves, and, once in a while, professional gamblers. They had a reputation for stinginess, except when drink and card-playing turned them into spenders. Of their relatives or where they themselves came from, nothing is known. They owned a cart and a yoke of oxen.

Their physical makeup differed from that of the rest of the toughs who gave the Costa Brava its unsavory reputation. This, and a lot that we don't know, helps us understand the close ties between them. To fall out with one of them was to reckon with two enemies.

The Nilsens liked carousing with women, but up until then their amorous escapades had always been carried out in darkened passageways or in whorehouses. There was no end of talk, then, when Cristián brought Juliana Burgos to live with him. Admittedly, in this way he gained a servant, but it is also true that he took to squandering his money buying her the most hideous junk jewelry and showing her off at parties. At those dingy parties held in tenements, where suggestive dance steps were strictly forbidden and where, at that time, partners still danced with a good six inches of light showing between them. Juliana was a dark girl and her eyes had a slight slant to them; all anyone had to do was look at her and she'd break into a smile. For a poor neighborhood, where drudgery and neglect wear women out, she was not bad-looking.

In the beginning, Eduardo went places with them. Later, at one point, he set out on a journey north to Arrecifes on some business or other, returning home with a girl he had picked up along the way. But after a few days he threw her out. He turned more sullen; he took to drinking alone at the corner saloon and kept completely to himself. He had fallen in love with Cristián's woman. The whole neighborhood, which may have realized it before he did, maliciously and cheerfully looked forward to the enmity about to break out between the two brothers.

Late one night, on coming home from the corner, Eduardo saw Cristián's horse, a big bay, tied to the hitching post. Inside in the patio, dressed in his Sunday best, his older brother was waiting for him. The woman shuttled in and out serving maté. Cristián said to Eduardo, "I'm on my way over to Farías' place, where they're throwing a party. Juliana stays here with you; if you want her, use her."

His tone was half commanding, half friendly. Eduardo stood there a while staring at him, not knowing what to do. Cristián got up, said goodbye—to his brother, not to Juliana, who was no more than an object—mounted his horse, and rode off at a jog, casually.

From that night on they shared her. Nobody will ever know the details of this strange partnership which outraged even the Costa Brava's sense of decency. The arrangement went well for several weeks, but it could not last. Between them the brothers never mentioned her name, not even to call her, but they kept looking for, and finding, reasons to be at odds. They argued over the sale of some hides, but what they were really arguing about was something else. Cristián took to raising his voice, while Eduardo kept silent. Without knowing it, they were watching each other. In tough neighborhoods a man never admits to anyone—not even to himself—that a woman matters beyond lust and possession, but the two brothers were in love. This, in some way, made them feel ashamed.

One afternoon, in the square in Lomas, Eduardo ran into Juan Iberra, who congratulated him on this beauty he'd got hold of. It was then, I believe, that Eduardo let him have it. Nobody—not to *his* face—was going to poke fun at Cristián.

The woman attended both men's wants with an animal submission, but she was unable to keep hidden a certain preference, probably for the younger man, who had not refused sharing her but who had not proposed it either.

One day, they ordered Juliana to bring two chairs out into the first patio and then not show her face for a while because they had things to talk over. Expecting a long session between them, she lay down for a nap, but before very long they woke her up. She was to fill a sack with all her belongings, including her glass-bead rosary and the tiny crucifix her mother had left her. Without any explanation, they lifted her onto the oxcart and set out on a long, tiresome, and silent journey. It had rained; the roads were heavy with mud, and it was nearly daybreak before they reached Morón. There they sold her to the woman who ran the whorehouse. The terms had already been agreed to; Cristián pocketed the money and later on split it with his brother.

Back in Turdera, the Nilsens, up till then trapped in the web (which was also a routine) of this monstrous love affair, tried to take up their old life of men among men. They went back to cardplaying, to cockfights, to their Saturday night binges. At times, perhaps, they felt they were saved, but they often indulged—each on his own—in unaccountable or only too accountable absences. A little before the year was out, the younger brother said he had business in the city. Immediately, Cristián went off to Morón; at the hitching post of the whorehouse he recognized Eduardo's piebald. Cristián walked in; there was his brother, sure enough, waiting his turn. It is said that Cristián told him, "If we go on this way, we'll wear out the horses. We'd be better off keeping her close at hand."

He spoke with the owner of the place, drew a handful of coins out of his money belt, and they took the girl away. Juliana rode with Cristián. Eduardo dug his spurs into his horse, not wanting to see them together.

They went back to what has already been told. Their solution had ended in failure, for the two had fallen into cheating. Cain was on the loose here, but the affection between the Nilsens was great—who knows what hard times and what dangers they may have faced together!—and they preferred taking their feelings out on others. On strangers, on the dogs, on Juliana, who had set this wedge between them.

The month of March was coming to a close and there was no sign of the heat's letting up. One Sunday (on Sundays people go to bed early), Eduardo, on his way home from the corner saloon, saw that Cristián was yoking the oxen. Cristián said to him, "Come on. We have to leave some hides off at Pardo's place. I've already loaded them; let's make the best of the night air."

Pardo's warehouse lay, I believe, farther south; they took the old cattle trail, then turned down a side road. As night fell, the countryside seemed wider and wider.

They skirted a growth of tall reeds; Cristián threw down the cigar he had just lit and said evenly, "Let's get busy, brother. In a while the buzzards will take over. This

107

afternoon I killed her. Let her stay here with all her trinkets, she won't cause us any more harm."

They threw their arms around each other, on the verge of tears. One more link bound them now—the woman they had cruelly sacrificed and their common need to forget her.

The Immortals

With Adolfo Bioy-Casares
(1966)

And see, no longer blinded by our eyes.
Rupert Brooke

Whoever could have foreseen, way back in that innocent summer of 1923, that the novelette *The Chosen One* by Camilo N. Huergo, presented to me by the author with his personal inscription on the flyleaf (which I had the decorum to tear out before offering the volume for sale to successive men of the book trade), hid under the thin varnish of fiction a prophetic truth. Huergo's photograph, in an oval frame, adorns the cover. Each time I look at it, I have the impression that the snapshot is about to cough, a victim of that lung disease which nipped in the bud a promising career. Tuberculosis, in short, denied him the happiness of acknowledging the letter I wrote him in one of my characteristic outbursts of generosity.

The epigraph prefixed to this thoughtful essay has been taken from the aforementioned novelette; I requested Dr. Montenegro, of the Academy, to render it into Spanish, but the results were negative. To give the unprepared reader the gist of the matter, I shall now sketch, in condensed form, an outline of Huergo's narrative, as follows:

The storyteller pays a visit, far to the south in Chubut, to the English rancher don Guillermo Blake, who devotes his energies not only to the breeding of sheep but also to the ramblings of the world-famous Plato and to the latest and more freakish experiments in the field of surgical medicine. On the basis of his reading, don Guillermo concludes that the five senses obstruct or deform the apprehension of reality and that, could we free ourselves of them, we would see the world as it is—endless and timeless. He comes to think that the eternal models of things lie in the depths of the soul and that the organs of perception with which the Creator has endowed us are, *grosso modo*, hindrances. They are no better than dark spectacles that blind us to what exists outside, diverting our attention at the same time from the splendor we carry within us.

Blake begets a son by one of the farm girls so that the boy may one day become acquainted with reality. To anesthetize him for life, to make him blind and deaf and dumb, to emancipate him from the senses of smell and taste, were the father's first concerns. He took, in the same way, all possible measures to make the chosen one unaware of his own body. As to the rest, this was arranged with contrivances designed to take over respiration, circulation, nourishment, digestion, and elimination. It was a pity that the boy, fully liberated, was cut off from all human contact.

Owing to the press of practical matters, the narrator goes away. After ten years, he returns. Don Guillermo has died; his son goes on living after his fashion, with natural breathing, heart regular, in a dusty shack cluttered with mechanical devices. The narrator, about to leave for good, drops a cigarette butt that sets fire to the shack and he never quite knows whether this act was done on purpose or by pure chance. So ends Huergo's story, strange enough for its time but now, of course, more than outstripped by the rockets and astronauts of our men of science.

Having dashed off this disinterested compendium of the

tale of a now dead and forgotten author—from whom I have nothing to gain—I steer back to the heart of the matter. Memory restores to me a Saturday morning in 1964 when I had an appointment with the eminent gerontologist Dr. Raúl Narbondo. The sad truth is that we young bloods of yesteryear are getting on; the thick mop begins to thin, one or another ear stops up, the wrinkles collect grime, molars grow hollow, a cough takes root, the backbone hunches up, the foot trips on a pebble, and, to put it plainly, the paterfamilias falters and withers. There was no doubt about it, the moment had come to see Dr. Narbondo for a general checkup, particularly considering the fact that he specialized in the replacement of malfunctioning organs.

Sick at heart because that afternoon the Palermo Juniors and the Spanish Sports were playing a return match and maybe I could not occupy my place in the front row to bolster my team, I betook myself to the clinic on Corrientes Avenue near Pasteur. The clinic, as its fame betrays, occupies the fifteenth floor of the Adamant Building. I went up by elevator (manufactured by the Electra Company). Eye to eye with Narbondo's brass shingle, I pressed the bell, and at long last, taking my courage in both hands, I slipped through the partly open door and entered into the waiting room proper. There, alone with the latest issues of the *Ladies' Companion* and *Jumbo*, I whiled away the passing hours until a cuckoo clock struck twelve and sent me leaping from my armchair. At once, I asked myself, What happened? Planning my every move now like a sleuth, I took a step or two toward the next room, peeped in, ready, admittedly, to fly the coop at the slightest sound. From the streets far below came the noise of horns and traffic, the cry of a newspaper hawker, the squeal of brakes sparing some pedestrian, but, all around me, a reign of silence. I crossed a kind of laboratory, or pharmaceutical back room, furnished with instruments and flasks of all sorts. Stimulated by the aim of reaching the men's room, I pushed open a door at the far end of the lab.

Inside, I saw something that my eyes did not understand.

The small enclosure was circular, painted white, with a low ceiling and neon lighting, and without a single window to relieve the sense of claustrophobia. The room was inhabited by four personages, or pieces of furniture. Their color was the same as the walls, their material wood, their form cubic. On each cube was another small cube with a latticed opening and below it a slot as in a mailbox. Carefully scrutinizing the grilled opening, you noted with alarm that from the interior you were being watched by something like eyes. The slots emitted, from time to time, a chorus of sighs or whisperings that the good Lord himself could not have made head or tail of. The placement of these cubes was such that they faced each other in the form of a square, composing a kind of conclave. I don't know how many minutes lapsed. At this point, the doctor came in and said to me, "My pardon, Bustos, for having kept you waiting. I was just out getting myself an advance ticket for today's match between the Palermo Juniors and the Spanish Sports." He went on, indicating the cubes, "Let me introduce you to Santiago Silberman, to retired clerk-of-court Ludueña, to Aquiles Molinari, and to Miss Bugard."

Out of the furniture came faint rumbling sounds. I quickly reached out a hand and, without the pleasure of shaking theirs, withdrew in good order, a frozen smile on my lips. Reaching the vestibule as best I could, I managed to stammer, "A drink. A stiff drink."

Narbondo came out of the lab with a graduated beaker filled with water and dissolved some effervescent drops into it. Blessed concoction—the wretched taste brought me to my senses. Then, the door to the small room closed and locked tight, came the explanation:

"I'm glad to see, my dear Bustos, that my immortals have made quite an impact on you. Whoever would have thought that *Homo sapiens*, Darwin's barely human ape, could achieve such perfection? This, my house, I assure you, is the only one in all Indo-America where Dr. Eric Stapledon's methodology has been fully applied. You recall, no doubt, the consternation that the death of the late lamented doctor, which took place in New Zealand, occasioned in scientific circles. I flatter myself, furthermore, for having implemented his precursory labors with a few Argentinean touches. In itself, the thesis—Newton's apple all over again—is fairly simple. The death of the body is a result, always, of the failure of some organ or other, call it the kidney, lungs, heart, or what you like. With the replacement of the organism's various components, in themselves perishable, with other corresponding stainless or polyethylene parts, there is no earthly reason whatever why the soul, why you yourself—Bustos Domecq—should not be immortal. None of your philosophical niceties here; the body can be vulcanized and from time to time recaulked, and so the mind keeps going. Surgery brings immortality to mankind. Life's essential aim has been attained—the mind lives on without fear of cessation. Each of our immortals is comforted by the certainty, backed by our firm's guarantee, of being a witness *in aeternum*. The brain, refreshed night and day by a system of electrical charges, is the last organic bulwark in which ball bearings and cells collaborate. The rest is Formica, steel, plastics. Respiration, alimentation, generation, mobility—elimination itself!—belong to the past. Our immortal is real estate. One or two minor touches are still missing, it's true. Oral articulation, dialogue, may still be improved. As for the cost, you need not worry yourself. By means of a procedure that circumvents legal red tape, the candidate transfers his property to us, and the Narbondo Company, Inc.—I, my son, his descendants—guarantees your upkeep, *in statu quo*, to the end of time. And, I might add, a money-back guarantee."

It was then that he laid a friendly hand on my shoulder. I felt his will taking power over me. "Ha-ha! I see I've whetted your appetite, I've tempted you, dear Bustos. You'll need a couple of months or so to get your affairs in order and to have your stock portfolio signed over to us. As far as the operation goes, naturally, as a friend, I want to save you a little something. Instead of our usual fee of ten thousand dollars, for you, ninety-five hundred—in cash, of course. The rest is yours. It goes to pay your lodging, care, and service. The medical procedure in itself is painless. No more than a question of amputation and replacement. Nothing to worry about. On the eve, just keep yourself calm, untroubled. Avoid heavy meals, tobacco, and alcohol, apart from your accustomed and imported, I hope, Scotch or two. Above all, refrain from impatience."

"Why two months?" I asked him. "One's enough, and then some. I come out of the anesthesia and I'm one more of your cubes. You have my address and phone number. We'll keep in touch. I'll be back next Friday at the latest."

At the escape hatch he handed me the card of Nemirovski, Nemirovski, & Nemirovski, Counsellors at Law, who would put themselves at my disposal for all the details of drawing up the will. With perfect composure I walked to the subway entrance, then took the stairs at a run. I lost no time. That same night, without leaving the slightest trace behind, I moved to the New Impartial, in whose register I figure under the assumed name of Aquiles Silberman. Here, in my bedroom at the far rear of this modest hotel, wearing a false beard and dark spectacles, I am setting down this account of the facts.

The Meeting

To Susana Bombal
(1969)

Anyone leafing his way through the morning paper does so
either to escape his surroundings or to provide himself with
small talk for later in the day, so it is not to be wondered
at that no one any longer remembers—or else remembers as
in a dream—the famous and once widely discussed case of
Maneco Uriarte and of Duncan. The event took place,
furthermore, back around 1910, the year of the comet and
the Centennial, and since then we have had and have lost
so many things. Both protagonists are now dead; those who
witnessed the episode solemnly swore silence. I, too, raised
my hand for the oath, feeling the importance of the ritual
with all the romantic seriousness of my nine or ten years. I
do not know whether the others noticed that I had given my
word; I do not know whether they kept theirs. Anyway,
here is the story, with all the inevitable variations brought
about by time and by good or bad writing.

My cousin Lafinur took me to a barbecue that evening at
a country house called The Laurels, which belonged to some

friends of his. I cannot fix its exact location; let us take any of those suburban towns lying just to the north, shaded and quiet, that slope down to the river and that have nothing in common with sprawling Buenos Aires and its surrounding prairie. The journey by train lasted long enough to seem endless to me, but time for children—as is well known—flows slowly. It was already dark when we passed through the villa's main gate. Here, I felt, were all the ancient, elemental things: the smell of meat cooking golden brown, the trees, the dogs, the kindling wood, and the fire that brings men together.

The guests numbered about a dozen; all were grown-ups. The eldest, I learned later, was not yet thirty. They were also—this I was soon to find out—well versed in matters about which I am still somewhat backward: race horses, the right tailors, motorcars, and notoriously expensive women. No one ruffled my shyness, no one paid any attention to me. The lamb, slowly and skillfully prepared by one of the hired men, kept us a long time in the big dining room. The dates of vintages were argued back and forth. There was a guitar; my cousin, if I remember correctly, sang a couple of Elías Regules' ballads about gauchos in the back country of Uruguay and some verses in dialect, in the incipient *lunfardo* of those days, about a knife fight in a brothel on Junín Street. Coffee and Havana cigars were brought in. Not a word about getting back. I felt (in the words of the poet Lugones) the fear of what is suddenly too late. I dared not look at the clock. In order to disguise my boyish loneliness among grown-ups, I put away—not really liking it—a glass or two of wine. Uriarte, in a loud voice, proposed to Duncan a two-handed game of poker. Someone objected that that kind of play made for a poor game and suggested a hand of four. Duncan agreed, but Uriarte, with a stubbornness that I did not understand and that I did not try to understand, insisted on the first scheme. Outside of *truco*—a game whose real aim is to pass time with mischief and verses—and of the modest mazes of solitaire, I never enjoyed cards. I slipped away without anyone's noticing. A rambling old house, unfamiliar and dark (only in the dining room was there light), means more to a boy than a new country means to a traveler. Step by step, I explored the rooms; I recall a billiard room, a long gallery with rectangular and diamond-shaped panes, a couple of rocking chairs, and a window from which you could just make out a summerhouse. In the darkness I lost my way; the owner of the house, whose name, as I recall after all these years, may have been Acevedo or Acebal, finally came across me somehow. Out of kindness or perhaps out of a collector's vanity, he led me to a display cabinet. On lighting a lamp, I saw the glint of steel. It was a collection of knives that had once been in the hands of famous fighters. He told me that he had a bit of land somewhere to the north around Pergamino, and that he had been picking up these things on his travels back and forth across the province. He opened the cabinet and, without looking at what was written on the tags, he began giving me accounts of each item; they were more or less the same except for dates and place names. I asked him whether among the weapons he might have the dagger of Juan Moreira, who was in that day the archetype of the gaucho, as later Martín Fierro and Don Segundo Sombra would be. He had to confess that he hadn't but that he could show me one like it, with a U-shaped crosspiece in the hilt. He was interrupted by the sound of angry voices. At once he shut the cabinet and turned to leave; I followed him.

Uriarte was shouting that his opponent had tried to cheat him. All the others stood around the two players. Duncan, I remember, was a taller man than the rest of the company, and was well built, though somewhat round-shouldered; his face was expressionless, and his hair was so light it was almost white. Maneco Uriarte was nervous, dark, with perhaps a touch of Indian blood, and wore a skimpy, petulant moustache. It was obvious that everybody was drunk; I do not know whether there were two or three emptied bottles on the floor or whether an excess of movies suggests this false memory to me. Uriarte's insults did not let up; at first sharp, they now grew obscene. Duncan appeared not to hear, but finally, as though weary, he got up and threw a punch. From the floor, Uriarte snarled that he was not going to take this outrage, and he challenged Duncan to fight.

Duncan said no, and added, as though to explain, "The trouble is I'm afraid of you."

Everybody howled with laughter.

Uriarte, picking himself up, answered, "I'm going to have it out with you, and right now."

Someone—may he be forgiven for it—remarked that weapons were not lacking.

I do not know who went and opened the glass cabinet. Maneco Uriarte picked out the showiest and longest dagger, the one with the U-shaped crosspiece; Duncan, almost absentmindedly, picked a wooden-handled knife with the stamp of a tiny tree on the blade. Someone else said it was just like Maneco to play it safe, to choose a sword. It astonished no one that his hand began shaking; what was astonishing is that the same thing happened with Duncan.

Tradition demands that men about to fight should respect the house in which they are guests, and step outside. Half on a spree, half seriously, we all went out into the damp night. I was not drunk—at least, not on wine—but I was reeling with adventure; I wished very hard that someone would be killed, so that later I could tell about it and always remember it. Maybe at that moment the others were no more adult than I was. I also had the feeling that an overpowering current was dragging us on and would drown us. Nobody believed the least bit in Maneco's accusation; everyone saw it as the fruit of an old rivalry, exacerbated by the wine.

We pushed our way through a clump of trees, leaving behind the summerhouse. Uriarte and Duncan led the way, wary of each other. The rest of us strung ourselves out around the edge of an opening of lawn. Duncan had stopped there in the moonlight and said, with mild authority, "This looks like the right place."

The two men stood in the center, not quite knowing what to do. A voice rang out: "Let go of all that hardware and use your hands!"

But the men were already fighting. They began clumsily, almost as if they were afraid of hurting each other; they began by watching the blades, but later their eyes were on one another. Uriarte had laid aside his anger, Duncan his contempt or aloofness. Danger, in some way, had transfigured them; these were now two men fighting, not boys. I had imagined the fight as a chaos of steel; instead, I was able to follow it, or almost follow it, as though it were a game of chess. The intervening years may, of course, have exaggerated or blurred what I saw. I do not know how long it lasted; there are events that fall outside the common measure of time.

Without ponchos to act as shields, they used their forearms to block each lunge of the knife. Their sleeves, soon hanging in shreds, grew black with blood. I thought that we had gone wrong in supposing that they knew nothing about this kind of fencing. I noticed right off that they handled themselves in different ways. Their weapons were unequal. Duncan, in order to make up for his disadvantage, tried to stay in close to the other man; Uriarte kept stepping back to be able to lunge out with long, low thrusts. The same voice that had called attention to the display cabinet shouted out now: "They're killing each other! Stop them!"

But no one dared break it up. Uriarte had lost ground; Duncan charged him. They were almost body to body now. Uriarte's weapon sought Duncan's face. Suddenly the blade seemed shorter, for it was piercing the taller man's chest. Duncan lay stretched out on the grass. It was at this point that he said, his voice very low, "How strange. All this is like a dream."

He did not shut his eyes, he did not move, and I had seen a man kill another man.

Maneco Uriarte bent over the body, sobbing openly, and begged to be forgiven. The thing he had just done was beyond him. I know now that he regretted less having committed a crime than having carried out a senseless act.

I did not want to look anymore. What I had wished for so much had happened, and it left me shaken. Lafinur told me later that they had had to struggle hard to pull out the weapon. A makeshift council was formed. They decided to lie as little as possible and to elevate this duel with knives to a duel with swords. Four of them volunteered as seconds, among them Acebal. In Buenos Aires anything can be fixed; someone always has a friend.

On top of the mahogany table where the men had been playing, a pack of English cards and a pile of bills lay in a jumble that nobody wanted to look at or to touch.

In the years that followed, I often considered revealing the story to some friend, but always I felt that there was a greater pleasure in being the keeper of a secret than in telling it. However, around 1929, a chance conversation suddenly moved me one day to break my long silence. The retired police captain, don José Olave, was recalling stories about men from the tough riverside neighborhood of the Retiro who had been handy with their knives; he remarked that when they were out to kill their man, scum of this kind had no use for the rules of the game, and that before all the fancy playing with daggers that you saw now on the stage, knife fights were few and far between. I said I had witnessed one, and gave him an account of what had happened nearly twenty years earlier.

He listened to me with professional attention, then said, "Are you sure Uriarte and What's-His-Name never handled a knife before? Maybe they had picked up a thing or two around their fathers' ranches."

"I don't think so," I said. "Everybody there that night knew one another pretty well, and I can tell you they were all amazed at the way the two men fought."

Olave went on in his quiet manner, as if thinking aloud. "One of the weapons had a U-shaped crosspiece in the handle. There were two daggers of that kind which became quite famous—Moreira's and Juan Almada's. Almada was from down south, in Tapalquén."

Something seemed to come awake in my memory. Olave continued. "You also mentioned a knife with a wooden handle, one with the Little Tree brand. There are thousands of them, but there was one—"

He broke off for a moment, then said, "Señor Acevedo had a big property up around Pergamino. There was another of these famous toughs from up that way—Juan Almanza was his name. This was along about the turn of the century. When he was fourteen, he killed his first man with one of these knives. From then on, for luck, he stuck to the same one. Juan Almanza and Juan Almada had it in for each other, jealous of the fact that many people confused the two. For a long time they searched high and low for one another, but they never met. Juan Almanza was killed by a stray bullet during some election brawl or other. The other man, I think, died a natural death in a hospital bed in Las Flores."

Nothing more was said. Each of us was left with his own conclusions.

Nine or ten men, none of whom is any longer living, saw what my eyes saw—that sudden stab and the body under the night sky—but perhaps what we were really seeing was the end of another story, an older story. I began to wonder whether it was Maneco Uriarte who killed Duncan or whether in some uncanny way it could have been the weapons, not the men, which fought. I still remember how Uriarte's hand shook when he first gripped his knife, and the same with Duncan, as though the knives were coming awake after a long sleep side by side in the cabinet. Even after their gauchos were dust, the knives—the knives, not their tools, the men—knew how to fight. And that night they fought well.

Things last longer than people; who knows whether these knives will meet again, who knows whether the story ends here.

Pedro Salvadores

To Juan Murchison
(1969)

I want to leave a written record (perhaps the first to be
attempted) of one of the strangest and grimmest happen-
ings in Argentine history. To meddle as little as possible in
the telling, to abstain from picturesque details or personal
conjectures is, it seems to me, the only way to do this.

A man, a woman, and the overpowering shadow of a
dictator are the three characters. The man's name was
Pedro Salvadores; my grandfather Acevedo saw him days
or weeks after the dictator's downfall in the battle of
Caseros. Pedro Salvadores may have been no different from
anyone else, but the years and his fate set him apart. He
was a gentleman like many other gentlemen of his day. He
owned (let us suppose) a ranch in the country and, op-
posed to the tyranny, was on the Unitarian side. His wife's
family name was Planes; they lived together on Suipacha
Street near the corner of Temple in what is now the heart
of Buenos Aires. The house in which the event took place
was much like any other, with its street door, long arched

entranceway, inner grillwork gate, its rooms, its row of two or three patios. The dictator, of course, was Rosas.

One night, around 1842, Salvadores and his wife heard the growing, muffled sound of horses' hooves out on the unpaved street and the riders shouting their drunken *vivas* and their threats. This time Rosas' henchmen did not ride on. After the shouts came repeated knocks at the door; while the men began forcing it, Salvadores was able to pull the dining-room table aside, lift the rug, and hide himself down in the cellar. His wife dragged the table back in place. The *mazorca* broke into the house; they had come to take Salvadores. The woman said her husband had run away to Montevideo. The men did not believe her; they flogged her, they smashed all the blue chinaware (blue was the Unitarian color), they searched the whole house, but they never thought of lifting the rug. At midnight they rode away, swearing that they would soon be back.

Here is the true beginning of Pedro Salvadores' story. He lived nine years in the cellar. For all we may tell ourselves that years are made of days and days of hours and that nine years is an abstract term and an impossible sum, the story is nonetheless gruesome. I suppose that in the darkness, which his eyes somehow learned to decipher, he had no particular thoughts, not even of his hatred or his danger. He was simply there—in the cellar—with echoes of the world he was cut off from sometimes reaching him from overhead: his wife's footsteps, the bucket clanging against the lip of the well, a heavy rainfall in the patio. Every day of his imprisonment, for all he knew, could have been the last.

His wife let go all the servants, who could possibly have informed against them, and told her family that Salvadores was in Uruguay. Meanwhile, she earned a living for them both sewing uniforms for the army. In the course of time, she gave birth to two children; her family turned from her, thinking she had a lover. After the tyrant's fall, they got down on their knees and begged to be forgiven.

What was Pedro Salvadores? Who was he? Was it his fear, his love, the unseen presence of Buenos Aires, or—in the long run—habit that held him prisoner? In order to keep him with her, his wife would make up news to tell him about whispered plots and rumored victories. Maybe he was a coward and she loyally hid it from him that she knew. I picture him in his cellar perhaps without a candle, without a book. Darkness probably sank him into sleep. His dreams, at the outset, were probably of that sudden night when the blade sought his throat, of the streets he knew so well, of the open plains. As the years went on, he would have been unable to escape even in his sleep; whatever he dreamed would have taken place in the cellar. At first, he may have been a man hunted down, a man in danger of his life; later (we will never know for certain), an animal at peace in its burrow or a sort of dim god.

All this went on until that summer day of 1852 when Rosas fled the country. It was only then that the secret man came out into the light of day; my grandfather spoke with him. Flabby, overweight, Salvadores was the color of wax and could not speak above a low voice. He never got back his confiscated lands; I think he died in poverty.

As with so many things, the fate of Pedro Salvadores strikes us as a symbol of something we are about to understand, but never quite do.

Rosendo's Tale
(1969)

It was about eleven o'clock at night; I had entered the old
grocery store-bar (which today is just a plain bar) at the
corner of Bolívar and Venezuela. From off on one side a
man signaled me with a "psst." There must have been
something forceful in his manner because I heeded him at
once. He was seated at one of the small tables in front of
an empty glass, and I somehow felt he had been sitting
there for a long time. Neither short nor tall, he had the
appearance of a common working man or maybe an old
farmhand. His thin moustache was graying. Fearful of his
health, like most people in Buenos Aires, he had not taken
off the scarf that draped his shoulders. He asked me to have
a drink with him. I sat down and we chatted. All this took
place sometime back in the early thirties. This is what the
man told me.

You don't know me except maybe by reputation, but I
know who you are. I'm Rosendo Juárez. The late Paredes

must have told you about me. The old man could pull the wool over people's eyes and liked to stretch a point—not to cheat anybody, mind you, but just in fun. Well, seeing you and I have nothing better to do, I'm going to tell you exactly what happened that night. The night the Butcher got killed. You put all that down in a storybook, which I'm not equipped to pass judgment on, but I want you to know the truth about all that trumped-up stuff.

Things happen to you and it's only years later you begin understanding them. What happened to me that night really had its start a long time back. I grew up in the neighborhood of the Maldonado, way out past Floresta. The Maldonado was just a ditch then, a kind of sewer, and it's a good thing they've covered it over now. I've always been of the opinion that the march of progress can't be held back—not by anybody. Anyway, a man's born where he's born. It never entered my head to find out who my father was. Clementina Juárez—that was my mother—was a decent woman who earned a living doing laundry. As far as I know, she was from Entre Ríos or Uruguay; anyhow, she always talked about her relatives from Concepción del Uruguay. I grew up like a weed. I first learned to handle a knife the way everyone else did, fencing with a charred stick. If you jabbed your man, it left a mark. Soccer hadn't taken us over yet—it was still in the hands of the English.

One night at the corner bar a young guy named Garmendia began taunting me, trying to pick a fight. I played deaf, but this other guy, who'd had a few, kept it up. We stepped out. Then from the sidewalk he swung open the door and said back inside to the people, "Don't anybody worry, I'll be right back."

I somehow got hold of a knife. We went off toward the brook, slow, our eyes on each other. He had a few years on me. We'd played at that fencing game a number of times together, and I had the feeling he was going to cut me up in ribbons. I went down the right-hand side of the road and he went down the left. He stumbled on some dry clods of mud. That moment was all I needed. I got the jump on him, almost without thinking, and opened a slice in his face. We got locked in a clinch, there was a minute when anything might have happened, and in the end I got my knife in and it was all over. Only later on did I find out I'd been cut up, too. But only a few scratches. That night I saw how easy it was to kill a man or to get killed. The water in the brook was pretty low; stalling for time, I half hid him behind one of the brick kilns. Fool that I was, I went and slipped off that fancy ring of his that he always wore with the nice stone in it. I put it on, I straightened my hat, and I went back to the bar. I walked in nonchalant, saying to them, "Looks like the one who came back was me."

I asked for a shot of rum and, to tell the truth, I needed it bad. It was then somebody noticed the blood on my sleeve.

I spent that whole night tossing and turning on my cot, and it was almost light outside before I dropped off and slept. Late the next day two cops came looking for me. My mother (may she rest in peace) began shrieking. They herded me along just like I was some kind of criminal. Two nights and two days I had to wait there in the cooler. Nobody came to see me, either, outside of Luis Irala—a real friend—only they wouldn't let him in. Then the third morning the police captain sent for me. He sat there in his chair, not even looking at me, and said, "So you're the one who took care of Garmendia, are you?"

"If that's what you say," I answered.

"You call me *sir*. And don't get funny or try beating around the bush. Here are the sworn statements of witnesses and the ring that was found in your house. Just sign this confession and get it over with."

He dipped the pen in the inkwell and handed it to me.

"Let me do some thinking, Captain sir," I came out with.

"I'll give you twenty-four hours where you can do some hard thinking—in the cooler. I'm not going to rush you. If you don't care to see reason, you can get used to the idea of a little vacation up on Las Heras—the penitentiary."

As you can probably imagine, I didn't understand.

127

"Look," he said, "if you come around, all you'll get is a few days. Then I'll let you go, and don Nicholás Paredes has already given me his word he'll straighten things out for you."

Actually, it was ten days. Then at last they remembered me. I signed what they wanted, and one of the two cops took me around to Paredes' house on Cabrera Street.

Horses were tied to the hitching post, and in the entranceway and inside the place there were more people than around a whorehouse. It looked to me like the party headquarters. Don Nicolás, who was sipping his maté, finally got around to me. Taking his good time, he told me he was sending me out to Morón, where they were getting ready for the elections. He was putting me in touch with Mr. Laferrer, who would try me out. He had the letter written by some kid all dressed in black, who, from what I heard, made up poems about tenements and filth—stuff that no refined public would dream of reading. I thanked Paredes for the favor and left. When I got to the corner, the cop wasn't tailing me any more.

Providence knows what it's up to; everything had turned out for the best. Garmendia's death, which at first had caused me a lot of worry, now opened things up for me. Of course, the law had me in the palm of their hands. If I was no use to the party they'd clap me back inside, but I felt pretty good and was counting on myself.

Mr. Laferrer warned me I was going to have to walk the straight and narrow with him, and said if I did I might even become his bodyguard. I came through with what was expected of me. In Morón, and later on in my part of town, I earned the trust of my bosses. The cops and the party kept on building up my reputation as a tough guy. I turned out to be pretty good at organizing the vote around the polls here in the capital and out in the province. I won't take up your time going into details about brawls and bloodletting, but let me tell you, in those days elections were lively affairs. I could never stand the Radicals, who down to this day are still hanging onto the beard of their chief Alem. There wasn't a soul around who didn't hold me in respect. I got hold of a woman, La Lujanera, and a fine-looking sorrel. For years I tried to live up to the part of the outlaw Moreira, who, in his time—the way I figure it—was probably trying to play the part of some other gaucho outlaw. I took to cards and absinthe.

An old man has a way of rambling on and on, but now I'm coming to the part I want you to hear. I wonder if I've already mentioned Luis Irala. The kind of friend you don't find every day. Irala was a man already well along in years. He never was afraid of work, and he took a liking to me. In his whole life he never had anything to do with politics. He was a carpenter by trade. He never caused anyone trouble and never allowed anyone to cause him trouble. One morning he came to see me and he said, "Of course, you've heard by now that Casilda's left me. Rufino Aguilera took her away from me."

I'd known that customer around Morón. I answered, "Yes, I know all about him. Of all the Aguileras, he's the least rotten."

"Rotten or not, now he'll have to reckon with me."

I thought that over for a while and told him, "Nobody takes anything away from anybody. If Casilda left you, it's because she cares for Rufino and you mean nothing to her."

"And what are people going to say? That I'm a coward?"

"My advice is don't get yourself mixed up in gossip about what people might say or about a woman who has no use for you."

"It's not her I'm worried about. A man who thinks five minutes straight about a woman is no man, he's a queer. Casilda has no heart. The last night we spent together she told me I wasn't as young as I used to be."

"Maybe she was telling you the truth."

"That's what hurts. What matters to me now is Rufino."

"Be careful there. I've seen Rufino in action around the polls in Mcrlo. He's a flash with a knife."

"You think I'm afraid of him?"

"I know you're not afraid of him, but think it over. One of two things—if you kill him, you get put away; if he kills you, you go six feet under."

"Maybe so. What would you do in my shoes?"

"I don't know, but my own life isn't exactly a model. I'm only a guy who became a party strong-arm man trying to cheat a jail sentence."

"I'm not going to the strong-arm guy for any party, I'm only out to settle a debt."

"So you're going to risk your peace and quiet for a man you don't know and a woman you don't love any more?"

He wouldn't hear me out. He just left. The next day the news came that he challenged Rufino in a saloon in Morón, and Rufino killed him. He was out to kill, and he got killed—but a fair fight, man to man. I'd given him my honest advice as a friend, but somehow I felt guilty just the same.

A few days after the wake, I went to a cockfight. I'd never been very big on cockfights, and that Sunday, to tell the truth, I had all I could do to stomach the thing. What is it in these animals, I kept thinking, that makes them gouge each other's eyes like that?

The night of my story, the night of the end of my story, I had told the boys I'd show up at Blackie's for the dance. So many years ago now, and that dress with the flowers my woman was wearing still comes back to me. The party was out in the backyard. Of course, there was the usual drunk or two trying to raise hell, but I took good care to see that things went off the way they ought to. It wasn't twelve yet when these strangers put in an appearance. One of them—the one they called the Butcher and who got himself stabbed in the back that same night—stood us all to a round of drinks. The odd thing was that the two of us looked a lot alike. Something was in the air; he drew up to me and began praising me up and down. He said he was from the Northside, where he'd heard a thing or two about me. I let him go on, but I was already sizing him up. He wasn't letting the gin alone, either, maybe to work up his courage, and finally he came out and asked me to fight. Then something happened that nobody ever understood. In that big loudmouth I saw myself, the same as in a mirror, and it made me feel ashamed. I wasn't scared; maybe if I'd been scared I'd have fought with him. I just stood there as if nothing happened. This other guy, with his face just inches away from mine, began shouting so everyone could hear, "The trouble is you're nothing but a coward."

"Maybe so," I said. "I'm not afraid of being taken for a coward. If it makes you feel good, why don't you say you've called me a son of a bitch, too, and that I've let you spit all over me. Now—are you any happier?"

La Lujanera took out the knife I always carried in my vest lining and, burning up inside, she shoved it into my hand. To clinch it, she said, "Rosendo, I think you're going to need this."

I let it drop and walked out, but not hurrying. The boys made way for me. They were stunned. What did it matter to me what they thought.

To make a clean break with that life, I took off for Uruguay, where I found myself work as a teamster. Since coming back to Buenos Aires I've settled around here. San Telmo always was a respectable neighborhood.

An Auto-biographical Essay

With Norman Thomas di Giovanni

An Auto-
biographical
Essay

Family and Childhood

I cannot tell whether my first memories go back to the eastern or to the western bank of the muddy, slow-moving Río de la Plata—to Montevideo, where we spent long, lazy holidays in the villa of my uncle Francisco Haedo, or to Buenos Aires. I was born there, in the very heart of that city, in 1899, on Tucumán Street, between Suipacha and Esmeralda, in a small, unassuming house belonging to my maternal grandparents. Like most of the houses of that day, it had a flat roof; a long, arched entranceway, called a *zaguán*; a cistern, where we got our water; and two patios. We must have moved out to the suburb of Palermo quite soon, because there I have my first memories of another house with two patios, a garden with a tall windmill pump, and, on the other side of the garden, an empty lot. Palermo at that time—the Palermo where we lived, Serrano and Guatemala—was on the shabby northern outskirts of town, and many people, ashamed of saying they lived there, spoke in a dim way of living on the Northside. We lived in one of the few two-story homes on our street; the rest of the neighborhood was made up of low houses and vacant lots. I have often spoken of this area as a slum, but I do not quite mean that in the American sense of the word. In Palermo lived shabby, genteel people as well as more undesirable sorts. There was also a Palermo of hoodlums, called *compadritos*, famed for their knife fights, but this Palermo was only later to capture my imagination, since we did our best—our successful best—to ignore it. Unlike our neighbor Evaristo Carriego, however, who was the first Argentine poet to explore the literary possibilities that lay there at hand. As for myself, I was hardly aware of the existence of *compadritos*, since I lived essentially indoors.

My father, Jorge Guillermo Borges, worked as a lawyer. He was a philosophical anarchist—a disciple of Spencer—and also a teacher of psychology at the Normal School for Modern Languages, where he gave his course in English, using as his text William James's shorter book of psychology. My father's English came from the fact that his mother, Frances Haslam, was born in Staffordshire of Northumbrian stock. A rather unlikely set of circumstances brought her to South America. Fanny Haslam's elder sister married an Italian-Jewish engineer named Jorge Suárez, who brought the first horse-drawn tramcars to Argentina, where he and his wife settled and sent for Fanny. I remember an anecdote concerning this venture. Suárez was a guest at General Urquiza's "palace" in Entre Ríos, and very improvidently won his first game of cards with the General, who was the stern dictator of that province and not above throat-cutting. When the game was over, Suárez was told by alarmed fellow-guests that if he wanted the license to run his tramcars in the province, it was expected of him to lose a certain amount of gold coins each night. Urquiza was such a poor player that Suárez had a great deal of trouble losing the appointed sums.

It was in Paraná, the capital city of Entre Ríos, that

Fanny Haslam met Colonel Francisco Borges. This was in 1870 or 1871, during the siege of the city by the *montoneros,* or gaucho militia, of Ricardo López Jordán. Borges, riding at the head of his regiment, commanded the troops defending the city. Fanny Haslam saw him from the flat roof of her house; that very night a ball was given to celebrate the arrival of the government relief forces. Fanny and the Colonel met, danced, fell in love, and eventually married.

My father was the younger of two sons. He had been born in Entre Ríos and used to explain to my grandmother, a respectable English lady, that he wasn't really an Entrerriano, since "I was begotten on the pampa." My grandmother would say, with English reserve, "I'm sure I don't know what you mean." My father's words, of course, were true, since my grandfather was, in the early 1870's, Commander-in-Chief of the northern and western frontiers of the Province of Buenos Aires. As a child, I heard many stories from Fanny Haslam about frontier life in those days. One of these I set down in my "Story of the Warrior and the Captive." My grandmother had spoken with a number of Indian chieftains, whose rather uncouth names were, I think, Simón Coliqueo, Catriel, Pincén, and Namuncurá. In 1874, during one of our civil wars, my grandfather, Colonel Borges, met his death. He was forty-one at the time. In the complicated circumstances surrounding his defeat at the battle of La Verde, he rode out slowly on horseback, wearing a white poncho and followed by ten or twelve of his men, toward the enemy lines, where he was struck by two Remington bullets. This was the first time Remington rifles were used in the Argentine, and it tickles my fancy to think that the firm that shaves me every morning bears the same name as the one that killed my grandfather.

Fanny Haslam was a great reader. When she was over eighty, people used to say, in order to be nice to her, that nowadays there were no writers who could vie with Dickens and Thackeray. My grandmother would answer, "On the whole, I rather prefer Arnold Bennett, Galsworthy, and Wells." When she died, at the age of ninety, in 1935, she called us to her side and said, in English (her Spanish was fluent but poor), in her thin voice, "I am only an old woman dying very, very slowly. There is nothing remarkable or interesting about this." She could see no reason whatever why the whole household should be upset, and she apologized for taking so long to die.

My father was very intelligent and, like all intelligent men, very kind. Once, he told me that I should take a good look at soldiers, uniforms, barracks, flags, churches, priests, and butcher shops, since all these things were about to disappear, and I could tell my children that I had actually seen them. The prophecy has not yet come true, unfortunately. My father was such a modest man that he would have liked being invisible. Though he was very proud of his English ancestry, he used to joke about it, saying with feigned perplexity, "After all, what are the English? Just a pack of German agricultural laborers." His idols were Shelley, Keats, and Swinburne. As a reader, he had two interests. First, books on metaphysics and psychology (Berkeley, Hume, Royce, and William James). Second, literature and books about the East (Lane, Burton, and Payne). It was he who revealed the power of poetry to me—the fact that words are not only a means of communication but also magic symbols and music. When I recite poetry in English now, my mother tells me I take on his very voice. He also, without my being aware of it, gave me my first lessons in philosophy. When I was still quite young, he showed me, with the aid of a chessboard, the paradoxes of Zeno— Achilles and the tortoise, the unmoving flight of the arrow, the impossibility of motion. Later, without mentioning Berkeley's name, he did his best to teach me the rudiments of idealism.

My mother, Leonor Acevedo de Borges, comes of old Argentine and Uruguayan stock, and at ninety-four is still hale and hearty and a good Catholic. When I was growing up, religion belonged to women and children; most men in

Buenos Aires were freethinkers—though, had they been asked, they might have called themselves Catholics. I think I inherited from my mother her quality of thinking the best of people and also her strong sense of friendship. My mother has always had a hospitable mind. From the time she learned English, through my father, she has done most of her reading in that language. After my father's death, finding that she was unable to keep her mind on the printed page, she tried her hand at translating William Saroyan's *The Human Comedy* in order to compel herself to concentrate. The translation found its way into print, and she was honored for this by a society of Buenos Aires Armenians. Later on, she translated some of Hawthorne's stories and one of Herbert Read's books on art, and she also produced some of the translations of Melville, Virginia Woolf, and Faulkner that are considered mine. She has always been a companion to me—especially in later years, when I went blind—and an understanding and forgiving friend. For years, until recently, she handled all my secretarial work, answering letters, reading to me, taking down my dictation, and also traveling with me on many occasions both at home and abroad. It was she, though I never gave a thought to it at the time, who quietly and effectively fostered my literary career.

Her grandfather was Colonel Isidoro Suárez, who, in 1824, at the age of twenty-four, led a famous charge of Peruvian and Colombian cavalry, which turned the tide of the battle of Junín, in Peru. This was the next to last battle of the South American War of Independence. Although Suárez was a second cousin to Juan Manuel de Rosas, who ruled as dictator in Argentina from 1835 to 1852, he preferred exile and poverty in Montevideo to living under a tyranny in Buenos Aires. His lands were, of course, confiscated, and one of his brothers was executed. Another member of my mother's family was Francisco de Laprida, who, in 1816, in Tucumán, where he presided over the Congress, declared the independence of the Argentine Confederation, and was killed in 1829 in a civil war. My mother's father, Isidoro Acevedo, though a civilian, took part in the fighting of yet other civil wars in the 1860's and 1880's. So, on both sides of my family, I have military forebears; this may account for my yearning after that epic destiny which my gods denied me, no doubt wisely.

I have already said that I spent a great deal of my boyhood indoors. Having no childhood friends, my sister and I invented two imaginary companions, named, for some reason or other, Quilos and The Windmill. (When they finally bored us, we told our mother that they had died.) I was always very nearsighted and wore glasses, and I was rather frail. As most of my people had been soldiers—even my father's brother had been a naval officer—and I knew I would never be, I felt ashamed, quite early, to be a bookish kind of person and not a man of action. Throughout my boyhood, I thought that to be loved would have amounted to an injustice. I did not feel I deserved any particular love, and I remember my birthdays filled me with shame, because everyone heaped gifts on me when I thought that I had done nothing to deserve them—that I was a kind of fake. After the age of thirty or so, I got over the feeling.

At home, both English and Spanish were commonly used. If I were asked to name the chief event in my life, I should say my father's library. In fact, I sometimes think I have never strayed outside that library. I can still picture it. It was in a room of its own, with glass-fronted shelves, and must have contained several thousand volumes. Being so nearsighted, I have forgotten most of the faces of that time (perhaps even when I think of my grandfather Acevedo I am thinking of his photograph), and yet I vividly remember so many of the steel engravings in *Chambers's Encyclopædia* and in the *Britannica*. The first novel I ever read through was *Huckleberry Finn*. Next came *Roughing It* and *Flush Days in California*. I also read books by Captain Marryat, Wells's *First Men in the Moon*, Poe, a one-volume edition of Longfellow, *Treasure Island*, Dickens, *Don Quixote*, *Tom Brown's School Days*, Grimms' *Fairy*

Tales, Lewis Carroll, *The Adventures of Mr Verdant Green* (a now forgotten book), Burton's *A Thousand Nights and a Night.* The Burton, filled with what was then considered obscenity, was forbidden, and I had to read it in hiding up on the roof. But at the time, I was so carried away with the magic that I took no notice whatever of the objectionable parts, reading the tales unaware of any other significance. All the foregoing books I read in English. When later I read *Don Quixote* in the original, it sounded like a bad translation to me. I still remember those red volumes with the gold lettering of the Garnier edition. At some point, my father's library was broken up, and when I read the *Quixote* in another edition I had the feeling that it wasn't the real *Quixote.* Later, I had a friend get me the Garnier, with the same steel engravings, the same footnotes, and also the same errata. All those things form part of the book for me; this I consider the real *Quixote.*

In Spanish, I also read many of the books by Eduardo Gutiérrez about Argentine outlaws and desperadoes—*Juan Moreira* foremost among them—as well as his *Siluetas militares,* which contains a forceful account of Colonel Borges' death. My mother forbade the reading of *Martín Fierro,* since that was a book fit only for hoodlums and schoolboys and, besides, was not about real gauchos at all. This too I read on the sly. Her feelings were based on the fact that Hernández had been an upholder of Rosas and therefore an enemy to our Unitarian ancestors. I read also Sarmiento's *Facundo,* many books on Greek mythology, and later Norse. Poetry came to me through English—Shelley, Keats, FitzGerald, and Swinburne, those great favorites of my father, who could quote them voluminously, and often did.

A tradition of literature ran through my father's family. His great-uncle Juan Crisóstomo Lafinur was one of the first Argentine poets, and he wrote an ode on the death of his friend General Manuel Belgrano, in 1820. One of my father's cousins, Álvaro Melián Lafinur, whom I knew from childhood, was a leading minor poet and later found his way into the Argentine Academy of Letters. My father's

maternal grandfather, Edward Young Haslam, edited one of
the first English papers in Argentina, the *Southern Cross*,
and was a Doctor of Philosophy or Letters, I'm not sure
which, of the University of Heidelberg. Haslam could not
afford Oxford or Cambridge, so he made his way to Germany, where he got his degree, going through the whole course
in Latin. Eventually, he died in Paraná. My father wrote a
novel, which he published in Majorca in 1921, about the
history of Entre Ríos. It was called *The Caudillo*. He also
wrote (and destroyed) a book of essays, and published a
translation of FitzGerald's Omar Khayyám in the same
meter as the original. He destroyed a book of Oriental
stories—in the manner of the Arabian Nights—and a drama,
Hacia la nada (Toward Nothingness), about a man's disap-
pointment in his son. He published some fine sonnets after
the style of the Argentine poet Enrique Banchs. From the
time I was a boy, when blindness came to him, it was
tacitly understood that I had to fulfill the literary destiny
that circumstances had denied my father. This was something that was taken for granted (and such things are far
more important than things that are merely said). I was
expected to be a writer.

I first started writing when I was six or seven. I tried to
imitate classic writers of Spanish—Miguel de Cervantes, for
example. I had set down in quite bad English a kind of
handbook on Greek mythology, no doubt cribbed from
Lemprière. This may have been my first literary venture.
My first story was a rather nonsensical piece after the
manner of Cervantes, an old-fashioned romance called "La
visera fatal" (The Fatal Helmet). I very neatly wrote these
things into copybooks. My father never interfered. He
wanted me to commit all my own mistakes, and once said,
"Children educate their parents, not the other way
around." When I was nine or so, I translated Oscar Wilde's
"The Happy Prince" into Spanish, and it was published in
one of the Buenos Aires dailies, *El País*. Since it was
signed merely "Jorge Borges," people naturally assumed
the translation was my father's.

I take no pleasure whatever in recalling my early schooldays. To begin with, I did not start school until I was nine. This was because my father, as an anarchist, distrusted all enterprises run by the State. As I wore spectacles and dressed in an Eton collar and tie, I was jeered at and bullied by most of my schoolmates, who were amateur hooligans. I cannot remember the name of the school but recall that it was on Thames Street. My father used to say that Argentine history had taken the place of the catechism, so we were expected to worship all things Argentine. We were taught Argentine history, for example, before we were allowed any knowledge of the many lands and many centuries that went into its making. As far as Spanish composition goes, I was taught to write in a flowery way: *Aquellos que lucharon por una patria libre, independiente, gloriosa* . . . (Those who struggled for a free, independent, and glorious nation . . .). Later on, in Geneva, I was to be told that such writing was meaningless and that I must see things through my own eyes. My sister Norah, who was born in 1901, of course attended a girls' school.

During all these years, we usually spent our summers out in Adrogué, some ten or fifteen miles to the south of Buenos Aires, where we had a place of our own—a large one-story house with grounds, two summerhouses, a windmill, and a shaggy brown sheepdog. Adrogué then was a lost and undisturbed maze of summer homes surrounded by iron fences with masonry planters on the gateposts, of parks, of streets that radiated out of the many plazas, and of the ubiquitous smell of eucalyptus trees. We continued to visit Adrogué for decades.

My first real experience of the pampa came around 1909, on a trip we took to a place belonging to relatives near San Nicolás, to the northwest of Buenos Aires. I remember that the nearest house was a kind of blur on the horizon. This endless distance, I found out, was called the pampa, and when I learned that the farmhands were gauchos, like the characters in Eduardo Gutiérrez, that gave them a certain glamor. I have always come to things after coming to books.

Once, I was allowed to acompany them on horseback, taking cattle to the river early one morning. The men were small and darkish and wore *bombachas*, a kind of wide, baggy trousers. When I asked them if they knew how to swim, they replied, "Water is meant for cattle." My mother gave a doll, in a large cardboard box, to the foreman's daughter. The next year, we went back and asked after the little girl. "What a delight the doll has been to her!" they told us. And we were shown it, still in its box, nailed to the wall like an image. Of course, the girl was allowed only to look at it, not to touch it, for it might have been soiled or broken. There it was, high up out of harm's way, worshiped from afar. Lugones has written that in Córdoba, before magazines came in, he had many times seen a playing card used as a picture and nailed to the wall in gauchos' shacks. The four of *copas*, with its small lion and two towers, was particularly coveted. I think I began writing a poem about gauchos, probably under the influence of the poet Ascasubi, before I went to Geneva. I recall trying to work in as many gaucho words as I could, but the technical difficulties were beyond me. I never got past a few stanzas.

Europe

In 1914, we moved to Europe. My father's eyesight had begun to fail and I remember his saying, "How on earth can I sign my name to legal papers when I am unable to read them?" Forced into early retirement, he planned our trip in exactly ten days. The world was unsuspicious then; there were no passports or other red tape. We first spent some weeks in Paris, a city that neither then nor since has particularly charmed me, as it does every other good Argentine. Perhaps, without knowing it, I was always a bit of a Britisher; in fact, I always think of Waterloo as a victory. The idea of the trip was for my sister and me to go to school in Geneva; we were to live with my maternal grandmother, who traveled with us and eventually died there, while my parents toured the Continent. At the same time, my father was to be treated by a famous Genevan eye doctor. Europe in those days was cheaper than Buenos Aires, and Argentine money then stood for something. We were so ignorant of history, however, that we had no idea that the First World War would break out in August. My mother and father were in Germany when it happened, but managed to get back to us in Geneva. A year or so later, despite the war, we were able to journey across the Alps into northern Italy. I have vivid memories of Verona and Venice. In the vast and empty amphitheater of Verona I recited, loud and bold, several gaucho verses from Ascasubi.

That first fall—1914—I started school at the College of Geneva, founded by John Calvin. It was a day school. In my class there were some forty of us; a good half were foreigners. The chief subject was Latin, and I soon found out that one could let other studies slide a bit as long as one's Latin was good. All these other courses, however—algebra, chemistry, physics, mineralogy, botany, zoology—were studied in French. That year, I passed all my exams successfully, except for French itself. Without a word to me, my fellow-schoolmates sent a petition around to the headmaster, which they had all signed. They pointed out that I had had to study all of the different subjects in French, a language I also had to learn. They asked the headmaster to take this into account, and he very kindly did so. At first, I had not even understood when a teacher was calling on me, because my name was pronounced in the French manner, in a single syllable (rhyming roughly with "forge"), while we pronounce it with two syllables, the "g" sounding like a strong Scottish "h." Every time I had to answer, my schoolmates would nudge me.

We lived in a flat on the southern, or old, side of town. I still know Geneva far better than I know Buenos Aires, which is easily explained by the fact that in Geneva no two streetcorners are alike and one quickly learns the differences. Every day, I walked along that green and icy river, the Rhone, which runs through the very heart of the city, spanned by seven quite different-looking bridges. The Swiss are rather proud and standoffish. My two bosom friends were of Polish-Jewish origin—Simon Jichlinski and Maurice Abramowicz. One became a lawyer and the other a physician. I taught them to play *truco*, and they learned so well and fast that at the end of our first game they left me without a cent. I became a good Latin scholar, while I did most of my private reading in English. At home, we spoke Spanish, but my sister's French soon became so good she even dreamed in it. I remember my mother's coming home one day and finding Norah hidden behind a red plush curtain, crying out in fear, *"Une mouche, une mouche!"* It seems she had adopted the French notion that flies are dangerous. "You come out of there," my mother told her, somewhat unpatriotically. "You were born and bred among flies!" As a result of the war—apart from the Italian trip and journeys inside Switzerland—we did no traveling. Later on, braving German submarines and in the company of only four or five other passengers, my English grandmother joined us.

On my own, outside of school, I took up the study of German. I was sent on this adventure by Carlyle's *Sartor Resartus* (The Tailor Retailored), which dazzled and also bewildered me. The hero, Diogenes Devil'sdung, is a German professor of idealism. In German literature I was looking for something Germanic, akin to Tacitus, but I was only later to find this in Old English and in Old Norse. German literature turned out to be romantic and sickly. At first, I tried Kant's *Critique of Pure Reason* but was defeated by it, as most people—including most Germans—are. Then I thought verse would be easier, because of its brevity. So I got hold of a copy of Heine's early poems, the *Lyrisches Intermezzo*, and a German-English dictionary. Little by little, owing to Heine's simple vocabulary, I found I could do without the dictionary. Soon I had worked my way into the loveliness of the language. I also managed to read Meyrink's nover *Der Golem*. (In 1969, when I was in

146

Israel, I talked over the Bohemian legend of the Golem with Gershom Scholem, a leading scholar of Jewish mysticism, whose name I had twice used as the only possible rhyming word in a poem of my own on the Golem.) I tried to be interested in Jean-Paul Richter, for Carlyle's and De Quincey's sake—this was around 1917—but I soon discovered that I was very bored by the reading. Richter, in spite of his two British champions, seemed to me very long-winded and perhaps a passionless writer. I became, however, very interested in German expressionism and still think of it as beyond other contemporary schools, such as imagism, cubism, futurism, surrealism, and so on. A few years later, in Madrid, I was to attempt some of the first, and perhaps the only, translations of a number of expressionist poets into Spanish.

At some point while in Switzerland, I began reading Schopenhauer. Today, were I to choose a single philosopher, I would choose him. If the riddle of the universe can be stated in words, I think these words would be in his writings. I have read him many times over, both in German and, with my father and his close friend Macedonio Fernández, in translation. I still think of German as being a beautiful language—perhaps more beautiful than the literature it has produced. French, rather paradoxically, has a fine literature despite its fondness for schools and movements, but the language itself is, I think, rather ugly. Things tend to sound trivial when they are said in French. In fact, I even think of Spanish as being the better of the two languages, though Spanish words are far too long and cumbersome. As an Argentine writer, I have to cope with Spanish and so am only too aware of its shortcomings. I remember that Goethe wrote that he had to deal with the worst language in the world—German. I suppose most writers think along these lines concerning the language they have to struggle with. As for Italian, I have read and reread *The Divine Comedy* in more than a dozen different editions. I've also read Ariosto, Tasso, Croce, and Gentile, but

I am quite unable to speak Italian or to follow an Italian play or film.

It was also in Geneva that I first met Walt Whitman, through a German translation by Johannes Schlaf (*"Als ich in Alabama meinen Morgengang machte"*—"As I have walk'd in Alabama my morning walk"). Of course, I was struck by the absurdity of reading an American poet in German, so I ordered a copy of *Leaves of Grass* from London. I remember it still—bound in green. For a time, I thought of Whitman not only as a great poet but as the *only* poet. In fact, I thought that all poets the world over had been merely leading up to Whitman until 1855, and that not to imitate him was a proof of ignorance. This feeling had already come over me with Carlyle's prose, which is now unbearable to me, and with the poetry of Swinburne. These were phases I went through. Later on, I was to go through similar experiences of being overwhelmed by some particular writer.

We remained in Switzerland until 1919. After three or four years in Geneva, we spent a year in Lugano. I had my bachelor's degree by then, and it was now understood that I should devote myself to writing. I wanted to show my manuscripts to my father, but he told me he didn't believe in advice and that I must work my way all by myself through trial and error. I had been writing sonnets in English and in French. The English sonnets were poor imitations of Wordsworth, and the French, in their own watery way, were imitative of symbolist poetry. I still recall one line of my French experiments: *"Petite boîte noire pour le violon cassé."* The whole piece was titled "Poeme pour être recité avec un accent russe." As I knew I wrote a foreigner's French, I thought a Russian accent better than an Argentine one. In my English experiments, I affected some eighteenth-century mannerisms, such as "o'er" instead of "over" and, for the sake of metrical ease, "doth sing" instead of "sings." I knew, however, that Spanish would be my unavoidable destiny.

We decided to go home, but to spend a year or so in

Spain first. Spain at that time was slowly being discovered by Argentines. Until then, even eminent writers like Leopoldo Lugones and Ricardo Güiraldes deliberately left Spain out of their European travels. This was no whim. In Buenos Aires, Spaniards always held menial jobs—as domestic servants, waiters, and laborers—or were small tradesmen, and we Argentines never thought of ourselves as Spanish. We had, in fact, left off being Spaniards in 1816, when we declared our independence from Spain. When, as a boy, I read Prescott's *Conquest of Peru*, it amazed me to find that he portrayed the conquistadors in a romantic way. To me, descended from certain of these officials, they were an uninteresting lot. Through French eyes, however, Latin Americans saw the Spaniards as picturesque, thinking of them in terms of the stock in trade of García Lorca—gypsies, bullfights, and Moorish architecture. But though Spanish was our language and we came mostly of Spanish and Portuguese blood, my own family never thought of our trip in terms of going back to Spain after an absence of some three centuries.

We went to Majorca because it was cheap, beautiful, and had hardly any tourists but ourselves. We lived there nearly a whole year, in Palma and in Valldemosa, a village high up in the hills. I went on studying Latin, this time under the tutelage of a priest, who told me that since the innate was sufficient to his needs, he had never attempted reading a novel. We went over Virgil, of whom I still think highly. I remember I astonished the natives by my fine swimming, for I had learned in swift rivers, such as the Uruguay and the Rhone, while Majorcans were used only to a quiet, tideless sea. My father was writing his novel, which harked back to old times during the civil war of the 1870's in his native Entre Ríos. I recall giving him some quite bad metaphors, borrowed from the German expressionists, which he accepted out of resignation. He had some five hundred copies of the book printed, and brought them back to Buenos Aires, where he gave them away to friends. Every time the word "Paraná"—his home town—had come up in the manuscript, the printers changed it to "Panamá," thinking they were correcting a mistake. Not to give them trouble, and also seeing it was funnier that way, my father let this pass. Now I repent my youthful intrusions into his book. Seventeen years later, before he died, he told me that he would very much like me to rewrite the novel in a straightforward way, with all the fine writing and purple patches left out. I myself in those days wrote a story about a werewolf and sent it to a popular magazine in Madrid, *La Esfera*, whose editors very wisely turned it down.

The winter of 1919–20 we spent in Seville, where I saw my first poem into print. It was titled "Hymn to the Sea" and appeared in the magazine *Grecia*, in its issue of December 31, 1919. In the poem, I tried my hardest to be Walt Whitman:

> O sea! O myth! O sun! O wide resting place!
> I know why I love you. I know that we are both very old,
> that we have known each other for centuries. . . .
> O Protean, I have been born of you—
> both of us chained and wandering,
> both of us hungering for stars,
> both of us with hopes and disappointments. . . !

Today, I hardly think of the sea, or even of myself, as hungering for stars. Years after, when I came across Arnold Bennett's phrase "the third-rate grandiose," I understood at once what he meant. And yet when I arrived in Madrid a few months later, as this was the only poem I had ever printed, people there thought of me as a singer of the sea.

In Seville, I fell in with the literary group formed around *Grecia*. This group, who called themselves ultraists, had set out to renew literature, a branch of the arts of which they knew nothing whatever. One of them once told me his whole reading had been the Bible, Cervantes, Darío, and one or two of the books of the Master, Rafael Cansinos-Assens. It baffled my Argentine mind to learn that they had no French and no inkling at all that such a thing as

English literature existed. I was even introduced to a local worthy popularly known as "the Humanist" and was not long in discovering that his Latin was far smaller than mine. As for *Grecia* itself, the editor, Isaac del Vando Villar, had the whole corpus of his poetry written for him by one or another of his assistants. I remember one of them telling me one day, "I'm very busy—Isaac is writing a poem."

Next, we went to Madrid, and there the great event to me was my friendship with Rafael Cansinos-Assens. I still like to think of myself as his disciple. He had come from Seville, where he had studied for the priesthood, but, having found the name Cansinos in the archives of the Inquisition, he decided he was a Jew. This led him to the study of Hebrew, and later on he even had himself circumcised. Literary friends from Andalusia took me to meet him. I timidly congratulated him on a poem *he* had written about the sea. "Yes," he said, "and how I'd like to see it before I die." He was a tall man with the Andalusian contempt for all things Castilian. The most remarkable fact about Cansinos was that he lived completely for literature, without regard for money or fame. He was a fine poet and wrote a book of psalms—chiefly erotic—called *El candelabro de los siete brazos*, which was published in 1914. He also wrote novels, stories, and essays, and, when I knew him, presided over a literary circle.

Every Saturday I would go to the Café Colonial, where we met at midnight, and the conversation lasted until daybreak. Sometimes there were as many as twenty or thirty of us. The group despised all Spanish local color—*cante jongo* and bullfights. They admired American jazz, and were more interested in being Europeans than Spaniards. Cansinos would propose a subject—The Metaphor, Free Verse, The Traditional Forms of Poetry, Narrative Poetry, The Adjective, The Verb. In his own quiet way, he was a dictator, allowing no unfriendly allusions to contemporary writers and trying to keep the talk on a high plane.

Cansinos was a wide reader. He had translated De Quincey's *Opium-Eater*, the *Meditations of Marcus Aureli-*

us from the Greek, novels of Barbusse, and Schwob's *Vies imaginaires*. Later, he was to undertake complete translations of Goethe and Dostoevski. He also made the first Spanish version of the Arabian Nights, which is very free compared to Burton's or Lane's, but which makes, I think, for more pleasurable reading. Once, I went to see him and he took me into his library. Or, rather, I should say his whole house was a library. It was like making your way through a woods. He was too poor to have shelves, and the books were piled one on top of the other from floor to ceiling, forcing you to thread your way among the vertical columns. Cansinos seemed to me as if he were all the past of that Europe I was leaving behind—something like the symbol of all culture, Western and Eastern. But he had a perversity that made him fail to get on with his leading contemporaries. It lay in writing books that lavishly praised second- or third-rate writers. At the time, Ortega y Gasset was at the height of his fame, but Cansinos thought of him as a bad philosopher and a bad writer. What I got from him, chiefly, was the pleasure of literary conversation. Also, I was stimulated by him to far-flung reading. In writing, I began aping him. He wrote long and flowing sentences with an un-Spanish and strongly Hebrew flavor to them.

Oddly, it was Cansinos who, in 1919, invented the term "ultraism." He thought Spanish literature had always been behind the times. Under the pen name of Juan Las, he wrote some short, laconic ultraist pieces. The whole thing—I see now—was done in a spirit of mockery. But we youngsters took it very seriously. Another of the earnest followers was Guillermo de Torre, whom I met in Madrid that spring and who married my sister Norah nine years later.

In Madrid at this time, there was another group gathered around Ramón Gómez de la Serna. I went there once and didn't like the way they behaved. They had a buffoon who wore a bracelet with a rattle attached. He would be made to shake hands with people and the rattle would rattle and Gómez de la Serna would invariably say, "Where's the snake?" That was supposed to be funny. Once, he turned to me proudly and remarked, "You've never seen this kind of thing in Buenos Aires, have you?" I owned, thank God, that I hadn't.

In Spain, I wrote two books. One was a series of essays called, I now wonder why, *Los naipes del tahur* (The Sharper's Cards). They were literary and political essays (I was still an anarchist and a freethinker and in favor of pacifism), written under the influence of Pío Baroja. Their aim was to be bitter and relentless, but they were, as a matter of fact, quite tame. I went in for using such words as "fools," "harlots," "liars." Failing to find a publisher, I destroyed the manuscript on my return to Buenos Aires. The second book was titled either *The Red Psalms* or *The Red Rhythms*. It was a collection of poems—perhaps some twenty in all—in free verse and in praise of the Russian Revolution, the brotherhood of man, and pacifism. Three or four of them found their way into magazines—"Bolshevik Epic," "Trenches," "Russia." This book I destroyed in Spain on the eve of our departure. I was then ready to go home.

Buenos Aires

We returned to Buenos Aires on the *Reina Victoria Eugenia* toward the end of March, 1921. It came to me as a surprise, after living in so many European cities—after so many memories of Geneva, Zurich, Nîmes, Córdoba, and Lisbon—to find that my native town had grown, and that it was now a very large, sprawling, and almost endless city of low buildings with flat roofs, stretching west toward what geographers and literary hands call the pampa. It was more than a homecoming; it was a rediscovery. I was able to see Buenos Aires keenly and eagerly because I had been away from it for a long time. Had I never gone abroad, I wonder whether I would ever have seen it with the peculiar shock and glow that it now gave me. The city—not the whole city, of course, but a few places in it that became emotionally significant to me—inspired the poems of my first published book, *Fervor de Buenos Aires*.

I wrote these poems in 1921 and 1922, and the volume came out early in 1923. The book was actually printed in five days; the printing had to be rushed, because it was necessary for us to return to Europe. (My father wanted to consult his Genevan doctor about his sight.) I had bargained for sixty-four pages, but the manuscript ran too long and at the last minute five poems had to be left out—mercifully. I can't remember a single thing about them. The book was produced in a somewhat boyish spirit. No proofreading was done, no table of contents was provided, and the pages were unnumbered. My sister made a woodcut for the cover, and three hundred copies were printed. In those days, publishing a book was something of a private venture. I never thought of sending copies to the booksellers or out for review. Most of them I just gave away. I recall one of my methods of distribution. Having noticed that many people who went to the offices of *Nosotros*—one of the older, more solid literary magazines of the time—left their overcoats hanging in the cloak room, I brought fifty or a hundred copies to Alfredo Bianchi, one of the editors. Bianchi stared at me in amazement and said, "Do you expect me to sell these books for you?"

"No," I answered. "Although I've written them, I'm not altogether a lunatic. I thought I might ask you to slip some of these books into the pockets of those coats hanging out there." He generously did so. When I came back after a year's absence, I found that some of the inhabitants of the overcoats had read my poems, and a few had even written about them. As a matter of fact, in this way I got myself a small reputation as a poet.

The book was essentially romantic, though it was written in a rather lean style and abounded in laconic metaphors. It celebrated sunsets, solitary places, and unfamiliar corners; it ventured into Berkeleyan metaphysics and family history; it recorded early loves. At the same time, I also mimicked the Spanish seventeenth century and cited Sir Thomas Browne's *Religio Medici* in my preface. I'm afraid the book was a plum pudding—there was just too much in it. And yet, looking back on it now, I think I have never strayed beyond that book. I feel that all my subsequent writing has only developed themes first taken up there; I feel that all during my lifetime I have been rewriting that one book.

Were the poems in *Fervor de Buenos Aires* ultraist poetry? When I came back from Europe in 1921, I came bearing the banners of ultraism. I am still known to literary historians as "the father of Argentine ultraism." When I talked things over at the time with fellow-poets Eduardo González Lanuza, Norah Lange, Francisco Piñero, my cousin Guillermo Juan (Borges), and Roberto Ortelli, we came to the conclusion that Spanish ultraism was overburdened—after the manner of futurism—with modernity and gadgets. We were unimpressed by railway trains, by propellers, by airplanes, and by electric fans. While in our manifestos we still upheld the primacy of the metaphor and the elimination of transitions and decorative adjectives, what we wanted to write was essential poetry—poems beyond the here and now, free of local color and contemporary circumstances. I think the poem "Plainness" sufficiently illustrates what I personally was after:

> The garden's grillwork gate
> opens with the ease of a page
> in a much thumbed book,
> and, once inside, our eyes
> have no need to dwell on objects
> already fixed and exact in memory.
> Here habits and minds and the private language
> all families invent
> are everyday things to me.
> What necessity is there to speak
> or pretend to be someone else?

155

> The whole house knows me,
> they're aware of my worries and weakness.
> This is the best that can happen—
> what Heaven perhaps will grant us:
> not to be wondered at or required to succeed
> but simply to be let in
> as part of an undeniable Reality,
> like stones of the road, like trees.

I think this is a far cry from the timid extravagances of my earlier Spanish ultraist exercises, when I saw a trolley car as a man shouldering a gun, or the sunrise as a shout, or the setting sun as being crucified in the west. A sane friend to whom I later recited such absurdities remarked, "Ah, I see you held the view that poetry's chief aim is to startle." As to whether the poems in *Fervor* are ultraist or not, the answer—for me—was given by my friend and French translator Néstor Ibarra, who said, "Borges left off being an ultraist poet with the first ultraist poem he wrote." I can now only regret my early ultraist excesses. After nearly a half century, I find myself still striving to live down that awkward period of my life.

Perhaps the major event of my return was Macedonio Fernández. Of all the people I have met in my life—and I have met some quite remarkable men—no one has ever made so deep and so lasting an impression on me as Macedonio. A tiny figure in a black bowler hat, he was waiting for us on the ·Dársena Norte when we landed, and I came to inherit his friendship from my father. Both men had been born in 1874. Paradoxically, Macedonio was an outstanding conversationalist and at the same time a man of long silences and few words. We met on Saturday evening at a café—the Perla, in the Plaza del Once. There we would talk till daybreak, Macedonio presiding. As in Madrid Cansinos had stood for all learning, Macedonio now stood for pure thinking. At the time, I was a great reader and went out very seldom (almost every night after dinner, I used to go to bed and read), but my whole week was lit up with the expectation that on Saturday I'd be seeing and hearing Macedonio. He lived quite near us and I could have seen him whenever I wanted, but I somehow felt that I had no right to that privilege and that in order to give Macedonio's Saturday its full value I had to forgo him throughout the week. At these meetings, Macedonio would speak perhaps three or four times, risking only a few quiet observations, which were addressed—seemingly—to his neighbor alone. These remarks were never affirmative. Macedonio was very courteous and soft-spoken and would say, for example, "Well, I suppose you've noticed . . ." And thereupon he would let loose some striking, highly original thought. But, invariably, he attributed his remark to the hearer.

He was a frail, gray man with the kind of ash-colored hair and moustache that made him look like Mark Twain. The resemblance pleased him, but when he was reminded that he also looked like Paul Valéry, he resented it, since he had little use for Frenchmen. He always wore that black bowler, and for all I know may even have slept in it. He never undressed to go to bed, and at night, to fend off drafts that he thought might cause him toothache, he draped a towel around his head. This made him look like an Arab. Among his other eccentricities were his nationalism (he admired one Argentine president after another for the sufficient reason that the Argentine electorate could not be wrong), his fear of dentistry (this led him to tugging at his teeth, in public, behind a hand, so as to stave off the dentist's pliers), and a habit of falling sentimentally in love with streetwalkers.

As a writer, Macedonio published several rather unusual volumes, and papers of his are still being collected close to twenty years after his death. His first book, published in 1928, was called *No toda es vigilia la de los ojos abiertos* (We're Not Always Awake When Our Eyes Are Open). It was an extended essay on idealism, written in a deliberately tangled and crabbed style, in order, I suppose, to match the tangledness of reality. The next year, a miscellany of his writings appeared—*Papeles de Recienvenido* (Newcomer's Papers)—in which I myself took a hand, collecting and ordering the chapters. This was a sort of miscellany of jokes within jokes. Macedonio also wrote novels and poems, all of them startling but hardly readable. One novel of twenty chapters is prefaced by fifty-six different forewords. For all his brilliance, I don't think Macedonio is to be found in his writings at all. The real Macedonio was in his conversation.

Macedonio lived modestly in boardinghouses, which he seemed to change with frequency. This was because he was always skipping out on the rent. Every time he would move, he'd leave behind piles and piles of manuscripts. Once, his friends scolded him about this, telling him it was a shame all that work should be lost. He said to us, "Do you really think I'm rich enough to lose anything?"

Readers of Hume and Schopenhauer may find little that is new in Macedonio, but the remarkable thing about him is that he arrived at his conclusions by himself. Later on, he actually read Hume, Schopenhauer, Berkeley, and William James, but I suspect he had not done much other reading, and he always quoted the same authors. He considered Sir Walter Scott the greatest of novelists, maybe just out of loyalty to a boyhood enthusiasm. He had once exchanged letters with William James, whom he had written in a medley of English, German, and French, explaining that it was because "I knew so little in any one of these languages that I had constantly to shift tongues." I think of Macedonio as reading a page or so and then being spurred into thought. He not only argued that we are such stuff as dreams are made on, but he really believed that we are all living in a dream world. Macedonio doubted whether truth was communicable. He thought that certain philosophers had discovered it but that they had failed to communicate it completely. However, he also believed that the discovery of truth was quite easy. He once told me that if he could lie out on the pampa, forgetting the world, himself, and his quest, truth might suddenly reveal itself to him. He added that, of course, it might be impossible to put that sudden wisdom into words.

Macedonio was fond of compiling small oral catalogs of people of genius, and in one of them I was amazed to find the name of a very lovable lady of our acquaintance, Quica González Acha de Tomkinson Alvear. I stared at him open-mouthed. I somehow did not think Quica ranked with Hume and Schopenhauer. But Macedonio said, "Philosophers have had to try and explain the universe, while Quica simply feels and understands it." He would turn to her and ask, "Quica, what is Being?" Quica would answer, "I don't know what you mean, Macedonio." "You see," he would say to me, "she understands so perfectly that she cannot even grasp the fact that we are puzzled." This was his proof of Quica's being a woman of genius. When I later told him he might say the same of a child or a cat, Macedonio took it angrily.

Before Macedonio, I had always been a credulous reader. His chief gift to me was to make me read skeptically. At the outset, I plagiarized him devotedly, picking up certain stylistic mannerisms of his that I later came to regret. I look back on him now, however, as an Adam bewildered by the Garden of Eden. His genius survives in but a few of his pages; his influence was of a Socratic nature. I truly loved the man, on this side idolatry, as much as any.

This period, from 1921 to 1930, was one of great activity, but much of it was perhaps reckless and even pointless. I wrote and published no less than seven books— four of them essays and three of them verse. I also founded three magazines and contributed with fair frequency to nearly a dozen other periodicals, among them *La Prensa, Nosostros, Inicial, Criterio,* and *Sintesis.* This productivity now amazes me as much as the fact that I feel only the remotest kinship with the work of these years. Three of the four essay collections—whose names are best forgotten—I have never allowed to be reprinted. In fact, when in 1953 my present publisher—Emecé—proposed to bring out my "complete writings," the only reason I accepted was that it would allow me to keep those preposterous volumes suppressed. This reminds me of Mark Twain's suggestion that a fine library could be started by leaving out the works of Jane Austen, and that even if that library contained no other books it would still be a fine library, since her books were left out.

In the first of these reckless compilations, there was a quite bad essay on Sir Thomas Browne, which may have been the first ever attempted on him in the Spanish language. There was another essay that set out to classify metaphors as though other poetic elements, such as rhythm and music, could be safely ignored. There was a longish essay on the nonexistence of the ego, cribbed from Bradley or the Buddha or Macedonio Fernández. When I wrote these pieces, I was trying to play the sedulous ape to two Spanish baroque seventeenth-century writers, Quevedo and Saavedra Fajardo, who stood in their own stiff, arid, Spanish way for the same kind of writing as Sir Thomas Browne in "Urne-Buriall." I was doing my best to write Latin in Spanish, and the book collapses under the sheer weight of its involutions and sententious judgments. The next of these failures was a kind of reaction. I went to the other extreme—I tried to be as Argentine as I could. I got hold of Segovia's dictionary of Argentinisms and worked in so many local words that many of my countrymen could hardly understand it. Since I have mislaid the dictionary, I'm not sure I would any longer understand the book myself, and so have given it up as utterly hopeless. The third of these unmentionables stands for a kind of partial redemption. I was creeping out of the second book's style and slowly going back to sanity, to writing with some attempt at logic and at making things easy for the reader rather than dazzling him with purple passages. One such experiment, of dubious value, was "Hombres pelearon" (Men Fought), my first venture into the mythology of the old Northside of Buenos Aires. In it, I was trying to tell a purely Argentine story in an Argentine way. This story is one I have been retelling, with small variations, ever since. It is the tale of the motiveless, or disinterested, duel—of courage for its own sake. I insisted when I wrote it that in our sense of the language we Argentines were different from the Spaniards. Now, instead, I think we should try to stress our linguistic affinities. I was still writing, but in a milder way, so that Spaniards would not understand me—writing, it might be said, to be ununderstood. The Gnostics claimed that the only way to avoid a sin was to commit it and be rid of it. In my books of these years, I seem to have committed most of the major literary sins, some of them under the influence of a great writer, Leopoldo Lugones, whom I still cannot help admiring. These sins were fine writing, local color, a quest for the unexpected, and a seventeenth-century style. Today, I no longer feel guilty over these excesses; those books were written by somebody else. Until a few years ago, if the price were not too stiff, I would buy up copies and burn them.

Of the poems of this time, I should perhaps have also suppressed my second collection, *Luna de enfrente* (Moon Across the Way). It was published in 1925 and is a kind of riot of sham local color. Among its tomfooleries were the spelling of my first name in the nineteenth-century Chilean fashion as "Jorje" (it was a halfhearted attempt at phonetic spelling); the spelling of the Spanish for "and" as "*i*" instead of "*y*" (our greatest writer, Sarmiento, had done the same, trying to be as un-Spanish as he could); and the omission of the final "d" in words like "*autoridá*" and "*ciudá*." In later editions, I dropped the worst poems, pruned the eccentricities, and, successively—through several reprintings—revised and toned down the verses. The third collection of the time, *Cuaderno San Martín* (the title has nothing to do with the national hero; it was merely the brand name of the out-of-fashion copybook into which I wrote the poems), includes some quite legitimate pieces, such as "La noche que en el Sur lo velaron," whose title has been strikingly translated by Robert Fitzgerald as "Deathwatch on the Southside," and "Muertes de Buenos Aires"

(Deaths of Buenos Aires), about the two chief graveyards of the Argentine capital. One poem in the book (no favorite of mine) has somehow become a minor Argentine classic: "The Mythical Founding of Buenos Aires." This book, too, has been improved, or purified, by cuts and revisions down through the years.

In 1929, that third book of essays won the Second Municipal Prize of three thousand pesos, which in those days was a lordly sum of money. I was, for one thing, to acquire with it a secondhand set of the Eleventh Edition of the *Encyclopædia Britannica*. For another, I was insured a year's leisure and decided I would write a longish book on a wholly Argentine subject. My mother wanted me to write about any of three really worthwhile poets—Ascasubi, Almafuerte, or Lugones. I now wish I had. Instead, I chose to write about a nearly invisible popular poet, Evaristo Carriego. My mother and father pointed out that his poems were not good. "But he was a friend and neighbor of ours," I said. "Well, if you think that qualifies him as the subject for a book, go ahead," they said. Carriego was the man who discovered the literary possibilities of the run-down and ragged outskirts of the city—the Palermo of my boyhood. His career followed the same evolution as the tango—rollicking, daring, courageous at first, then turning sentimental. In 1912, at the age of twenty-nine, he died of tuberculosis, leaving behind a single volume of his work. I remember that a copy of it, inscribed to my father, was one of several Argentine books we had taken to Geneva and that I read and reread there. Around 1909, Carriego had dedicated a poem to my mother. Actually, he had written it in her album. In it, he spoke of me: "And may your son ... go forth, led by the trusting wing of inspiration, to carry out the vintage of a new annunciation, which from lofty grapes will yield the wine of Song." But when I began writing my book the same thing happened to me that happened to Carlyle as he wrote his *Frederick the Great*. The more I wrote, the less I cared about my hero. I had started out to do a straight biography, but on the way I became more and more interested in old-time Buenos Aires. Readers, of course, were not slow in finding out that the book hardly lived up to its title, *Evaristo Carriego,* and so it fell flat. When the second edition appeared twenty-five years later, in 1955, as the fourth volume of my "complete" works, I enlarged the book with several new chapters, one a "History of the Tango." As a consequence of these additions, I feel *Evaristo Carriego* has been rounded out for the better.

Prisma (Prism), founded in 1921 and lasting two numbers, was the earliest of the magazines I edited. Our small ultraist group was eager to have a magazine of its own, but a real magazine was beyond our means. I had noticed billboard ads, and the thought came to me that we might similarly print a "mural magazine" and paste it up ourselves on the walls of buildings in different parts of town. Each issue was a large single sheet and contained a manifesto and some six or eight short, laconic poems, printed with plenty of white space around them, and a woodcut by my sister. We sallied forth at night—González Lanuza, Piñero, my cousin, and I—armed with pastepots and brushes provided by my mother, and, walking miles on end, slapped them up along Santa Fe, Callao, Entre Ríos, and Mexico Streets. Most of our handiwork was torn down by baffled readers almost at once, but luckily for us Alfredo Bianchi, of *Nosotros,* saw one of them and invited us to publish an ultraist anthology among the pages of his solid magazine. After *Prisma,* we went in for a six-page magazine, which was really just a single sheet printed on both sides and folded twice. This was the first *Proa* (Prow), and three numbers of it were published. Two years later, in 1924, came the second *Proa.* One afternoon, Brandán Caraffa, a young poet from Córdoba, came to see me at the Garden Hotel, where we were living upon return from our second European trip. He told me that Ricardo Güiraldes and Pablo Rojas Paz had decided to found a magazine that would represent the new literary generation, and that everyone had said that if that were its goal I could not possibly be left out. Naturally, I was flattered. That night, I went around to the Phoenix Hotel, where Güiraldes was staying. He greeted me with these words: "Brandán told me that the night before last all of you got together to found a magazine of young writers, and everyone said I couldn't be left out." At that moment, Rojas Paz came in and told us excitedly, "I'm quite flattered." I broke in and said, "The night before last, the three of us got together and decided that in a magazine of new writers you couldn't be left out." Thanks to this innocent stratagem, *Proa* was born. Each one of us put in fifty pesos, which paid for an edition of three to five hundred copies with no misprints and on fine paper. But a year and a half and fifteen issues later, for lack of subscriptions and ads, we had to give it up.

These years were quite happy ones because they stood for many friendships. There were those of Norah Lange, Macedonio, Piñero, and my father. Behind our work was a sincerity; we felt we were renewing both prose and poetry. Of course, like all young men, I tried to be as unhappy as I could—a kind of Hamlet and Raskolnikov rolled into one. What we achieved was quite bad, but our comradeships endured.

In 1924, I found my way into two different literary sets. One, whose memory I still enjoy, was that of Ricardo Güiraldes, who was yet to write *Don Segundo Sombra*. Güiraldes was very generous to me. I would give him a quite clumsy poem and he would read between the lines and divine what I had been trying to say but what my literary incapacity had prevented me from saying. He would then speak of the poem to other people, who were baffled not to find these things in the text. The other set, which I rather regret, was that of the magazine *Martín Fierro*. I disliked what *Martín Fierro* stood for, which was the French idea that literature is being continually renewed—that Adam is reborn every morning, and also for the idea that, since Paris had literary cliques that wallowed in publicity and bickering, we should be up to date and do the same. One result of this was that a sham literary feud was cooked up in Buenos Aires—that between Florida and Boedo. Florida represented downtown and Boedo the proletariat. I'd have preferred to be in the Boedo group, since I was writing about the old Northside and slums, sadness, and sunsets. But I was informed by one of the two conspirators—they were Ernesto Palacio, of Florida, and Roberto Mariani, of Boedo—that I was already one of the Florida warriors and that it was too late for me to change. The whole thing was just a put-up job. Some writers belonged to both groups—Roberto Arlt and Nicolás Olivari, for example. This sham is now taken into serious consideration by "credulous universities." But it was partly publicity, partly a boyish prank.

Linked to this time are the names of Silvina and Victoria Ocampo, of the poet Carlos Mastronardi, of Eduardo Mallea, and, not least, of Alejandro Xul-Solar. In a rough-and-ready way, it may be said that Xul, who was a mystic, a poet, and a painter, is our William Blake. I remember asking him on one particularly sultry afternoon about what he had done that stifling day. His answer was "Nothing whatever, except for founding twelve religions after lunch." Xul was also a philologist and the inventor of two languages. One was a philosophical language after the manner of John Wilkins and the other a reformation of Spanish with many English, German, and Greek words thrown in. He came of Baltic and Italian stock. "Xul" was his version of "Schulz" and "Solar" of "Solari." At this time, I also met Alfonso Reyes. He was the Mexican ambassador to Argentina, and used to invite me to dinner every Sunday at the embassy. I think of Reyes as the finest Spanish prose stylist of this century, and in my writing I learned a great deal about simplicity and directness from him.

Summing up this span of my life, I find myself completely out of sympathy with the priggish and rather dogmatic young man I then was. Those friends, however, are still very living and very close to me. In fact, they form a precious part of me. Friendship is, I think, the one redeeming Argentine passion.

Maturity

In the course of a lifetime devoted chiefly to books, I have read but few novels, and, in most cases, only a sense of duty has enabled me to find my way to their last page. At the same time, I have always been a reader and rereader of short stories. Stevenson, Kipling, James, Conrad, Poe, Chesterton, the tales of Lane's Arabian Nights, and certain stories by Hawthorne have been habits of mine since I can remember. The feeling that great novels like *Don Quixote* and *Huckleberry Finn* are virtually shapeless served to reinforce my taste for the short-story form, whose indispensable elements are economy and a clearly stated beginning, middle, and end. As a writer, however, I thought for years that the short story was beyond my powers, and it was only after a long and roundabout series of timid experiments in narration that I sat down to write real stories.

It took me some six years, from 1927 to 1933, to go from that all too self-conscious sketch "Hombres pelearon" to my first outright short story, "Hombre de la esquina rosada" (Streetcorner Man). A friend of mine, don Nicolás Paredes, a former political boss and professional gambler of the Northside, had died, and I wanted to record something of his voice, his anecdotes, and his particular way of telling them. I slaved over my every page, sounding out each sentence and striving to phrase it in his exact tones. We were living out in Adrogué at the time and, because I knew my mother would heartily disapprove of the subject matter, I composed in secret over a period of several months. Originally titled "Hombres de las orillas" (Men from the Edge of Town), the story appeared in the Saturday supplement, which I was editing, of a yellow-press daily called *Crítica*. But out of shyness, and perhaps a feeling that the story was a bit beneath me, I signed it with a pen name—the name of one of my great-great grandfathers, Francisco Bustos. Although the story became popular to the point of embarrassment (today I only find it stagy and mannered and the characters bogus), I never regarded it as a starting point. It simply stands there as a kind of freak.

The real beginning of my career as a story writer starts with the series of sketches entitled *Historia universal de la infamia* (A Universal History of Infamy), which I contributed to the columns of *Crítica* in 1933 and 1934. The irony of this is that "Streetcorner Man" really was a story but that these sketches and several of the fictional pieces which followed them, and which very slowly led me to legitimate stories, were in the nature of hoaxes and pseudo-essays. In my *Universal History,* I did not want to repeat what Marcel Schwob had done in his *Imaginary Lives.* He had invented biographies of real men about whom little or nothing is recorded. I, instead, read up on the lives of known persons and then deliberately varied and distorted them according to my own whims. For example, after reading Herbert Asbury's *The Gangs of New York,* I set down my free version of Monk Eastman, the Jewish gunman, in flagrant contradiction of my chosen authority. I did the same for Billy the Kid, for John Murrel (whom I rechristened Lazarus Morell), for the Veiled Prophet of Khorassan, for the Tichborne Claimant, and for several others. I never thought of book publication. The pieces were meant for popular consumption in *Crítica* and were pointedly picturesque. I suppose now the secret value of those sketches—apart from the sheer pleasure the writing gave me—lay in the fact that they were narrative exercises. Since the general plots or circumstances were all given me, I had only to embroider sets of vivid variations.

My next story, "The Approach to al-Mu'tasim," written in 1935, is both a hoax *and* a pseudo-essay. It purports to be a review of a book published originally in Bombay three years earlier. I endowed its fake second edition with a real publisher, Victor Gollancz, and a preface by a real writer, Dorothy L. Sayers. But the author and the book are entirely my own invention. I gave the plot and details of some chapters—borrowing from Kipling and working in the twelfth-century Persian mystic Farid ud-Din Attar—and then carefully pointed out its shortcomings. The story appeared the next year in a volume of my essays, *Historia de la eternidad* (A History of Eternity), buried at the back of the book together with an article on the "Art of Insult." Those who read "The Approach to al-Mu'tasim" took it at face value, and one of my friends even ordered a copy from London. It was not until 1942 that I openly published it as a short story in my first story collection, *El jardín de senderos que se bifurcan* (The Garden of Branching Paths). Perhaps I have been unfair to this story; it now seems to me to foreshadow and even to set the pattern for those tales that were somehow awaiting me, and upon which my reputation as a storyteller was to be based.

Along about 1937, I took my first regular full-time job. I had previously worked at small editing tasks. There was the *Crítica* supplement, which was a heavily and even gaudily illustrated entertainment sheet. There was *El Hogar*, a popular society weekly, to which, twice a month, I contributed a couple of literary pages on foreign books and authors. I had also written newsreel texts and had been editor of a pseudo-scientific magazine called *Urbe*, which was really a promotional organ of a privately owned Buenos Aires subway system. These had all been small-paying jobs, and I was long past the age when I should have begun contributing to our household upkeep. Now, through friends, I was given a very minor position as First Assistant in the Miguel Cané branch of the Municipal Library, out in a drab and dreary part of town to the southwest. While there were Second and Third Assistants below me, there were also a Director and First, Second, and Third Officials above me. I was paid two hundred and ten pesos a month and later went up to two hundred and forty. These were sums roughly equivalent to seventy or eighty American dollars.

At the library, we did very little work. There were some fifty of us doing what fifteen could easily have done. My particular job, shared with fifteen or twenty colleagues, was classifying and cataloging the library's holdings, which until that time were uncatalogued. The collection, however, was so small that we knew where to find the books without the system, so the system, though laboriously carried out, was never needed or used. The first day, I worked honestly. On the next, some of my fellows took me aside to say that I couldn't do this sort of thing because it showed them up. "Besides," they argued, "as this cataloging has been planned to give us some semblance of work, you'll put us out of our jobs." I told them I had classified four hundred titles instead of their one hundred. "Well, if you keep that up," they said, "the boss will be angry and won't know what to do with us." For the sake of realism, I was told that from then on I should do eighty-three books one day, ninety another, and one hundred and four the third.

I stuck out the library for about nine years. They were nine years of solid unhappiness. At work, the other men were interested in nothing but horse racing, soccer matches, and smutty stories. Once, a woman, one of the readers, was raped on her way to the ladies' room. Everybody said such things were bound to happen, since the men's and ladies' rooms were adjoining. One day, two rather posh and well-meaning friends—society ladies—came to see me at work. They phoned me a day or two later to say, "You may think it amusing to work in a place like that, but promise us you will find at least a nine-hundred-peso job before the month is out." I gave them my word that I would. Ironically, at the time I was a fairly well-known writer—except at the library. I remember a fellow employee's once noting in an encyclopedia the name of a certain Jorge Luis Borges—a fact that set him wondering at the coincidence of our identical names and birth dates. Now and then during these years, we municipal workers were rewarded with gifts of a two-pound package of maté to take home. Sometimes in the evening, as I walked the ten blocks to the tramline, my eyes would be filled with tears. These small gifts from above always underlined my menial and dismal existence.

A couple of hours each day, riding back and forth on the tram, I made my way through *The Divine Comedy*, helped as far as "Purgatory" by John Aitken Carlyle's prose translation and then ascending the rest of the way on my own. I would do all my library work in the first hour and then steal away to the basement and pass the other five hours in reading or writing. I remember in this way rereading the six volumes of Gibbon's *Decline and Fall* and the many volumes of Vicente Fidel López' *History of the Argentine Republic*. I read Léon Bloy, Claudel, Groussac, and Bernard Shaw. On holidays, I translated Faulkner and Virginia Woolf. At some point, I was moved up to the dizzying height of Third Official. One morning, my mother rang me up and I asked for leave to go home, arriving just in time to see my father die. He had undergone a long agony and was very impatient for his death.

It was on Christmas Eve of 1938—the same year my father died—that I had a severe accident. I was running up a stairway and suddenly felt something brush my scalp. I had grazed a freshly painted open casement window. In spite of first-aid treatment, the wound became poisoned, and for a period of a week or so I lay sleepless every night and had hallucinations and high fever. One evening, I lost the power of speech and had to be rushed to the hospital for an immediate operation. Septicemia had set in, and for a month I hovered, all unknowingly, between life and death. (Much later, I was to write about this in my story "The South.") When I began to recover, I feared for my mental integrity. I remember that my mother wanted to read to me from a book I had just ordered, C. S. Lewis' *Out of the Silent Planet*, but for two or three nights I kept putting her off. At last, she prevailed, and after hearing a page or two I fell to crying. My mother asked me why the tears. "I'm crying because I understand," I said. A bit later, I wondered whether I could ever write again. I had previously written quite a few poems and dozens of short reviews. I thought that if I tried to write a review now and failed, I'd be all through intellectually but that if I tried something I had never really done before and failed at that it wouldn't be so bad and might even prepare me for the final revelation. I decided I would try to write a story. The result was "Pierre Menard, Author of *Don Quixote*."

"Pierre Menard," like its forerunner "The Approach to al-Mu'tasim," was still a halfway house between the essay and the true tale. But the achievement spurred me on. I next tried something more ambitious—"Tlön, Uqbar, Orbis Tertius," about the discovery of a new world that finally replaces our present world. Both were published in Victoria Ocampo's magazine *Sur*. I kept up my writing at the library. Though my colleagues thought of me as a traitor for not sharing their boisterous fun, I went on with work of my own in the basement, or, when the weather was warm, up on the flat roof. My Kafkian story "The Library of Babel" was meant as a nightmare version or magnification of that municipal library, and certain details in the text have no particular meaning. The numbers of books and shelves that I recorded in the story were literally what I had at my elbow. Clever critics have worried over those ciphers, and generously endowed them with mystic significance. "The Lottery in Babylon," "Death and the Compass," and "The Circular Ruins" were also written, in whole or part, while I played truant. These tales and others were to become *The Garden of Branching Paths*, a book expanded and retitled *Ficciones* in 1944. *Ficciones* and *El Aleph* (1949 and 1952), my second story collection, are, I suppose, my two major books.

In 1946, a president whose name I do not want to remember came into power. One day soon after, I was honored with the news that I had been "promoted" out of the library to the inspectorship of poultry and rabbits in the public markets. I went to the City Hall to find out what it was all about. "Look here," I said. "It's rather strange that among so many others at the library I should be singled out as worthy of this new position." "Well," the clerk answered, "you were on the side of the Allies—what do you expect?" His statement was unanswerable; the next day, I sent in my resignation. My friends rallied round me at once and offered me a public dinner. I prepared a speech for the occasion but, knowing I was too shy to read it myself, I asked my friend Pedro Henríquez Ureña to read it for me.

I was now out of a job. Several months before, an old English lady had read my tea leaves and had foretold that I was soon to travel, to lecture, and to make vast sums of money thereby. When I told my mother about it, we both laughed, for public speaking was far beyond me. At this juncture, a friend came to the rescue, and I was made a teacher of English literature at the Asociación Argentina de Cultura Inglesa. I was also asked at the same time to lecture on classic American literature at the Colegio Libre de Estudios Superiores. Since this pair of offers was made three months before classes opened, I accepted, feeling quite safe. As the time grew near, however, I grew sicker and sicker. My series of lectures was to be on Hawthorne, Poe, Thoreau, Emerson, Melville, Whitman, Twain, Henry James, and Veblen. I wrote the first one down. But I had no time to write out the second one. Besides, thinking of the first lecture as Doomsday, I felt that only eternity could come after. The first one went off well enough—miraculously. Two nights before the second lecture, I took my mother for a long walk around Adrogué and had her time me as I rehearsed my talk. She said she thought it was overlong. "In that case," I said, "I'm safe." My fear had been of running dry. So, at forty-seven, I found a new and exciting life opening up for me. I traveled up and down Argentina and Uruguay, lecturing on Swedenborg, Blake, the Persian and Chinese mystics, Buddhism, gauchesco poetry, Martin Buber, the Kabbalah, the Arabian Nights, T. E. Lawrence, medieval Germanic poetry, the Icelandic sagas, Heine, Dante, expressionism, and Cervantes. I went from town to town, staying overnight in hotels I'd never see again. Sometimes my mother or a friend accompanied me. Not only did I end up making far more money than at the library but I enjoyed the work and felt that it justified me.

One of the chief events of these years—and of my life—was the beginning of my friendship with Adolfo Bioy-Casares. We met in 1930 or 1931, when he was about seventeen and I was just past thirty. It is always taken for granted in these cases that the older man is the master and the younger his disciple. This may have been true at the outset, but several years later, when we began to work together, Bioy was really and secretly the master. He and I attempted many different literary ventures. We compiled anthologies of Argentine poetry, tales of the fantastic, and detective stories; we wrote articles and forewords; we annotated Sir Thomas Browne and Gracián; we translated short stories by writers like Beerbohm, Kipling, Wells, and Lord Dunsany; we founded a magazine, *Destiempo,* which lasted three issues; we wrote film scripts, which were invariably rejected. Opposing my taste for the pathetic, the sententious, and the baroque, Bioy made me feel that quietness and restraint are more desirable. If I may be allowed a sweeping statement, Bioy led me gradually toward classicism.

It was at some point in the early forties that we began writing in collaboration—a feat that up to that time I had thought impossible. I had invented what we thought was a quite good plot for a detective story. One rainy morning, he told me we ought to give it a try. I reluctantly agreed, and a little later that same morning the thing happened. A third man, Honorio Bustos Domecq, emerged and took over. In the long run, he ruled us with a rod of iron and to our amusement, and later to our dismay, he became utterly unlike ourselves, with his own whims, his own puns, and his own very elaborate style of writing. Domecq was the name of a great-grandfather of Bioy's and Bustos of a great-grandfather of mine from Córdoba. Bustos Domecq's first book was *Six Problems for don Isidro Parodi* (1942), and during the writing of that volume he never got out of hand. Max Carrados had attempted a blind detective; Bioy and I went one step further and confined our detective to a jail cell. The book was at the same time a satire on the Argentine. For many years, the dual identity of Bustos Domecq was never revealed. When finally it was, people thought that, as Bustos was a joke, his writing could hardly be taken seriously.

Our next collaboration was another detective novel, *A Model for Death*. This one was so personal and so full of private jokes that we published it only in an edition that was not for sale. The author of this book we named B. Suárez Lynch. The "B." stood, I think, for Bioy and Borges, "Suárez" for another great-grandfather of mine, and Lynch for another great-grandfather of Bioy's. Bustos Domecq reappeared in 1946 in another private edition, this time of two stories, entitled *Two Memorable Fantasies*. After a long eclipse, Bustos took up his pen again, and in 1967 brought out his *Chronicles*. These are articles written on imaginary, extravagantly modern artists—architects, sculptors, painters, chefs, poets, novelists, couturiers—by a devotedly modern critic. But both the author and his subjects are fools, and it is hard to tell who is taking in whom. The book is inscribed, "To those three forgotten greats— Picasso, Joyce, Le Corbusier." The style is itself a parody. Bustos writes a literary journalese, abounding in neologisms, a Latinate vocabulary, clichés, mixed metaphors, non sequiturs, and bombast.

I have often been asked how collaboration is possible. I think it requires a joint abandoning of the ego, of vanity, and maybe of common politeness. The collaborators should forget themselves and think only in terms of the work. In fact, when somebody wants to know whether such-and-such a joke or epithet came from my side of the table or Bioy's, I honestly cannot tell him. I have tried to collaborate with other friends—some of them very close ones—but their inability to be blunt on the one hand or thick-skinned on the other has made the scheme impossible. As to the *Chronicles of Bustos Domecq,* I think they are better than anything I have published under my own name and nearly as good as anything Bioy has written on his own.

In 1950, I was elected President of the Sociedad Argentina de Escritores (Argentine Society of Writers). The Argentine Republic, then as now, is a soft country, and the S.A.D.E. was one of the few strongholds against the dictatorship. This was so evident that many distinguished men of letters did not dare set foot inside its doors until after the revolution. One curious trait of the dictatorship was that even its professed upholders made it clear that they did not really take the government seriously but were acting out of self-interest. This was understood and forgiven, since most of my countrymen have an intellectual, if not a moral, conscience. Nearly all the smutty jokes made up about Perón and his wife were the invention of Peronistas themselves, trying to save face. The S.A.D.E. was eventually closed. I remember the last lecture I was allowed to give there. The audience, quite a small one, included a very puzzled policeman who did his clumsy best to set down a few of my remarks on Persian Sufism. During this drab and hopeless period, my mother—then in her seventies—was under house arrest. My sister and one of my nephews spent a month in jail. I myself had a detective on my heels, whom I first took on long, aimless walks and at last made friends with. He admitted that he too hated Perón, but said that he was obeying orders. Ernesto Palacio once offered to introduce me to the Unspeakable, but I did not want to meet him. How could I be introduced to a man whose hand I would not shake?

The long-hoped-for revolution came in September, 1955. After a sleepless, anxious night, nearly the whole population came out into the streets, cheering the revolution and shouting the name of Córdoba, where most of the fighting had taken place. We were so carried away that for some time we were quite unaware of the rain that was soaking us to the bone. We were so happy that not a single word was even uttered against the fallen dictator. Perón

175

went into hiding, and was later allowed to leave the country. No one knows how much money he got away with.

Two very dear friends of mine, Esther Zemborain de Torres and Victoria Ocampo, dreamed up the possibility of my being appointed Director of the National Library. I thought the scheme a wild one, and hoped at most to be given the directorship of some small-town library, preferably to the south of the city. Within the space of a day, a petition was signed by the magazine *Sur* (read Victoria Ocampo), by the reopened S.A.D.E. (read Carlos Alberto Erro), by the Sociedad Argentina de Cultura Inglesa (read Carlos del Campillo), and by the Colegio Libre de Estudios Superiores (read Luis Reissig). This was placed on the desk of the Minister of Education, and eventually I was appointed to the directorship by General Eduardo Lonardi, who was Acting President. A few days earlier, my mother and I had walked to the Library one night to take a look at the building, but, feeling superstitious, I refused to go in. "Not until I get the job," I said. That same week, I was called to come to the Library to take over. My family was present, and I made a speech to the employees, telling them I was actually the Director—the incredible Director. At the same time, José Edmundo Clemente, who a few years before had managed to persuade Emecé to bring out an edition of my works, became the Assistant Director. Of course, I felt very important, but we got no pay for the next three months. I don't think my predecessor, who was a Peronista, was ever officially fired. He just never came around to the Library again. They named me to the job but did not take the trouble to unseat him.

Another pleasure came to me the very next year, when I was named to the professorship of English and American Literature at the University of Buenos Aires. Other candidates had sent in painstaking lists of their translations, papers, lectures, and other achievements. I limited myself to the following statement: "Quite unwittingly, I have been qualifying myself for this position throughout my life." My plain approach gained the day. I was hired, and spent ten or twelve happy years at the University.

My blindness had been coming on gradually since childhood. It was a slow, summer twilight. There was nothing particularly pathetic or dramatic about it. Beginning in 1927, I underwent eight eye operations, but since the late 1950's, when I wrote my "Poem of the Gifts," for reading and writing purposes I have been blind. Blindness ran in my family; a description of the operation performed on the eyes of my great-grandfather, Edward Young Haslam, appeared in the pages of the London medical journal, the *Lancet*. Blindness also seems to run among the Directors of the National Library. Two of my eminent forerunners, José Mármol and Paul Groussac, suffered the same fate. In my poem, I speak of God's splendid irony in granting me at one time 800,000 books and darkness.

One salient consequence of my blindness was my gradual abandonment of free verse in favor of classical metrics. In fact, blindness made me take up the writing of poetry again. Since rough drafts were denied me, I had to fall back on memory. It is obviously easier to remember verse than prose, and to remember regular verse forms rather than free ones. Regular verse is, so to speak, portable. One can walk down the street or be riding the subway while composing and polishing a sonnet, for rhyme and meter have mnemonic virtues. In these years, I wrote dozens of sonnets and longer poems consisting of eleven-syllable quatrains. I thought I had taken Lugones as my master, but when the verses were written my friends told me that, regrettably, they were quite unlike him. In my later poetry, a narrative thread is always to be found. As a matter of fact, I even think of plots for poems. Perhaps the main difference between Lugones and me is that he held French literature as his model and lived intellectually in a French world, whereas I look to English literature. In this new poetic activity, I never thought of building a sequence of poems, as I always formerly did, but was chiefly interested in each piece for its own sake. In this way, I wrote poems on such different subjects as Emerson and wine, Snorri Sturluson and the hourglass, my grandfather's death and the beheading of Charles I. I also went in for summing up my literary heroes: Poe, Swedenborg, Whitman, Heine, Camões, Jonathan Edwards, and Cervantes. Due tribute, of course, was also paid to mirrors, the Minotaur, and knives.

I had always been attracted to the metaphor, and this leaning led me to the study of the simple Saxon kennings and overelaborate Norse ones. As far back as 1932, I had even written an essay about them. The quaint notion of using, as far as it could be done, metaphors instead of straightforward nouns, and of these metaphors' being at once traditional and arbitrary, puzzled and appealed to me. I was later to surmise that the purpose of these figures lay not only in the pleasure given by the pomp and circumstance of compounding words but also in the demands of alliteration. Taken by themselves, the kennings are not especially witty, and calling a ship "a sea-stallion" and the open sea "the whale's-road" is no great feat. The Norse skalds went a step further, calling the sea "the sea-stallion's-road," so that what originally was an image became a laborious equation. In turn, my investigation of kennings led me to the study of Old English and Old Norse. Another factor that impelled me in this direction was my ancestry. It may be no more than a romantic superstition of mine, but the fact that the Haslams lived in Northumbria and Mercia—or, as they are today called, Northumberland and the Midlands—links me with a Saxon and perhaps a Danish past. (My fondness for such a northern past has been resented by some of my more nationalistic countrymen, who dub me an Englishman, but I hardly need point out that many things English are utterly alien to me: tea, the Royal Family, "manly" sports, the worship of every line written by the uncaring Shakespeare.)

At the end of one of my University courses, several of my students came to see me at the Library. We had just polished off all English literature from Beowulf to Bernard

Shaw in the span of four months, and I thought we might now do something in earnest. I proposed that we begin at the beginning, and they agreed. I knew that at home, on a certain top shelf, I had copies of Sweet's *Anglo-Saxon Reader* and the *Anglo-Saxon Chronicle*. When the students came the next Saturday morning, we began reading these two books. We skipped grammar as much as we could and pronounced the words like German. All at once, we fell in love with a sentence in which Rome (Romeburh) was mentioned. We got drunk on these words and rushed down Peru Street shouting them at the top of our voices. And so we had set out on a long adventure. I had always thought of English literature as the richest in the world; the discovery now of a secret chamber at the very threshold of that literature came to me as an additional gift. Personally, I knew that the adventure would be an endless one, and that I could go on studying Old English for the rest of my days. The pleasure of studying, not the vanity of mastering, has been my chief aim, and I have not been disappointed these past twelve years. As for my recent interest in Old Norse, this is only a logical step, since the two languages are closely linked and since of all medieval Germanic literature Old Norse is the crown. My excursions into Old English have been wholly personal and, therefore, have made their way into a number of my poems. A fellow-academician once took me aside and said in alarm, "What do you mean by publishing a poem entitled 'Embarking on the Study of Anglo-Saxon Grammar'?" I tried to make him understand that Anglo-Saxon was as intimate an experience to me as looking at a sunset or falling in love.

Around 1954, I began writing short prose pieces—sketches and parables. One day, my friend Carlos Frías, of Emecé, told me he needed a new book for the series of my so-called complete works. I said I had none to give him, but Frías persisted, saying, "Every writer has a book if he only looks for it." Going through drawers at home one idle Sunday, I began ferreting out uncollected poems and prose pieces, some of the latter going back to my days on *Crítica*.

These odds and ends, sorted out and ordered and published in 1960, became *El hacedor* (The Maker). Remarkably, this book, which I accumulated rather than wrote, seems to me my most personal work and, to my taste, maybe my best. The explanation is only too easy: the pages of *El hacedor* contain no padding. Each piece was written for its own sake and out of an inner necessity. By the time it was undertaken, I had come to realize that fine writing is a mistake, and a mistake born out of vanity. Good writing, I firmly believe, should be done in an unobtrusive way.

On the closing page of that book, I told of a man who sets out to make a picture of the universe. After many years, he has covered a blank wall with images of ships, towers, horses, weapons, and men, only to find out at the moment of his death that he has drawn a likeness of his own face. This may be the case of all books; it is certainly the case of this particular book.

Crowded Years

Fame, like my blindness, had been coming gradually to me. I had never expected it, I had never sought it. Néstor Ibarra and Roger Caillois, who in the early 1950's daringly translated me into French, were my first benefactors. I suspect that their pioneer work paved the way for my sharing with Samuel Beckett the Formentor Prize in 1961, for until I appeared in French I was practically invisible—not only abroad but at home in Buenos Aires. As a consequence of that prize, my books mushroomed overnight throughout the western world.

This same year, under the auspices of Edward Larocque Tinker, I was invited as Visiting Professor to the University of Texas. It was my first physical encounter with America. In a sense, because of my reading, I had always been there, and yet how strange it seemed when in Austin I heard ditch diggers who worked on campus speaking in English, a language I had until then always thought of as being denied that class of people. America, in fact, had taken on such mythic proportions in my mind that I was sincerely amazed to find there such commonplace things as weeds, mud, puddles, dirt roads, flies, and stray dogs. Though at times we fell into homesickness, I know now that my mother—who accompanied me—and I grew to love Texas. She, who always loathed football, even rejoiced over *our* victory when the Longhorns defeated the neighboring Bears. At the University, when I finished one class I was giving in Argentine literature, I would sit in on another as a student of Saxon verse under Dr. Rudolph Willard. My days were full. I found American students, unlike the run of students in the Argentine, far more interested in their subjects than in their grades. I tried to interest people in Ascasubi and Lugones, but they stubbornly questioned and interviewed me about my own output. I spent as much time as I could with Ramón Martínez López, who, as a philologist, shared my passion for etymologies and taught me many things. During those six months in the States, we traveled widely, and I lectured at universities from coast to coast. I saw New Mexico, San Francisco, New York, New England, Washington. I found America the friendliest, most forgiving, and most generous nation I had ever visited. We South Americans tend to think in terms of convenience, whereas people in the United States approach things ethically. This—amateur Protestant that I am—I admired above all. It even helped me overlook skyscrapers, paper bags, television, plastics, and the unholy jungle of gadgets.

My second American trip came in 1967, when I held the Charles Eliot Norton Chair of Poetry at Harvard, and lectured to well-wishing audiences on "This Craft of Verse." I spent seven months in Cambridge, also teaching a course on Argentine writers and traveling all over New England, where most things American, including the West, seem to have been invented. I made numerous literary pilgrimages—to Hawthorne's haunts in Salem, to Emerson's in Concord, to Melville's in New Bedford, to Emily Dickinson's in Amherst, and to Longfellow's around the corner from where I lived. Friends seemed to multiply in Cambridge: Jorge Guillén, John Murchison, Juan Marichal, Raimundo Lida, Héctor Ingrao, and a Persian physicist who had worked out a theory of spherical time that I do not quite understand but hope someday to plagiarize—Farid Hushfar. I also met writers like Robert Fitzgerald, John Updike, and the late Dudley Fitts. I availed myself of chances to see new parts of the continent: Iowa, where I found my native pampa awaiting me; Chicago, recalling Carl Sandburg; Missouri; Maryland; Virginia. At the end of my stay, I was greatly honored to have my poems read at the Y.M.H.A. Poetry Center in New York, with several of my translators reading and a number of poets in the audience. I owe a third trip to the United States, in November of 1969, to my two benefactors at the University of Oklahoma, Lowell Dunham and Ivar Ivask, who invited me to give talks there and called together a group of scholars to comment on, and enrich, my work. Ivask made me a gift of a fish-shaped Finnish dagger—rather alien to the tradition of the old Palermo of my boyhood.

Looking back on this past decade, I seem to have been quite a wanderer. In 1963, thanks to Neil MacKay of the British Council in Buenos Aires, I was able to visit England and Scotland. There, too, again in my mother's company, I made my pilgrimages: to London, so teeming with literary memories; to Lichfield and Dr. Johnson; to Manchester and De Quincey; to Rye and Henry James; to the Lake Country; to Edinburgh. I visited my grandmother's birthplace in Hanley, one of the Five Towns—Arnold Bennett country. Scotland and Yorkshire I think of as among the loveliest places on earth. Somewhere in the Scottish hills and glens I recaptured a strange sense of loneliness and bleakness that I had known before; it took me some time to trace this feeling back to the far-flung wastes of Patagonia. A few years later, this time in the company of María Esther Vázquez, I made another European trip. In England, we stayed with the late Herbert Read in his fine rambling house out on the moors. He took us to Yorkminster, where he showed us some ancient Danish swords in the Viking Yorkshire room of the museum. I later wrote a sonnet to one of the swords, and just before his death Sir Herbert corrected and bettered my original title, suggesting, instead of "To a Sword in York," "To a Sword in Yorkminster." We later went to Stockholm, invited by my Swedish publisher, Bonnier, and by the Argentine ambassador. Stockholm and Copenhagen I count among the most unforgettable cities I have seen, like San Francisco, New York, Edinburgh, Santiago de Compostela, and Geneva.

Early in 1969, invited by the Israeli government, I spent ten very exciting days in Tel Aviv and Jerusalem. I brought home with me the conviction of having been in the oldest and the youngest of nations, of having come from a very living, vigilant land back to a half-asleep nook of the world. Since my Genevan days, I had always been interested in Jewish culture, thinking of it as an integral element of our so-called Western civilization, and during the Israeli-Arab war of a few years back I found myself taking immediate sides. While the outcome was still uncertain, I wrote a poem on the battle. A week after, I wrote another on the victory. Israel was, of course, still an armed camp at the time of my visit. There, along the shores of Galilee, I kept recalling these lines from Shakespeare:

> Over whose acres walk'd those blessed feet,
> Which, fourteen hundred years ago, were nail'd,
> For our advantage, on the bitter cross.

Now, despite my years, I still think of the many stones I have left unturned, and of others I would like to turn again. I hope yet to see Mormon Utah, to which I was introduced as a boy by Mark Twain's *Roughing It* and by the first book of the Sherlock Holmes saga, *A Study in Scarlet*. Another daydream of mine is a pilgrimage to Iceland, and another still to return again to Texas and to Scotland.

183

At seventy-one, I am still hard at work and brimming with plans. Last year I wrote a new book of poems, *Elogio de la sombra* (In Praise of Darkness). It was my first entirely new volume since 1960, and these were also my first poems since 1929 written with a book in mind. My main concern in this work, running through several of its pieces, is of an ethical nature, irrespective of any religious or antireligious bias. "Darkness" in the title stands for both blindness and death. To finish *Elogio,* I worked every morning, dictating at the National Library. By the time I ended, I had set up a comfortable routine—so comfortable that I kept it up and began writing tales. These, my first stories since 1953, I published this year. The collection is called *El informe de Brodie* (Doctor Brodie's Report). It is a set of modest experiments in straightforward storytelling, and is the book I have often spoken about in the past five years. Recently, I completed the script of a film to be called *Los otros* (The Others). Its plot is my own; the writing was done together with Adolfo Bioy-Casares and the young Argentine director Hugo Santiago. My afternoons now are usually given over to a long-range and cherished project: for nearly the past three years, I have been lucky to have my own translator at my side, and together we are bringing out some ten or twelve volumes of my work in English, a language I am unworthy to handle, a language I often wish had been my birthright.

I intend now to begin a new book, a series of personal— not scholarly—essays on Dante, Ariosto, and medieval northern subjects. I want also to set down a book of informal, outspoken opinions, whims, reflections, and private heresies. After that, who knows? I still have a number of stories, heard or invented, that I want to tell. At present, I am finishing a long tale called "The Congress." Despite its Kafkian title, I hope it will turn out more in the line of Chesterton. The setting is Argentine and Uruguayan. For twenty years, I have been boring my friends with the raw plot. Finally, I came to see that no further elaboration was needed. I have another project that has been pending for an even longer period of time—that of revising and perhaps rewriting my father's novel *The Caudillo,* as he asked me to years ago. We had gone as far as discussing many of the problems; I like to think of the undertaking as a continued dialogue and a very real collaboration.

People have been unaccountably good to me. I have no enemies, and if certain persons have masqueraded as such, they've been far too good-natured to have ever pained me. Anytime I read something written against me, I not only share the sentiment but feel I could do the job far better myself. Perhaps I should advise would-be enemies to send me their grievances beforehand, with full assurance that they will receive my every aid and support. I have even secretly longed to write, under a pen name, a merciless tirade against myself. Ah, the unvarnished truths I harbor!

At my age, one should be aware of one's limits, and this knowledge may make for happiness. When I was young, I thought of literature as a game of skillful and surprising variations; now that I have found my own voice, I feel that tinkering and tampering neither greatly improve nor greatly spoil my drafts. This, of course, is a sin against one of the main tendencies of letters in this century—the vanity of overwriting—which led a man like Joyce into publishing expensive fragments, showily entitled "Work in Progress." I suppose my best work is over. This gives me a certain quiet satisfaction and ease. And yet I do not feel I have written myself out. In a way, youthfulness seems closer to me today than when I was a young man. I no longer regard happiness as unattainable; once, long ago, I did. Now I know that it may occur at any moment but that it should never be sought after. As to failure or fame, they are quite irrelevant and I never bother about them. What I'm out for now is peace, the enjoyment of thinking and of friendship, and, though it may be too ambitious, a sense of loving and of being loved.

Commentaries

With Norman Thomas
di Giovanni

Commentaries

The Aleph

What eternity is to time, the Aleph is to space. In eternity, all time—past, present, and future—coexists simultaneously. In the Aleph, the sum total of the spatial universe is to be found in a tiny shining sphere barely over an inch across. When I wrote my story, I recalled Wells's dictum that in a tale of the fantastic, if the story is to be acceptable to the mind of the reader, only one fantastic element should be allowed at a time. For example, though Wells wrote a book about the invasion of Earth by Martians, and another book about a single invisible man in England, he was far too wise to attempt a novel about an invasion of our planet by an army of invisible men. Thinking of the Aleph as a thing of wonder, I placed it in as drab a setting as I could imagine—a small cellar in a nondescript house in an unfashionable quarter of Buenos Aires. In the world of the *Arabian Nights*, such things as magic lamps and rings are left lying about and nobody cares; in our skeptical world, we have to tidy up any alarming or out-of-the-way element. Thus, at the end of "The Aleph," the house has to be pulled down and the shining sphere destroyed with it.

Once, in Madrid, a journalist asked me whether Buenos Aires actually possessed an Aleph. I nearly yielded to temptation and said yes, but a friend broke in and pointed out that were such an object to exist it would not only be the most famous thing in the world but would renew our whole conception of time, astronomy, mathematics, and space. "Ah," said the journalist, "so the entire thing is your own invention. I thought it was true because you gave the name of the street." I did not dare tell him that the naming of streets is not much of a feat.

My chief problem in writing the story lay in what Walt Whitman had very successfully achieved—the setting down of a limited catalog of endless things. The task, as is evident, is impossible, for such chaotic enumeration can only be simulated, and every apparently haphazard element has to be linked to its neighbor either by secret association or by contrast.

"The Aleph" has been praised by readers for its variety of elements: the fantastic, the satiric, the autobiographical, and the pathetic. I wonder whether our modern worship of complexity is not wrong, however. I wonder whether a short story should be so ambitious. Critics, going even further, have detected Beatrice Portinari in Beatriz Viterbo, Dante in Daneri, and the descent into hell in the descent into the cellar. I am, of course, duly grateful for these unlooked-for gifts.

Beatriz Viterbo really existed and I was very much and hopelessly in love with her. I wrote my story after her death. Carlos Argentino Daneri is a friend of mine, still living, who to this day has never suspected he is in the story. The verses are a parody of his verse. Daneri's speech on the other hand is not an exaggeration but a fair rendering. The Argentine Academy of Letters is the habitat of such specimens.

Streetcorner Man

As already stated as far back as 1935 in the foreword to *Historia universal de la infamia,* this story was written under the triple influence of Stevenson, G. K. Chesterton, and Josef von Sternberg's unforgettable gangster films. My aim was to recapture the atmosphere of the outer slums of Buenos Aires some fifty years ago. At the same time, I wanted the story to be vividly and persistently visual, and to unfold with a kind of pattern or symmetry. The characters appear on the scene like actors and make set speeches, deliberately unlike the unstudied and careless manner of everyday life. Francisco Real knocks twice at the same door: the first time to swagger in and challenge his man, the second time to die. Another example of this symmetry is the high window, out of which first goes the knife and later the body. All this is sheer choreography. The fact that this story was later made into a ballet, a movie, and a stage play corroborates this. But strangely enough, Argentine readers have always felt the story to be realistic. Some eager young men once asked me if I had actually witnessed the scene. I knew very well when I wrote the story that things could never have happened in that stagy and even operatic way, but I suppose I was indulging in a bit of wishful thinking. All Argentines are fond of an imaginary heroic and mythic past, especially as applied to hoodlums and pimps.

The voice used throughout the story is supposed to be oral, but the sentences are really those of a written work. They are unbroken and complete, while in real life Argentines rarely finish a sentence; the moment they feel the hearer has caught what they are aiming at, they just break off. The language of "Streetcorner Man" is partly a conventionalized slang, or dialect, of Buenos Aires called *lunfardo*. This language is primarily a device of the writers of *sainetes* and tango lyrics. It has, as to be expected, been canonized by several glossaries, by an Academy of Lunfardo, and by the Argentine Academy of Letters. As a matter of fact, *lunfardo* is barely used by the people it is credited to. Once taxed by fellow journalists for his utter ignorance of *lunfardo*, Roberto Arlt, the novelist of Buenos Aires lowlife, said, "I'm afraid I've spent all my life in the outer slums among common people and toughs and so never had time to study such a thing."

The "esquina rosada" of the Spanish title means pink, or rose-colored, corner. It refers to the painted walls of the streetcorner *almacenes,* which a long time ago were both groceries and saloons, where men drank and played cards. These corners were often painted other vivid colors, such as green, purple, or blue, and stood out in an otherwise drab city. For me the *esquina rosada* symbolizes a particular kind of life. It has nothing whatever to do, as some adventurous translator has supposed, with the red lamp that hung outside Julia's dance hall. Such an establishment would be called a "Farol Colorado," which is close to the term "red-light district." In a way, the American "drugstore cowboy" would be something of a latter-day "hombre de la esquina rosada."

The Approach to al-Mu'tasim

The idea that a man may be many men is, of course, a literary commonplace. This is usually understood in an ethical way (William Wilson, Jekyll and Hyde, and so on) or in terms of heredity (Hawthorne, Zola). In "The Approach to al-Mu'tasim" the concept undergoes certain modifications. There, I think of men being incessantly changed by each man they talk to and perhaps by each book they read. Thus I arrived at the tale of a kind of saint who spreads circles of diminishing splendor all around him, and is finally discovered by somebody who divines him through these many far-flung echoes of his influence. Since this plot is something of an allegory, it led me quite naturally to an Eastern setting. I do my best to be indebted to Kipling; India, as we are aware, stands for almost countless multitudes.

I knew only too well that this delicate work lay far beyond my powers. I therefore plotted the piece as a literary hoax, rather after the example of *Sartor Resartus*. Years after the story was published, I found out that Henry James had attempted a similar scheme in his novel *The Sacred Fount*, and had failed through sheer inability to keep his characters distinguishable.

As to Farid ud-Din Attar, I am afraid my knowledge of his famous poem can be reduced to FitzGerald's *A bird's-eye view of Farid-Uddin Attar's Bird-parliament*, to Browne's *Literary History of Persia*, and to a few handbooks on Sufism. Silvina Ocampo, by the way, composed a very fine poem based on Attar's book.

The Circular Ruins

The ontological argument, the claim that Something or Someone could be its own cause—its *causa sui*—as the Schoolmen and Spinoza have it, has always seemed to me a mere juggling of words, a violence done to language. In my opinion, a speech implies a speaker and a dream, a dreamer; this, of course, leads to the concept of an endless series of speakers and dreamers, an infinite regress, and may be what lies at the root of my story.

Naturally, when I wrote it, I never thought of the story in these abstract terms. In a pair of sonnets on chess, written years afterward, I took up the same idea. The chessmen do not know they are guided by a player; the player does not know he is guided by a god; the god does not know what other gods are guiding him. Several years ago, during a one-day visit to Lubbock, in the Texas panhandle, a girl asked me whether in writing another poem, "The Golem," I had been consciously rewriting "The Circular Ruins." The answer was no, but I thanked her for revealing this unsuspected affinity to me. In fact, it amazed me to have traveled hundreds of miles to come upon this piece of news about myself out on the edge of the desert.

Readers have thought of "The Circular Ruins" as my best story. I can hardly share this view since I now think of fine writing, which this tale comes continually to the brink of, as a beginner's mistake. One might argue, however, that if it is going to be done at all, this kind of story needs this kind of writing. This also accounts for the dim Eastern setting and for the fact that the scheme is somehow timeless. The title itself suggests the Pythagorean and Eastern idea of cyclical time.

Lewis Carroll gave me my epigraph, which may have been the story's seed, but had I not often thought about life as a dream, that seed, known to millions of readers, might have fallen wide of the furrow.

When I wrote "The Circular Ruins" way back in 1940, the work carried me away as it had never done before and as it has never done since. The whole story is about a dream and, while writing it down, my everyday affairs—my job at the municipal library, going to the movies, dining with friends— were like a dream. For the space of that week, the one thing real to me was the story.

Death and the Compass

Since 1923 I had been doing my best, and never quite succeeding, to be the poet of Buenos Aires. When, in 1942, I undertook a nightmare version of the city in "Death and the Compass," my friends told me that at long last I had managed to evoke a sufficiently recognizable image of my home town. A few topographical elucidations may perhaps be in order. The Hôtel du Nord stands for the Plaza Hotel. The estuary is the Río de la

Plata, called "the great lion-colored river" by Lugones, and, far more effectively, "the unmoving river" by Eduardo Mallea. The Rue de Toulon is the Paseo Colón, or rather, in terms of rowdiness, the old Paseo de Julio, today called Leandro Alem. Triste-le-Roy, a beautiful name invented by Amanda Molina Vedia, stands for the now demolished Hotel Las Delicias in Adrogué. (Amanda had painted a map of an imaginary island on the wall of her bedroom; on her map I discovered the name Triste-le-Roy.) In order to avoid any suspicion of realism, I used distorted names and placed the story in some cosmopolitan setting beyond any specific geography. The characters' names further bear this out: Treviranus is German, Azevedo is Portuguese and Jewish, Yarmolinsky is a Polish Jew, Finnegan is Irish, Lönnrot is Swedish.

Patterns in time and space are to be found throughout the story. A triangle is suggested but the solution is really based on a rhombus. This rhombus is picked up in the Carnival costumes of the seeming kidnappers and in the windows of Triste-le-Roy as well as in the Fourfold Name of God—the Tetragrammaton. A thread of red also runs through the story's pages. There is the sunset on the rose-colored wall and, in the same scene, the blood splashed on the dead man's face. Red is found in the detective's and in the gunman's names.

The killer and the slain, whose minds work in the same way, may be the same man. Lönnrot is not an unbelievable fool walking into his own death trap but, in a symbolic way, a man committing suicide. This is hinted at by the similarity of their names. The end syllable of "Lönnrot" means "red" in German, and "Red Scharlach" is also translatable, in German, as "Red Scarlet."

No apology is needed for repeated mention of the Kabbalah, for it provides the reader and the all-too-subtle detective with a false track, and the story is, as most of the names imply, a Jewish one. The Kabbalah also provides an additional sense of mystery.

As in the case of most stories, "Death and the Compass" should stand or fall by its general atmosphere, not by its plot, which I suppose is now quite old-fashioned and therefore un-interesting. I have embedded many memories of Buenos Aires and its southern outskirts in this wild story. Triste-le-Roy itself is a heightened and distorted version of the roomy and pleasant Hotel Las Delicias, which still survives in so many memories.

I have written a longish elegy, entitled "Adrogué," about the real hotel.

The straight-line labyrinth at the story's close comes out of Zeno the Eleatic.

The Life of Tadeo Isidoro Cruz (1829-1874)

This tale is my Argentine version of the call of the wild. It is also a gloss on the gauchesco poem *Martín Fierro*, written in 1872 by José Hernández. In the poem, Sergeant Cruz is a former desperado who, as often happens to his kind, becomes the leader of a posse and is sent out to hunt down the deserter and murderer Martín Fierro. Cruz witnesses this outlaw's courage, goes over to his side, kills some of his own men, and returns to his old life. In this unexpected decision, I think of Cruz as being the most interesting and puzzling character in Hernández' book. For all I know, I may be the only reader to have wondered at the strange behavior of a policeman who goes over to the enemy. As *Martín Fierro* is now a classic, all things in it seem to be taken for granted.

I suppose I was moved to write the story out of my personal bewilderment. A quite detailed account of Sergeant Cruz's former life is given in Hernández; these circumstances had to be changed so that the reader familiar with the poem would not realize until the very end that he was being told something he already knew. The name Cruz itself I buried under the longer Tadeo Isidoro; I also worked in actual historical episodes unconnected with Hernández, such as Mesa's execution and Laprida's thirty white men pitted against two hundred Indians. A number of incidental details came out of my own family history. Suárez, who routs the gauchos at the opening of the story, was my great-grandfather; the ranch where Cruz once worked belonged to another relative, Francisco Xavier Acevedo. It was Suárez, by the way, who ordered the drums to drown out Manuel Mesa's last words. I have, however, left certain tracks and hints in my version in order to prevent the story from concluding on a mere trick. Reference to the poem is made as early as the second paragraph, and, at the end of the story, the obvious reason for my not describing the fight is that it is already very minutely set forth in *Martín Fierro*.

In the dramatic moment when Tadeo Isidoro Cruz finds out

who he is and refuses to act against Martín Fierro, there may be something deeply and unconsciously Hispanic. I am reminded of that famous passage in *Don Quixote* when the knight urges the officers of the law to set the convicts free, saying to them, "Let each man tend to his own sins; there's a God in heaven who takes good care to punish the wicked and to reward the good, and an honest man should not go out of his way to be another man's jailer. . . ."

The Two Kings and Their Two Labyrinths

Several elements or personal whims may be found in this unpresuming fable. Firstly, its Eastern setting, its deliberate aim to be a page—overlooked by Lane or Burton—out of the *Arabian Nights*. Secondly, that obvious symbol of perplexity, the maze, given in the story two forms—that of the traditional labyrinth, and, even more sinister, that of the unbounded desert. After some twenty-five years, I am beginning to suspect that the king of Babylon, with his lust for winding ways and devious complexity, stands for civilization, while the Arabian king stands for unrelieved barbarism. For all I know, the first may be a *porteño* and his antagonist, a gaucho.

The Dead Man

A ten days' stay on the Uruguay-Brazil border in 1934 seems to have impressed me far more than all the kingdoms of the world and the glory of them, since in my imagination I keep going back to that one not very notable experience. (At the time, I thought of it as boring, though on one of those days I did see a man shot down before my very eyes.) A likely explanation for this is that everything I then witnessed—the stone fences, the longhorn cattle, the horses' silver trappings, the bearded gauchos, the hitching posts, the ostriches—was so primitive, and even barbarous, as to make it more a journey into the past than a journey through space.

"The Dead Man" should not be taken, as I sometimes fear it may be, as a deliberate allegory on human life, though, like poor Otálora, we are given all things only to have them snatched from us at the moment we die. I prefer the story to be read as a kind of adventure.

Several rash enthusiasts have fallen into the mistake of thinking that "The Dead Man" might easily be worked into a film. They overlook the fact that Azevedo Bandeira, in a movie, would require psychological plausibility, while in a story he may be both accepted and yet not understandable. No real man, of course, would act the way he does.

The story has been criticized by some friends as being no more than a sketchy outline; my incapacity, or laziness, has led me to believe that such an outline is sufficient.

A few elements in the story may be worth pointing out. Here, as in other cases, I have begun with a long opening sentence. My feeling is that first sentences should be long in order to tear the reader out of his everyday life and firmly lodge him in an imaginary world. If an illustrious example be allowed me, Cervantes apparently felt the same way when he began his famous novel. As to the names, Otálora is an old family name of mine; so is Azevedo, but with a Spanish *c* instead of the Portuguese *z*. Bandeira was the name of Enrique Amorim's head gardener, and the word *bandeira* (flag) also suggests the Portuguese *bandeirantes*, or conquistadors. During that 1934 trip, we actually spent one night at a ranch called El Suspiro. The present tense, used throughout the story, makes it perhaps more vivid. The gaucho laboriously picking out a *milonga* at the very end is my comment on the way country people really play the guitar, though I'm sure that in the film version he will be made to sound like Andrés Segovia.

The Other Death

All theologians have denied God one miracle—that of undoing the past. The eleventh-century churchman Pier Damiano, however, grants Him that all but unimaginable power. This gave me the idea of writing a story about a scientist who, in some minor and unobtrusive way, attempts a similar feat. He hides two black balls in an upper drawer and three yellow ones in a lower drawer and, after years of hard work, finds that they have changed places. I was not long in perceiving that this tame miracle would never do, and that I would have to dream up something more dramatic. I thought of a common man coming to such a wonder, unawares, at the very moment he dies. Aparicio Saravia's revolution had caught my imagination from boyhood, and I saw a way of combining, in a setting of that backwoods civil war, the gaucho idea of courage as the one cardinal virtue and my metaphysical plan. And so my story, which was first titled "The Redemption," was born.

In the story, for literary purposes, the miracle takes place over a span of some forty-odd years. Pedro Damián's sin would be the more unbearable for him since, as the lone Argentine among Uruguayans, he would feel greater shame. Ultimately, Damián dies as he would have liked to die—struck down by a bullet in the chest while leading a charge. Had this actually happened, his fellow soldiers would hardly have remarked on such a detail. I introduced it into my story in order to make the whole atmosphere that much more visionary.

Emerson's verses are mentioned at the outset for two main reasons: first, because I simply admire their beauty; second, so as to send the reader—if he goes back to them—off the track, since they strongly express the idea that the past is unchangeable.

A favorite trick of mine is to work into my fiction the names of real friends. In "The Other Death" we find Ulrike von Kühlmann, Patricio Gannon, and Emir Rodríguez Monegal.

Ibn Hakkan al-Bokhari, Dead in His Labyrinth

Before "Ibn Hakkan," I had previously tried my hand at two detective stories, "The Garden of Branching Paths" (1941) and "Death and the Compass" (1942). The former won a second prize in *Ellery Queen's Mystery Magazine;* the latter was flatly rejected. My interest in detective fiction is rooted in my reading of Edgar Allan Poe, Wilkie Collins, Robert Louis Stevenson's *The Wrecker,* G. K. Chesterton, Eden Phillpotts, and, of course, Ellery Queen. In a world of shapeless psychological writing, I found in this particular form the classic virtues of a beginning, a middle, and an end—of something planned and executed. Bioy-Casares and I even went to the length of editing, in Buenos Aires, a successful collection of detective novels. The series was called "The Seventh Circle." The amount of reading required in the selection of these books rid me, in time, of my boyish craze for the general run of such games and puzzles. "Ibn Hakkan" turned out to be my swan song.

My first two exercises of 1941 and 1942 were, I think, fair attempts at Chestertonian storytelling. When I wrote "Ibn Hakkan," however, it became a cross between a permissible detective story and a caricature of one. The more I worked on it, the more hopeless the plot seemed and the stronger my need to parody. What I ended up with I hope will be read for its humor. I certainly can't expect anyone to take seriously or to look for symbols in such pictorial whims as a black slave, a lion in Cornwall, a red-haired king, and a scarlet maze so large that on first sight its outer ramparts appear to be a straight blank wall.

The pseudo-Arabian parable preached by the timorous Mr. Allaby from his pulpit was written before "Ibn Hakkan." How it found its way into the story is now a mystery to me.

The Man on the Threshold

I have previously written of this story:

> The sudden and recurring glimpse into a deep set of corridors and patios of a tenement house around the corner from Paraná Street, in Buenos Aires, gave me the tale entitled "The Man on the Threshold"; I placed it in India so as to make its unlikeliness less obvious.

Looking back on this statement, I seem to recall a rather different starting point. One night in Salto, Uruguay, with Enrique Amorim, for lack of anything better to do, we went around to the local slaughterhouse to watch the cattle being killed. Squatting on the threshold of the long, low adobe building was a battered and almost lifeless old man. Amorim asked him, "Are they killing?" The old man appeared to come to a brief and evil awakening, and answered back in a fierce whisper, "Yes, they're killing! They're killing!"

Somehow the idea—somehow the image—of an apparently helpless old man holding a secret power impressed itself on my imagination. I wove this image into the present story and, several years later, used it again—almost word for word—near the close of another story, "The South." Of course, the same linking of seeming helplessness and real power is to be found in the *Arabian Nights* and in the idea of old and wizened witches.

Students of Kipling will note that my Indian background is, in part, cribbed from him. Mention of Nikal Seyn comes from *Kim*. The madman counting on his fingers and mocking at the trees comes from the poem "Evarra and His Gods." The young man crowned with flowers was suggested, I think, by *From Sea to Sea*.

I'm sorry to say that "The Man on the Threshold" is also a bit of a trick story and a game with time. What is told as having happened years and years earlier is actually taking place at that moment. The teller, of course, as he patiently spins his yarn, is really hindering the officer from breaking in and stopping the trial and execution.

The Challenge

I was lecturing during the dictatorship out in the western part of the Province of Buenos Aires, in the city of Chivilcoy, when I was told the story of Wenceslao Suárez, nicknamed the Manco, or One-Handed. After I published "The Challenge," I received two letters bearing on the subject. (These letters are printed at the back of *Evaristo Carriego*.) One recounts Wenceslao's story with certain variations in the place names and in the behavior of his foe. The other tells of a similar incident in Entre Ríos, where the opponents—an Argentine and an Uruguayan—end their fight exchanging knives as a token of friendship. Both letters corroborate rather than debunk the tradition.

I found in this story a key to much of what I had already heard, thought about, and invented in stories of my own about such disinterested duels. I think the reader will find in "The Challenge" a full explanation of my feeling for the subject of knives, knife fighters, courage, and so on, as it has concerned me over the past forty or forty-five years.

Of course, Wenceslao's story may be found wanting in likelihood, but, as Boileau pointed out, "Reality stands in no need of being true to life."

This piece, like many others of mine, is halfway between a real short story and an essay.

The Captive

This tale, of course, is true. Frontier life has always attracted
me, no doubt because some hundred years ago my grandparents
lived among civilization's outposts out on the edge of the
Province of Buenos Aires. Colonel Borges, my grandfather,
there held the command of the Northern and Western Frontier
until he met his death in 1874. Additionally, I have always
been interested in the strangeness of memory and in the fact
that the past is somehow rescued, or saved for us, by it. De
Quincey thought of the human brain as a palimpsest, wherein
all our yesterdays, down to the minutest detail, survive; for
their release, these yesterdays only await the proper, unsuspected stimulus. Memory, not the captive, may very well be
the real subject of the story.

Borges and Myself

This all-too-famous sketch is my personal rendering of the old
Jekyll-and-Hyde theme, save that in their case the opposition
is between good and evil and in my version the opposites are
the spectator and the spectacle. During extremes of happiness or
unhappiness, I am apt to feel—in the space of a single, fleeting
moment—that what I am undergoing is happening, independent
of me, to somebody else. According to one of the Indian schools
of philosophy, the ego is merely an onlooker who has identified
himself with the man he is continually looking at. The fact
that when I write I am stressing certain peculiarities of mine
and omitting others has led me to think of Borges as a creature
of fancy. This suspicion is strengthened by the existence of so
many articles and studies that deal with him. A preoccupation
with identity and sometimes its discord, duality, runs through
much of my work—for example, in "The Theologians" and in
"Tadeo Isidoro Cruz" and in the very title of my later poetry,
The Self and the Other.

Jorge Luis Borges

The Maker

This story may be thought of as autobiographical—Homer as
an exaltation of myself, his blindness as my blindness, his acceptance of darkness as my acceptance. On the other hand, the
departures from autobiography are striking. Blindness came to
me as a slow twilight, not as a revelation; no Iliads and no
Odysseys ever awaited me. When I first conceived this piece,
I hesitated between Homer and Milton. Milton, however, is
almost a contemporary, and also—as Dr. Johnson felt—a not
very lovable figure. But Homer, as old as Western civilization
itself, is a myth and so may quite easily be made into another
myth. Eleven years after writing "The Maker," I seem to have
recast my fable—without being aware of it—into a more nar-
rowly autobiographical poem called "In Praise of Darkness." As
for Milton, I have paid due tribute to him in a sonnet entitled
"A Rose and Milton."

An early translator was worried that there was no strict
English equivalent for the words "El hacedor," my Spanish
title. I could only inform him that *"hacedor"* was my own
translation of the English "maker," as used by Dunbar in his
"Lament."

Ever since 1934, the writing of short prose pieces—fables,
parables, brief narratives—has given me a certain mysterious
satisfaction. I think of such pages as these as I think of coins—
small material objects, hard and bright, tokens of something
else.

The Intruder

In the fall of 1965, the Buenos Aires bibliophile Gustavo Fillol
Day asked me for a short story to be published by him in one
of those fine and secret editions meant for the happy few.
Around that time I had been rereading Kipling's *Plain Tales
from the Hills,* and I told Fillol that I had a story in mind. The
brevity and straightforwardness of the young Kipling tempted
me, since I had always written very involved and many-faceted
narratives. A few months later I was ready to get down to work,

202

and at the beginning of 1966 I dictated "The Intruder" to my mother.

Without my suspecting it, the hint for this story—perhaps the best I have ever written—came out of a chance conversation with my friend don Nicolás Paredes sometime back in the late twenties. Commenting on the decadence of tango lyrics, which even then went in for "loud self-pity" among sentimental *compadritos* betrayed by their wenches, Paredes remarked dryly, "Any man who thinks five minutes straight about a woman is no man—he's a queer." Love among such people was obviously ruled out; I knew that their real passion would be friendship. Out of this rather abstract set of ideas I evolved my story. I placed it in an almost nameless town to the south of Buenos Aires more than seventy years ago so that nobody could dispute the details. Really there are only two characters—the two brothers. Of them, we are allowed to hear only what the elder brother says; it is he who takes all the decisions, even the last one. I made them brothers for the sake of likelihood and, of course, to avoid unsavory implications.

I was stuck at the end of the story, unsure of the words Cristián would say. My mother, who from the outset thoroughly disliked the tale, at that point gave me the words I needed without a moment's hesitation.

"The Intruder" was, by the way, the first of my new ventures into straightforward storytelling. From this beginning I went on to write many others, ultimately collecting them under the title *El informe de Brodie* (Doctor Brodie's Report).

The Immortals

Blake wrote that were our senses closed—were we made blind, deaf, dumb, and so forth—we should see all things as they are: endless. "The Immortals" came out of that strange idea and also out of Rupert Brooke's derivative line, "And see, no longer blinded by our eyes." We acknowledge this first debt by calling one of the characters don Guillermo Blake.

Thrice over I attempted writing the story. First with Marta Mosquera Eastman and later with Alicia Jurado. They may still have copies of those early drafts. The story was to have been called "The Chosen One." For some reason or other, each of these schemes was dropped. Then, in 1966, I took the story up again with Bioy-Casares. By that time, Bioy and I had invented a new way of telling gruesome and uncanny tales. It lay in understating the grimness and essential horror while playing up certain humorous aspects—a kind of graft between Alfred Hitchcock and the Marx Brothers. This not only made for more amusing and less pretentious writing, but at the same time underlined the horror. We developed the technique in our comic detective saga, *Six Problems for don Isidro Parodi,* and, more openly, in the first of the *Two Memorable Fantasies,* "The Witness." In fact, some of the personages in "The Immortals" are taken from the *Six Problems,* and in the present story are fated to a terrible eternity. Another detail may be pointed out, the circumstance that all the characters—including the very Frankenstein of the story, the maker of monsters Dr. Narbondo—are also blatant fools and indulge in a silly jargon all their own.

The story deals in its own way with the problem of immortality. Since our only proof of personal death is statistical, and inasmuch as a new generation of deathless men may be already on its way, I have for years lived in fear of never dying. Such an idea as immortality would, of course, be unbearable. In "The Immortals" we are face to face with people who are only immortal and nothing else, and the prospect, I trust, is appalling. I think that this joint story (I can say this without undue vanity because I wrote it with someone else) is among my very best and that, despite its having been overlooked by Argentine critics, it may yet come into its own.

The Meeting

I seem to be telling the same story over and over again. Obviously, "The Meeting" is at heart the identical tale I have told in another new story of mine, "Juan Muraña." It is also linked to a fairly recent sonnet called "Allusion to a Shadow of the Nineties," which is about Muraña's knife, and to a short prose poem, "The Dagger," written I think in the late forties. Perhaps not so obvious is the fact that when I wrote these things I was quite unaware of repeating myself or of attempting variations. Precisely what takes over my mind in these cases, I do not know.

Spinoza's doctrine of things having a life of their own, or

of wanting to persist in their own being, has struck me as particularly true of those things, such as weapons, meant for quite specific ends. A dagger, for example, has to fulfill a destiny. In the story, the two knives have a will of their own, ruling the hapless young men who are supposed to be wielding them. Duncan and Uriarte are gentlemen, but the knives turn them into gauchos. In order to make this sufficiently clear, I have given Uriarte, who is a coward, the victory.

Back of all this lies my personal—or perhaps Argentine—obsession with knives. In the United States or in England, where men tend to square off with their fists, people think of fighting as something to be done bare-handed. In Western or gangster films, we often see men throw down their arms and resort to their fists. To me this seems highly unnatural and even unconvincing, since there is no earthly reason for a cowboy or a gangster also to be something of a boxer. Among *compadritos,* if a man struck another he did it with the back of his hand, as a mere provocation, and then the real fighting began. To me there is real intimacy in the knife; in fact, in one of my poems, the last line runs: "and across my throat the intimate knife." Firearms, of course, stand for marksmanship rather than courage. Fistfighting seems both harmless and undignified to an Argentine, while knife dueling has what Dr. Johnson said of the lives of sailors and seamen—"the dignity of danger."

A few minor autobiographical elements have found their way into "The Meeting." Álvaro Melián Lafinur was a childhood idol of mine and really was my cousin. He wore a dagger and a cloak and used to play the guitar, singing the Uruguayan ballads of Elias Regules which I mention. Álvaro was a quite bad poet and, as to be expected, an academician. It is in this latter role that I introduced him into "The Aleph."

Pedro Salvadores

I think the tale of Pedro Salvadores is summed up fully enough in its last paragraph. I might therefore take this opportunity to say something about the way it was written. At first, I played with the idea of attempting historical research, but I soon realized that for aesthetic purposes oral tradition is truer than mere facts. (The early version of Chevy Chase seems clumsier than the later.) I perhaps first heard this story from my grandfather when I was five or six. I set it down, in part, as my mother recalled it. I recently learned that the nineteenth-century novelist Eduardo Gutiérrez had already recorded the story—I think in a book called *El puñal del tirano*—and that the man's real name was José María Salvadores. As to Unitarians and Federals, these words should not be taken at face value. The Unitarians, as Sarmiento and Echeverría well knew, represented civilization, while the Federals stood for the barbarism of caudillo clans. Honorably, my own forebears on both sides were Unitarians.

Our own time has furnished us with many destinies like that of Pedro Salvadores; Anne Frank's is perhaps the best known of them.

Rosendo's Tale

This story is, obviously, a sequel and an antidote to "Streetcorner Man." The earlier story was mistakenly read as realistic; the present one is a deliberate surmise as to how events might actually have happened on the night Francisco Real was murdered. When I wrote "Streetcorner Man," I was—as I pointed out at the time—fully aware of its stagy unreality. As the years went by, however, and that story became embarrassingly popular, I wanted people to understand that I was not quite the fool I was being admired for.

I had been rereading my Browning and knew from *The Ring and the Book* that a story could be told from different points of view. Rosendo Juárez, the seeming coward of the first version, might perhaps be allowed to have his own say. So, instead of the braggart of "Streetcorner Man," we get a Shavian character who sees through the romantic nonsense and childish vanity of dueling, and finally attains manhood and sanity. In the first telling, Francisco Real is mortally wounded in the chest; sadly and realistically enough, he was really stabbed in the back while fornicating with La Lujanera in a ditch.

In the days when the story took place, toughs and killers were aided and abetted by the authorities, since most of them were official bodyguards of leading political figures. They were also used during elections to intimidate voters, knowing very well that because of police support they could act with impunity. Seldom outlaws, they were simply strong-arm men. I recall an anecdote told me by a priest in Adrogué. He walked up to the polling booth during one election and was politely and firmly informed by the local Rosendo Juárez, "Father, you have already cast your vote."

Incidentally, the reference to the young man dressed in black, who wrote Paredes' letter for him, is to the poet Evaristo Carriego.

Bibliographical Note

The original titles and first magazine or newspaper appearances of the stories in this volume are as follows (place of publication, throughout, unless otherwise indicated, is Buenos Aires):

STREETCORNER MAN: "Hombre de la esquina rosada" (entitled "Hombres de las orillas" and signed "F. Bustos"), *Crítica* (September 16, 1933).

THE CIRCULAR RUINS: "Las ruinas circulares," *Sur* (December 1940).

DEATH AND THE COMPASS: "La muerte y la brújula," *Sur* (May 1942).

THE LIFE OF TADEO ISIDORO CRUZ (1829-1874): "Biografía de Tadeo Isidoro Cruz (1829-1874)," *Sur* (December 1944).

THE ALEPH: "El Aleph," *Sur* (September 1945).

THE TWO KINGS AND THEIR TWO LABYRINTHS: "Los dos reyes y los dos laberintos" (entitled "Historia de los dos reyes y de los dos laberintos" and attributed, as an excerpt from *The Land of Midian Revisited (1879)*, to R. F. Burton), *Los Anales de Buenos Aires* (May 1946).

THE DEAD MAN: "El muerto," *Sur* (November 1946).

THE OTHER DEATH: "La otra muerte" (entitled "La redención"), *La Nación* (January 9, 1949).

IBN HAKKAN AL-BOKHARI, DEAD IN HIS LABYRINTH: "Abenjacán el Bojarí, muerto en su Laberinto," *Sur* (August 1951).

THE MAN ON THE THRESHOLD: "El hombre en el umbral," *La Nación* (April 20, 1952).

Jorge Luis Borges

THE CHALLENGE: "El desafío," *La Nación* (December 28, 1952).

THE CAPTIVE: "El cautivo," *La Biblioteca* (January-February-March 1957).

BORGES AND MYSELF: "Borges y yo," *La Biblioteca* (January-February-March 1957).

THE MAKER: "El Hacedor," *La Biblioteca* ([February] 1958).

THE MEETING: "El encuentro," *La Prensa* (October 5, 1969).

PEDRO SALVADORES: "Pedro Salvadores" [in English translation], *The New York Review of Books* (New York: August 21, 1969).

ROSENDO'S TALE: "Historia de Rosendo Juárez," *La Nación* (November 9, 1969).

"El acercamiento a Almotásim" (THE APPROACH TO AL-MU'TASIM) did not appear in a magazine before its publication in *Historia de la eternidad* (Viau y Zona, 1936); "Los inmortales" (THE IMMORTALS) did not appear before it was published in *Crónicas de Bustos Domecq* (Losada, 1967). The first appearance of "La intrusa (THE INTRUDER) was in an edition of fifty-two copies, printed by the Buenos Aires bibliophile Gustavo Fillol Day in April 1966 for private distribution among his and the author's friends; it also appeared, in the same month, in the sixth impression of the third edition of *El Aleph* (Emecé, 1966).

"Hombre de la esquina rosada" was first collected in *Historia universal de la infamia* (Tor, 1935). "Las ruinas circulares" was first reprinted in *El jardín de senderos que se bifurcan* (Sur, 1942); "La muerte y la brújula" in *Ficciones* (Sur, 1944); "Biografía de Tadeo Isidoro Cruz (1829-1874)," "El Aleph," "El muerto," and "La otra muerte" in the first edition of *El Aleph* (Losada, 1949); "Abenjacán el Bojarí, muerto en su laberinto," "Los dos reyes y los dos laberintos," and "El hombre en el umbral" in the second edition of *El Aleph* (Losada, 1952). "El desafío" (entitled "El culto del coraje") was first collected in the second edition of *Evaristo Carriego* (Emecé, 1955), where it appeared in a somewhat different form as part of the chapter "Historia del tango." "El cautivo," "Borges y yo," and "El hacedor" were collected in *El hacedor* (Emecé, 1960); "Pedro Salvadores" in *Elogio de la sombra* (Emecé, 1969); "El encuentro" and "Historia de Rosendo Juárez" in *El informe de Brodie* (Emecé, 1970).

ABOUT THE AUTHOR

Jorge Luis Borges was born on August 24, 1899, in Buenos
Aires. In 1955, with the overthrow of Peron, he was named
Director of the Argentine National Library, and in the same
year became professor of English and American literatures
at the University of Buenos Aires. In 1961, he shared the
International Publishers' Prize with Samuel Beckett. He has
made three trips to the United States—the latest, in 1969, to
attend a conference devoted to his writings at the University
of Oklahoma.

ABOUT THE TRANSLATOR

Norman Thomas di Giovanni was born in Newton, Massa-
chusetts, in 1933, and was graduated from Antioch College
in 1955. He met Borges in 1967 while the latter was at
Harvard. In 1968, on Borges' invitation, he went to live in
Buenos Aires, where he works with the author in daily
sessions. Together they are producing ten of Borges' books
in English versions. The first of these, The Book of Imaginary Beings, was published in 1969.

20th Century Literature

ALEXANDER SOLZHENITSYN

Winner of The 1970 Nobel Prize for Literature, this celebrated author's works are available in Bantam paper-
backs. Ask for them at your local bookseller, or use the
handy coupon below.

☐ THE FIRST CIRCLE   (T7074 $1.50)
  A large-scale panoramic novel in the great tradition of WAR
  AND PEACE and DR. ZHIVAGO.

☐ ONE DAY IN THE LIFE OF IVAN DENISOVICH   (N4639   95¢)
  Solzhenitsyn's brutal portrait of life inside a Siberian prison
  camp.

☐ CANCER WARD   (Q4753 $1.25)
  The celebrated novel of the Soviet Union. Includes Solzhenitsyn's highly acclaimed stand against censorship.

☐ THE LOVE-GIRL AND THE INNOCENT   (NM6600   95¢)
  Solzhenitsyn's first play about two prisoners who learn to love
  in a Siberian slave labor camp.

☐ DELUXE GIFT-BOX EDITION containing all four Solzhenitsyn
  volumes.   (K5148 $4.65)

Bantam is the only publisher with all of Solzhenitsyn's
works in paperback.

Buy them at your local bookstore or use this handy coupon:

Bantam Books, Inc., Dept. AS, Room 2450, 666 Fifth Ave., N.Y., N.Y. 10019

Please send me the titles checked above. I am enclosing $_____
(Check or money order—no currency or C.O.D.'s, please. If less than 5 books,
add 10¢ per book for postage and handling.)

NAME_____

ADDRESS_____

CITY_____State_____ZIP_____
Please allow about four weeks for delivery.   AS—9/71

Collections of Literature

Buy them at your local bookstore or use this handy coupon:

Michel Quoist

CHRIST
IS ALIVE!

Translated by J. F. Bernard

IMAGE BOOKS

A Division of Doubleday & Company, Inc.

Garden City, New York

Image Books edition 1972
by special arrangement with Doubleday & Company, Inc.
Image Books edition published February, 1972

Nihil Obstat: Daniel V. Flynn, J.C.D.
           Censor Liborum

Imprimatur: Joseph P. O'Brien, S.T.D.
           Vicar General
           Archdiocese of New York
           October 12, 1970

Originally published in France by Les Éditions Ouvrières, Paris,
under the title *Le Christ Est Vivant,* © Michel Quoist, 1970.

"In his new book, Father Quoist presents an impassioned essay that both demonstrates the thinking behind his earlier writings and argues for the further articulation of a new spirituality that will satisfy the religious needs of modern man. His theme is the same: modern man wants to live his life fully and participate in the world around him, and therefore he is not interested in a religion which seems to divorce him from the human and technocratic situations in which he finds himself involved. Accordingly, Quoist argues that 'to keep faith with Jesus Christ we must begin by keeping faith with the realities of daily life.' Adopting a Teilhardian theme, he states that 'the world is still under construction,' and thus the authentic Christian must participate fully in the process. And a failure to do so, a withdrawing from love and enterprise and involvement, is *the* Christian sin. . . .

These, of course, have now become familiar themes in the years since the Council, but seldom have they been expressed with such intensity and urgency. Quoist is almost apocalyptic in his pleadings that a failure to promote this type of realistic spirituality will doom Christianity to a totally ineffectual force in our time. He offers very few practical and precise guidelines throughout the book, but perhaps that is the direction that the new writers on spirituality will have to take—a broad enunciation of dynamic Christian principles, rather than the old unrealistic attempt to impose a series of specifics that would fit all situations. To that extent, *Christ Is Alive!* provides a compelling rationale from which the thoughtful reader can construct a practicable spirituality for himself."
                                                              —*America*

November 20, 1969
32, rue Barbet de Jouy
Paris VII

Dear Father Quoist,

Light must not be hidden under a bushel basket; it must be used to light our way. To that effect, you preach Jesus Christ the Savior ardently and effectively, and these pages are indeed the Good News. May they be read by everyone who is uncertain and trying to find his way.

Your words also bear witness to your faith. We priests and bishops, pastors of the faithful gathered together within the Church, have been made responsible for the Word; and the preaching of the Gospel today requires both courage and experience.

I am delighted to have the opportunity once more to express my gratitude for your apostolic work and to assure you of my continuing friendship.

☩ François Cardinal Marty
Archbishop of Paris

CONTENTS

FOREWORD

Please read these few preliminary pages.

Many people do not read prefaces, or they read them in a cursory fashion. That is a mistake. If we do not know the person to whom we are speaking, we can understand him only imperfectly. It works the same way for books. Books have something to say, even though their message is limited, and the truth that they contain is communicated through the intermediary of a person and colored by his own experience. That is self-evident. What is not clear, however, is the kind of effort that a reader must make in order to perceive the thought through the veil of the author's approach and method. The following remarks are intended to help the reader grasp the meaning and the purpose of this book, and, above all, to explain how I wrote it.

First of all, I must point out that I have not said, in this book, everything that could, or should, be said. Some people read books primarily to find confirmation of what they already believe. They are not open to the thoughts and experiences of the author, and they do not find what a particular book has to offer. Instead, they spend their time seeing what is not there, and bewailing what they do not see.

I know that this book cannot escape that fate. Many people will read it and say, "What a shame that Quoist does not mention this," or "Quoist has not considered this or that important aspect of the question." I want to tell such critics beforehand that they are quite right. And I do not say that in order to disarm them, but because I am aware of the limitations of this book. Indeed, I have imposed those limitations myself. My intention has been simply to select a few aspects of the Living Christ on which to reflect and meditate—aspects which it seemed necessary to clarify for the men of our time.

What I intend to say is this: Every man or group of men today can live in Jesus Christ; and he can do so without cutting himself off from his own life. Christ himself is living at the heart of the world; and his total Mystery—that of Creation, Incarnation, Redemption, and Resurrection—embodies and animates all of life and all of history. To be a Christian is to bind oneself to Christ, but to the total Christ, head and body, in order to live consciously, every day, that mystery of love which is the historical realization of the eternal plan of the Father.

There will be some readers, too, who will say, "But Quoist does not talk about the Church." And they will be right; or at least half right. It depends on what one means by "the Church." (Let's leave aside altogether such false definitions as those that conceive of the Church as "the pope, the bishops, and the priests"—or as the place where Christians assemble.) For us, the Church is the Body of Christ; that is, everyone who has been re-created and reunited in Jesus Christ through his redemptive Incarnation. The Church, then, is the People of God. But the Church is also that terrestrial institution, founded by Jesus Christ, to which new members are joined throughout the course of history. The Church is therefore both visible and invisible, in time and beyond time. In Christ, the Church is fully realized and sanctified; in her members on earth, the Church is incomplete and *in via*. Like the People of God in the Old Testament, the Church on earth is on the move, under the supervision of responsible authority, and she has her own laws, and her sacraments, which are visible and efficacious signs of the life of the Risen Christ. The Church, therefore, is the Body of Christ; but she is, at the same time, the one who generates that Body in history.

The Church which is the Body of Christ is considered on

almost every page of this book. The Church as a terrestrial institution is not mentioned at all. Why? Simply because it fell within the scope of the book to treat of the former and to skip over the latter. One cannot cover everything; and one had better not even try. Another volume would be necessary to speak of the institutional Church; and frankly, at this moment, I don't think that I could write it. It is very hard to translate the diverse riches of the Church into clear terms. Many people, of course, write about the Church, but without telling us what Church they are talking about. Such men confuse the issue, instead of clarifying it, for Christians. We hear people talking about the Church as the Body of Christ, as the "spouse" of Christ, as the People of God, as the mother Church, as the institutional Church, as the Church of communion, of individual Churches, of "cells" of the Church—one could go on indefinitely. If you think that I am either exaggerating or being unduly severe, then make a simple experiment (I have done it often). Ask a Christian what the Church is—and you'll see what I mean. What we need, along with the studies by specialists, is a popular explanation of the Mystery of the Church. But again, that is another book.

Next, I think I should explain, in general terms, how— and why—I write. Some men sit at their desks, study doctrine, investigate in depth one or another point, read everything that has been written on the subject, and then write books in order to share with us the fruits of their study. That is their trade, as it were. But it is not mine. Mine is to live, and to observe other people living, and to help them reflect on their lives, to reflect on my own life, to "contemplate" their spiritual destiny, and then to try to express in writing what I have discovered and what others have discovered in their lives. I do not understand everything that I observe, of course; others perceive, and will perceive, aspects of the Christian life of our contemporaries that I do not. Hence, the limitations of this book. It does not pretend to be an exhaustive study of contemporary spirituality; it offers only a few reflections on that spirituality. It is also a meditation on the Mystery of the Living Christ.

I gave the manuscript of this book to a theologian for his advice and guidance. He wrote to me: "It would be possible to pack the book with quotations from the Council and from theologians, ancient and modern, to show that they are all in agreement with what you say here about the spiritual life. . . ." In the same vein, I am often "classed" as belonging to one or the other school of theology. I am greatly honored by all this; but I must confess that, nine times out of ten, I am ignorant of the work of the great masters that seems to furnish the basis for this comparison. Unfortunately, I have never had the time to read such works, let alone to study them. So it is not the thought of these masters that I will attempt to elucidate; it is what I have read in life, what I have discovered in the spiritual experiences of men of our time. *I wish to write nothing but what has been lived.* If these two approaches to truth converge and we find ourselves before the same Lord who today awaits us, then I am wholly satisfied. It is a sign that the Holy Spirit walks with those who faithfully try to know and to live Christ Jesus.

My purpose in writing is—to be read. Hundreds of books on doctrine and spirituality are published every year. How many of these are read, and by whom? It is a sad fact that ninety percent of them—those that can be classified as "popularizations"—are read only by priests, religious, seminarians, and by a few cultivated (and more or less clericalized) laymen. We do not take into account how much of what we write passes over the heads, and even more "over the lives," of most of the People of God. We do not put ourselves in the reader's place. We flit about in a world of ideas and notions which is alien to him. We use a specialized vocabulary which he finds incomprehensible. It's often happened that I've loaned a particularly good book—one which, moreover, sold very well—to authentic Christians who were, as well, very intelligent and cultivated. Usually, the book has been returned only partially read; or, if the reader persevered to the end, he did so without interest or profit and out of a sense of duty. Any priest who works with Christians interested in understanding their lives and their faith will tell you the same thing. If they try to draw up a list of religious books they can recommend to such Christians, they find the list reduced to a very few titles.

I often travel abroad, and when I do I suffer because I cannot make myself understood without an interpreter. I do not know the language of my audience; but I do not say, "Let them learn French. I'll come back when they can understand me." I say instead, "I'll have to learn their language." But then, since I don't have the time, I have recourse, regretfully, to an interpreter.

Similarly, when we preach Jesus Christ, when we want to help Christians deepen their faith, we make ourselves understood little or not at all. What we must do is learn the language of our contemporaries. We must not try to set up courses for them to learn ours. We must attempt to enter into their way of thinking, into their mentality; we must not try to coax them out of their universe and into ours. We do not demean ourselves in doing so, and we do not compromise the spiritual wealth that we wish to communicate. I wonder why we are always inclined to confuse the *form* in which those riches have been transmitted with the *content*, the message that they contain.

In writing this book—as with my earlier books—I have consulted not only with theologians, but also with its readers-to-be. There is not a page that has not been read and reread by several of the latter, both young and old, taken from various walks of life. I carefully noted the terms, the explanations, the words which they found confusing or unclear, and, without sacrificing the substance or even subtracting from what I had intended to say, I have retranslated such terms, explanations, and words. Some people say that to translate is to betray. I agree—if the translator is not perfectly the master of the language into which he is translating. And it is for that reason that I have asked the help of those who could correct what I had written. The result is certainly not a study in perfection; but it is an effort. (I thought I should mention this, because it is an effort that I must pursue further.)

Some readers will be surprised at the absence of "technical terms" in this work. And, in fact, I have been at pains to avoid such terms. This is a somewhat dangerous procedure. Theologians make use of a vocabulary in which words have a precise meaning, and it is much easier to make use of that vocabulary than to try to express oneself in the words of everyday life. Nonetheless, our contemporaries—and the young, particularly—no longer understand the words and expressions of the theologians. That may be unfortunate, but it is a fact. I have therefore tried to avoid all technical terminology.

There are those who measure the "depth" of a book in terms of its obscurity. "What a wealth of thought!" they exclaim, when they have to read a chapter three times in order to understand it. Such confused and pedantic spirits notwithstanding, I have tried at all times to be as clear as possible. I am sorry if, because of that, I am branded as "superficial." It is not easy to be simple. If anyone reads parts of this book more than once, I hope it will be to meditate on them and not because they are obscure and difficult to understand.

I must end this preface with an appeal to theologians and to laymen jointly. It is necessary that there be men who study problems scientifically; and it is necessary that there be men who translate these findings into a language intelligible to our contemporaries. I don't believe that the same man can take on both jobs at the same time; he would risk neglecting one or the other task—and would probably end up by doing neither of them very well.

We need the *work* of the theologians. There are vital questions before today's Christians, and who will help us to resolve them if there are no specialists hard at work? But the specialists, for their part, should resist the temptation to speak too often, to write too hurriedly. Let them work in silence; and let them give us, from time to time, the benefit of their learning. But let them leave to the "translators" the task of communicating such fruits to the People of God.

The best translators are those who work at translating a foreign language into their mother tongue. Therefore, the best "translators" of doctrine for men of our time will be laymen. Only laymen are fully involved in life. Let them acquaint themselves with the work of the great theologians; and let them translate it for their brothers. But let them also live Jesus Christ today and bear witness to him for us. Why must almost all works of spirituality be written by priests and religious? Let the layman take up the pen—not to criticize (which is what some would make the layman's function), but to preach Christ Jesus.* The absence of the layman's voice in the Church is becoming more and more painfully clear.

"You are too optimistic," some readers will tell me. I won't defend myself against that charge. On the contrary, I'll thank those readers, for I regard such an accusation as a compliment. Sometimes I am tempted to be pessimistic; but if I give in to the temptation, I feel guilty about it.

I am indeed optimistic about the world today. Too optimistic? I don't think so. We are never too optimistic when we believe in the Risen Christ living his mystery at the very heart of the world. I think the gravest sin of Christians today is fear. Evil, sin, death—we must keep those things in mind, of course; but beyond them, and in the same glance, we must see Christ victorious. Many people say, "Everything is falling apart. A world is passing away." But I say, "A world is being born." Death exists, but Jesus Christ has conquered death. Christ is alive!

* We have made a step in this direction by establishing a series called "Visages du Christ" (The Faces of Christ), to be published by Les Éditions Ouvrières. The series will consist of authentic journals, letters, texts, etc. written by modern Christians who had no intention of publishing their manuscripts. We hope in this way to make available to modern man a true picture of contemporary Christian life.

PART I

Chapter One

Are There Any New Christians?

Are we witnessing the birth of a new kind of Christianity? No doubt we are. Humanity is in the process of evolution, of mutation. Man's discoveries astonish even man. He has made himself master of atomic energy and, like every other conquest of a form of energy, this victory signals a veritable leap forward in man's domination over nature. Now electronic computers give man answers that it would otherwise take years, or a lifetime, to calculate. These machines, more efficient than the combined effort of thousands of human brains, control—and will control more and more as time goes on—the progress of man and the world. Man is beginning to explore the universe itself as a prelude to taking possession of it. His power over life is growing, and the time will come when, having reached its very source, he will be able to control it, protect it, and prolong it more and more.

In the final analysis, man today, even less than yesterday, can truly be man only if he is aware of humanity. Men, wherever they may be, can no longer ignore other men. Everywhere, regardless of social class, nation, and race, men are growing; everywhere they are conscious of their human dignity; they are shaking off the chains of servitude; they are reaching up to, and demanding, total development. Nothing, no one, will be able to prevent this radical transformation of the world. The striving of the peoples of the world, their bat-

tles, the blood that they shed throughout the world for their
freedom, is a tidal wave on the ocean of humanity; it is an
immense and sorrowful sigh from a body which only yesterday had not been fully born but which today, in all its members, demands that it be allowed to live in the full light
of day.

The man who lives, and will live, in this new world will
have a life very different from that of his predecessors—
even his immediate predecessors. And the Christian of today,
who belongs to this mutating race of humans and who, with
humanity, explores these new paths, will not be able to live
his Christianity except within the framework of these new
developments. The grace of Christ must inevitably lead him
to a new form of contemplation, to new prayers, to new
commitments; that is, to a new form of the Christian life. Today's Christian will not live as did yesterday's Christian. He
cannot, and he does not wish to. He must not.

The Church, the People of God, is also going forward in
time. Certainly, she has received from Jesus Christ, once and
for all time, the inexhaustible treasury of Revelation. But the
Church, on the one hand, must never cease exploring that
treasury, in the diversity of its means, in order to be able to
live in the today of her history; and, on the other hand, the
Church, conscious of the requirements of human life at a
particular moment in time, and studying that life in a spirit
of love, must make it her task to shed light on whatever aspects of the Mystery of Christ are needed to enable men to
live in their time. We are at the confluence of two worlds; we
are at the dawn of a new age of humanity. And so, the
Church, led by the Holy Spirit, felt the need to gather in
Council in order to study her very nature so as to emerge
renewed and cleansed of that human dross which has
weighed her down, dimmed her glory, and stifled the Word.
Then, looking upon the world, the Church has set about the
chore of studying those existential relations with which the
Christian, by his very nature, binds himself to her, so as to
guide him on the road of history. For that history is the stuff
of which is made the history of the Kingdom itself.

The Christian, however, has need of more than light to
find his way. He needs a witness to travel with him and guide

him. The Holy Spirit, who has raised up saints for every age, also raises up everyday saints; and these men are visible signs of Jesus' love for his people. It is their way of living Christ today that, little by little, initiates us into a "spirituality for the men of our time."

When we say that new "witnesses" are needed for our time, it is not a matter of calling into question the value of the Christian life of yesterday. That life, that way of living Christ, was a sign for the contemporaries of our predecessors; but it cannot remain such for men of today. On the contrary. Certain attitudes and certain approaches, if they remain clothed in the forms of the past, will become "counter-witnesses."

Charity, for example, will always remain charity: "Love one another as I have loved you." But the road which leads from Jerusalem to Jericho has been extended to the ends of the earth, and our neighbors are now not only those who live in our vicinity, but also those of our social class, of our ethnic group, of our country, and of all the intermediate human groups to which we belong. Would the black man in America really be loving his neighbor if he contented himself with caring for the wounds of his brother and did not fight with all his strength for the liberation of all the brothers of his race? Would the laborer really be loving his neighbor if he were willing to lend an associate some money "till payday," but did not join the battle for a living wage and social justice? To be sure, charity remains the same in its source, which is the infinite love of Jesus. But charity today must be lived differently from what it was yesterday. To old-fashioned charity a new dimension must be added: that by virtue of which man is reached through the intermediary of socialized structures.

(It would be easy to give other examples based on the way in which we must live other Christian virtues. We have but to reflect a bit on poverty, obedience, and so forth.)

For today's Christians to be intelligible signs of love-charity to their contemporaries, they must, in the midst of the world, translate the eternal love of Jesus *into the actions of modern men.*

It is often said that modern man is a non-believer, that he rejects God. That may be. But too often the God that modern man rejects—the God that he believes to be the God of the Christians—is only a caricature. Somewhere, there has been a terrible misunderstanding. We have expressed ourselves very badly. We have lived badly. And so we have not made ourselves understood. We have spoken an unintelligible language in our churches and sacristies and meeting halls; and we did not have enough interpreters capable of translating into living language the eternal Word which is intended for every man. Jesus Christ came among us, and "his own knew him not"—because we have too often exiled God from the company of man, from the very life that he came to participate in; because we have declared our love in a foreign language.

The Holy Spirit, nonetheless, continues to work in the heart of man and in the heart of humanity. He still prepares every man for the coming of the Savior. He is present in the highest aspirations of men, of races and peoples today. And even if the latter, proud and impatient as rebellious adolescents who reject their fathers, reject, for the moment, both false gods and the living God—then let us have sense enough to realize (and patience and faith enough to believe) that man is experiencing merely a crisis of growth. It is a crisis that will resolve itself if only we are able, not to condemn, but to love.

It is true that, in a way, many men are in the process of converting to a kind of natural religion, to the religion of man and his total development, of justice, peace, and happiness. But it is also true that man, God's creature, retains in himself a taste for the infinite. Man is insatiable. He knows his strength, and he wants to be ever stronger. He wants to master the universe. But when he has mastered the universe, he will still be unsatisfied. He will quickly see that his ambitions do not originate within himself; and he will realize that purely human accomplishments cannot satisfy those aspirations. Unconsciously, man senses and looks for a Strength, a Love: Someone. If we know how to proclaim and reveal Jesus Christ, then one day man will discover him—not at the end of the road of human achievement, but in the middle of it, within himself.

Modern man, who seems so far from God, in fact is not very far. Indeed, he has never been so close to the *true* God. In the midst of man's unbelief, faith awaits.

Let them take heart, those men of little faith who believe in the seed, but not in the ear of corn; who welcome the infant but reject the inevitable adolescent and then the adult. We must believe in the process of life. And when that life is that of Christ who beats a path to the heart of man and of the world, then to believe in life is a virtue—that of hope.

How excruciating is the fear of those "well-disposed" Christians who mourn and lament the "loss of faith"—of others. How deceptive is the good will of those who mobilize to defend the faith as though they were preparing to fly to the aid of a beaten and retreating army. Let them stop their trembling. Let them still their battle cries. Let them put away their weapons. Let them learn that their fear betrays a basic lack of faith. How can one believe in a Risen God who loses battles and who needs someone to defend him? How can one believe in a love which is unable to declare itself, a love which has become sterile and incapable of giving life? Christians should at least have faith! Let there be no more of this "unbelief of the believers" that does so much harm. Jesus Christ has come. *He has saved the world.* He is risen. He does not stand there trembling, waiting for his disciples to defend him. He waits to be announced, to be revealed; and man, consciously or not, today more than ever, waits for the Good News. He is not going to meet Jesus Christ automatically, either at the end of or during his quest for human development. It is up to the new Christians to introduce Christ to him by joining in man's battles, progress, and aspirations.

But what are those aspirations which Christians, since they too are men of their time, also feel? We shall see that, far from being extraneous to Christianity, they are part and parcel of it.

Chapter Two

CHRISTIANITY AND THE ASPIRATIONS OF MODERN MAN

The normal man of today wants above all to be fully a man. He wants to develop to the maximum degree that "humanity" which is his. He knows that he has come far since his remote ancestors crouched in caves; and he knows that he will go even further.

Man today believes in man. He is proud of man. He is conscious of his greatness, of his power over himself, over his fellow men, over the world and the universe. He believes with all his strength in technology, in science, in the organization of the terrestrial city, in the possibility of a happiness of which he will be the author. He wants this happiness for himself, of course; but he wants it also for all men without exception, for he knows that there are many kinds of men on the face of the earth and that they all have a right to develop themselves fully.

But can man believe both in man and in God? Can he believe both in heaven and in earth? Is the development of the human the same as the diminution of the divine? In attempting to build up and dominate the world, will man destroy heaven? God is a jealous God, we are told, and he requires that, to be united with him, man must renounce himself and the world. In that case, what meaning does the world have? Must man turn toward God and despise the world, or must he turn toward man and forget God? Or should he attempt a compromise (as many do) and sacrifice one to the other, each in his turn, and condemn himself to the dissatisfaction of neither living fully his humanity nor loving fully his God? Such, in fact, is the fate of many Christians—those who live in a state of half joy and half sadness because they are never able to reconcile their desire to be both of the race of man and of Christ. And this is one of the chief sources of scandal to non-Christians, who, when they see so many Christians living in a state of dissatisfaction, are unable to believe in a Love that does not fulfill.

The Gospel tells us that if we want to follow Christ, we must deny ourselves, die to ourselves. The Gospel says that the Kingdom of Heaven is not of this world. And yet, we love the excitement of life; we love beauty; and we believe in a love which gives life. We love mankind; and when humanity suffers, we suffer. We love the world, and we take pride, as others do, when we see it becoming better. And we want to take part, with all our strength, in that process of amelioration.

How foolish we have been. We have allowed these terrible—and utterly false—alternatives to become rooted in the minds of many Christians. Today, we must show them that they not only can be proud of being men, but also that it is an obligation for them to *be* men as fully as possible and to fight so that all of their brothers, all over the world, may attain the highest degree of development as human beings. We must show them that to take possession of the world, to dominate it, to use it and to love it, is not to abandon God; rather, it is to obey God, to give glory to God—and to bear in mind that one day God will expect a full accounting of how we have managed the job. Christians must be the most militant of those who strive for human development; they must work harder than anyone else, by means of technology, science, and sweat, for the conquest and control of nature. And they must not do this as a more or less optional "good work," as a means of "witnessing" before non-Christians, but because it is their obligation as men and as children of God. Those who worry about a possible "religion of man" shall see that it is Jesus Christ who is at the heart of that great work of creation; it is Jesus Christ who summons man to work with him;

it is Jesus Christ who will lead mankind to the transcendental fulfillment that awaits it. To many, unfortunately, the very possibility of that fulfillment comes as a total surprise; and the fault is ours. But let us be patient with ourselves. If we are faithful to Christ, and faithful too to mankind and to the world, then Christ will be revealed.

Like that man who believes in man and in the reconstruction of the world, young people, in ever greater numbers, are asking questions about the meaning of life; and the answers of the adult world do not satisfy them. Their agony is expressed in an escape from the rigid life structures of that society which they reject, or in open revolt against institutions and persons. There is nothing surprising in that. A flower, if it were intelligent, would not be willing to live, to grow, to suffer, and to bloom for no one and no reason. It would certainly want to be beautiful; but it would want to be beautiful for someone.

This existential agony of the young is much less in evidence in underdeveloped countries and among the lowest social classes than in more affluent classes and nations. It seems that as soon as man is freed from the need to strive for the necessities of life, for a minimum of assured comfort, then he immediately begins to ask himself a basic question: What is the meaning of this life, and what is the reason for its limitations? Thus, unless we discover how to give a meaning to the life of men today—and especially to that of the young, who are less materialistic, more authentic, and more demanding—we can expect to see mankind torn apart by that terrible agony which follows the suspicion that life is, in effect, meaningless and absurd; that man is great, beautiful, and happy for, and with, no one—that is, with no one who is the inexhaustible source and purpose of happiness.

Indeed, it is obvious that the "age of human agony" looms on the horizon of contemporary history; and already many young people have fallen victim to that plague. For someone to live as a man, he must know why he lives, what is the meaning of the moment of history in which he lives, what is the importance of each instant, each event, each encounter. Either the world is meaningless and therefore life is not worth

living, or else the drama of life is being directed by a great
Love, a great Idea. Today, Christianity can no longer be the
caricature that some have made of it by reducing it to a
complex of moral rules and religious rites—rules and rites
which one can observe easily enough without their having
one iota of influence upons one's personal or social life. Christianity today must be the beacon which lights up every human
path; the Life which animates all life. Christianity must give
a meaning to all of history, to the universe, to mankind, and
also to each particle of matter and to each movement and
instant of existence. Through Christ, modern man must be
rescued from the temptation of the absurd.

Many men, however, are not ready to ask themselves
questions about the basic meaning of the happiness they have
attained through blood and sweat. The workers of the world
are still fighting to live, and to live as men—that is, as responsible men. For that, in the final analysis, is what it is all about.

It is true that some workers, intimidated by statistics showing a supposedly regular rise in their buying power, hypnotized by the flicker of their television screens, lulled by the
murmur of their washing machines, consider themselves to be
relatively well off. These are the defeated; those who have
abandoned, momentarily or permanently, the battle for total
dignity for themselves and their fellow workers. It is also true,
however, that the great masses of the people have, through
the inspiration of a few men, come to realize that the earth
belongs to all mankind. They know that each man, as a responsible individual, should have the means to accomplish
the task that has been entrusted to him; that is, the conquest and building-up of the world by work. And he should
be able to do this not in the role of a mere functionary, but
as a responsible man, in cooperation with his brothers, through
the interplay of just political, social, and economic structures.
This movement of the masses will continue so long as the
workers will not have attained—beyond the bare necessities
of life—the respect concomitant with that essential dignity.

Christians, generally, have been conspicuously absent from
this mass movement of workers. One result of this absence
has been that the workers have not discovered that the power
of eternal Love, incarnated in Jesus Christ, could unite and mo-

bilize them in the service of their brothers. Another has been that the workers have often become convinced that Christianity and the Church, the repositories of that infinite strength, are, in effect, a stronghold of inertia and an obstacle to progress—so much so that they must be destroyed before justice can triumph.

Certainly, the good works of some Christians have often been heroic; but those good works, though they have been a striking form of witness for some, for others have been a counterwitness to the extent that they have not been accompanied by participation in the battle for social justice. The Church, in fact (as many have noted), never "lost" the working classes, for she was never really present among the workers—and she was especially absent from the "labor movement," which is essentially an expression of the ideal of life and dignity.

For several years now, some Christians (who were long misunderstood, and often attacked, by their brethren) have been living their worker's life, their battles, and their Christianity, in the unity of a unique Love. Such men are exceptions; and yet, they are true Christians. Tomorrow, perhaps, there will be enough such Christians among the poor and the exploited not merely to give a meaning to the labor movement (which has a meaning of itself), but to give *all* its meaning to it.

The worker "proletariat" is no longer alone in the world. There is now a proletariat of peoples, comprising the millions of men who are virtually slaves—slaves, many of whom die of hunger every year. Perhaps the sociologists can work out statistical tables to tell us how many tens of millions of men have died, in the last few decades, in the concentration camps of underdevelopment. Maybe then those who advocate the violent suppression of every revolutionary movement, on the grounds that such movements risk "bloodshed," will begin to have second thoughts. One may wonder whether lives sacrificed to maintain "law and order" are less precious than those sacrificed in "disorder." Is violence always justified when it is used to put down revolutions, and always unjustified when it is used to make revolutions?

Such are the agonizing questions that are being asked today, the world over, by many men of good will, and by many young people, who can no longer bear to see generation after generation of their brothers die for no reason at all. Sooner or later, these men will rise up in revolution, to free their people. The only question that remains is: What revolution will it be?

Today, Christianity must be the crucible of true revolution. Now that it is a matter of freeing entire nations, we must not attempt—as we did with respect to the labor movement—to excuse ourselves from participation. For the underdeveloped peoples of the world can wait no longer. They know now that they are suffering unjustly. They know why they are oppressed. And they want to free themselves. But how? They are searching for a concept of humanity and of life that will give meaning to their battle and will give them the courage to act.

In some countries, the choice is still open. I am thinking particularly of the Latin American countries, in which ninety-five percent of the population are baptized Catholics, and where many good men, in every class of society and at every age level, have come face to face with a painful question: Should they turn to another "mystique," to another "faith," to accomplish that revolution which Christianity has not been able to achieve? These men know that they have no need to ask the Church for instructions on the techniques of liberation; but some of them still hope that they may find—that they will be helped to find—in the Church that strength of Love which they need in order to fight, suffer, and win.

We must restore to Christianity the irresistible power of revolution that our selfishness, our stupidity, and our exaggerated prudence has stifled. Jesus Christ is condemned by our timidity. He dies every day, in millions of the members of his Body. "I was hungry," he says, "and you did not feed me. I was naked, and you did not clothe me." Many of us, he forgives, "for they know not what they do." But now, let us know what we do. The good works, heroic though they may be, by which we silence our conscience are but a drop in the ocean so far as what they accomplish; even worse, they are an offense to the basic dignity of man unless they are accompanied by the gift of ourselves in the all-out battle for the radical reform of our political, economic, and social structures.

Let us acknowledge that we cannot save our souls unless we save man's body. Jesus Christ came to save the *whole* man; and that is the final purpose of the real revolution—of the revolution that each of us must preach and that each of us, in his own way, must accomplish.

Chapter Three

A Spirituality for Contemporary Christians

The situation touched on in the preceding chapter is clear enough. We are waiting to see whether the modern world is indeed "allergic" to Christianity. One of two things will happen. First, man will come to understand not only that there is no conflict between his human aspirations and Christianity, but also that Christianity can give their true meaning to those aspirations; and then many men will open their minds and hearts to the revelation of Jesus Christ. Or, modern man will continue to believe that there is a contradiction between those two elements, and then, helpless but still generous and open, he will continue to search elsewhere for a reason to live and to fight.

If this is true of the man of good will who is earnestly trying to find his way, it is no less true of the faithful Christian. The Christian, as we have already said, is a man of his time; he has the same anxieties and the same ideals as other men. If Christianity does not give him the answers to the vital questions that he asks, then he will abandon Christianity—as one abandons an old suit that, though useful in its time, has now become useless and out of fashion.

What is needed today is for the Christian to encounter God *in his everyday life.* Jesus can no longer be a distant stranger, respected and feared—or even loved—but uninvolved in life. And the Christian can no longer be merely a servant whose daily chores are only a test of his loyalty and a testimonial to his unswerving faith. Man knows that he is only a creature, and a weak and vulnerable creature at that; but he knows too that he has been offered the opportunity to become a son of God and a collaborator in the Kingdom that is being founded. He knows that he must diminish so that God may increase—but more and more he realizes that it is not a question of self-annihilation but of the pure exercise of a freedom which, by opening up man to infinite Love, assures his full development both in time and in eternity.

In his spiritual life, therefore—that is, in his progress toward God—the Christian wants to commit his whole being. It is not sufficient for him to give an intellectual allegiance to that or that point of doctrine; and even less is he satisfied by emotional consolations, the charms of a fertile imagination, or merely physical manifestations of his submission to God. If he is to move toward God through Christ Jesus, his Savior, then he wishes to do so with all of himself, in every act of his daily life, in his work, his leisure, his relationships, his loves, his struggles and the struggles of his brothers. Every day of his life, today's Christian becomes aware that he is not alone; he is in a certain neighborhood, in a certain factory, in a certain club or social class; he is aware, in other words, that he is a member of the human community. He is surrounded by a people on the move and in company with them; and that people wants to meet his God.

This heartfelt desire to find Christ in daily life is not a vision or an illusion. Jesus Christ, in effect, is waiting for man at the very heart of the world. And man today, more than his predecessors, longs—too often in darkness, unfortunately—for the Risen Christ who lives his Mystery in human history. He senses, confusedly, that he will meet Christ on the way, a Christ who is there for everyone and in everything. He senses the presence of the divine Lover who is indifferent to nothing that concerns man, of the silent Companion of his labors who mixes his redeeming blood with man's daily sweat and works with man to build a world which will be transformed by the Father through the elements of the infinite which exist at the very center of the temporal order. Man can no longer bear to struggle each day if that struggle is to remain forever at the level of earth, if God is to be absent from it, if it is not to be with God that he and his brothers live, love, and die.

God is there, and man knows it. God is waiting to love man and to work with him. And the success of man's life depends on his finding God. Can God be found? He calls to man in the world; but the world itself is noisy, distracting, and seductive. Many men in the world are concerned only with amusing themselves while waiting for death; while others, unknowing but proud, are convinced that they will somehow be able to eternalize their earthly happiness. But the Christian—have we been able to persuade him that his instincts are not mistaken, that God is indeed present in man's life? Have we been able to show him how to find God and how to work with God?

Unfortunately, the spirituality that we have attempted to teach laymen is not that of laymen but of monks. It is a spirituality shot through with the mystical experiences of vowed religious, with their methods, with the spiritual exercises they have formulated. The most renowned saints, those who are recognized as founders of "schools" of spirituality, those who are held up as examples, are almost always religious. Most often, they have attained sanctity by "leaving the world." And, of course, priests have all been educated in seminaries which were little more than monasteries; they have all spent many years living like monks (a life which they were unable to continue in the active ministry). They then attempted to pass on to the faithful what they had learned and lived in those monasteries; and to the most devout of the faithful they suggested entering a "Third Order," in which the layman would find, rather than a spirit of sharing, the framework of monastic life adapted to persons living in the world. Certain lay spiritual movements—even those which call themselves "action" movements—have been so influenced by this monastic orientation that they have tried to reproduce the monastic rule of life, with its charters, chapters, sessions of self-confession and self-abasement, and all the rest. But other action movements—that is, organizations aimed at the integration of faith and life—have, in the past few years, discovered the elements of an authentic "layman's" spirituality. In the latter instance, however, only a few priests were able to be of use to those organizations; and those few were the priests

who were capable of grasping the fact that their function was
not to *teach* the Christian life to laymen, but to learn life itself
from them. And then those priests were able to be of service,
to join with laymen in finding, not a doctrine, but a living
Person.

Today, there are still religious who live in such a way as to
let us know, somehow, that a man may be a contemplative in
the midst of the world. But their testimony is no more directly
applicable to laymen than was that of their predecessors.
Such religious are present in the world, but they are not committed to the world. For the layman, however, it is in the
midst of a commitment to the world that Jesus must be found
and must be lived.

The faithful are told: "God is in the desert. You must separate yourself from the world and enter into solitude if you
want to find God. God is in silence; if you want to hear him,
you must flee the noise of the world. Only through contemplation can you know God, and an active life destroys contemplation. Forget the preoccupations of the world, for they
are obstacles to an encounter with God."

But the layman lives in the midst of noise, surrounded by
crowds, overwhelmed by necessary activities. He works in an
office, surrounded by employees, and pores over columns of
figures. He works in a factory, noise is everywhere, and he is
the slave of a machine which becomes like a part of himself.
He is packed into a bus, jammed into a subway. He is in an
apartment whose paper-thin walls bring him the sounds of
the lives of his neighbors. He is in a kitchen, always a little
behind in washing the clothes, washing the vegetables, bath-
ing the baby, getting the children off to school. He is at the
beach, in a restaurant, in front of the television set. He is
always busy, always worried—about the end-of-the-month
bills, about the shoes he must buy, about a repairman for the
washing machine, about the expenses he must meet, about
the stock market. He belongs to a family and to a social milieu;
he lives in a neighborhood, in a city, in a nation. He belongs
to a union and goes to innumerable meetings. He agitates,
struggles, fights for various movements and groups. *He is a*

part of life. And yet, we tell him that he must separate himself from life if he is to find God.

Perhaps there are several classes of Christians. The first would comprise a privileged class, the super-Christians, the aristocrats of the spiritual life, who are called to love Christ in solitude, far from the world, and to participate in a special relationship with him. The second class would be composed of a sort of spiritual *bourgeoisie* who, following the example of the aristocrats, are able to shut themselves up in their rooms (because each of them is able to afford a private room), attend retreats regularly and spend Holy Week in a monastery, read books of spirituality, and take courses in the Bible—because they have enough education to do so, or because they are unmarried, or because they can afford servants to care for their families—or because they have the time to do all these things since they refuse to become involved in social and political matters in order to concentrate on "what is essential." And finally, in last place, there would be the great mass of the people, those who are condemned to live in the hurly-burly of the world, joustled, crushed, sacrificed; who are able from time to time, by a heroic act of the will, to tear themselves away and, despite a thousand worries and distractions, to catch a glimpse of Christ—just enough of a glimpse to leave a bitter aftertaste of dissatisfaction.

If God is truly present only "in the desert" and in silence, then he is not accessible to the majority of men today. And in that case, if the purpose of the Incarnation was to join Christ to man in the whole of life, we may say that the Incarnation has been a fiasco.

Fortunately, that is not the case. We know—through the words of a certain number of Christians—that the Holy Spirit is in the process of teaching us anew today that, although the gifts and vocations of each man are different, every man is called to meet Jesus and to unite himself to Jesus within the framework of that human life to which Providence has assigned him. The Holy Spirit is telling us that life today—like life yesterday—is not a "punishment"; it is a gift of love from the Creator. It is not an obstacle to divine union; it is the customary place for a meeting with Christ. Man is not condemned to live as "an exile" in this "valley of tears"; he is invited to participate, as a friend and a brother, in the mission entrusted to Jesus by the Father. It may be that participation has become burdensome and painful; if so, it is not by God's will but by man's sin, for its essential characteristic is the infinite joyfulness of the Resurrection.

We may be certain that, guided by the Holy Spirit, the laity will give to the Church those new saints of which she has such need. And, in the meantime, we must, with our brother laymen, search, pray, and live the adventure of sanctity in new ways.

PART II

Chapter Four

JESUS CHRIST AND FAITH

At the center of history, at the center of the world, and the center of humanity, there is the Event, the unique Event: Jesus Christ, the Son of God, made man.

Jesus Christ appeared in history two thousand years ago, in a segment of space called Palestine, as a Man among men, as the Man-God. His mission was to reveal the infinite love of the Father—a love of which he himself is the sign. He is the sacrament par excellence, in which all other sacraments are included and from which they all emanate and take their power. He came to reveal the eternal plan of the Father's love, to reveal "the message which was a mystery hidden for generations and centuries" (Col. 1:26); the plan by which all men are to become the Father's "adopted sons, through Jesus Christ" (Eph. 1:5); "the hidden plan he so kindly made in Christ from the beginning, to act upon when the times had run their course to the end: that he would bring everything together under Christ, as head, everything in the heavens and everything on earth" (Eph. 1:10). He came to gather together the scattered children of God into one people, one Church.

We know now that all things had been conceived in Christ from eternity, that all things are accomplished in him; and therefore we know that the Mystery of Jesus Christ permeates all things, affects all men—present, past, and future—per-

vades all of history and all of the universe both in time and
beyond time into eternity. Jesus Christ is at the beginning,
in the middle, and at the end. He is before, during, and after:
"I am the Alpha and the Omega, the First and the Last,
the Beginning and the End" (Rev. 22:13). And the eternal
plan of the Father's love is the total Mystery of Christ.

Thus, nothing and no one is beyond that mystery of love.
No man, whoever he be, with faith or without it, can escape
from it. Every man is vitally affected. Since the Event, man
cannot have the same view of himself, of other men, and of
the world. He can no longer live, work, and love in the same
way, for the Event has given a meaning to everything; it has
given its own meaning—a total and final meaning—to all of
creation. And it has done this, not by destroying what went
before, but by perfecting and accomplishing all things in itself.

This historic Event, the coming of Christ on earth, is the
sensible, visible, and efficacious sign of the total and invisible
Mystery of Jesus Christ. And the whole of our Christian lives,
all of our "spirituality," is characterized by, and receives its
direction from, the degree to which we understand the Event.

Either we meet the Son of God, as it were, in Jesus as a
historical personage, and we allow ourselves to be loved by
him and to imitate him in our lives. In that case we bind ourselves to him by a personal relationship of friendship so that
our lives are influenced only indirectly, from without, and
(probably) only in part by Christ. Or, on the other hand, we
believe in and we live Jesus Christ in his total Mystery—and
then our lives are affected directly, from within, and wholly,
so that the years of our lives become a prolonged effort to
achieve *incorporation* into Jesus. We offer him our lives so that
through them—in every instant of time and in every act and
thought—Jesus Christ may make present to us in time his
eternal Mystery by making us live, with him and in him within
the framework of our day-to-day existence, in union with all
of mankind and with the world, the ineffable mystery of love
which is the eternal plan of the Father.

It is to this sharing of himself that Christ invites us.

If, however, we are to understand that to which we are
called, we must consider Christ in what we might call his

"dimensions." And the first question that comes to mind, of course, is: Who is Jesus Christ?

We have already said that he is a historical personage, whose life (at least in its most important events) is known to us, and whose message we know essentially from Jesus' own words. He was a man, we know, who lived for about thirty-three years on earth, and whose memory is still vivid in human history. And we know that he was the Son of God. St. John saw, listened to, and touched this God-made-man; and while he was still trembling with the excitement of this unbelievable encounter, he wrote: "Something which has existed since the beginning, that we have heard, that we have seen with our own eyes; that we have watched and touched with our hands: the Word, who is life—this is our subject. That life was made visible: we saw it and we are giving our testimony, telling you of the eternal life which was with the Father and has been made visible to us. What we have seen and heard we are telling you so that you too may be in union with us, as we are in union with the Father and with his Son Jesus Christ. We are writing this to you to make our own joy complete" (I John 1:1–4).

The Christ of which St. John writes is the same Risen Christ who mysteriously lives among us today. Christ is his whole Body—that is to say, the entire universe, all the matter and all the life that would not exist if he did not sustain it by being present in it: "He is the image of the unseen God and the first-born of all creation, for in him were created all things in heaven and on earth: everything visible and everything invisible . . . and he holds all things in unity" (Col. 1:15–17). It was from matter and from life that he took his flesh; "and the Word was made flesh"—flesh that the Father raised up and took to himself for eternity. And therefore matter and life should be wholly contained in him: "He has let us know the mystery of his purpose . . . that he would bring everything together under Christ, as head, everything in the heavens and everything on earth" (Eph. 1:9–11).

Of this Body of Christ, therefore, we are all members—including, in a very special and privileged way, the poorest of our brothers and even those who seem to be the farthest from Christ: "I was in prison and you came to see me" (Matt.

25:36)—or "you did not come to see me." And therefore it
is the human race in its entirety which grows each day, and
will continue to grow until the end of time when Christ's Body
will have become "fully mature" (Eph. 4:13).

This Body of Christ is the Kingdom of God; it is the City of
God; it is the Church, that enormous complex within which
human beings and the Holy Spirit work together: "So you are
no longer aliens or foreign visitors: you are citizens like all the
saints and part of God's household. You are part of a building
that has the apostles and prophets for its foundations, and
Christ Jesus himself for its main cornerstone. As every structure is aligned on him, all grow into one holy temple in the
Lord; and you too, in him, are being built into a house where
God lives, in the Spirit" (Eph. 2:19–22).

Jesus' question is still valid: "And you, who do you say I
am?" It is directed to each of us personally; and the answer
we give is a measure of the depth and dimension of our faith.

The question which inevitably follows that of "Who is
Jesus Christ" is this: "What is Christian faith?" Christian faith,
obviously, is not merely a felt emotion; nor a purely intellectual conviction; nor adherence to a moral or religious code;
nor even a "belief" in a creator-God (which would be deism;
and how many self-styled Christians, unfortunately, are no
more than deists).

Christian faith is, first of all, an encounter with God by
means of the grace of the Father. It is Love, brought to mankind by the Son of God. It is also an act of trust made in Christ
Jesus as a living person, as someone in the truth of whose
words and life we can believe. And finally, it is a commitment
within the Church, the People of God, as an institution which
lives in time the Mystery of Christ. That is, it is a free and
conscious participation, within Love, in the mission of Christ
on earth: the realization of the plan of the Father. "If anyone
wishes to be my disciple"—that is, to be a Christian—"let him
follow me."

Thus, in the final analysis, the "mature" Christian is a man
who (progressively) has encountered Christ as a historic personage; who has recognized him as the Son of God; who has
made an act of trust in him; and who is bound to Jesus by a

personal relationship of love which culminates in a basic identification and union with him. If is, furthermore—and necessarily—the man who finds Jesus Christ in his "mystical dimension," in his total Mystery, in order to live with him and in him. This Mystery is one which we must live as a people, as a Church, at a particular moment in time; in our life as a whole and in every instant and event of our life; occupying a certain space in the cosmos; within the geographical and sociological circumstances within which we find ourselves; and, finally, in the company of our brothers—that is, in all of the natural communities and societies within which we spend our lives.

Faith at that level may be classified as "mature." Why? Because it is the adolescent whose proper function it is to become aware of himself as a person, as someone distinct from his parents; as an autonomous being capable of entering into personal relationships with other autonomous beings. The adolescent, after a long exploration of himself (which leads, hopefully, to an understanding of himself), becomes more and more capable of friendship; he serves, as it were, an apprenticeship in human relations. At the same time, as a Christian, he becomes aware of his God in Jesus Christ, in a preliminary stage, as a friend, a model, and a leader.

On the road to maturity, the adolescent discovers subsequently that he is a person who lives in a society, in a world. Or else, he fails to adapt himself to his environment and therefore remains at the preceding stage of psychological development; that is, he lives as a stranger in the world, capable only of transitory and limited relationships, requiring direction and rules in order to keep him in line. The adolescent who is maturing properly, on the other hand, learns to integrate himself into the world and to take his place among his peers, to work out the problems implicit in personal confrontations and in common undertakings.

Similarly, the adult Christian must also go beyond a personal meeting with Jesus of Nazareth. Taking cognizance of the fact that he belongs to "a people," to a Church situated in time and space, he must live, in the company of his brothers, all the dimensions of the Mystery of Jesus Christ. He must commit himself voluntarily not only to the observance of a law clearly and simply enunciated, but also to participation in a common work by determining, step by step, in every phase of his daily life, what is God's will both for himself and for the human race of which he is a member.

There are, no doubt, sincere and generous Christians today who are upset by the appearance of certain Christian life-styles, by attempts to resolve, in the light of faith, the novel problems of a changing world, by the efforts of some Christians to live in brotherhood with non-Christians. Those who are disturbed by such things seem to be basically maladjusted and immature in their faith. They are taking refuge in the security of the past, where, they hope, they will find doctrinal "security," clear rules, predigested rituals, etc. They need the help of theologians, certainly; but, even more, such Christians need the help of psychology and psychiatry to help them travel the road toward maturity.

The world today has need of mature men. And it has equal need of mature faith.

The Mystery of Jesus Christ is unique. It is the eternal plan of the Father's love, which was lived historically by Christ in ancient Palestine and which is "mysteriously" unfolded in and by the Risen Christ throughout time and history. We who contemplate that Mystery will never adequately grasp "the breadth and the length, the height and the depth, until, knowing the love of Christ, which is beyond all knowledge, you are filled with the utter fulness of God" (Eph. 3:18–19). We must therefore—without losing sight, however, of the Mystery as a whole and of its unity—reflect successively on the Creation, the Incarnation, the Redemption, and the Resurrection. Those are all different aspects of the same love as lived by Christ on earth two thousand years ago, and lived now with him and in him by the whole Church, and, within the Church, by each individual Christian—and even, at another level, by all men.

The imperfection of our sight requires that we study individually each aspect of that unique Mystery of Jesus; but we must then contemplate them as a whole, each one in and with all the other aspects. Only in that way can the symphonic harmony of the Mystery be audible in all of its truth, as each part loses itself in the beauty of the whole.

What holds true with respect to meditation on the Mystery of Jesus is even more true when it is a question of living that Mystery. For there are such things as false virtues and false spiritualities which, in concentrating on only one aspect of the Christian life to the exclusion of all else, mutilate that life almost beyond repair. Thus, it would be a serious mistake to attempt to live the mystery of the Creation while ignoring that of the Incarnation, which lies at the very center of the Creation. (And isn't that really the great temptation of the modern world? I mean to accept and develop man and the world, but to ignore, at every step along the way, the necessity for the virtue of Love-Charity?)

The Incarnation itself cannot be lived authentically if it is not tied to the Redemption. Sin is always with us, and the grace of salvation cannot reach mankind unless, in the footsteps of Christ, man is able to do battle against evil and unless he is able to die to himself.

And finally, the Redemption cannot be lived without the Resurrection; for in Christ Jesus, beyond all suffering and all death, there is the infinite life and joy of Easter.

Chapter Five

THE MYSTERY OF CREATION

Creation is not yet finished. Not all the seed has been sown; not all the trees planted; not all the crops harvested. Not all the animals have been born; and man has not yet domesticated them all. And not all the factories have been built, nor all the bridges constructed, nor all the dams erected. There are still houses and cities to be built, satellites to be put into orbit, planets to be conquered. The creation of the universe, of life and matter, is still taking place in time, is being transformed by man, and is still not yet complete.

Mankind itself is developing. We, who have the obligation to work for our full development, are still creating ourselves. Such is the work of education—both the education which we receive and that which we give to ourselves as we grow in maturity; it is, in essence, a long process of balancing, harmonizing, unifying, and developing all of our physical, intellectual, and spiritual energies by humanizing and personalizing them. It is also all of the instruction that we have received, the cultural acquisitions that we have made to enrich ourselves at the intellectual, artistic, and professional levels. And, finally, it is the interplay of our personal relationships within the framework of the natural societies within which we live; relationships which must deepen to the point of "communion" and broaden to the extent that our human nature allows.

Every day, in living and still more in determining the course of his life, man is creating himself. And mankind, collectively, also continues its prodigious expansion. Man, in the process of transforming himself by means of the successive victories of past generations and of his own efforts to rise still higher, is becoming greater and more powerful with every passing century. He is also multiplying himself rapidly—so much so that the rising birth rate presents new problems to man's intelligence and to his conscience. And finally, the "body" of mankind is taking on definition as it develops. Increasingly structured human societies are being formed or strengthened and are establishing closer and closer bonds with other societies the world over. Thus, we are far from the concept of a God who, in one unique and definitive act, created the universe. And creation, as a gesture of love on the part of the Father and of the Son, continues in time.

Creation, therefore, is an integral part of the Mystery of Christ. Nothing escapes the impact of the Event. It is in Christ that creation begins, develops, and flourishes: "He is the image of the unseen God and the first-born of all creation, for in him were created all things in heaven and on earth: everything visible and everything invisible. . . . Before anything was created, he existed, and he holds all things in unity" (Col. 1:15–17); "It is in him that we live and move, and exist" (Acts 17:28); "Through him all things came to be, not one thing had its being but through him" (John 1:3)

Thus, the Risen Christ is present throughout the prodigious development of mankind and the universe. He is the center of it and the Mover. Nothing of matter, of life, can be created, transformed, or brought to its final form without the all-powerful action of Jesus Christ. Creation was conceived "in him" from all eternity; and it is "in him" that it is being realized.

But if creation is the work of Christ, at every moment both within us and around us, it is also the work of man. God has so willed it from the very beginning, and he has entrusted the universe to man: "God said, 'Let us make man in our own image, in the likeness of ourselves'"—that is, man would share, among other things, God's role as creator—"'and let them be masters of the fish of the sea, the birds of heaven, the cattle, all the wild beasts and all the reptiles that crawl upon the earth'" (Gen. 1:26). And to mankind he also entrusted man: "God created man in the image of himself, in the image of God he created them, male and female he created them. God blessed them, saying to them, 'Be fruitful, multiply, fill the earth and conquer it'" (Gen. 1:27–28).

Man undertook his task—that of turning his individual and collective energies to the conquest of the earth and the universe by both knowledge and action, by bending it to his will, transforming and developing it for his own benefit and for the glory of God—but he undertook it slowly and painfully. For the undertaking includes in itself all of man's labors in science, technology, art, and all that he has accomplished through the labor of his hands and the effort of his reason.

At the same time, man himself has taken charge of the progress of mankind; of man's personal ascent toward the expanded horizons of knowledge, of conscience, and of freedom, by means of instruction and education; of the development of mankind by procreation, with love, within the family unit.

Man's responsibilities are exhilarating and exalting. Man begins with the gift of life and of his abilities; but, from that point, he decides and creates what he is to be. He decides to change the course of a river, to build a city, to explore the heavens, or to create a child. God, for his part, confirms, guides, and strengthens; but to man he leaves complete freedom of decision and of action. How far will he allow man to go in the exercise of his power of procreation? To what point will he allow man's power over matter and life to continue to grow? The modern world gives us some exciting indications of the answer—and some rather frightening indications too. What is certain, however, is that God, the infinitely loving Father, must be pleased to see his children develop themselves personally and accept the enormous responsibilities he has placed upon their shoulders. As at the beginning of time, when God invested man with dominion over the world, he continues to look upon his work and to see that it is very good indeed.

What, then, can we possibly fear?

Nothing. For the Christian least of all should be afraid of

man's power over himself and the universe. On the contrary, he should be proud of it. We should never have left it to the Marxists to preach the nobility of labor, for we go much further than they in believing in it. For us, the world that we must build and the human race that we must glorify are all part of a divine Mystery. It is "in Christ" that man and the universe have been created; but, just as they have not been created at one instant and for all time in one definitive act, so too it is in Christ that all men live and grow and that the universe develops and is brought under control. Thus, God, through the Son, has arranged an encounter of love at the very center of labor, of every educational undertaking, and of human love. The creature is to encounter the Creator. Man's will is to become one with the divine will, and man's action is to be joined to the divine action. And the two, radically united, are to complete the work of Creation.

But man can choose to be absent from that encounter. Some men refuse to recognize God and to unite themselves to him. They want to work alone, and they reject God either directly (by saying, in effect, "mind your own business") or indirectly, by refusing to work in justice and for justice and dignity with their brother men. This is the eternal temptation for man: to make himself a god without God. "You will be like gods," says Satan. And so, man tries to build for himself "a town and a tower with its top reaching heaven" (Gen. 2:4). Such is the folly of man, who becomes man-creator only in and with Christ Jesus: "If Yahweh does not build the house, in vain the masons toil" (Ps. 127:1). Neither the philosophical materialism of Marxism nor the practical materialism of capitalism, therefore, is capable of preparing us for a glorious tomorrow. It is all up to the mature Christian, who must live the mystery of the Creation without forgetting the mystery of the Incarnation—who must live, in fact, the entire Mystery of Jesus.

There are many who are incapable of discerning the presence of God in the continuing work of creation. These are the truly underdeveloped. Because of insufficient information, or inadequate education, or simply because they have been overwhelmed by the mere struggle for existence, they are not in a position to believe in the presence of the infinite love of Jesus Christ which, in spite of sin (and it is indeed a question of sin), waits for them in order to perfect and redeem that creation by participating in it. But this is yet another aspect of the Mystery of Christ; that is, the mystery of the Redemption, which we will discuss later on.

Finally, we may say that many men simply do not know that Jesus Christ is waiting for them in the midst of all their efforts to develop man and the world by means of instruction, education, and sweat. They do not know, because no one has bothered to tell them. Christians, who should have told them, were too often of the opinion that the development of mankind and of the universe was none of God's business—or at least that he was not directly concerned with it.

Such are the various drawing boards of creation, which are the predestined meeting places of Creator and creature. We tell Christians today that human love, divinized by the sacrament of marriage, is capable of leading one to Christ and uniting one to him. There are not two different times, for example, in conjugal love—that is, a time to live one's love, and a time to offer that love to God. There is only one time; and it is in the act of loving itself that we will love Jesus Christ. Not in "offering up" an already existing human love.

We also tell Christians today that in all the acts of one's married life, even in the physical act of love, a man and wife live their love authentically and communicate God to one another.

To be sure, we should rejoice that the spiritual value of married life has finally been recognized. Even so, we must recognize that that concept is only one stage, one aspect, of a greater spirituality, a spirituality which affects all phases and the whole of one's life, a spirituality which modern man must discover in order to nourish himself from it. Otherwise, he condemns himself to a continued compartmentalization of his life—to a divorce between his life and his Christian faith.

We have not preached enough to our fellow Christians the fact that, in their efforts to better themselves both individually and collectively, in their work, they can and must unite themselves to Jesus Christ. There is no sacrament, obviously, which divinizes those aspects of human life; nonetheless, they are an integral part of the mystery of Creation, one of the facets of the total Mystery of Jesus Christ, which is itself signified by, included in, and accomplished by that Sacrament of sacraments, the Eucharist.

Man, we have said, is not finished. He is still in the state of becoming, both individually and collectively; and he is creating himself—or not creating himself—by the act of living. In struggling to humanize and personalize himself, in struggling for his complete development—a development which he creates himself—man meets Jesus Christ. He meets Jesus Christ at every moment, at every turn. For Christ, in effect, has been at work since the beginning of creation in order to engender the sons whom the Father has wanted from all eternity.

We must therefore rid ourselves of that concept of man which tells us that man is simply man, once and for all; that man is fixed and complete in his being, a creature whose behavior is liable to judgment according to a fixed hierarchy of values and according to whether or not one is a man-man or a Christian-man. We must no longer think of man as a being who subsequently will become "a virtuous man" or a saint merely because he observes this or that special system of laws for Christian-man. For a Christian is not a person who lives in a special way. A Christian is a man who lives as a man and is continually becoming more of a man. It is as simple as that. It is by becoming a "whole man"* that he will bear witness, for then he will represent to his brothers the perfect realization of that which God has intended for man from the beginning of time.

Christ came on earth to show us what a Perfect Man is. And he came to show us how to become perfect men. The hierarchical Church, when she counsels man, when she warns him, intends always to defend him and to defend his true

* By a "whole man" I mean one who is wholly open to divinization in Jesus Christ. We will return to this subject when we discuss the mystery of the Incarnation. Suffice it to say here that God, from all eternity, has willed and loved not several kinds of men, but one kind; and the "whole man," man fully developed and fully himself, is properly "Man, the Son of God."

development as a man. It is never her intention to diminish his humanity. Like Christ, the Church wishes for man to succeed. So for the Church. There are, however, individuals within that Church—churchmen, to be exact—who, as incompetent teachers, have made "virtuous Christians," "devout laymen," and even "holy priests and religious" out of individuals who were, in fact, nothing more than sick and unbalanced men and women; and such "spiritual formation" is nothing more than monstrous deformation. Certainly, we do not mean to call into question the sincerity and generosity of these poor souls whose efforts were offered to —and no doubt received by—God. They deceived themselves, no doubt; but only because they themselves were deceived. Still, we have no right to present to the Father men who are unbalanced, or deformed—monstrosities, in other words. Except in the case of a "miracle," God leaves it to doctors to cure the sick. Grace does not cure a disordered mind; that is up to the psychotherapists and the psychologists. (But here again, let us recall that the doctor, the psychotherapist, and the psychologist, in their work of healing, collaborate with Christ to bring man to his proper development.)

Some of the Christians in certain organizations and "societies" and "confraternities" and "movements" have attempted to escape the world by joining those groups. Then, when they finally emerge into the world, when they become men again like other men, they are confused and upset. They discover that there are non-Christians in the world who are very much like themselves, who live as they do and as well as they do. And so, they immediately set about trying to discover something that distinguishes them from the rest of mankind. Unfortunately, there are some ill-advised priests who help them by trying to establish, at all costs, some special characteristics which pretend to be the marks of a *visible* superiority. What a waste of time. It is not in being different from men that a Christian is a Christian; it is in being more a man than other men.†

† We should bear in mind that it is only after having studied all aspects of the Mystery of Christ that we can understand how only a Christian can *consciously* live, in their totality, all the dimensions of his own life and of the life of the world.

In speaking of work, as in speaking of man, we must go beyond the narrow concepts of yesterday; beyond the idea of the "duties" of one's state in life and of "offering up" a job well done before and after the fact, so as to render homage to God or to give a meaning to something that essentially has no meaning of its own. We must go beyond the idea of work as an expenditure of energy which does not concern God directly, but which we offer in much the same way that a child offers to his father an ash tray that he has made and which has no value other than that which paternal love attaches to it. And we must come to accept the fact that it is in the act of work itself that man must encounter God.

Obviously, we are talking about an ideal situation. Christians today are not accustomed to living their professions in that perspective. Nonetheless, we must learn to see our work in that light; and we must meditate at length on the active presence of the Risen Jesus in the *whole* of creation. For Jesus, in his Action, is present in the smallest particle of matter, in the faintest palpitation of life. And the worker who touches, with his hand or mind, that particle, who takes and develops and directs that spark of life, encounters therein the creative action of God and the eternal plan of the Father which is mysteriously realized in Jesus Christ.

Man, however, does not encounter Jesus only when he works directly, as an individual, on created matter. He also encounters him, as we shall see, in that work which is the immense collective undertaking of the whole of humanity in its struggle to master the universe, to develop it, and to place it at the service of mankind.

If man is to encounter God in his own work and in mankind's conquest of the universe, it is necessary that two "projects"—his own and God's—meet in harmony in Jesus Christ. It is necessary that man's will and God's conform to the same end. And it is at that level that there develops either collaboration between the Creator and the co-creator, or a dramatic divorce between the two. It is there, too, that man first experiences God's invitation to a life of intimate union with Jesus Christ in his daily life. It should be clear, then, that only laymen who live in the midst of the world can enjoy the authentic experience of this particular spirituality. And it is equally clear that priests and religious, as they are *today*, are incapable of counseling and guiding laymen in this form of mysticism unless they are willing to forget the classic spirituality they have learned, and unless they are willing, humbly, to contemplate the life and the activity of their layman-brother and to discover therein Jesus Christ—Jesus Christ living already in a place to which they thought they would be able to "bring" him.

"You must put God into your lives," the priests used to tell us. They were mistaken. God *is* in our lives. Our job is to find him there, to accustom ourselves to seeing him a bit more clearly every day, to learn to make out his creator-design in our lives so that we may work with him for its fulfillment.

As man works, as he educates himself, as he educates and teaches other men, how can he know that he is working in accordance with the wishes of God and that he is accomplishing what the Father has planned from all eternity? How can he know that, in the midst of his activity, he can encounter and unite himself to Jesus Christ, in whom creation continues according to that eternal plan? In order to answer that question, we will first make a few preliminary remarks. And then we will set out the four criteria in which all others are contained: man's universal climb upward; the mastery and development of the universe for the service of humanity; the free and responsible participation of every man, according to his abilities, in that difficult but exhilarating task; and, finally, the fact that such participation must be accomplished collectively and fraternally by all men on the face of the earth.

Before we can understand what is involved in the integral development of man, we must understand what we mean by "human development"; and, more basically, we must know what a man is. These definitions are all-important. What is a perfectly constituted, balanced, and developed man? What is involved in living as a man, as a couple, as the member of a community? What is meant by "working as a man," by relaxing, by participating in the life of society? All of our sciences should be turned to the task of finding the answers to these questions. They should take an inventory of nature, as it were, in order subsequently to be able to develop its resources and channel them to where they are needed, and also to be able to correct nature when necessary (for nature too has been affected by sin). We must not fear to carry out the most painstaking and detailed research on man himself, for, in doing it, mankind—Christians and non-Christians alike—are working in accordance with the wishes of the Father for his children. Jesus Christ accompanies man on his pilgrimage to the sources of this knowledge. If man is faithful to him, he cannot go astray.

The Church, because she knows Jesus Christ, the perfect man, is an expert on mankind; that is, she perceives the direction in which man must grow. And, from time to time, she recalls that direction to man. When that happens, our men of science should take their cue from her. For there can be no contradiction between their discoveries and the thought of the Church (obviously, I am speaking about the Church, and not about churchmen). There can be, of course, difficulties and hesitations along the way, before final conclusions are reached; but that should come as no surprise to anyone, for man's greatness consists not only in working unceasingly for his own development but also in searching out, step by step, what he is and what he must become. The road we must travel is sufficiently well lighted for us to be able to follow it without fear.

1. *The universal ascent of man and of humanity.*

When a man and a woman want to have a child, they invariably want certain things for that child. They would like him to be big and handsome, intelligent, educated—an artist, even; they want him to be talented, a "doer," efficient, successful in life; and they want him to be a good man. And when they have a child, finally, which they create in love, they do everything possible to assure that he will become what they want him to be.

It is not likely that the heavenly Father is less loving than earthly fathers. Man is the masterpiece of creation because God has wanted him to be such. God has made man in his own likeness, because he wanted man to be greater and more beautiful than we could have imagined until Jesus

Christ revealed it to us. Even before Christ, the Psalmist was able to write: "Ah, what is man that you should spare a thought for him, the son of man that you should care for him? Yet, you have made him a little less than a god, you have crowned him with glory and splendour, made him lord over the work of your hands, set all things under his feet" (Ps. 8:4–6).

What God the Father has dreamed of for his sons, he wishes to see come true. And so, he "raises" each one of us in such a way that we may attain *total* development. He wants man to be fully developed, to be a "complete man," in body and soul and in all aspects of his life both natural and supernatural. We must be wary, of course, of confusing the levels of man's existence; but, at the same time, we must avoid the temptation to cut man into slices and, even more, to place the resulting pieces in opposition to one another. In man, it is impossible truly to develop one aspect of his being or of his life to the detriment of another aspect. For that reason, certain schools of spirituality are gravely in error. For example, true Christian "detachment," as we shall see, is never a refusal to participate in life; instead, it is the will to live more fully, to be more truly man. No withdrawal from life can be "for the glory of God"; on the contrary, withdrawal is an insult to God, for it constitutes the rejection of a gift which God means to be used. Man has no more right to mutilate his mind than he has to mutilate his body. For that reason, the chastity of the celibate must never be a psychological castration. The celibate must not simply renounce the use of his sexual forces; he must use them at another level of existence. Every man, whoever he is and whatever his state in life, must communicate life. Not to do so—to prevent life from flourishing and flourishing "humanly"—is, simply, abortion.

Sacred Scripture does not recognize the separation between flesh and spirit, body and soul. It is not possible to conceive of the human body without its principle of life. It is true that, in studying man, we make a distinction between the animating spirit and the animated body; but we must never lose sight of the fact that man is neither an angel nor a beast, but, in the unity of his person, is Man.

Too many Christian laymen and priests have attempted to
"disincarnate" man. The attitudes with which they operate
have indeed become so deeply rooted that they have passed
into everyday language. A pious and zealous pastor will say
that his parish comprises three thousand "souls," or that so-
and-so is a "good soul." The old adage to the effect "I have
only one soul to save" should be condemned, not only because of the individualistic approach to salvation which it expresses, but also because of the false view of Christianity and
of Christians which it reveals. It is *all* of man, the whole man,
that Christ came to save; because it is *the whole man*
whom God loves and whom he invites to the prodigious and
final drama of the resurrection. It is the whole man whom
the Father, eternally loving, wishes to see grow in time. God
cannot bear to see an underdeveloped man, be he underdeveloped voluntarily or through indifference or through the
fault of others, regardless of whether it is a matter of physical,‡ intellectual, or moral underdevelopment. For each and
every man, God wants, and has always wanted, *integral* development.

We, for our part, should, in Jesus Christ, fulfill God's
desires in our regard. We should develop a hundredfold the
gifts he has given us. Man, unfinished, is an insult to God; but
the complete man is God's glory. Thus, everything that leads
to human development is in harmony with that creative process which takes place in Jesus; and, through Jesus, God is
present in it. I mean that man, whether he knows it or not, is
working with Christ when he works, on his behalf or on that
of all mankind, for physical and spiritual health, for greater
liberty, for interior harmony and unity, for more equilibrium
within himself, for greater mastery over himself, for more
understanding and knowledge, for a greater ability to communicate with other men, for more control over nature, and
so forth.

Man, as an individual, does not develop solely through his

‡ Sickness itself is always an evil. It is not "wanted" by God; and
we should not "resign ourselves" to it. We should instead fight
sickness with all the resources at our disposal. And in that battle
—as we shall see when we speak of the mystery of the Redemption
—Christ is our companion in arms.

own resources. He makes use also of those of all other men, individually and collectively, as a member of a group and of a society. He makes use, too, of the economic, political, and social structures of mankind. And Jesus Christ is present in all those men and, through them, in all those structures, insofar as they are useful in man's upward climb. Thus, because the Father desires the spiritual development of man—not only the acquisition of knowledge, but the expansion of all his faculties—we must believe that Jesus is present in all schools and colleges, in the work of the students and their teachers, in the election of class officers, and in meetings of parent-teacher associations. He is present in day nurseries and in graduate schools; in schools for retarded children and in institutes for higher learning; in governmental departments of education and in the legislative bodies that pass laws affecting the educational process. Jesus is present in all men, in all organizations, in all structures. For it is the complex of all these efforts, of all this competency and generosity (and also of all incompetency and selfishness) which speeds or retards or impedes man along the road to self-development according to the plan of the Father. Everything is related in space and in time. A teacher owes his knowledge to his own teachers; he makes use of books written by others; he owes his education, perhaps, to the fact that, many years before, other men had passed laws making education compulsory. When a boy gets his high school diploma, or a young man obtains a college degree, it is because a collective effort of men, both yesterday and today, has allowed him to become, intellectually, that which he should be.

If this is true of one aspect of human development, it is true also of all other aspects. When man grows in one of his dimensions, it is because of God, who daily creates him; but it is also because of the work of all other men. St. John tells us (1:3) that "not one thing had its being but through him." We may add that not one thing has its being but through the whole of mankind.

It is not a single person, but the whole of humanity that must reach a state of complete development. God has not created special classes of men. Everyone, without exception, receives at birth the basic right to physical and spiritual well-being. And everyone, according to his abilities, has a right to maximum development. Not to attain that development because of one's own laziness is a grave fault; but to deprive someone else of it through selfishness is a monstrous injustice. We should suffer when we see an unfinished man. We should blush and ask for forgiveness in the face of that multitude of underdeveloped men whom society has crushed and despised. God has not willed these things. We can be sure, to the contrary, that God, in Christ, is present in everything that concerns the intellectual development of man—in the struggle of student organizations for the democratization of education, in the workings of scholarship committees and student-loan committees; and also in classes for "slow learners," in neighborhood schoolrooms where volunteers teach immigrants to read and write, in trade schools, in the elementary education movement in Brazil, in the work in UNESCO, in everything everywhere.

If a Christian is satisfied with himself, with his little personal devotions, his little domestic world; if he does not become involved, according to his situation and his gifts, in man's great effort to rise, then that Christian has rejected the work of Christ, who, as the emissary of the Father, is in the process of creating a Total Humanity from which to forge his mystical Body.

We men have atrophied that mystical Body of Christ, not only because of our poverty in the order of grace, but also (and previously—insofar as we can speak of a "before" and an "after" in this context) because we have impeded the natural growth of the members of that body; and we have done this either out of laziness or selfishness, or worse, because of a distorted concept of a disincarnated "supernatural order."

We cannot say that we belong to Christ if we are not passionately involved—yes, even to the laying down of one's life—in man's upward ascent; for mankind is the cherished offspring of the Father, whom God has so loved that he sent his only Son among men in an act of ineffable love.

2. *The mastery and development of the universe for the benefit of man.*

God, as we have noted, gave the earth—that is, the universe

—to man so that he might reign over it and subject it to himself. It has been only a short time since man has begun really to dominate nature. Before that, he was occupied mostly with defending himself against natural forces and with struggling to feed and clothe himself adequately. There was little question of "mastering nature." Today, however, he is working toward that mastery—beginning with that tiny particle of matter which is his body, and then reaching out toward the land, the sea, and the universe, which he is just beginning to explore.

In this new role, man no longer functions as a workman alone in his shop, but as a member of a group, with his brothers. And slowly, sporadically, but irreversibly, he is achieving the liberation—individual and collective—of mankind. This is the beginning of the task that God entrusted to man at the beginning of time. And man is entering into a new age.

Why should man dominate nature? The answer is simple: to place nature at the service of man, for the benefit of all men. But nature, or the universe, if it can be the occasion for human growth, can also crush man. It can be inadequately controlled. Or, if controlled, it can be used only to obtain that which is immediately useful; and thus, it can render man once more its servant rather than its master by making him dependent upon it for material goods—so dependent that man would do anything to obtain those goods, even at the expense and to the detriment of his brothers, whom he would be willing to transform into slaves, and thus into enemies. Such, unhappily, are the disadvantages of unbridled capitalism, of that "consumers' society" against which young people today, in so many countries are in violent revolt, even though they may be the submissive beneficiaries of such a system, and later become, like their elders, its slaves.

We must not conclude from this, however, that it is wrong for the earth, through man's efforts, to produce more and more goods; wrong for the material standards of life slowly to be rising; wrong for men to be becoming richer in "consumer goods." What is wrong is that a few men "capitalize" unjustly on the wealth of all mankind, to the detriment of the rest of humanity, and that many men become dependent upon wealth rather than dominating wealth and using it for purposes of spiritual growth.

It is not a matter of having to choose between *having* more and *being* more. The two are not incompatible. But we must be careful that having more does not exclude, but encourages, our being more.

Nature, once subdued by man, cannot only not be used for man's benefit, and not only make of man a perpetually dissatisfied and selfish hedonist, but it can also be used by man against other men. We have not far to look for examples. Think for a moment of the vast treasure of money, intelligence, imagination, and energy that nations have expended, and continue to expend, in a deadly arms race. If God gave the earth to man, it was surely not with the intention that man should use it to kill his brother.

We have said that it is work, human effort, which characterizes man's struggle in time and space to subdue nature; and it matters little whether we speak of intellectual work or manual work, scientific work or artistic work. God, since the creation of man, has intended that man work. And every man should work; for work is one of the essential vocations of humanity. Moreover, every man has the right to work, not only in order to support himself and his dependents, which is one of the consequences of work, but also—and more importantly—in order to become a complete man; that is, to become co-creator, with Jesus Christ and all other men, of the work. Man becomes more fully man by means of work freely undertaken and performed. (That is a fact which Marxists know almost intuitively.) Work is not a punishment, but an honor. It has become difficult because of sin—"With sweat on your brow shall you eat your bread" (Gen. 3:19)—but it retains its essential dignity. Work is one of the Christian mysteries.

Great masses of humanity, unfortunately, have been excluded from that mystery. They have no work. Others—the majority—work, but they are so poorly remunerated that they can hardly support themselves and their families, and they have become slaves rather than free and responsible workers. God has not willed this; and he does not will it now. In Jesus, God strives for the liberation of all workers; and when men strive to free themselves, they can—if they know it and if they wish it—go forward consciously, in the midst of the battle, to meet their Savior. Let us remember the enormous effort expended, the great sufferings endured, and the blood shed, on behalf of the labor movement. Let us become as aware of the problems of an apprentice's first day on the job as we are of union meetings, strike votes, labor legislation, and the international labor movement as a whole. Let us be mindful of the vast army of laborers on the move throughout the world and in history. And then let us ask God to let us see these things through his eyes. Then we will not be tempted to oversimplify the problems, quickly to divide mankind into the exploiters and the exploited, automatically to canonize any demand of labor unions. Then, freed from our hidden fears, rid of our traditional middle-class ideas, with our hearts purified, we will discover—through and beyond love and hate, truth and error, sin and grace—the great battle of militant labor to realize the eternal plan of the Father: to accomplish the mastery and development of the universe for the benefit of mankind, to raise this man, and all men, to the level of his divine vocation as co-creator of the universe in freedom, pride, and the full development of his faculties.

3. *The free and responsible participation of every man according to his abilities.*

Man was not the first to claim for himself the responsibility for his life in all its aspects; he was not the one who discovered the concept of participation. It was God. From the very first pages of the Bible, God expressed his confidence in man by giving him a world—not, however, a ready-made world, but one which remains to be built; not a completed and perfect humanity, but a humanity which is still to be created. This was not the act of a benevolent employer toward his workers. God is the Father; but he is not paternalistic. No employer, certainly, would leave it to his workers to decide when they would work and what they would work on. No employer would place all of his own resources and all of his power at the disposal of his workers so that they might decide their goals for themselves and work toward those goals. God's world is not a Tinker Toy or an Erector set; it does not come with instructions for assembly. It is raw material, which has been placed in the hands of free men.

Man's job is to complete humanity. God has given him complete responsibility for the job. Men know that, sooner or later, it will be up to them to decide whether to give or withhold life. A man has a child. Will he have a second child? He has two; does he want a third? God will bend to man's will. He has infinite respect for human freedom, which is the apex of responsibility. It is an act of folly of divine love, by which God places the destiny of creation into the hands of man.

Throughout the world today, man seems to be awakening from a long sleep. Everywhere, among all social classes, in all nations, under all political regimes, men—the young first, and then the adults—are beginning to rediscover, albeit confusedly, their basic dignity. They have come to realize that they too can attain happiness, find joy in life. They sense that they too can become *responsible participants* in the whole of life, whether it be in school, in the factory, or in the office—or in any sector of the political, economic, and social worlds. They are no longer content to be given something to eat when they are hungry, to be given work when they are unemployed, to be allowed to go to school when they are illiterate, to be allowed to develop their countries when the latter are underdeveloped. What they all want is to be free, and to be the masters of their own destiny. And when they have enough to eat, when they can find work, and when they can go to school, what they want is not a higher salary, or a refrigerator, or a washing machine, or even an automobile. What they want is to be responsible. What they are demanding is more than physical or intellectual food and more than material well-being. They demand their dignity as men. But very few men know that what they are really asking for, in effect, is that they be allowed to become what God has always wanted them to be.

The collective awakening that we see in the world today is the expression of an uneasiness, a sense of surprise, the revolt of an adolescent who suddenly discovers that he has become a man after having been told for years that he was still a child. The disorder and suffering which that awakening implies are the first, painful contractions which must precede the birth of a new world.

There are certain men who reject, out of hand and without due consideration, anything which seems to them to be an obstacle, either proximate or remote, to this vindication and development of their being. Therefore, many of those at every level of society who hold positions of responsibility become frightened and attempt to hold on to the *status quo*. They are wrong to do so, for it is wrong to attempt to stifle just and reasonable aspirations. Such aspirations must be recognized and oriented toward a constructive goal. To do otherwise is a waste of energy for society, and an impediment to man's evolution toward maturity.

First in the order of execution, we must try to understand in depth this movement of dissent. And we must not try to suppress it, or to neutralize it by attempting to appease those who are contesting the *status quo* by smothering them in material advantages. An abundance of pocket money may satisfy a child, but its equivalent cannot satisfy a man. Alms, in whatever form, even if necessity compels one to accept them, constitute a humiliation; and, later on, this humiliation will increase tenfold the bitterness of the recipient's demands for justice. To create a welfare society is to create a revolutionary society, whether we are speaking of individuals or of nations as a whole. What people want is no longer merely to be handed "benefits" by society. They want participation and responsibility within the framework of society; and, more exactly, they want a just sharing of responsibility.

Many of today's angry men realize that they have been deprived by their brothers of those responsibilities, and even of goods which were intended for them. God may have given the earth to all men; but many men have never been allowed to benefit from that gift. A privileged few have taken it and kept it for themselves and made capital on it; these men—perhaps they are more enterprising than other men, or more unscrupulous, or more intelligent, or more audacious—have monopolized that gift and turned it into profit for themselves. They forget that the earth is the possession of all men; that it belongs to everyone, both individually and collectively, and that everyone has a right to a share in it. The earth is not

shared on a basis of first come first served; nor does it belong
to the hardest worker, or to the most virtuous, or to the
strongest. The law of the strongest, above all, is not the law
of God.

There are men who exercise responsibility and who justify
excluding others from a similar exercise by saying, "They
would not be able to do it, to think, to give orders, to work."
We may ask, then, whether a newborn infant is able to walk.
What would we think about parents who, in order to keep the
child from falling, would force him to stay in bed forever,
and then say, "Well, he has nothing to complain about. We
give him enough to eat." Such parents would soon be
hauled up in court, for they would have committed a crime.
They would, in effect, have killed their child; for they would
have destroyed the man that that child was destined to
become. There is not more than one principle of justice, and
that principle applies to all cases. If a man does not yet
possess that which God has offered to him of the world's
goods and responsibilities, then he has a duty to fight until
he obtains them. And if what he has received from God's
hands has been taken away by human hands, then he has a
right to take it back. Moreover, God will help him in his
struggle to regain it.

Thus, everything that works toward that conquest, or re-
conquest, of the goods of the earth works within the context
of God's plan. It matters little whether we are talking about
the possession of a house which a man can call his home, or
about the land on which a farmer works, or about the responsibility of a student in his courses or of a worker in his
job or of a citizen in his community. Everything that serves
as an inspiration, a search, or a battle for the establishment of
an economic, political, and social system within which all
men, each according to his abilities, may have a share in the
collective responsibility of mankind for the development of
the universe—everything is within God's plan. And Jesus, too,
is there, waiting for man so that he may fight side by side
with him.

4. *Collective and fraternal participation by all the men of the world.*

God, as we have said, has not given each individual man the responsibility for building up the world. He has given it to all men, collectively. No one man, therefore, can accomplish that task by himself, without the help of other men.

Man, like it or not, is bound to all men on the face of the earth; and he is even more closely bound to those who live in proximity to him. In order to develop himself, he has need of everyone, just as everyone else has need of him. He is one member of a great body. The function of grace is to transform, to divinize, the natural solidarity of that body, which is humanity; it is, in other words, to build up the Body of Christ.

Man must not only recognize the existence of that solidarity; he must also accept it, and, even more, live it in love. Those who do so act in accordance with God's will, who, from the very beginning, established in nature the roots of human brotherhood. Jesus Christ came on earth to activate that brotherhood. Man, therefore, is able to unite himself to Jesus' work. A student, for example, does not study and work alone. Within Jesus, he is united with the others in his class, with everyone living in a scholarly milieu, with other young people in his own country and all over the world. Workers, likewise, whether rural or urban, are one with their brothers who do the same kind of work, and indeed with the whole of the world of labor.

In other words, every man has the grave and difficult obligation to reconcile the necessity of personal growth with the necessity of not growing alone. He can achieve this unity only by working, with all his resources and with all other men, beginning from the place in which he finds himself, to build up the world. It is in accomplishing this act of creation that man completes himself and attains happiness. He can never be fully and truly happy without other men; for God has permanently united in Jesus Christ the destiny of the world and the destiny of all men and of humanity.

The over-all conclusion we may draw from the above is this, that we must believe in the world. Whether we wish to believe it or not, the whole of creation—this creation which, within us and under our very eyes, is continuing and working toward completion and perfection; this creation which is the very life of man, humanity, and the universe is not merely "profane." Its trademark, as it were, is divine; for it is the product of God's eternal love in his Son. It is an act of love, yesterday and today and tomorrow, for it is being created by God every day. And it is a continuing and insistent appeal to man from God, an invitation to work freely in the vineyard of the world; and thus, it is an invitation also to a divine intimacy the dimensions of which are incalculable.

Because a Christian believes in heaven does not mean that he should not believe in the world. On the contrary. In contemplating his transcendent God in his uncreated Love, the Christian discovers the source of creation. He should admire it, marvel at it, be proud of it infinitely more than the non-Christian. The non-believer can marvel only at a river whose course is too often broken and whose waters are too often polluted; he cannot know the pure source of all things. Much more than the non-Christian, therefore, the believer should believe in the unprecedented development of the earth, and he should take pride in it. He must not tamely acquiesce in things as they are, for he knows that the lengthy process of evolution—man's prodigious leap from the caverns to scientific accomplishment, from being the victim of nature to the unbelievable accomplishments of technology, science, and industry—which has overcome all obstacles and failures and won many battles, is but the unfolding in time of a work common to God and to man as Creator and co-creator.

Christians declare that they believe in "the resurrection of the body." But no one can separate the body from the air, the sun, and the earth which enable the body to live. The universe itself is but the total body of mankind, of which man is the animating principle, the mover. The whole of creation, therefore, will "enjoy the same freedom and glory as the children of God" (Rom. 8:21). There will indeed be "a new heaven and a new earth" (Rev. 21:1).

No one knows, of course, if this entry of the earth into glory will take place in historical continuity with the existence of the present-day earth and present-day humanity. It seems improbable. St. Paul (I Cor. 15:36) says, in speaking of the resurrection, that "whatever you sow in the ground has to die before it is given new life." Perhaps it will be the same for the earth. But it makes little difference. We Christians believe that our own bodies will become "incorruptible"—or, as Paul says (I Cor. 15:54), that they will "put on imperishability and . . . immortality." In the same way, we believe that it is our very own world, the world that we ourselves will have developed, which will be transformed into "a new earth." If a seed has to die (to continue Paul's analogy), it is of the greatest importance that it be a seed of much beauty and goodness, so that those qualities may be reproduced tenfold in the plant that is to rise up in triumph. For the flower is wholly contained in the seed which is planted.

The Christian, more than anyone else, should believe most fervently in the earth. He alone can grasp, through the knowledge of faith, the mystery of creation in all its breadth and depth—in its totality. He alone is aware of the infinite dimension of the earth's origin, expansion, and development. He, above all, should be filled with joy at this mystery, with knowledge, and with enthusiasm.

Why is it, then, that Christians so often seem eager to place themselves apart from the world? Why do Christians fear the world? Why are they suspicious of it? No doubt, there is always the danger that one will be led astray by the world and monopolized by it. Nonetheless, when a Christian withdraws, even partially, from mankind's struggle to conquer the world, he does not do so because of his faith; he does so because he lacks faith.

What is true of creation in general is even more true of man in particular. God has always had man in his heart. He gives a sign of that presence when he creates and develops man. That creation is not the sort of single and final act by which a mother gives birth to a child; it is rather the act of a parent who continues always to give birth to that child. Man can therefore find God in himself, in the depths of his own being and his own existence and in the existence of all men. God is the source within us of that river of life from which we take our own lives. God is Love, and man is an act of that

Love-made-flesh. When we take pride in our lives and in those of our brothers, we take pride in God. When we love our lives and those of all men, it is God whom we love and whom we glorify. When we abandon ourselves to life in order that life may be improved, we are, in fact, abandoning ourselves to the Creator. If there is a danger in all this, it is not that man will be too much loved or defended or developed; it is instead the danger that man will be badly loved, or— even more—not loved enough. The longer a Christian lives, the more he should love man; and the more he loves man, the more he will grow to love God, the Creator of man.

Creation, as the continually engendered child of the Father, must take cognizance of this relationship and, each day, make an act of love to the Father. But alone and unaided, creation cannot do so. At the apex of the created order, however, at the pinnacle of matter and of life, there is spirit and freedom in the person of man. And man, the fruit of the world, a product of the earth to which he is indissolubly joined, the free co-creator with God of mankind and of the universe, can offer himself to God. He can offer also man's universal climb to the heights, and the universe which man has conquered, transformed, and developed but which, of itself, has not the quality that would enable it to recognize its own beauty, or the mouth to give thanks to God, or the heart to love God.

On the altars of our churches, a candle, lighted in love, glorifies God. In our ceremonies, incense of human offering rises toward heaven in praise and homage. But before the liturgy of the Church there is the immense liturgy of the universe in the process of completion. The candle of that liturgy is the factory chimney which rises above the city, and its incense is the luminous trail left by jets in the sky. The candles and incense of the churches have value as offerings to God only to the extent that they are offered with love. But the factory chimney and the jet have a significance of their own; they represent and embody man's historical effort to participate in the work of God the Creator—and that work is the creation of the world which continues to take place in the sight of God and man.

May there be Christians who are fully men at the center of that sacred undertaking! Christians who will carry that work forward to its completion in Christ, so that, together with him, they may carry it beyond time and beyond death to place it finally into the hands of God.

May there be in the world a new army of men like Francis of Assisi, Christians who are fully citizens of the world! Men who will not only sing hymns of praise to creation, but also, having transformed and renewed creation, will offer it to God— offer it as a prize made rich by the human mind, increased by man's blood, marked by human brotherhood, and afire with the struggle for greater human dignity and freedom.

It is man who is the worker of creation and the priest of creation. All things are his. But he is Christ's; and Christ is God's.

Chapter Six

THE MYSTERY OF THE INCARNATION

"The Word was made flesh." What more is there to say? God, in the person of his Son, came to earth to enter into and to assume the totality of human nature. He came in the body of a man, with the heart of a man, to live a human life. God became God-Man.

We know, however, that there is unity in the universe and in humanity. Men are members of a body, which is called mankind; and the universe itself is but an extension of that body. We cannot separate a man from his father and mother, and these latter from their parents, and their parents from their own parents. . . . Man is bound to all other men. If he is to become fully man, he must accept all men as his brothers. But he must go beyond that. He must communicate with them in a spirit of love. To believe otherwise is to say that a hand can be a real hand apart from the body.

It is likewise impossible to separate man from the universe, for man cannot live without the earth, the air, and the sun. Man sprang from the earth, and he is brother to the earth. He needs the earth in order to be born, to live, and to grow. There is nothing in creation that man does not need—"not a star in the heavens," as Paul Claudel declared.

God, because he became man in Jesus Christ, takes to himself, by virtue of that humanity, all men of every time and every place. And, less obviously (but nonetheless truly), he also takes to himself all of the universe. By divinizing man, Christ will achieve the final unity of the human race in the likeness of the Trinity: "That all may be one, as you and I are one." Jesus willingly accepts the bond which unites him to man. He came through love; and it is through love that he encounters and unites himself to those who, henceforth, are to be his brothers. In Jesus Christ, God communicates with all men, so that all men may communicate with him.

The first act of communication between man and God took place through Mary, and it was in Mary that that act was accomplished. In her, as the embodiment of the highest human perfection which had been prepared from the beginning of the world, all men and all of the earth were brought into the presence of God; and God was brought into the presence of man and of the world. Mary's "yes"—a total and efficacious affirmative—was in her and through her the first "yes" of mankind to the uniting of Creator and creature, of the "natural" and the "supernatural."

Since man, in Mary, had given his assent, God came; and he thereby fulfilled his Promise and sealed the Alliance. He came, as a man among men; and because he was wholly man and infinitely loving, he came to enter into every man, into all of humanity and the world, through the presence of his love. That is the Event which dominates history. It is the realization and accomplishment of the Father's eternal plan of love: to "bring together . . . everything in the heavens and everything on earth" (Eph. 1:10).

The coming of Christ among men two thousand years ago is the visible expression of a unique and eternal act of love which unfolds in time and space, beginning with the creation of the universe and enduring until the coming of triumphant Christ at the end of the world. For the incorporation of all mankind into Christ must take place gradually, step by step, at the same tempo as man, a wanderer in history, says his "yes" as an act of love. Christ does not compel love, and he does not unite himself to a man who is unwilling.

Love is, in effect, a giving and a taking, and that giving and that taking are inseparable. A man who gives, or even gives himself, but forgets or refuses to take, is simply indulging in an act of paternalism. Love presupposes an exchange; that is, it presumes that one person be, with respect to another person and at the same time as that other person, sufficiently wealthy to give and sufficiently poor to take.

Man, moreover, limited as he is—among other reasons, because of his existence in time—cannot give himself definitively to another by a unique act of love. That love takes place in time; it is developed in time. Lovers say "yes" to one another on a particular day, and they do so in joy and in full liberty. By their mutual "yes," they commit their lives and their eternity, for that affirmative contains all other affirmatives. And the lovers marry. But then, they must set about becoming in fact that which they are in theory. They must work out their "yes" in daily life, and live out their commitment. In the same way, man's personal answer to God is given within the context of each man's concrete existence, day after day. The "yes" of Jesus to mankind, on the other hand, is perfect and complete; it is at once a total gift from God to man, and the expression of a willingness, an openness, to man's love, to the degree that man is willing to give it. That willingness of man, however, that act of consenting, can only take place step by step. Man makes himself man every day, and he should make himself a Christian every day; that is, he should surrender himself, his life, and the life of the world, to love, and thus allow Jesus Christ to make real for him, in time and in humanity, that which he has already accomplished once and for all.

It is in this sense that we can say the mystery of the Incarnation is not yet complete. No doubt, the advent of God in a man's body and in human life—i.e., the physical or historical Incarnation—is complete. But the mystical Incarnation, Jesus' coming into each man, into man's life and the life of the world, even though it has been perfectly accomplished in the love of Christ, must still be realized in time by means of man's free response.

"I am the vine, you are the branches," said Jesus. "Make your home in me, as I make mine in you" (John 15:4–5). But just as not all of the vine's branches reach maturity, so too not all men are one with Christ; not all men "make their home" in him.

Christ is the head and we are the members. "If we live by the truth and in love, we shall grow in all ways into Christ, who is the head by whom the whole body is fitted and joined together, every joint adding its own strength, for each separate part to work according to its function. So the body grows until it has built itself up, in love" (Eph. 4:15–16). But that body is not yet complete. Each day, it grows.

Christ is the cornerstone of a holy temple. "As every structure is aligned on him, all grow into one holy temple in the Lord; and you too, in him, are being built into a house where God lives, in the Spirit" (Eph. 2:21–22). But the building is not yet over. The temple has not yet been constructed.

The mystical Incarnation of Christ is realized simultaneously in two "dimensions": in "depth" and in "breadth." In depth, Jesus Christ establishes contact with man and seeks his response in love. Such is the mystery of communication and identification between Christ and the Christian, until the latter is totally transformed by Christ, until he becomes a new man in a new life, so that he may say with St. Paul, "It is now not I who live, but Christ who lives in me."

History, then, is nothing more than Jesus' continuing act of love in quest of man; his enduring declaration of love, spoken in the depths of the heart and of being; his permanent desire to incorporate all men into himself so that they may become, in him, sons of the Father and brothers among themselves.

There is only one success that is possible for man. There are not two, a "human" one for the world and a "divine" one for the Church. And that single, unique success consists in being divinized. That is the end, the total development, that God has always desired for man. God has made man "incorporable" in his very being; therefore, man can be truly man only in becoming a Christian of Christ and in Christ.

By extension, we may say that Jesus takes to himself all of mankind, and, through mankind, all of the universe. And thus, mankind collectively—man in his natural communities, in his nations, in his Church—must give an answer to Christ's love, until all men are joined together in the unity of faith in, and knowledge of, the Son of God. That is, "until we become the perfect Man, fully mature with the fulness of Christ himself" (Eph. 4:13). "And when everything is subjected to him, then the Son himself will be subject in his turn to the One who subjected all things to him, so that God may be all in all" (I Cor. 15:28). Thus, the eternal plan of the Father will be realized, "that he would bring everything together under Christ . . . everything in the heavens and everything on earth" (Eph. 1:10).

The mystery of Creation unfolds in time, as a gesture of God's love, in Christ. At the heart of that creation, by virtue of man's universal aspirations and his development of himself and of the world through work, there is already a close link between God and man. But, as creation continues, Jesus Christ, by that same gesture of love, gathers it to himself totally. By his Incarnation, he completes it and gives it its final meaning in order to bring it to its supreme accomplishment: the creation of a "new man" and a "new earth." This is the realization of man's deepest aspirations, of the need to become "great," to develop more and more—until what? Man does not always know the answer to that "until what." But we know that we have a taste for the infinite within ourselves. And, in fact, Christ invites us to rise infinitely above ourselves and to take a new greatness upon ourselves—a greatness which the Father has planned for us from all eternity: divinization in Christ Jesus. "Before the world was made, he chose us . . . determining that we should become his adopted sons, through Jesus Christ" (Eph. 1:4–5).

Christ tells us who God is, and he tells us who man is—since he himself is wholly both God and man. His purpose in coming is to make of man that which man should be. And all men are, with respect to Christ, in the process of development and of "humanization" and divinization. By incorporating us into himself, Christ allows us to achieve our fullest expansion.

To man's ineradicable desire to build a world of justice, and peace, and happiness which surpasses all previous happiness, there corresponds in Christ a desire to build a world that will reach "as high as heaven." For the whole of creation, affected as it is by the redemptive Incarnation of Christ, has received, through man, the promise of eternal life.

If mankind sets its sights low and keeps its own development and that of the world at ground level, then man will never be fully content. Man has a reminder of his divine origin and destiny in the hunger for the infinite which lies in his heart. Men, in other words, need God. If they ignore God, or reject him, then they must necessarily turn to the quest for material goods which are sought for their own sake; for men will then lack *the* supreme Good. They will want to possess everything, because they will lack that which *is* everything. And they will fight, and kill, in order to defend their material possessions. They will glut themselves with "consumer goods"—goods that they will, quite laudably, have developed, but which they will have perverted by making of them an end in themselves. Man will then allow himself to be dominated, crushed, and destroyed by the dissatisfaction of having created a surface humanity and a surface world—a humanity and a universe that do not attain the infinite depths for which they were intended. They will be plants without fruit, condemned to sterility and to final death.

Jesus Christ did not choose to use heaven as a podium from which to give man directions for the proper use and development of creation; and he did not choose to hand over a detailed set of instructions. Instead, he came down and entered into creation itself, into human flesh and human life, in order to give roots and sap to the plant which is to bear the fruit of eternity. Without Christ, creation would abort.

Henri Bergson used to say that what the world needed was more soul. Today, what the world needs is more love. And it is a matter of life and death.

Human progress is ever increasing its pace. Thousands of centuries were necessary for man to rise above the level of the savage. But only a few centuries were necessary to produce an Einstein. The energy of love, however, does not develop as quickly as the energy of the mind. What will be man's destiny, one wonders, if, as he becomes more and more rich intellectually and more and more attracted to the world which he is developing, he becomes less and less able to achieve unity through love. He will be overwhelmed by the forces he has created—a being who can launch a spaceship and compute its orbit to the tenth of a second, but who cannot master his own nature. Man, if he is too rich in intellect, in emotion, in imagination, but too poor in love, runs the risk of becoming a nothing, a puppet on a string, a shadow of what man should be.

Man's power over nature is growing proportionately to his increasing intellectual energies. It took hundreds of centuries for man to learn to fly, but only a few years for him to learn how to reach the planets. We belong to the generation of men who have discovered the secret of matter and of the energy it contains. Surely, that is something to be proud of. But we also belong to the generation of men who made their first use of that secret in order to kill two hundred thousand of their brothers at Hiroshima. We may well ask what will become of the world, now that it has fallen into the hands of man. Will it revert to a primordial chaos? Will man be forced back into the dawn of time, to begin all over again the work of building up the world? And what of society itself? Under-endowed as it is with love, will it sicken and open itself to the deadly cancer of selfishness and hate? We know now from experience that even the most humane and just of our economic, political, and social institutions are nothing unless they are animated with that same human love which transforms man himself. An old house may be torn down and replaced by a splendid new one; but that does not necessarily change the people who live in it. Society today is being reborn; but it will only be reborn in a better form if there is an increase of love in the hearts of men. Otherwise, the new society will be born dead.

We believe wholeheartedly that only the unifying force of love can harmonize and synthesize and personalize man's inner drives. We believe likewise that only love can unite mankind—only love can tear man's eyes away from his own little possessions and preoccupations to make him throw himself into his brother's arms. Love alone can make it possible for man to build up the universe—not for selfish purposes, and for it to become a bone of contention among men, but for it to be placed at the service of all men. And we believe, finally, that this love is a force which has its source above and beyond man, that it is infinitely above man; that it is, in fact, a Person, who is God incarnated and inserted into the heart of humanity, like yeast into bread, in order to make man rise; that it is Jesus Christ.

It is almost unbelievable that we have not yet studied all the consequences of that Event, which is the coming of Christ on earth. So little do we know, that we often find ourselves in the position of men for whom God has not yet come. Like the men of the Old Testament, we seem still to be waiting. We have no faith in the active presence of that Love which never fails.

Jesus Christ has come. He has allowed himself to be circumscribed by the Incarnation, by a human body, by a place, a country, a race, an era. That expedition into humanity, as it were, carried the assurance of Jesus' active presence in history—"I am with you always; yes, to the end of time"—and the proof of man's total incorporation into Jesus. The Risen Christ sent us his Spirit of Love; and the Holy Spirit has not returned to heaven, but remains on earth, in the heart of man, in a relationship more intimate even than that of man to himself and to other men. That Love is present in the whole of human history and at every instant of it. And, if man allows, Love will make of that history the sacred history of the People of God en route to the new Promised Land. For all this, God is present. But man is often absent.

Man himself must be present to the infinite Presence in order for Christ to continue his "descent" into humanity, in order for the Incarnation to be actualized each day in man and, through man, in the world. And he must be present in this way in the very heart of reality. Just as Christ wills to perpetuate his eucharistic presence on earth by means of human bread, so too he wills to make his mystical Body grow by means of the bread of human life. The existential aspiration of modern man is basically healthy. It represents a preliminary and unconscious approach to God. Modern man believes in existence, and sometimes only in existence. Unfortunately, he does not always realize that, within existence, God is waiting for him, and that, in the midst of life, is hidden subsistent Total Love. Nonetheless, it is there that man can meet his God. He has no need to look further.

Thus, to keep faith with Jesus Christ we must begin by keeping faith with the realities of daily life. Our first act should be the cultivation of loyalty to ourselves, to our lives, to our community and all the human groupings within which we live, to our relatives, our work, etc. It is there that we have the opportunity to take part in the work of creation and, by our faithfulness to that task, in the continuing Incarnation.

No one is a greater realist than the true Christian. The true Christian is not, as one may think, a man who walks with his eyes fixed on the heavens—who lives "up in the clouds." On the contrary, the Christian is a man who has his eyes fixed on the earth and who studies the ways of mankind in the light of faith so as to discover the will of the Father. He searches out the answers to questions: What is my mission? How shall I go about doing it? Who are my collaborators? What are we supposed to accomplish? And these questions pertain not only to one's whole life or to one's general vocation, but also to every week, every day, every instant of one's existence.

We have said that Jesus Christ first came into the world because of Mary's free and loving "yes." He continues to come into the world, however, because of *our* free and loving "yes." He comes to the place where we are—to us, as unique individuals in a particular situation with our own consciences and our human liberty—to live with us that small part of life which is ours, that small event which is part of the great Event.

Every day, we must choose ourselves anew; every day, we must choose our lives anew—that is, the people who are around us, the places where we are, the things in which we participate. All of that life must become ours; for that life is the "daily bread" that we must assimilate into ourselves. At the same time, we must offer it to Christ, who asks for it. We must allow Christ to transform it within himself and assimilate it totally so that—with our help—he may actualize the mystery of his Incarnation. For man's free and loving "yes" to his present life is the key to the mystical Incarnation of Jesus which lies at the heart of creation.

Certainly, not every life can be taken by Christ unto himself. It must be a life which is spent according to the will of

the Father; that is, a life spent in the betterment of man and
in the building-up of the world. That which goes against the
will of the Father—that which is sin—is rejected automatically,
like an anti-body, for it can provide no nourishment to the
Body of Christ.

Man is saved by his life; not the life that he would like
to live, or the life that he dreams of living, but the life that he
lives from day to day. Indeed, outside of life, there is no salvation.

Thus, the mystery of the Incarnation—that loving undertaking of Jesus to unite himself to all men, and by him perfectly accomplished from the beginning—is realized now in
time, and enriched by our conscious response, in love. Our
consent was necessary for this union to take place. Because we
grow each day, and because we live in a world which itself is
gestating, that consent must be expressed daily in the midst
of the process of creation. Nothing, no one must escape
Christ; otherwise, we are in danger of becoming the victims
of a deadly imbalance between creation-in-growth and that
Love which must permeate creation in order to give it its
meaning. And nothing must be taken from Christ to be destroyed or turned away from its true purpose; not a piece of
ourselves or of our bodies or of our minds; not an instant of
individual and collective lives; not a speck of earth; not a
moment of history. All things must be subjected to Christ—
with man working, consciously and free, to realize God's
plan. All things are sacred in their origin; but all things must
be consecrated by man, who has been divinized by Jesus
Christ.

Nonetheless, there are many Christians who have long
been absent from the world. They emigrated to a "spiritual"
universe that they created for themselves, or that was created
for them, where they lived in the shelter of moral rules and
religious rites which, since they had nothing to do with life,
were meaningless in themselves, uninspiring for the faithful,
and a scandal and counterwitness for everyone else. Such
Christians have become aliens, strangers on earth. They must
return to their mother country. They must be naturalized and
become men once more.

There can be no real "spiritual life" unless life itself is lived fully. A Christian who is absent from life is a man who has separated himself from Christ.* If he does not enter first into communion with Christ's presence in life, he cannot enter into real communion with Christ's presence in the Eucharist: "The Word was made flesh; he lived among us" (John 1:14).

* Obviously, I am talking about a Christian who lives, as we say, "in the world." Someone who, by a special vocation, "leaves the world," is only physically separated from it; he does not flee from life, but chooses an alternate way of being present with his brothers in the construction of the universe. He is present spiritually—directly, we may say, in Christ, in whom man and the world are united.

Chapter Seven

THE MYSTERY OF THE REDEMPTION

The mystery of Christ's Incarnation cannot be understood or fully lived unless it is joined to the mystery of the Redemption. In fact, the Incarnation of Jesus must be—because of sin—a redemptive incarnation. Therefore, before discussing the Redemption itself and trying to understand how we must live it out in our daily lives, it would be useful to examine the notion of sin and suffering.

Man was created out of love, and for love. His vocation is love—not human love alone, but, beginning with human love and through it and in it, also a love divinized and transfigured by the presence of Jesus Christ. The final purpose is for man, in Jesus Christ, with all other men and in a renewed universe, to love with the love of the Trinity. And that is heaven.

As a product of love, man—along with all of mankind and the whole of the universe—must return God's love. It is man's destiny to do so; and without it he can succeed neither with his life nor with the life of the world.

Since man was made by love, it follows that love has willed man to be free. For there can be no love without freedom. To love someone is to want him to be free; it is to lay down one's life, if necessary, to set him free. But freedom, even though it also is a product of love, is not given as such to man. Only the seed of freedom is planted in the human heart. Man's freedom is a freedom which must be tended and made to grow. And it will grow only through love. Man must be free; but he will be truly free only when he learns to love without reservation. Selfishness imprisons man and makes a slave of him; but love sets him free.

We are not talking about physical freedom, but about that extraordinary and inalienable right that we all have to accept or to refuse, to rebel or to submit, to say yes or no with respect to our lives. And that right is operative no matter what external pressures may be brought to bear, and no matter what internal conditions may prevail. Such is the freedom to love.

Man is invited to love. Of course, he can refuse the invitation. And that is sin.* Sin is always a conditional love, a love mingled with self-love, or a simple refusal to love throughout one's life.

Sin is the refusal to commit oneself wholly to the creation of oneself (sloth). It is the deformation of that creation (sensuality). It is the creation of oneself for one's own sake while forgetting about one's brothers (selfishness and pride).

Sin is the refusal to risk one's life in order to give life to another in love, so that the other person may go forward or so that other lives may be lived (the sins of married couples and of families). For to love means to give life to another, or to others.

Sin is the refusal to commit oneself to the creation of the world. And it is the deformation and perversion of that creation by developing it solely for one's own ends (the sins of labor, in the most general sense of that term).

Sin is the refusal to allow God's Love to enter into our lives so that he may take control of it, and through it reach our brothers and the world (rejection of Christ and of a relationship with him).

---

* Sin has never been disobedience to a "rule." The commandments of the Church, for example, are only signposts on the road of love. They remind us, among other things, that we cannot claim to love God and to be loved by God if we do not take communion —or communicate with God—at least once a year. If one sins, it is not because he disobeys that particular commandment; it is because, in disobeying it, he proves that he does not love.

Sin is the refusal to recognize and acknowledge God as the supreme end of each man and all men and of the world. It is the refusal to render homage to God. It is the building of a god for oneself in place of God, by thinking only of oneself, by taking for oneself alone that which belongs to other men and to God. It is the making of oneself the center of creation, and thereby displacing mankind and the universe and causing imbalance and disorientation in the world.

All these refusals are failures to love. They cause man and the world to lose their direction, and they place them outside the plan of the Father, which is to unite all things in love. There are, in effect, only two great forces in the world. One is the force of expansion toward God and toward others; and that force is called love. The other is the force of withdrawal into oneself; and that force is called selfishness, pride, and all the other names which signify aspects of that egocentric regression.

Because God's plan is a plan of love, which can be realized only through love, man's refusal to participate in that plan "offends" God in his very being—which is love. Sin is the non-requital of God's love. But, because of the Incarnation, sin also offends God because it affects man. Since Jesus Christ united humanity and divinity within himself, and since through him God has united himself to all humanity by taking mankind to himself in its totality, the rejection of one member of the body of humanity implies the rejection of the Head. If we refuse to love man, then we necessarily refuse to love God: "Anyone who says, 'I love God,' and hates his brother, is a liar" (I John 4:20). Jesus himself said so in so many words: "In so far as you did this to one of the least of these brothers of mine, you did it to me" (Matt. 25:40). And he warned us that we would be judged according to the degree that we proved our love for him by loving our brothers for their own sake: "I was hungry and you gave me food; I was thirsty and you gave me drink; I was a stranger and you made me welcome. . . . in prison and you came to see me" (Matt. 25:35). Some will say, "But Jesus is talking about his own people, about those who accept him and believe in him and consciously follow him." Nonsense. A father does not dis-

tinguish between his children who love him and those who
ignore and reject him. Jesus did not attach conditions to his
redemption of man through love. As a prisoner of his love, he
gives himself to all men, without exception. "His own people"
are all men—men of every time, forever. When there is rejection, it does not come from God. God does not reject
man. He cannot. If he did, then he would not be infinite Love.
But man is capable of rejecting God.

Love gives to man the one chance that he has to save himself. Man must love God with all his strength; and he must
love his fellow men in the same way. Jesus tells us that these
two loves are but one love, that they are inseparable.

Men, whether they like it or not, are bound to one another.
All of mankind is one unit. Men cannot really be men except
to the extent that they are united to other men as members are
united to a body. Men, in fact, compose a body: humanity.
This human solidarity can have one of two consequences: It
can work either to man's benefit or to man's detriment. The
member who loves and develops within the body gives life
to all the other members. But the member who places obstacles
in the way of love destroys himself and weakens the rest of
the body as well. All non-love—that is, all sin—affects all of
mankind. And that is why, when we confess our sins, we
acknowledge them before God and before all men living and
dead.

In the same way, man is bound to all of creation, in his
being and in his acts. He lives in the universe, and he builds
the universe; but he can halt that construction, or deflect it
from the purpose for which it was intended. When man does
that, he stamps sin, as it were, on the heart of creation. An
apartment building, for example, is badly built because the
builder has no professional ethics. He skimped on essentials,
and used cheap materials in order to turn a larger profit. The
apartments are too small, too noisy, badly laid out, and un-
attractive. People who come to live in that building will un-
doubtedly be influenced by their surroundings. If they commit immoral acts, how can we measure their responsibility,
compared to the responsibility—the less evident, but nonetheless real responsibility—of those who were indirectly or di-

rectly involved in the construction of the building, and who have carved their own sin onto the very walls of the building? Such buildings—and such "developments," such cities, such schools and universities, such factories and offices—condone and multiply the sins of man. And the same holds true, of course, for labor and building regulations, for laws—for all the "structures" which, at every level, control man's life in society.

Thus, sin—like love—is introduced by man into the heart of all creation. And we may therefore say that creation, whose function is to nourish man and help him in his development, can also become an obstacle and the occasion of man's fall. For that reason, Jesus Christ, through man, must carry the Redemption even into the center of creation. For creation too must be saved. "The whole of creation is eagerly waiting for God to reveal his son. It was not for any fault on the part of creation that it was made unable to attain its purpose, it was made so by God; but creation still retains the hope of being freed, like us, from its slavery to decadence, to enjoy the same freedom and glory as the children of God. From the beginning till now the entire creation, as we know, has been groaning in one great act of giving birth" (Rom. 8:19–22).

It is often said that man today, and particularly the young, are no longer aware of a sense of individual sin, but that they are more intensely conscious than ever of their responsibility for the collective sins which afflict humanity. This attitude —so long as it does not exclude the recognition of personal faults—is a proof of maturity.

Whence come unemployment, inadequate salaries, slums, illiteracy, the exorbitant rate of infant mortality in some countries, hunger, underdevelopment, war? From selfishness, pride, profiteering—from all the sins of man. All of these things are the results of sin—of sins added one to another and linked one to another; from chain-sinning, as it were. And all of mankind is responsible for these sins.

What is an individual man's responsibility for that tragic collective sin? No one knows. Only God knows, for he alone sees each one of us in our own place within the torrent of yesterday's and today's humanity. He alone knows what we are, and why we are what we are. He alone knows what advantages we enjoy and what problems we face. He alone sees our place and function in the construction of the world, and the degree of our commitment to the brotherhood of mankind. And God alone is able to go beyond our outward behavior and judge us according to the amount of love that we have.

What we men know, however, is that we have some responsibility. We know that the non-love in our lives never exists in a vacuum, but, by some mysterious process, combines with the non-love of other men to form those horrendous collective sins which are the scourge of mankind. And since we are all responsible together, we must strive together to make up for those sins.

There are two kinds of suffering in the world. There is that suffering which is part of nature itself; and that kind is a mystery. And there is that suffering that man adds and superadds every day to necessary suffering by his sins; and this kind can be explained and understood.

It is true that evil existed in the world even before man took a hand in it. For there is no change in nature, no progress, without struggle and suffering and death. A grain of wheat must split, rot, and die before a new plant can rise. An animal, in order to live and survive, must fight and kill. The earth, and the universe itself, emerged and developed only after incredible upheavals. Creation often seems intent on revenging itself for man's progressive domination of it. Why? I do not know. No one knows. If there were no Jesus Christ, I would rebel at the apparent injustice of it all.

The other kind of suffering—that which man creates for himself—is even worse, more horrible and tragic, for man, because man knows its origins and he knows how it could be avoided. Nonetheless, he sometimes seems to take pleasure in increasing that suffering rather than diminishing it. This is the suffering that sin causes in the world. It is a suffering that ranges from the hurt feelings of a neighbor because of a thoughtless word to the mass slaughter of a nation. In between those two extremes, there are such things as the manifestations of non-love in broken homes, in disrupted communities, in the reduction of labor to virtual slavery, etc. There is no sin so small, so obscure, that it does not produce suffering; for every sin generates disorder where there should be order, disharmony where there should be harmony, self-ishness and hate where there should be love: "Sin entered the world through one man, and through sin death, and thus death has spread through the whole human race because everyone has sinned" (Rom. 5:12).

Let us make no mistake about it. There are infinitely more men who die from hunger and war than from earthquakes or natural catastrophes. There are more children who die from lack of the most basic care than from "natural" diseases. There exists, nonetheless, a terrible illogic in man by which he, perhaps out of hypocrisy, demands that God explain why there is so much natural suffering in the world; and, at the same time, he ignores completely the suffering that he him-self creates every day—suffering which, moreover, he could limit, and then eliminate, through love.

We must not think that God should step in and prevent man from hurting himself. We would not want a God who would turn us into remote-controlled robots by intervening in our lives constantly in order to keep us from doing wrong or hurting ourselves or doing something dangerous—a God who would permit us only to do what is safe, who would choose the path we are to follow and tell us what precautions to take. We would not even want a God who would catapult us out of a car that was about to have a collision, or who would make us miraculously grow wings if our airplane was going to crash. No. We want to live dangerously. We want to be free. We want to win—but we want to do it ourselves. And this is not pride. It is the will to be what we are: men. To be men, however, we have need of God's love, and we must ask for that love with all our strength. But that love does not do away with our freedom; instead, it gives us freedom.

The god who is a wonder-worker is not our God. Our God is a Father; which is to say that he is loving, that he loves his children enough to allow them to run the risk of sin and the consequences of sin, that he loves them enough never to allow them to suffer alone.

All suffering, per se, is evil. It is foolish for us to try to explain suffering by pretending that, somehow, it is good. That would be making excuses for God. Suffering is evil, and it will always be evil. But in "the new heaven and the new earth" there will be no more suffering and no more death: "Here God lives among men. He will make his home among them; they shall be his people, and he will be their God; his name is God-with-them. He will wipe away all tears from their eyes; there will be no more death, and no more mourning or sadness. The world of the past has gone" (Rev. 21: 3–4).

I do not believe that God "sends us suffering" in order to "punish us" or "for our own good." I cannot believe in a God who is Love and who tortures man to make man better. Sin is indeed punished; but it is man who decides on the punishment. In disrupting creation, he creates severe penalties for himself and his fellow men. There is no need for God to add even more punishment. We sometimes see a small child run away from his mother in the street; the child falls and hurts itself—and the mother spanks the child. The spanking serves no purpose, for the child has already been punished for running away by hurting himself. The mother's reaction is emotional; it is illogical, and an imperfection. God does not act out of emotion, or illogically, or imperfectly. He does not spank his children. On the contrary, he comforts them and helps them to bear the hurt.

I do not approve of those Christians who, prostrated by suffering, can "bless the will of God." We do not need people who are resigned and submissive. We need men; men who will fight against suffering. And when suffering refuses to submit, when evil refuses to change, then man must make use of the grace of Jesus Christ to convert it into good. Thus, useless waste products are thrown into the fire—where they are converted into heat and light.

Even at the purely human level, man can make use of suffering in order to grow. The mountain climber who voluntarily risks his life in an ascent suffers from cold, hunger, fatigue. He arrives at the summit a better man for his effort and his suffering. And if that effort and suffering are such as hardly to be borne, he is changed from the man that he was into a hero. If, on the other hand, he reaches the summit in a helicopter, he reaches his goal—but he remains unchanged. In accepting suffering, man is not asked to do anything which is beyond his strength.

Each one of us has a road to travel, the road of our individual lives. That road is filled with problems. Together, we have a world to conquer. It is by effort and struggle that we can succeed in both tasks. There are always difficulties and resistance, but if we face up to them we will end up better men after the battle than before. God, as we have already said, did not give us a ready-made world, but a world that has to be constructed; and we become men when we build it in the midst of difficulties. A child whose parents remove every difficulty and solve every problem will never become strong; he will never mature. Our God may never spank his children, but neither does he spoil them.

Thus, I do not believe that God *wills* suffering. As in the case of sin, he must allow it, "unwillingly," in order truly to love his children. He did not make either man or the world perfect. Man must become perfect, even as his heavenly Father is perfect. And he must struggle so that the world may become perfect too. But he is not required to struggle singlehandedly—for it would then be impossible for him to accomplish anything—but to cooperate with Christ. For Christ is the final proof that God has not resigned himself to the existence of suffering. Christ has wholly committed himself to the fight against suffering and death. Without Christ, there is only despair. But with Christ, there is hope and victory. And that is the mystery of the Redemption.

From all eternity the Father has planned that man be his son in his Son. It is a unique project. There is no initial failure, and then a "making-up." It is also an original project, as sin and suffering are original, but it enters into time through the life and passion of Jesus Christ.

The mystery of the Redemption is the reorientation of man and the universe, in Christ and by him, in the direction of his final development—which is divine Love. That is the last battle, and the victorious battle, of Christ against sin, suffering, and death, so that man, humanity, and the universe may attain the goal for which they were created. The great enemy, therefore, the historical obstacle, is sin; that is, non-love, suffering, and death.

How can Christ overcome this enemy? It was necessary that he take upon himself all the sins of man in order to fight and conquer them. But Christ is infinitely pure; he can have no part of sin. That is the mystery. But, as before, love clarifies the mystery.

The man who really loves his wife or his friend loves without conditions and without reservation. He accepts the loved one "as is," with all his virtues and all his imperfections, and even with his sins if he is a sinner. A lover does not break up with the loved one because the latter sins. Instead, he draws nearer to the sinner, embraces him, welcomes him—and takes his sin upon himself. "Not only do I not condemn you," he says, "but I will help you to bear your sin." In this way, too, Jesus, united to man, takes our sins upon himself. "For our sake God made the sinless one into sin," St. Paul says (II Cor. 5:21). Not one of our faults is foreign to him, whatever may be our individual sins or those tragic collective sins that we spoke of earlier. Because his love is infinite, because he is united to all men, because he is present by his Incarnation, he accepts for himself man's battle against non-love throughout history. And he does this without ever having sinned himself.

Anyone who has ever experienced disgust for the sins of a friend, and has known the tension of continuing to love him, can imagine Jesus' agony. Cut to the heart by man's sin, but filled with love, he suffered to the point of asking the Father to deliver him from this tragic confrontation. He fell to the ground and sweated blood. But he did not abandon man. He continued to love man. Man is his brother, and Christ did not judge man. Rather, he loved man all the more. He united himself to man and took man's sin upon himself.

It was necessary that Jesus also receive all the suffering of the world—the suffering endured by man for the continuing creation of the world—in order to give meaning to that suffering, and the useless suffering, which is the fruit of sin, in order to reclaim it and put it to use.

How could he do this? His body was not large enough to receive the number of whiplashes that would have been necessary; nor his brow, to take the necessary number of thorns. In his passion, Jesus was tortured and put to death. But he was not more tortured, nor did he die more, than have thousands and thousands of men through the centuries (and, most recently, in the concentration camps of World War II). How, then, could he take upon his shoulders the suffering of all mankind since the beginning of time?

I began to understand the answer one day on Good Friday. I had gone to visit a sick child. The doctor was there, and he had just announced that he would have to do a bit of very minor surgery. We took the child to a window and sat him upon a chair. His mother was at his side, of course, pressed against him. Each time the doctor touched him the child registered pain—and so did the mother. Each time the child groaned, the mother groaned. When the doctor had finished, the child felt nauseous and had to be put to bed. And the mother felt nauseous and had to be put to bed. In that instant, I understood: When we love, we suffer with the suffering of the one we love.

That, I think, was the true suffering of Jesus Christ. It was not so much the lashes and the crown of thorns and the carrying of the cross. It was the suffering of love. Jesus, because he has infinite love for all men and is aware of every man, saw, knew, and suffered all of man's sufferings. With the weight of these sufferings on his back, he made the way of the cross. His cross was the wooden cross of the Gospels; but it was also, and above all, the gigantic cross which has been erected at the center of human history.

When, finally, Jesus was nailed to the cross of wood and suspended between heaven and earth, at the moment when he died the death of a man through love, he took upon himself all the deaths of his brothers. He could not defend himself, for to do so would have been to defend himself against love. He was incapable of not opening his heart to all men. In a very real sense, he was a victim of his own love. His Incarnation was a success. He had incorporated all of humanity into himself. On Calvary, all of mankind was joined together in him. The whole of his Body was nailed to the cross.

Then Jesus, the first of all his brothers, the Son of Man, the Head of the great body of humanity, himself total awareness and total freedom, infinite love, was totally alone. And he grasped all the members of his Body, mankind and the universe, their sins and their sufferings and their death, and with one great cry he gave it all to the Father: "Father, into your hands I commit my spirit." It was a spirit enriched with all of humanity, past, present, and future. It was all of man, all of human history, and all of creation, now reoriented by Love toward Eternal Love. It was the redemption of the world.

Three days afterward, the Father gave life back to his Son—his own life, and the life of all mankind. It was, however, a life that had been purified and made new by love. And that is the life which is the New Life and which shall endure unto eternity.

Religous literature abounds in texts which celebrate the suffering of the Savior. Similarly, there are many so-called "spiritualities of the cross," some of which give rise to attitudes and deeds which may be generous and sincere but which are, nonetheless, often unhealthy. We used to offer to man the ideal of the resigned Christian whose back was bent to receive lashes from the whip of fate. And man rebelled. He turned away from us—whereas we Christians are the only ones who can save man from despair in the face of suffering and death.

It is not the blood shed by Jesus which saves the world. It is not suffering that redeems. Only love redeems. Suffering is an evil, even after the Redemption. When the Church says, "O happy fault because of which we have been given a Savior," she is not canonizing sin. Because Jesus made use of suffering as the occasion for redeeming us, we must not be tempted to attribute some magical power to it. We must not "resign ourselves" to suffering and seek it out. Jesus did not look for suffering and death. He did not save man by committing suicide. Instead, in the midst of the Event which was his life on earth, he lived suffering. He was arrested, tried, condemned, tortured, and executed. All these things happened to him in human history, just as they have happened to other men before and after him. He did not try to escape from them as though he were some sort of wonder-working demigod rather than the Man-God who is Love. He submitted. He did not refuse to accept a single instant of it. What was forced upon him from without, he accepted within himself. When his executioners thought they had taken his life by force, he, in a gesture of infinite love, took it and gave it willingly. He used what happened to him. He joined together in it all the suffering and death and all the "passions" of his brothers who fight for the development of mankind and the world. He made up for the monstrous and senseless suffering which is the result of sin. And, having taken upon himself the intolerable weight of all this, he caused it to become, through love, an acceptable exchange for sin. Thus, out of suffering and death he forged the material of redemption. From infinite love, which is the conqueror of non-love, he worked the Redemption.

Suffering in itself is worth nothing. Only love can give life.

The Redemption was carried out to its completion. All men have been saved, and the whole of creation has been re-established in love. But Jesus does not want to save man if man is unknowing or unwilling. He does not wish it, because if he did save man in that way he would have to do violence to man's freedom and, therefore, to man's dignity: "All of us who possess the first-fruits of the Spirit, we too groan inwardly as we wait for our bodies to be set free. For we must be content to hope that we shall be saved" (Rom. 8:23). Man must not only receive and accept salvation from the hands of Christ; he must also participate. Otherwise, God would be a paternalistic God—the kind of God that, as we have already said, cannot be God. "And if we are children [of God] we are heirs as well: heirs of God and coheirs with Christ, sharing his sufferings so as to share his glory" (Rom. 8:17). But Jesus goes even further. Just as we are responsible for the realization of creation, so too are we responsible for the actualization of the Redemption. It is up to us to bring salvation to mankind and to the universe.

And so, the Redemption, which has been lived by Jesus, the Head of the body of humanity, must now be realized, day by day, in the members of that body. But just as the mystery of the Creation and of the Incarnation of Jesus Christ can be complete only with man's free assent, the mystery of the Redemption can become effective only through the full and loving consent of each one of us: "In my own body [I] do what I can to make up all that has still to be undergone by Christ for the sake of his body, the Church" (Col. 1:24). That which is missing from the sufferings of Christ is not human suffering; he has already accepted, borne, and offered human suffering to the Father. What is missing is that we freely give him our suffering, and that, in him and with him, we offer our suffering for the salvation of the world.

We Christians, therefore, must not make a mere pious memory of Christ's passion. The "way of the Cross" is not a spiritual exercise suitable for those tender souls who are more concerned with the past than with the present and the future. The true Way of the Cross is not finished, for it has two dimensions. In one dimension, it was completed by Jesus Christ two thousand years ago, in the streets of Jerusalem. In the second dimension, however, the Way of the Cross is being followed by the whole of humanity, by all the members of Jesus Christ. This Way of the Cross comprises all the streets of humanity, all the paths of history and of time. It runs through man's torn body, through his divided heart, through his convulsed being. It passes through divided couples, destroyed families. It passes through the world of labor, and through the organization or disorganization of labor by which man is made a slave. It passes through the lines of the unemployed, through understaffed and inadequate schools, through the slums, the hospitals, the prisons. It passes through underdeveloped countries. It passes through the battlefields. It passes everywhere that there is suffering, great or small, since all suffering affects man and strikes at the total body of humanity.

The cross dominates the world and time as it dominated Jerusalem. For sin too remains and unfolds in time, just as the Redemption is a divine and continuing action—an uninterrupted mystery of love which shall last as long as the race of man.

How can man, free and loving, enter into the heart of this mystery and live it as a conqueror with Jesus Christ the Conqueror?

The first battle to be fought is that against sin. It is, however, a battle that we cannot hope to win by ourselves. We need Christ. God was unable to leave us alone to face our non-love, to harm ourselves or others, to kill one another like unnatural brothers in a family feud. He therefore sent his Son, not to force us to cease sinning (for that would violate our human freedom), but to deliver us from our sin by taking it upon himself and obtaining forgiveness for it. If we renew that redemptive act with Jesus Christ and in him, then we will save ourselves and our brothers.

Today, man must consciously give to Christ the sins for which Christ has already made himself responsible. In order to do this, man must first recognize his sins and admit that he has committed them. He must also recognize and acknowledge the collective sins of social classes and communities, from the very smallest to the largest (which is humanity itself), in which man lives out his life. No man today can "wash his hands." No man can say that he is not responsible for those terrible plagues which are the collective sins of humanity. These sins surround us on all sides. They take place before our very eyes. They cause all mankind to cry out in pain; and in those cries we hear a question which God asked long ago: "What have you done to your brother?"

Today's Christian, if he is mature, will rise above the narrow concept of one's own little sins, his violations of a set of regulations that was composed for children. Instead, he must examine his whole life in order to discover the acts of non-love—his own, and those for which he bears the responsibility along with his associates.

Once more we see the fundamental necessity for a Christian to live his life fully. If he is able to face up to the reality of his daily life, in the circumstances in which the Father has placed him, then he will be able to uncover, acknowledge, and take upon himself his own sins and his share of the sins of the world. The more fully he lives his life in those human societies into which he was born, the more he will be consciously "committed" to his world, and the more he will become a true brother to those around him. He will become "one of them"; or rather, he will become them by sharing their joys, their suffering, their victories, and their defeats. In short, the more "incarnated" a man is, the more easily will he be able to detect, accept, and bear his sin and the sin of his brothers.

Once more let us say that Jesus Christ waits for man in the midst of daily life and in all the dimensions of that life. Since Christ's passion, man can no longer despair, no matter what his sin or that of his brothers. He is no longer alone with that sin; for Christ the Redeemer is mysteriously there, waiting silently for man's free response to his saving love. That response must be an essential act of faith: "Jesus, I believe that your love is stronger than my sin and that of my brothers. I believe that no sin exists which you have not already taken upon yourself. I believe that forgiveness has already been granted, for your conquering love has destroyed evil as fire consumes wood. Today, I freely give my sin, and that of my world, to you; and with you and in you, I give it to the Father, so that I may consciously receive from your hands a new life, that life of pure love which, on Calvary, you restored to all of mankind."

The Christian must live that spiritual attitude every day of his life. But he must also make it effective through use of the sacrament of Penance. In this way, the Redemption is reintroduced into time, into the life of man and the life of the world.

The Redemption as we have seen is not only a struggle and a victory over sin. It is also a struggle and a victory over suffering and death—over that suffering and death that Jesus Christ grasped, took to himself, and "dynamized" by means of his infinite love. Nothing that we have said about acknowledging our sins and giving them to the Father, in Christ the Savior, would be valid if we were not willing to participate also in the struggle which is the second aspect of the unique act of our salvation.

Before thinking of accepting and offering suffering to God, the Christian must fight against suffering. That is an absolute obligation. Otherwise, the Christian becomes that "resigned soul" whose attitude is entirely contrary to man's God-given and essential dignity. We cannot repeat often enough that suffering is an evil, and that we must do all we can to control it and reduce it. In that effort consists one of the aspects of man's involvement in creation: the painful and tragic confrontation and struggle between an intelligent creature and the universe which he gradually conquers and dominates; the individual and collective struggle ranging from direct action on raw material and on life to action in a world and a human race already transformed. This, in a word, is the function of work, of technology, of all the sciences. It involves a commitment to and a participation in man's political, social, and economic structures. It requires that man be actively present in the battle to develop and complete the world—a battle in which all men relate to each other, in which those who suffer and die are soldiers killed in action, and in which progress is achieved only at the price of temporary defeat, of wounds and pain. All of this, and this alone, allows mankind to go forward.

If man is to become more human, and if the Christian is to become more a child of God, he will not do so by being passive in the face of suffering, but by fighting against suffering. The blood shed for the mastery of the universe, for the establishment of a just society, for the liberation of man and his integral development, is a redemptive force. Thus, a sick man, before offering his suffering to God, must fight with all his strength against his sickness. The laborer must fight against the pain of work, and also against inhuman working conditions. The student must struggle with the difficulty of overcoming the world by knowledge; but he must also fight against the abnormal conditions imposed on man "in order to train his mind." In other words, man must fight against all suffering—against both the suffering which man experiences in trying to master the world, and the suffering which results from his own selfishness, which is a supernumerary suffering caused by man's individual and collective sins.

If we can never resign ourselves to suffering, if we can never give up the struggle against it, and if we can (and sometimes we can indeed) decrease suffering, we must admit that suffering is, in one sense, invincible. For one thing, the struggle against suffering itself causes suffering. And that is the mystery. And that is the signal for rebellion and despair among those who do not know, or do not believe that, since Jesus' passion, there is an extraordinary force concealed within suffering which is capable of raising up the world. That force is the strength of the Redemption. It is the infinite strength of Jesus' redemptive love. It is the unitive strength of man burdened with sin and of the body of humanity which develops in history and in the world. It is the strength of a world perpetually harassed by a destructive non-love. It is the living strength which is ever victorious over death.

This strength, however, is a hidden force. It can be perceived only by the eyes of a believer. It is also a captive force, which only man's freedom can take and set free so that it may become operative. To take advantage of that strength, man has only to go to Jesus Christ, the Redeemer, who waits for him in the midst of suffering. For before that suffering belonged to man, it belonged to the Savior. Jesus took it, lived it, and made it part of himself. He entered into it, transformed it, and dynamized it with all the power of his love by reclaiming it in order to give it to the Father, as a free gift.

We have said that, even at the purely human level, man can grow through suffering if, instead of resigning himself to it, man struggles against it and integrates it into his upward climb. For the believer, however, suffering can also be the occasion for his own salvation and that of the world; he has only to consent to meet the suffering and triumphant Christ in the midst of each one of his sufferings, and to refuse to live life only on its surface.

Man was given the Redemption before he could freely take it to himself. Now, he must, while living, take it from the hands of Jesus Christ—not in a sort of mystical rapture or through imaginary sufferings, but by being totally present in his everyday life. It is there, and nowhere else, that man will find his path in the unique and true Way of the Cross which leads to the resurrection.

The energy of which we have spoken, which lies at the heart of suffering, is too often forgotten; and man too often deprives himself of his greatest means of liberation, renewal, unity, and progress. Man wants to save himself alone and to build the world without setting free the love won by Jesus Christ, the love which is mysteriously available within the smallest suffering. But man cannot reformulate the economy of salvation in time. If the mortar of love is not present around every stone of his edifice, he builds in vain. Since the advent of sin into the world, that love can flourish only as the result of a painful but victorious effort by the suffering members of Christ. We must not waste a single human suffering, or the Redemption cannot be fully realized for the men of our time.

Often, too, the strength hidden in suffering is misused. We make use of suffering for itself, and ignore its redemptive content. Too often man decides to "go it alone" with his misfortune, to remain crushed under the weight of injustices and of sufferings which someone has advised him to "offer up for the salvation of your soul." And that is one of the worst possible spiritual perversions. It is not a question of allowing man to suffer, for suffering is an evil. What we must give man, beyond a suffering against which he has fought, is a meeting with the suffering Christ. We must never thank God for suffering, any more than we can thank him for sin. But we should thank him for allowing us to meet the Savior, who, despite sin and despite suffering, waits for us to allow us to benefit from his struggle and his victory *against* sin and suffering.

It is not true that "God tries those whom he loves." But it is true that the more we suffer, the more Christ is present in us. Because he has already suffered and conquered our suffering, he is aware of us and available to us—not to remove our suffering, but to allow us to conquer it in turn, through his love, and to turn it into a redemptive force.

As long as a child plays quietly, his mother remains in the kitchen preparing dinner. But if he does something

naughty and hurts himself, his screams will bring the mother
running to help him. Despite his behavior, she is there, more
attentive and loving than ever. But the child, nonetheless,
can rebel against his hurt. He can throw himself on the floor;
he can kick the piece of furniture on which he hurt himself;
he can strike out at his mother who is trying to help him.
In that case, he suffers even more, for his pain remains and
he now has to bear it alone—along with his frustration. But
if he loves his mother, he goes beyond his pain and throws
himself into her arms. She does not take away the hurt, but,
in holding her child, she bears his hurt with him.

In the same way, suffering can either separate us from
God or bring us closer to him. Man can reject Jesus, who
is present within that suffering. He can accuse Jesus of
causing the pain and try to "get even" with Jesus. Or, having heard Jesus softly speak his invitation to love, he can,
by assenting with all his strength to Jesus' redemptive act,
abandon himself to the Savior, and offer himself by allowing himself to be offered. In that sense, where there is much
sin, there Jesus is most present in order to receive and pardon. Where there is much suffering, Jesus is most present in
order to save his child; that is, to love him.

Mary accompanied Jesus on the Way of the Cross. She
stood near him on Calvary. But she was not beaten with
Jesus, and she was not crucified with him. And yet, the
Church calls her the "co-Redemptrice"—the redeemer-with-
Christ. The reason is that she silently united herself to all
the suffering of her son—just as the mother did in the preceding example. She bore his suffering, and she offered it to
God with him. She was powerless to stop the torture of her
son; but she was all-powerful when it came to redeeming
the world with her son. It was a miracle of love.

We have all, at one time or another, been crushed by,
and rebelled against, the suffering of another. What doctor
or nurse has not felt the frustration of being powerless in
the face of approaching death? What man engaged in the
struggle against injustice in his own community or in the
world has not felt the temptation to despair because of the
apparent futility of his efforts? We are men of little faith;

and we have wasted valuable time because of it. Instead, we should make use of all of our redemptive power. This does not mean that we should regard it as some sort of magical panacea to be hauled out once all human resources have been exhausted. It means, rather, that at the moment of greatest discouragement we discover, within suffering but going infinitely beyond it, a treasure by virtue of which we are enabled to accept life just when we thought we were about to be overcome by death.

What we lack today are contemplatives in the midst of life, men who, while fighting in the thick of the battle against suffering, are able to withdraw to the foot of the world's cross. We lack militants of pure love to appear before the unknown or rejected love, communicants with Christ the Redeemer. Without such men, all the suffering of man and humanity will be to no avail.

In the face of our suffering brothers, in the sight of tortured humanity, we are invited to share the co-redemption of Mary, who stands powerless but all-powerful at the foot of the cross.

We have said several times that it is wrong to seek out suffering for its own sake; it is even a sickness. We do not willingly make ourselves suffer just to prove our love for someone. There are saints who have inflicted suffering on themselves. That is no surprise, any more than it is a surprise that, centuries ago, lovers used to risk their lives in tournaments for the sake of their ladies. Today, however, there are other ways for lovers to prove their love; there are studies to be undertaken, professions to be prepared for, a commitment to society to be worked out. These things involve much in the way of sacrifice and suffering. And the same holds true for Christians. If we are sometimes asked to make a sacrifice—during Lent, for example—it is not in order to create suffering so that we may be able to "offer it up." Its purpose is to make possible a real step forward, to allow us to develop a fuller life that we may offer to God. What we must do, in effect, is to make a choice: We must deprive ourselves of something in order to get something better. We prune roses in order to produce more beautiful roses. And we must prune

our lives—not so that we may die, but so that we may live
more fully. We must choose life. And to choose life is to
choose the development of life. The kingdom of the Father
is not built on ruins.

Thus, we should not attempt to bypass the sufferings that
come to us in the ordinary course of life and invent new ones
of our own manufacture. We must accept our limitations—
those of our bodies, our minds, our acts, our lives, our commitment to life—as dictated by such persons and events as
constitute the circumstances of our lives. We must accept
such limitations in order to create the world which the Father
desires, and we must take the weight of our suffering as an
indication of the extent of our life-giving activity. The man
who sits by the side of the road and refuses to get involved
in life will not suffer. (Or perhaps he will deliberately choose
to sit on sharp rocks, in order to create some suffering for
himself.) Such suffering cannot be reclaimed. Jesus has not
taken them within himself. He is not present in them.

Where man truly suffers and dies is in the accomplishment of his human tasks. And he dies a real death; for we
spend our lives in dying so that we may live more fully. The
man who wants to save his life will lose it. Only the man
who is willing to accept the life of each day as a free gift
will grow. This gift of life is the gift of oneself to others and
for the sake of others. It is made directly in interpersonal
relationships; and indirectly through the intermediary of familiar, social, economic, and political institutions. When we
join a union, a neighborhood association, a club, or a movement, what we are doing is joining ourselves to others and
giving ourselves to others.

Man, however, cannot give himself unless he renounces
himself, unless he dies to himself. To express it concretely,
I cannot both smoke a cigarette and give it to a friend. I cannot put on my slippers and settle down for a night of television and, at the same time, attend a union meeting. I cannot
talk and, at the same time, listen. I cannot concentrate on
obtaining what I want for myself and, at the same time, work
for others.

Man is prone to be self-centered. We make little gods of
ourselves. That is not necessarily wrong; for we must indeed

become gods—but we must do so with God and by God, through Jesus Christ, who became man so that we might become gods. Our whole lives must be a sustained effort to forget ourselves so that we may think, in Jesus Christ, of other men and of the world which is to be built. That is the essential sacrifice. That is the true "spirituality" of daily life: to die to ourselves so that we may have life more abundantly. It is a painful but exhilarating and perpetual process of being born anew.

Jesus Christ was the first to commit himself to suffering and death through love of life; and his commitment involved the taking upon himself of all the sufferings and all the deaths of all men in the past and the future. The Christian, in his turn, must now freely embark with Jesus on that unique and total Passion in his daily life. If the Christian dies to himself every day, he will attain life—true life, which is the life of man; an expanded, transfigured, divinized, and eternal life.

At the end of our life on earth, when we die the final death of a series of deaths, we will have the most beautiful and complete opportunity to live, in Jesus Christ, the mystery of the Redemption. This final death to ourselves by the process of biological dissolution is the final stage in our development, the final step in our climb toward transfiguration, the ultimate liberation from our limitations so that we may emerge into life. It is a blessing for man to be able consciously to experience that dissolution, to be able willingly to offer the gift of his final breath to the Father with Jesus and in him, for the salvation of the world.

Jesus Christ, then, has willed to need man in order to live the mystery of the Redemption, just as he needs him in order to live the mysteries of Creation and the Incarnation, to reintroduce it into time, first of all by acknowledging his sins and those of his world, and then by offering those sins consciously to the Father through Jesus Christ. He does so also by fighting with all his strength against suffering, and by freeing the energy which is hidden within suffering through communion with the Redeemer. And finally, he does so by accepting and living with Jesus Christ all of his deaths-to-himself, even to the final and ultimate death. Man must make a daily and

loving response to the freely given love of the Savior. In this
way, man is saved and himself becomes a savior with Christ—
no longer, as St. Paul says, "in hope," but in fact; and all of
mankind and the universe itself then enter into that life which
is Eternal Life.

The mystery of the Redemption is also the mystery of the
Resurrection; for the Way of the Cross does not end at the
tomb, but continues beyond death and leads to the joy of
life eternal. Jesus Christ is the great conqueror of sin, suffering, and death. In him, every man, and all of mankind—
past, present, and future—are dead and brought to life again:
God "brought us to life with Christ—it is through grace that
you have been saved—and raised us up with him and gave us
a place with him in heaven, in Christ Jesus" (Eph. 2:5–6).
And so, there is no one, no sin, not a moment of our lives,
not a particle of the universe, which is not affected by Christ's
victory. Nothing is outside of the Redemption which has
been accomplished. He has gathered all things within himself: man, humanity, the world. He has offered all things,
given all things, made all things "happen" in God; and all
things have been restored to life.

If we are willing, every moment of our lives can resound
with the joy of Easter. And the true Christian cannot live
without joy. Through Christ, he encounters joy and lives
in joy. He is given over to joy. In his life there can be no
enduring failure—neither suffering nor death are insur-
mountable obstacles for him. Everything is the raw material
of redemption, of resurrection, for, in the middle of his sufferings and his deaths, Christ the Conqueror waits. If a
Christian is unhappy, it can only be because he has suc-
cumbed to the temptation to flirt with death and to turn his
back on life. For that reason, the greatest suffering and the
greatest joy can coexist in the same life and be intimately
interconnected to one another. By "joy" we do not mean
the transient (though legitimate) pleasure that comes from
comfort, or the false happiness of the simple mind that is
unaware of his degradation, or the "virtuous" resignation of a
pseudo-mystic, or the blind optimism of the man who figures
that "it is better to laugh than to cry." We mean rather the

calm, the interior serenity, and the profound peace which permeate and emanate from a man who, notwithstanding a torn heart and body, and despite the suffering of mankind and the world, believes with all his strength in the victory of the Savior. And he believes this without for an instant forgetting or denying the existence of suffering and sin, and without giving up the fight against them.

The man who has entered into this joy and remains in it becomes, in Christ, what the Father wants him to be. He has reached his true level, as a man who is totally developed; for he has reached the ultimate stage in his communion with the Mystery of Jesus—not only the mystery of Creation; not only the mystery of Incarnation; not only the mystery of Redemption. But also the mystery of *Resurrection*.

PART III

Chapter Eight

THE ENCOUNTER WITH GOD

We firmly believe that modern man and the modern world, without being conscious of it, are calling to God with all their strength. That call is often a silent one, from the subconscious of individuals or from that of mankind collectively. But sometimes it is the desperate cry of men victimized and crushed by our great "consumer society"—of men who are supposed to be the beneficiaries, but become the slaves, of that society. That cry comes principally from the young, who, before they can be anesthetized and smothered by the urge to "have," scream out their hunger to "be." Often, they have no idea of what it is they want to be or of what they should be. Their rebellion is a revolt, which takes place in the most complete disorder, against everything that appears to limit man in his body, his mind, his love, and in the desire to surpass himself by attaining a degree of development and expansion as yet undreamed of. It is also an expression of the eternal quest for total love—but outside of love's so-called middle-class frame of reference, which is said to be too restrictive. Thus, these young people demand, and often live, sexual freedom. They are looking for a love to satisfy their famished bodies, but without taking into account that their hunger comes from beyond the body. It is a hunger of the soul, and it rises above the body through which it is felt. Thus, they attempt to penetrate into "another world" by means of drugs and esoteric cults; or they simply try to establish a new life-style by cultivating "originality" and experimenting in human relationships—hence the phenomena of the hippies, beatniks, and so forth. All of this, very likely, is founded in discouragement and disillusionment with realistic efforts to build a new society; but it also reflects a will to question values deeply at a time when, in the face of so many failures, the desire and the vision of a beautiful future is growing.

All of these things are indications of aspirations and ideals rooted in the heart of man—aspirations to truth, to justice, to responsibility, to unity, to harmony, to peace on earth—aspirations ever present, but never satisfied. And this holds true now, in particular, when man stands astonished by his own knowledge and power, and trembling before the possibilities that are opening up.

Men today—especially men who no longer need to struggle continually in order to live—are finding that they are disoriented, and sometimes anguished, when they reflect on their own lives and on that of the world. It used to be that only poets and philosophers asked the questions that entire groups of people ask today: Why are we alive? Where does life come from? Where does it lead? Who are we?

And when men have the opportunity to avoid being stifled by a superabundance of material goods, or hypnotized by the uncontrolled desire for them, they sense, or realize, that the possession of such goods—as useful and as legitimate as they may be in themselves—does not satisfy them. They then try somehow to rise above them, to become better, to build a world that is more solid and durable. They look for "something better"—for a real reason "to be" and "to be more fully."

I think that the present crisis, with its revolts, its searching, its suffering, is the first contraction in the birth of a new world. Mankind is becoming more aware, and this awareness involves a great responsibility, a great opportunity for man today. Mature men are beginning to see the light at the end of the tunnel—and their first reaction is a cry of anguish. They are looking for their beginning and their end. They are looking for their Father.

Why, then, are there some Christians who are afraid? At

every new birth of his creatures, God is present. We have said, and we may repeat, that in all of man's aspirations, in all of his intolerable suffering, in all of his absences, in all of his anguish, God is there, inviting man to discover that there is something beyond man, beyond history, beyond the universe. The heart and body of man may be tormented; but in his mind there is a sign of his divine origin which points out to him the long road to the very source of his being. There are the sounds of a Creator-Love which come to him from beyond time and suggest to him the possibility of his full development and his divinization in Jesus Christ. Man cannot ignore that suggestion without denying his own nature, for he was created to become a son of God; God "chose us, chose us in Christ . . . determining that we should become his adopted sons, through Jesus Christ" (Eph. 1:4–5).

We believe with all our strength that God today is calling man; and that man, blind and surrounded by darkness, is casting about, often unconsciously, to see where that voice is coming from.

Many of our contemporaries recognize the need for a radical change. They want, in fact, to create a "new man" and a "new world." Some of them think, rather naïvely, that this new man will appear on his own, at the end of some natural process. Others are convinced that he will spring up once we have disposed of all the "alienations" that now impede man's progress. Still others say that the new man will be the result of a new society, in which all present social, political, and economic structures will be overturned. But more and more men of all persuasions are beginning to be apprehensive because they see no indication that the new man is about to appear. They are beginning to sense their own powerlessness. And, in fact, even though technology and science are making giant strides forward, man is remaining pretty much what he has always been. It is true that, despite serious failures and unforgivable delays, there have been certain cultural improvements and a certain influx of material goods into some segments of society which hitherto were almost totally deprived. But the beneficiaries of these improvements are still themselves. They are eager to possess

more, but not concerned about *being* more. In some countries
in which this process of material amelioration has taken
place, the older generation is astonished that their children,
who were born within these new structures, are no different
from themselves.

In the same way, we are discovering every day, through
modern methods of communication, that man is essentially
the same everywhere, in all countries, under all political or
economic or social regimes, at every level of development.
And so vanishes our hope that man, by an increase in knowledge and in goods and in material power over himself and
over life, might improve morally and attain the state of
being "more." The contrary, in fact, seems to be the case.
As man grows richer in earthly things, he seems more and
more threatened. The forces within man—those of his mind
and his heart and his life—seem less under control than ever
before, less unified, less balanced. Many of us are like hand
grenades from which the pins have been removed; sooner
or later, we are going to explode all over our lives. Men no
longer seem capable of mastering themselves. They no longer
have the strength to "build themselves," or the will to
do so. And what is worse, they do not know where to find
the source of energy that is necessary to effect a synthesis.
They do not even know what the plan of construction is.

As we develop the will to create a radically new man and
a radically new world, there develops, along with it, confusion on what kind of man and world to build. Some men
are beginning to grasp, however tenuously, that man must
be transformed and changed far more than they had originally thought; that man needs a permanent revolution *in
his heart,* the necessity for which no other kind of revolution can obviate. And then, these men pin their hopes to
whatever hero happens to be in vogue at the moment in
the world of the intellect or in that of action. They expect
these "stars" to furnish on request a doctrine, an ideal, and
a mysterious "power" that will be able to change man. But
none of these men are the latter-day saviors that are needed
and expected.

Christ is still shut up in the churches, they say, and that
is why some men are unwilling to call on him and why

others do not even think of turning toward him. They say that Christ is the private property of medieval ghosts who wear cassocks or wimples. They say that he is a personage dreamed up to satisfy children eager for miracles, to awaken enthusiasm in adolescents, to console the aged, the sick, and single ladies of pious inclination. They may even think that Jesus was a remarkable man, that his ideas and his ideals— although a bit mysterious and utopian—are beautiful; but they say, in the next breath, that Jesus' teachings have been betrayed by his followers, and that he is as dead as the founders of other movements.

We, however, believe that it is the living Christ whom many of our contemporaries seek unconsciously. It is the saving Christ whom they expect to build a new man and a new world—a man and a world more beautiful, greater, and more exciting than they could ever imagine. Man alone can never find the means to save himself; and, if he looks for them at ground level, he will be wasting his time. We believe what revelation tells us: "This is the stone rejected by you the builders, but which has proved to be the keystone. For of all the names in the world given to men, this is the only one by which we can be saved" (Acts 4:11–12). We learn the same thing from the experience of failure—and it is the Holy Spirit who speaks through that experience, and who invites us. We firmly believe—though many deny it—that now is the time of Christ, and that we must now proclaim and reveal him as the true Christ, Man-God, living and triumphant. We must show that he is not a caricature, and not a corpse.

Our contemporaries will discover Christ in his overwhelming truth only if we, as Christians, have truly encountered him ourselves.

Man is looking for God. Man needs God. But who can encounter God? No one. Jesus himself said it: "No one has ever seen God." But then Jesus added: "It is the only Son, who is nearest to the Father's heart, who has made him known" (John 1:18).

And that is it. There is no other way to see God, to know him, to unite oneself to him, other than in Jesus Christ. And

Jesus repeated this idea many times. He said that he was
the way, *the* truth, *the* life; that no one went to the Father
except through him; that whoever saw him saw the Father;
that the Father was in him and he was in the Father. Jesus
came to save the world, and except in him there can be no
salvation for man: "God loved the world so much that he
gave his only Son, so that everyone who believes in him may
not be lost but may have eternal life. For God sent his Son
into the world not to condemn the world, but so that through
him the world might be saved" (John 3:16–17). And then
St. John says (1:11–12), "He came to his own domain . . .
to all who did accept him he gave power to become children
of God." But it is useless to go on; one could quote the entire
Gospel to prove this point. It is simply a matter of this: We
must believe in the central Event of history, the Incarnation
of God; we must truly believe in Jesus Christ, God, who
came among men to save man and the world; we must believe
that in Jesus there is the power necessary to touch the heart
of man and transform him completely; we must believe that
the mystery of Jesus Christ is unfolding in time, and that
our God is present, in us, with us, among us, living with our
life, conquering, until the end of time.

The crucial question in all this is that of our relationship
with Christ. The man who separates himself from Christ,
who loses sight of him, separates himself from God and
turns his back on salvation—that is, he turns his back on the
opportunity for his own full development and the building
of a better world. *The man who loses Jesus loses everything.*

In the contemporary Church there are constant meetings
and conferences, composed of bishops, priests, religious, and
laymen, the purpose of which is to study, discuss, and research the best means of evangelizing modern man. There
are sessions, innumerable committees, staff personnel, and
new structures constantly being created. There are innova-
tors offering new ideas, techniques, and revolutionary methods. There are conservatives trying to apply the brakes, and
there are militants defending the cause of "progress" and
change. This is all very well. It is even necessary. But we
must ask ourselves what the source is of all this activity. Is

it a more intimate contact with Christ, which is itself the result of more frequent and extended contacts? Is it primarily not the defense of methods, or research, or organization and structures, or ideas and even dogma, but rather a great love, a "passion" for someone—for Jesus Christ as contemplated in his mystical and historical dimensions? Are our most militant revolutionaries and our most steadfast contestants those who are most intimate with and most enthusiastic for Christ? For that must be the criterion against which we measure the authenticity of their work. "Make sure that no one traps you and deprives you of your freedom by some secondhand, empty, rational philosophy based on the principles of this world instead of on Christ. In his body lives the fulness of divinity" (Col. 2:8–9).

Among all those people who gather to study and decide "priorities," to organize the preaching of Christ—for everyone says that that is what it is all about—how many are there who do, in fact, preach Christ? And how much time is there left for them to get started on that all-important work?

Is there anyone left who preaches Christ instead of discussing the methodology of preaching Christ? Is there anyone left among us who, because he has met Christ and lives with him and has daily been transformed by him in the Gospel and in life, can preach his discovery, his certitude, his love, instead of mumbling words that are full of excuses?

The desire to change and progress within the Church is indeed praiseworthy. But we are running the risk of ignoring the only thing that is essential. In our desire to make improvements, it is not impossible that we are smothering the *spirit* of Christ under a fabric woven of our subtle thoughts, our organizations, tactics, and techniques. It is possible that, as we sit weaving our splendid plans for the future, our contemporaries are dying of hunger in their search for a living Person, a Savior.

Jesus Christ, we have said, is the Son of God who came among men two thousand years ago. But he is also the "Great Christ" who has incorporated all mankind into his love and made "members" of all men. He is the Mystery of Christ, the mystery of Creation, of Incarnation, of Redemption and Resurrection, and he is not limited to thirty years of human history. He covers and embodies the entire history of the human race.

This is the "total Christ," in his dual dimension: the historical Jesus and the Risen Christ, who lives in his members and in the world. This is the Christ whom we must encounter if we are not to lose our spiritual balance and if we do not wish our witness to be in vain.

We have said that there are Christians, especially in the past, who knew the historical Jesus. They prayed to the historical Jesus, contemplated him, and tried to imitate him. But Jesus, despite all this, remained outside their lives and external to them. He was merely a model whom those Christians admired and whose life-style they tried to duplicate. That style was soon translated into religious rituals, which then came often to be regarded as magical means to attain eternal life.

It seems that this sort of spirituality was only a "phase," a stage of development which corresponds roughly to a spiritual adolescence. Carried to an extreme, it can produce a real separation between life and faith and leave whole sectors of human life—particularly life in society—without the influence of Jesus.

We have seen (and suffered from) too many of these Christians who "practice" a "religion" which has nothing to do with life. We have come to realize that we cannot know Christ unless we know all the members of his Body. We cannot love him unless we love all his brothers and unless we participate with him, in our lives, in all the aspects of his Mystery.

To accept Christ, the Head, without accepting all of his members and his total Mystery, is to mutilate Christ.

It will be one of the glories of our generation of Christians to have rediscovered concretely the "mystical dimension" of Jesus Christ, to have realized that we can actually discover the Living Christ in our brother men and in all the events of our lives and the life of the world.

That is the difficult, demanding, but exhilarating task of

a mature faith, which gives meaning to life and to the world and which makes of us, at each instant, Christ's collaborators in realizing the plan of the Father.

The problem, however, is that the dangers and the possible errors implicit in that discovery are proportionately great. Christians today are passionately involved in building up the world; and they risk forgetting what lies beyond that constructive process; or they risk the temptation to postpone until later what must be lived here and now because it is an interior reality. We are not building a spaceship, which must be constructed from the ground up, with the capsule itself coming last in the order of execution. To believe that we are doing something analogous to that can lead to a new and even more obvious separation between the life of man and the world and "Christian" life.

Another danger is that the Christian, fascinated by the discovery of Christ living in men and in history, may neglect the historical Jesus Christ and may neglect to meditate on his life. If we forget the Jesus of history, then it becomes impossible for us to find him in life. If we arrange to meet someone at a crowded train station, and we have never seen that person before, how can we pick him out of a crowd of people milling about? In the same way, a man who has never "seen" the Jesus of history cannot recognize him, cannot approach him or contemplate him. He is risking living a life of illusion—until the day he realizes that, by definition, an illusion is unreal; that an illusion is a thing, or a person, that does not exist. And then he will say, "I've lost my faith." It would be more accurate to say, "I've lost sight of Christ. I don't see him any more."

In such cases, we may say that Christ is "decapitated." But where we decapitate Christ or mutilate him, the result is the same: We condemn ourselves to live without him. We have witnessed that phenomenon among Christians who, at one time or another of their lives and by one method or another, reach that state. They are deprived of animation, like corpses. For anyone who can no longer live through Christ condemns himself to death and his action becomes fruitless. "Make your home in me," Jesus said (John 15:4–5), "as I make mine in you. As a branch cannot bear fruit all by itself, but must remain part of the vine, neither can you unless you remain in me. . . . Whoever remains in me, with me in him, bears fruit in plenty; for cut off from me you can do nothing."

If man is to make something of himself and the world, he must encounter Christ—but the *whole* Christ.

Must we first of all meet the historical Jesus, and then, knowing him, live with him and through him? Or must we first discover him among men, work with him, and then go and find him in the Gospel? Some people ask those questions. Some even accuse one another of having made the wrong choice, and saying that the faith of this or that Christian has no value, they condemn one another without the possibility of an appeal.

There is no point in fighting about it. Jesus Christ, sent by the Father, arranges for man, individually or in groups, according to the needs of the time, to meet with him in love. But, through his Holy Spirit, he chooses different times and places for those meetings. We must respect his choice. Man has nothing to say about it; and neither do the theologians. All we can do is desire with all our strength to encounter the total Christ, so that we may have a life of faith that is solid and balanced. We must, however, allow for and respect the various ways in which different people attain that end. Throughout history, Jesus has revealed himself only gradually; and today too he shows himself only gradually to the man who seeks him out. The important fact is that we are invited to meet with Jesus, to talk with him, to love him, so that we may be transformed and united in a common undertaking. It makes not the slightest difference how we receive that invitation and where we meet.

Let me say it once more: Why be afraid? What is the use of being afraid and thereby casting doubt on the validity of modern man's spiritual orientation?

For many decades we have admired men, both young and old, who have dedicated their lives to working for their fellow men, and especially for the poor. These men, working within the framework of their own lives, within their professions and their communities, have, in the course of their militant lives, discovered Jesus Christ. Some of them took a long time to recognize and identify Jesus; but those who witnessed their generous struggle for the poor, and their spiritual progress, have no doubt at all that Jesus was mysteriously present in them and in their work from the very beginning. One must entirely lack "good faith" not to admit it, not to admire and be edified by the lives of certain "militants" who burn with love for their brother men.

It disturbs some people to see these brilliant flowers blooming so profusely outside of our carefully prepared gardens. And they ask, "But do these people have *true* charity?" Certainly, we all know militants who are not "devout," and even some who are not religious at all, at least at the beginning of their work. That is not surprising, and we should not be taken aback by it. We cannot cut love into pieces. There is only one love. And love expresses itself by forsaking oneself, forgetting oneself, for the sake of someone else. Whenever anyone does this, he loves; and God is present in all real love. (See the First Epistle of St. John, Chapter 4.)

Let the theologians discuss and study the nature of God's presence in love. That is what they are supposed to do. But they must abstain (and we should too) from issuing identity cards certifying that one is a Christian because he believes, or does, this or that. If the Gospel teaches us anything, it is that we must be very wary of well-established categories. Categories have nothing to do with love.

In this context, we must take into account the massive effect of almost fifty years of Catholic Action. We have only begun to realize the enormous riches that have come to the Church because of it. And to it we owe in large measure that marvelous "experience" of the presence of the Risen Christ living among us, ready to reveal himself in the full light of day—but also sometimes in insupportable darkness—to all those who take part in serving their fellow men and in building up the world. We should thank the Holy Spirit, who has given such men to our time.

To sum up, we may say that we believe wholeheartedly that Jesus Christ is present to those men who are involved in life, that he reveals himself to them in the midst of their activities and invites them to a life of extraordinary union. But we believe too that these men must take into account

Jesus' historical reality in order consciously to live the *total*
Christ: " . . . so that Christ may live in your hearts through
faith, and then, planted in love and built on love, you will
with all the saints have strength to grasp the breadth and
the length, the height and the depth; until knowing the love
of Christ, which is beyond all knowledge, you are filled with
the utter fullness of God" (Eph. 3:17–19).

Chapter Nine

"I Am with You Always; Yes, to the End of Time"

Every life, and every moment of every life, is a moment of that "sacred history" of the People of God who are visibly gathered together within the Church; of that history which began at the beginning of the world and which will endure until the end of time, until Jesus Christ, having gathered all things, all men, and all the universe unto himself, will offer all to the Father so that all may be transformed and transfigured in love.

Every event, no matter how insignificant, in the life of a man or a group of men is contained in the essential Event of history, which is the coming of God in Jesus Christ so that all things might be subjected to him. Every event, therefore, has an incalculable value because of its content—or rather, because of its "interiority." Every event is a moment of the Mystery of Christ which is taking place in time and to which nothing and no one is alien.

Man can live the Creation, the Incarnation, the Redemption, and the Resurrection in every one of his acts. He can live the Creation because by the very act of living he is completing his own creation and, in the company of his brothers, that of the world. He can live the Incarnation because, by accepting with love the presence of Jesus Christ, he allows Christ to take him over completely. He can live the Redemption since, because of sin, there is not a second of his life that does not necessitate struggle, suffering, and death to himself. If it is lived with Christ, that battle against selfishness, pride, and non-love can only lead to the victory of the Resurrection, by virtue of which that particle of life enters into Life—into true life, which is eternal.

Thus, the Christian who, through faith, discovers Christ living in the center of life can join Christ and live out the Mystery of Christ with him. But he can also reject the encounter and union with Christ. He must therefore acquire the spiritual habit, as it were, of that encounter, through loyalty with respect to living his faith in his life. Just as he must go beyond the words of the Evangelists if he is to find Christ in the Gospel, so too must he go beyond life's events in order to find life itself.

Since all things are received into Christ, since everything is contained within the Event, all life and all of life possess a dimension which is invisible to bodily eyes, a certain mysterious "inner dimension."

This inner dimension is not something that is reserved for use after death. It is primarily a function of the here and now; for it is within every person, every event, every life.

If modern man and the modern world have trouble in believing in an inner dimension, it is because we have always presented it to them as divorced from the present, as "another life" sometime in the future which has no connection with this life. We have made Christians look up to heaven; and so they have lost interest in the earth. But there is no "other life" which obliges us to ignore and despise the present life. There is indeed only one life, and that is the life that we are now living—a life which goes far beyond that which we experience through our senses, a life that our intellect alone cannot comprehend unless it is enlightened by faith. And that one, single life is the life which, at the end of our days on earth, will be profoundly transformed, transfigured, and restored in Christ, so that it may be lived out in eternity.

God is now present in the midst of that life. He has come down into life, permeated it, and given a supernatural dimension to it. He did not merely stitch one life, like a patch, onto another, so that we may say "well, this life ends here, and the next one begins there." He added a dimension which gives life to all of life, just as the spirit gives life to the body.

God made the "supernatural" come down to the "natural," heaven to earth, in the most radical way possible. He sent his Son down to earth to live the life of a man, the Man-God: "and the Word was made flesh."

For a man to live an integral, total life, he must consciously relate within himself, within his brothers, within his life, within the life of the world, to that inner dimension. To live fully and intensively, in effect, is to live here and now—but the here and now in all its dimensions, in depth as well as in breadth. If life does not satisfy our needs, it is because we do not live life in its totality. When we are overcome with hunger for the infinite, for life, for love, truth, justice, and peace, it is not only a *future* life which motivates us, but also (and primarily) the need to live our present life perfectly, without limitations, as a life which has something about it of the infinite. What we want, in short, is heaven; but heaven here and now, rooted in the whole of our lives. And we are right in wanting it, for Christ has given it to us. He has given us *his* life, and, through it, the Kingdom which is now among us.

Christ said, "I will be raised up so that I may draw all things to myself." Then he entered into suffering and death. Finally, he emerged triumphant; he rose from the dead. Since that time, as Head of the human body, he draws to himself all of his members so that, in him, they may penetrate for all eternity into that inner dimension, into what lies beyond life today. That is, he draws all men to himself so that they may become the whole men that the Father wishes them to be.

Man has been created in God's image. But God is love, truth, justice, peace, etc. Therefore man has been created with a tendency toward love, truth, justice, peace, etc. This divine likeness in man should not be merely a blueprint. In and through Christ, it must become a reality. There is no human aspiration or ideal which is not, either clearly or obscurely, part of that likeness. That is, there is not one that is not an aspiration toward Christ, toward intimate union with him, so that in him may be constructed the man and the world that the Father has eternally desired.

This is true for man as an individual, and is true for the various human communities, from the largest to the smallest, no matter whether they be social, labor, recreational, scholarly, or residential communities. God, in Jesus Christ, is equally present in the aspirations of all those groups. In fact, it is Christ who, in drawing them toward himself, inspires their search for liberty, dignity, justice, responsibility, pleasure, etc.

That is not to say that all the aspirations of man and of human groups are necessarily healthy ones. Many of them are often deformed, perverted from their true purpose, misappropriated by man for his own profit and advantage when man either does not know God or thinks that he can do without God. Such is the heritage of original sin. It is capable of diverting the course of human aspirations; but it is not capable of destroying those aspirations. For Jesus Christ is too strong to allow it. By his redemptive Incarnation, he has set again on its proper path that which had been diverted. The man who struggles is therefore assured of Victory—if only he struggles alongside the one who is the great Liberator.

If we believe in man's aspirations, in man's desire to better himself, to live more fully, to build a just and united world, then we believe in the Father who creates in love. And we believe in Jesus Christ, the Savior. And we also believe in the Holy Spirit. For the Holy Spirit also came down to earth. Christ had promised to send him: "I shall ask the Father, and he will give you another Advocate to be with you for ever, that Spirit of truth . . . you know him, because he is with you, he is in you" (John 14:15–17). And Christ kept his word.

The Holy Spirit is always with us. And the Scriptures tells us what his function is from all eternity. He was present at all of creation. He spoke through the prophets. He prepared Mary for the coming of the Savior, and he "overshadowed" her on the day of the Event.

Today, the Holy Spirit is still at work in the heart of man and of the world. He accompanies and guides man in the completion of creation. It is he who straightens what has been twisted. It is he who makes straight the way of the Savior. He is present in all human aspirations, and he corrects in them what must be corrected. He directs them. He prepared the encounter between man and Christ within the framework of involvement in the realization of what would otherwise remain merely a plan.

It is not enough for man to aspire to justice, liberty, peace, and fraternity. It is not enough to preach the necessity for the liberation of man, of the oppressed, and of the poor. We must commit ourselves to the realization of those ideals. That is the work which is proper to man in the completion of creation according to the will of the Father, as we explained earlier in this book (see Chapter Five). Man's initial response to his aspirations, which are really words of Christ spoken through his Holy Spirit, must be to become involved. It is by action (as St. John tells us in his First Epistle), and not solely by words, that man must love his brothers. By action in the service of mankind, man begins to realize, concretely and historically, the Mystery of Christ. And the Mystery of Christ itself is thereby "activated" within the Father's eternal plan of love for man and the world. For that plan is not purely "spiritual"; it involves the work of creation, and also the taking of that creation unto himself by Christ the Savior.

Man's aspirations and ideals are the same throughout the world, although they are felt, expressed, and lived in different ways according to man's varying situation. They exist in the heart of every man, regardless of one's race, class, age, philosophy, or religion—and also regardless of the notion that man has of them. They have all the same source, for all men are called to be sons of God and to participate in building the Body of Christ. In this way, a non-believer who takes these aspirations seriously, who rises above himself and works for the betterment of mankind and the world, also works within the plan of the Father, with Jesus Christ and in Jesus Christ. And this is true even if the non-believer has no idea, or a false idea, of where these aspirations come from. The reason is that, just as there are not several kinds of love, neither is there more than one way of giving oneself. To give

oneself to one's brothers is *always* the same as giving oneself to Jesus Christ, and, in him, to the Father.

A Christian, therefore, should fearlessly join hands with
all men of good will who work for the integral and harmoni-
ous development of man and the world. He should work
alongside them in every kind of undertaking, whether great
or small, according to his situation and his abilities. He should
join his effort to theirs, and he should encourage those who
are fearful or who have never been asked to participate. He
should, under the guidance of the Holy Spirit, make straight
the ways that are adopted—for the end does not justify the
means. And he should believe with all his strength in the
presence of the Risen Christ in this activity. He should contemplate Christ in such a way that the men who observe
the Christian see, in reality, Someone whom they had never
noticed before.

The whole theory of action, in Catholic Action, is based
on faith in the presence of Christ in any activity which is
for man's benefit. Many militants, no doubt, have gone
beyond their duty in working for their brothers without suspecting that they were working for Christ and with Christ.
As we mentioned earlier, it is sometimes only after a very
long time that they became aware of it. Some did not even
discover it until after death, at which time they learned the
truth from Jesus himself as he told them, "The man to whom
you gave food because he was hungry, the man to whom
you gave clothes because he was in need, the man for whom
you fought to obtain a living wage—I was all of those men."

When we encourage someone to work for others, and
when we join him in that work, we are actually causing him
to enter into the Mystery of Christ; we are putting him on
the road to an encounter with Jesus; we are perhaps even
making it possible for him one day to make a *conscious* response to Love.

Some people worry about what distinguishes a Christian
from a non-Christian. If there is no difference between the
two, they reason, then there is no point in having faith. In
this respect, we must avoid two major pitfalls. The first is
to make God's love for man, and man's love for God, the

private property of duly baptized and registered Christians. The second is not to be able to recognize what essentially constitutes a Christian response to God's love.

God does not make distinctions between men. All, without exception, have been loved from all eternity. All have been born, and are born anew each day, in Christ. All have been taken by Christ unto himself. All have been "carried," with their sins, their sufferings, their struggles, their whole lives, by Christ the Redeemer. All have been saved.

No man knows of anyone who is not included in Jesus' conquering love. When the Father looks at man, he "sees" him in his Son, permeated with his love. We should look at man in the same way as God. We should consider all men with great benevolence and invincible hope; for God is in them.

All men of good will who rise above themselves for the sake of an ideal—regardless of the label which they attach to that ideal—and who forget themselves for the sake of their brothers, all such men are working with Jesus Christ and for him. They are mysteriously united to him. It is correct to say, then, that it is not absolutely necessary for a man to know Jesus Christ in order to be saved. That is, it is not necessary that he know Jesus clearly, on this earth. For a man will be judged according to his treatment of his brothers, and especially of the poorest among them, even if that man is unaware that in dealing with his brothers he is dealing with Jesus Christ himself (see Matt. 25:31–46).

We Christians must therefore rid ourselves once and for all of our irritation when we see that, in daily life, there is little or nothing to distinguish us from non-Christians.

We must not be shocked when, on the construction site which is the world, we see non-believers and even atheists among our fellow workers who surpass us in generosity and self-denial for the sake of our brothers. On the contrary, we should be altogether delighted. Nothing is so repellent to non-believers as that aura of self-stylized superiority with which we surround ourselves either consciously or unconsciously and of which we seem unable to rid ourselves. We seem to think that we can have everything for ourselves alone—everything: truth, goodness, and even God. We think that we are rich and that we can afford to give generously to everyone else; whereas, in reality, we possess nothing. And least of all do we possess God. It is God who possesses us. It is God who loved first, and if we believe, then we must first of all believe in that love. We must believe that God loves us infinitely and personally, and that he loves all men equally, without exception and without distinction. If we can bring ourselves to accept that and believe it, our relations with non-believers will be totally different from what they are.

All men are loved. All men are saved. All men must respond to that love. And it is in that response that Christians differ from non-Christians.

God's love does not force itself upon unwilling man. Man can receive it only if he is willing. Christ cannot save us in spite of ourselves, without our help. A lover cannot demand that his love be returned. But when the loved one freely returns love, then there is a true relationship of love—that is, true love, which is simultaneously a giving and a taking. Like every lover and every friend, Jesus cannot ignore man's liberty without doing violence to human nature, without treating man as a child; without, in fact, negating his love for man.

Man, for his part, can fulfill himself only in responding with love to Jesus' love. The same thing is true also for the world; it cannot reach its full development unless man uses love at each step of its construction.

The redemptive Incarnation of Jesus Christ is perfect. Now, for man and the world to be perfect, it is necessary that they both be subordinated to man's loving response in life.

And that is the first distinction to be drawn; a distinction between those who respond to love and those who do not. And it matters little that man is required by circumstances to shout out, or to whisper, his response.

Man, of course, can say "no." That possibility, which can also express itself by a definite and final rejection, is, as the Gospel points out, a great mystery. It can be understood only in the light of a love which requires the existence and exercise of complete liberty. It is, therefore, a proof of God's love, and not, as some would have it, an indication of God's indifference. God's love is never lacking to man; it is man's love that is lacking to God: " . . . whoever comes to me I shall not turn him away; because I have come from heaven, not to do my own will, but to do the will of him who sent me. Now the will of him who sent me is that I should lose nothing of all that he has given to me, and that I should raise it up on the last day" (John 6:37–39).

Of all those who say "yes" to God, only the Christian can give a conscious response with full knowledge of what is involved. The Christian *knows* that the Father has always loved. He believes it, because he has met Someone, Jesus Christ, who told him, revealed it to him. And he trusts that Someone. Jesus also "has let us know the mystery of his purpose, the hidden plan he so kindly made in Christ from the beginning . . . that he would bring everything together under Christ, as head, everything in the heavens and everything on earth" (Eph. 1:9–10). So the Christian knows that, when he works with his brothers for the good of the world, Jesus is there among them; and he knows that he may encounter Jesus there. He knows, too, that he is working with Christ for the execution of the Father's plan for the universe.

There are non-Christians, we have said, who say "yes" to God's love. Some of those who say "yes" are even atheists. They speak their answer through their lives, and particularly through their work on mankind's behalf, although they have no idea of where the question comes from, or even of the identity of the one who asks it. They give their response through the intermediary of persons, or through loyalty to a doctrine, an ideal in which they believe. They believe in the well-being of other men, and they are determined to achieve that well-being even at the cost of their lives; but they do not know that the goal toward which they are working goes infinitely beyond earthly benefits. They want to build a just, free, and peaceful world; but they do not know that their undertaking has a supernatural, interior dimension of which they are unaware. They are like workmen who, forgetting themselves, build a solid and beautiful house, without knowing for whom, and at whose order, they build it. Jesus will judge them according to that work and its value; and its value may not be less than that of the work of those who build in full knowledge of what they are doing. But Jesus will judge them, above all, according to how much "heart" they will have put into their work.

In this way, Jesus accepts also the "yes" of those who come to offer it to him in a roundabout way; he accepts it even if the man who offers it, being blind, does not see the face and the hands of the one who accepts in order to give it, in turn, to his Father. For all life comes from the Father, and all must be returned to the Father.

If it is not absolutely necessary to know Jesus in order to collaborate with him, and if the work of the faithful and generous non-believer or non-Christian can have the same value as that of the Christian, then what is the point of preaching Jesus Christ? Why should we accept the "mission" that the Father, in and with his Son, has entrusted to us?

We have no intention of straying into the theologians' field. But we cannot help stopping to reflect for a moment on that question. It is a question that comes up, sometimes painfully, among militant Christians who are working with non-believers. And it occurs, perhaps more than elsewhere, among men who have given up everything in order to go into the world and preach the Risen Christ.

The images that we have already used determine the direction of our reflections. Could we bear the blindness of our brother if it were possible for us to cure him? A blind man can walk, and sometimes he is better and faster at it than the man who can see. Guided by others, "enlightened" by their words, he can form an image in his mind of the road to be traveled. And yet, he does not *see*. He travels through life without ever seeing the sun, without seeing the roads on which he walks, without seeing where he is going, without seeing the people around him, without ever seeing love in someone's face. His life, it is true, can be useful, and beautiful. But he is still mutilated.

In the same way, a man cannot be fully himself unless he knows who he is, whence he comes, and where he goes. An animal is a perfect animal without knowing or caring about "why" or "how," without being able to participate in his own development, and without being able to offer that development. It is man's prerogative, his basic dignity, to *know*, to become himself by means of himself. But for man to become himself, he must become a son of God in Jesus Christ. That is a fact that everyone should know.

If we can cure someone of his disability, then we have no right to allow him to remain disabled—particularly if his infirmity is one which affects his very being. We have no right to let a man make a mistake about his destiny, even if God, in his infinite love, and to prevent that man from suffering because of *our* willful negligence, allows him to work, in darkness, for the creation of the world. We are responsible for that man; and we are liable for his mistakes. "Woe to me if I do not preach Jesus Christ," cried St. Paul. He did not say, "Woe to those to whom we do not preach Jesus Christ." Woe to *us* if we allow ourselves to violate man's dignity to the point of letting him live his life without ever hearing of that Mystery of Jesus Christ which has been revealed to us.

Once again, let us say that the best way to approach the mystery of human destiny is by way of love.

Some time ago, a woman told me how, after twenty unhappy years, she had found her missing son. The young man, hesitant and still astonished, with trembling fingers touched, caressed, and explored the face of his new-found mother. "You are my mother!" he said.

For twenty years he had been the son of that mother. His life had sprung from her life. But he had never seen her. He did not know her name. He had everything, in a sense, because he had life. But, in another sense, he had nothing, since he did not know the source of that life. He did not know his mother's face. His mother had never held him in her arms, and he had never been able to embrace her.

The tragedy of many "alienated" people today, and especially of the young, is that they do not know their mothers or their fathers; they do not believe in—or they cannot believe in—their love. They are not loved, or they do not know that they are loved. And the psychologists tell us that that ignorance, or that absence, is the primary cause of social maladjustment.

There are many men who do not know their true Father

in heaven, the Father who loves them more than any earthly father. They have received life from him, but they do not know either his name or his face. They do not know that they are infinitely loved by him, and that that love follows them and gives new life to them at every moment of their lives. They do not know that they are heirs to a great heritage because of Jesus Christ, and that that heritage is life itself—divine life, for today, tomorrow, and forever.

Just as we should do all that we can to help the child of an unknown father find his father—particularly if we know the father, and know him to be both loving and lovable—so too we must do all in our power to reveal God's love to our brothers. We must, in other words, act as the sons of God that we are. For we are not a father's children simply because we have received life from him without having asked for it, but also because, knowing to whom we owe life, we can accept it willingly and express our gratitude by offering the best gift that a father can receive: our joy in living from his life. Love can exist only if it is received and returned consciously.

We have a tendency to take too lightly our responsibility for the errors and ignorance of our fellow men about themselves, their life, and the life of the world. We often say to ourselves (or we act as though we had said), "Well, after all, what does it matter whether they know where they come from and where they are going. The only thing that matters is that they are sincere, in 'good faith.' They've started out on the right road, and they'll get to where they are going. God will take care of that."

That is a shocking attitude, based on perverted reasoning. It means not only that we do not love our brothers with all our hearts, as we are obliged to do, but also that we hold them in contempt and have no regard for their essential dignity.

Moreover, we forget, when we feel that way, what we have received as the People of God: the Church, the deposit of Revelation, which is the most extraordinary gift that it is possible to receive. It is a gift from God which, of all gifts, must not be hidden under a bushel basket, but must be displayed for all to see. And it is a gift of which God will demand an accounting.

God the Father is always looking for his children. He revealed himself in Jesus Christ, but Jesus, although still living among men, is no longer wholly perceived as a man. Christians, therefore, as members of Christ, should individually and collectively offer their lives to God so that God may, through them, by them, and with them, be the contemporary of all modern men. Through us, Christ should be able to continue to reveal Love, and the name of Love.

If there were only one man in all the world who did not know Christ, then we would have to search the world to find him and reveal Christ to him so that that man might come to know his Father, love him, and allow the Father to love him also.

A few decades ago, we all admired militant Christians who, living in the midst of the world, were eager to bear witness to the historical Christ, to preach him openly, to shout his name from the rooftops. Fearlessly they declared their love for him, explained him to their friends, and invited everyone openly to share Christ with them. They cared not one bit whether their efforts were met with a welcome or with hostility. The Jocists* used to sing,

> *Let us march to victory.*
> *Let us march with pride,*
> *and nothing will stop us. . . .*

Those were the days when the first priest-workers used to preach Christ in public places and held the Way of the Cross in subway stations.

Attitudes have changed since that time. One no longer speaks Jesus' name out loud or in public. We whisper it into someone's ear so as not to disturb other people or to seem to want to force our own ideas on them. There are also innumerable rules to be followed today, sensibilities to be respected, stages to be observed, and so forth. Above all, how-

* The acronym for *Jeunesse Ouvrière Chrétienne* (Young Christian Workers), a very militant Catholic youth movement, active in France particularly in the forties and fifties. (*Tr.*)

ever, it is no longer a matter so much of preaching Christ
as it is of waiting for someone personally to discover his presence in others and in life. Christians must be prudent. They
must not interfere; but they must be quietly present.

Every once in a while there is friction between those who
believe in preaching and those who believe in silence. Both
sides, either nostalgic for the past or fanatical about the present, shout invectives at each other and exchange excom-
munications. "You have lost the faith," they scream. "You
understand nothing about evangelizing!"

We surely do not expect Christians to climb up onto their
filing cabinets or their air compressors and ask their fellow
workers to observe a minute of silence at three o'clock on
Good Friday afternoon. But we do not expect them to remain silent forever on the pretext that the time "is not ripe"
to speak out. And we do not expect them to neglect to preach
Jesus on the pretext that true evangelization consists essentially in living Jesus daily among men. Somewhere between
the two extremes there is a middle ground on which those
two attitudes are reconciled and synthesized. And Christians
should stand on that middle ground.

We must indeed preach Christ Jesus. We are obliged to
do so. But we are not obliged to preach, as it were, any Christ
Jesus at any given moment and in any way possible. We know
that we must individually encounter Christ in both of his
dimensions. By the same token, it is the *total* Christ whom
we must reveal to our contemporaries; the Jesus of Nazareth
who came two thousand years ago to save man and the world
through love, and the Risen Christ who today lives a mystery
of love in human history. These two approaches are indispensable and inseparable. They serve to reinforce one
another. To neglect one or the other would be to mutilate
Jesus and to distort his message.

We cannot deny that, in the past, we have been too often
content to preach Jesus—if not to "teach Jesus"—without bothering to help our brothers to meet Jesus, who is present and
active in their lives. How on earth could they believe in a
Jesus who died and rose from the dead if we did not tell
them about the Jesus who is alive today? And how could

they believe in the Living Jesus if they did not have the chance to meet him?

All this is perfectly true, of course. But, again, we must be wary of going to extremes.

Earlier in the book we asked whether there was anyone left today who was preaching Jesus Christ. We meant someone who speaks openly of the person of Jesus, without excuses. Someone who declares, "The one in whom I believe and whom I love is not Allah. It is not the Buddha, or Marx, or Lenin, or even Mao or Marcuse. It is Jesus Christ. I trust him, and I try to live my whole life, my commitment, my struggles, with him and in him. For I am convinced that they were his struggles before they were mine."

I have had the opportunity several times, in meetings and gatherings of various kinds, to hear Christians openly bear witness to their faith. They spoke openly of Jesus, ignoring the uneasiness, the prudent advice, and the disapprobation of priests and laymen who thought that it was "not the right time," that the people were "not ready," that those who heard them "would not understand." On each and every occasion, their testimony was received not only respectfully and sympathetically, but even enthusiastically. The general reaction was, "Finally, someone is talking to us about Jesus Christ."

We are very happy and proud about all the research and all the studies that have been made on the subject of evangelization. We are also happy and proud of the technical progress that has been made in catechetical science. But now we are tempted to say, "Hold it. That's enough. Let's not be so concerned with perfection in the initial stages, or we'll get bogged down at the stage of pre-evangelization, or pre-catechesis, or in the stage preparatory to pre-evangelization or pre-catechesis, or . . . You've already made straight the way of the Holy Spirit. He now knows the road, and he can read the signposts. Let's let him get to work. Let's admit that he is perfectly able to do what he is supposed to do. And let's expect to see him go off the road that we have prepared for him and cut new roads for himself. And then, let's get down to business and talk about Jesus. Let's talk loudly and clearly. People are tired of our hesitations and

our discussions and our fears, of our defensiveness and our
overcautiousness. They are ready for us to reveal a living
person to them—readier than we suspect."

What we Christians must do is speak as apostles, as witnesses. A witness is someone who personally has *seen* what
he talks about. Someone who has not *seen* almost always
develops, embroiders, and sometimes, more or less consciously, pushes his lack of knowledge under the rug of technical jargon. We are often clumsy preachers and maladroit
technicians simply because we have not *seen*—or because
we have lost the habit of seeing. And that, of course, is why
people do not listen to us. "But they will not ask his help
unless they believe in him, and they will not believe in him
unless they have heard of him, and they will not hear
of him unless they get a preacher, and they will never get a
preacher unless one is sent" (Rom. 10:14–15).

And St. Paul is not talking about "professional" preachers.
Every Christian is a preacher. And every Christian is "sent."

Under the guidance of the Holy Spirit, we must be life's
most enthusiastic pilgrims in the search for those signs of
the presence of Christ which are man's just aspirations. Working with all our strength for the integral development of
man and the universe, we should study, in the light of faith,
all the "values" of the life and of activity which are the seeds
of the Kingdom. We must expose those seeds to the sun-
light of love so that they may grow and bear fruit. We must
learn to see Jesus in those signs. We must listen when he
speaks to us. We must join him to work for the eternal plan
of his Father. Then, strengthened by our discovery, by our
encounter, by our unity, we will become witnesses to our
brothers that Jesus Christ, who came down on earth two
thousand years ago, is still here today, mysteriously living
in our lives and in theirs.

It is in being thus involved with all men—be they indifferent, unbelievers, or believers in another faith—that we
will be enabled, not to "bring God" to them (for God is
already there, in their lives; and, moreover, we do not own
God), but to reveal God to them. It is not enough that men
of good will work for their brothers; not enough that individ-

uals and groups be transformed by that work. They must know of that transformation. They must discover, bit by bit, that it is the result of a force that is beyond them because it is the strength of Love, of Jesus Christ.

That is why Christians must not be content with joining Christ, in his Spirit, to work with him on behalf of mankind individually and collectively. We must go beyond even that. We must go to that faint trace of revelation that is in the heart of every man. And we can go there only by paying the strictest attention to what we see in other persons and in events. Then we will be witnesses, because we shall have *seen*. By our attitude, by a gesture, a word, a comment, we will be able to make known to our brothers that which we live deep within us: a mysterious communication with Jesus Christ in all our work for the benefit of man.

Let us not be too willing to allow Jesus to live incognito in the hearts of so many men. Possibly it is a lack of faith that makes us willing often to undertake a project in common with men of good faith, but unwilling to carry our mission through to its logical conclusion—that is, to reveal Jesus Christ. Certainly, Christ is well able to reveal himself within a man's heart. But he has chosen to make use of us in order that he may become known.

Every Christian is born in order to reveal Love and the name of Love. If we love Jesus Christ, we cannot allow him to remain hidden from the eyes of men. We must reveal him, openly and fearlessly, so that all men may live of him and in the light of his presence.

Chapter Ten

TO LIVE JESUS CHRIST

We must encounter Jesus of Nazareth, not only to contemplate him but also to live him. And he waits for us in the Gospel, the purpose of which is to unite us to Jesus.

It is a matter of either believing or not believing that God has spoken to us. If we believe that "At various times in the past and in various different ways, God spoke to our ancestors through the prophets; but in our own time, the last days, he has spoken to us through his Son" (Heb. 1:1–2); if we believe that Jesus Christ, in revealing the Father and his infinite love, expressed himself by means of a human life and in human words; if we believe that four of his Apostles, guided by the Holy Spirit, recorded the essential parts of his message for the instruction, and liturgical and missionary participation, of the first Christian communities; and if we believe, finally, that through the Gospels, in Jesus Christ, God not only spoke to the first Christians but also continues to speak to man in any era—if we believe all this and we do not regularly have recourse to the Gospel, then we are totally without understanding and we cannot call ourselves Christians. That is, we cannot say that we are "of Christ."

It is possible that we have lost the habit of making free use of the Gospel. Perhaps we have explained the Gospel so much, written so many commentaries, studied it so scientifically, "utilized" it so often to illustrate and explain and defend

our theses, searched it so assiduously to find a formula for
Christian life, and discussed it so much that we can no longer
communicate with it.

I do not mean to denigrate the importance of scientific
studies of the Gospel. What we must do, however, in inte-
grating the results of such studies into our knowledge is to
keep in mind, as we read the Gospel, the rich but simple
attitude of a lover who reads a letter from his beloved. For
such a man, words are only an intermediary. That which
the eyes of his body, and even those of his mind, cannot reveal, is revealed by the eyes of the heart.

We must approach the Gospel "religiously"; that is, with
eyes that are not of our body. We must use the eyes of our
minds, certainly. But we must also use the eyes of faith. In
the Gospel, it is Jesus who appears before me, and speaks
to me. I must communicate with his Word just as, in the
Eucharist, I communicate with his Body. The Holy Spirit,
who guided the Apostles when they were writing the Gospel,
guides us today when we read what they wrote so that we
may live from it.

I mentioned in another work the comment of a young
girl who, in familiarizing herself with the Gospel, had discovered the perfect way to approach the Word of Christ: "I
get up a half hour early every day to read what Jesus has to
say about that day. . . . During the day, at work, I often
think of what Jesus said that morning."

Man, through love, goes freely before God, and God appears freely before him. If a man is faithful to that extraordinary meeting, he will gradually be changed—like a man who
sunbathes every day. Jesus will say to him, "I shall not call
you servants any more, because a servant does not know his
master's business; I call you friends, because I have made
known to you everything I have learnt from my Father"
(John 15:15).

I am convinced that Christians are too willing to give up
personal contact with the Gospel. As we abandon it, we find
ourselves loudly demanding from man what we did not dare
ask of the Man-God. We cannot but be impressed and ap-
palled by those millions of Chinese who are never without
their little "red book," who read it daily in order to under-

stand the thought of their idol, and who study Mao's maxims. And let's not say that all this is carefully staged. Is it possible that Christians believe less in Christ than the Chinese do in Mao Tse-tung?

"Lord, who shall we go to? You have the message of eternal life" (John 6:68–69).

An artist who stands studying a painting understands more about it than does a layman. He discovers harmony, emotion, and thought beneath the lines, forms, and colors. Through these things, the artist goes beyond an ordinary man in his reaction.

The lover who receives a dried flower in a letter from his beloved goes far beyond the few desiccated petals. He sees "beyond." Through the flower, which is a symbol, and because of it, he is united to a person, a love. He communes with that love.

The Christian, too, sees things. In the face of mankind, of history, and of the world, he sees further than other men. Where other men see only the surface of beings, things, and events, the Christian perceives them as they are, in their "inner dimension."

If the Christian sees more deeply, it is because he has a special eye, a sort of sixth sense—which comes to him as a result of faith.

The real "new man," whom our non-believing brothers dream of "creating," is the Christian. The Christian is re-created in Christ. Jesus said to Nicodemus, "I tell you most solemnly, unless a man is born from above, he cannot see the kingdom of God" (John 3:3); and St. Paul adds, "For anyone who is in Christ, there is a new creation" (II Cor. 5:17).

We say of lovers that they are in each other's heart. Jesus has all men in his heart. In him, because of the Redemption, man has assisted at the death of non-love and of a merely human life. In him, man has been raised up: "Whoever listens to my words, and believes in the one who sent me, has eternal life" (John 5:24).

The Christian is a man who, believing in Christ, is reborn in him to Love and to a "new life"—to divine life: "You too must consider yourselves to be dead to sin but alive for God

in Christ Jesus" (Rom. 6:11). He has become a true child of
the Father, and he must behave as such. He has the power
to do so, and henceforth he can hope as the Son hopes, love
as the Son loves, and see as the Son sees.

The Christian shares in Christ's prophetic gift. A prophet
is not someone who predicts the future, but someone who
"sees"—that is, a man who is able to read events in the light
of God. A prophet lives in the midst of life. He lives the life
of his brothers. But he is able to discover the essential meaning of that life, and he announces it to his brothers who do
not "see." And Christ, of course, is the prophet par excellence,
for he has seen all things.

What the world needs is Christians who are prophets. And
it needs many of them, and perfectly lucid ones. Men today
no longer know why they are alive, and Christians have too
often offered them life-styles rather than reasons for life.
Prophets who "see" in Christ will rediscover, for themselves
and their brothers, the meaning of life. They will save history!

No man can become a prophet simply by wishing to be
one. There are some people today who believe, and say, that
they are prophets. But too often they proclaim only what
they *think*, and not what they have *seen*. The true prophet
is a man who, within the framework of the community of
the Church, consents to die to himself in his way of "seeing
things" and to embrace God's way of seeing things. To become a prophet involves arduous and lengthy training, and
a series of painful purifications.

We must learn to *see*. The spiritual value of our life depends, first of all, on how well we see, on our "degree of vision." Even on earth, we can develop that vision to a fantastic
degree. Later, if we are loyal, we will see God face to face,
"as he really is": "We are already the children of God but
what we are to be in the future has not yet been revealed;
all we know is, that when it is revealed we shall be like him
because we shall see him as he really is" (I John 3:2). But on
earth we must learn to see the Living Christ in people, in
human aspirations, in activity, and in events. The whole of
life must be seen and lived in the light of faith: "The life I

now live in this body I live in faith: faith in the Son of God who loved me" (Gal. 2:20).

Militant Christians of Catholic Action, above all, have taught us to look at our lives through the eyes of the new man. They have trained us in the confrontation of Jesus in the Gospel. They have taught us how to listen for Jesus' words through all the circumstances of our life. And they have shown us how to progress from a religious interpretation of events to an involvement in action for the sake of our brothers. The whole of this approach is called a "review of life." And many Christians—laymen, priests, and religious—have discovered the enormous benefits which it entails.

This "review of life" can be badly understood and badly lived. It must not become a "technique" for analyzing situations and attitudes, or a measure of the human effectiveness of activity, or a form of intellectual gymnastics which proceeds from fixed guidelines to the dissection of an event. Even within the Catholic Action movement, there were some who did not avoid such temptations—as many people, particularly foreigners, were quick to point out. People within the movement wanted to demonstrate the "review of life," and observers merely smiled, or reacted violently to what they regarded as a very complicated and specifically French method which, when carried to an extreme, was a distortion of our vaunted Cartesian spirit. In this case, as in others, technique overpowered mystique. Certainly, the "review of life" is a remarkable discovery which has affected our time more than we perhaps realize. Many men have made use of it in many fields, as a pedagogical, psychological, or sociological method. But for the Christian it is and must remain a religious approach. It is up to those movements which use it in common to see that their members do not distort it.

It is always easier to perfect the form of a religious approach than to live its spirit. Those who become discouraged and abandon the enterprise, however, will lose a great deal with respect to the depth of their spiritual commitment and to the authentic evangelization of their milieux.

For our part, what we would like to do is emphasize the review of one's personal life as a spiritual approach. (We would say "as a spiritual exercise"; but that term, through overuse, has lost much of its meaning.) I am absolutely convinced that, along with the reading of the Gospel as described above, the review of one's personal life should be at the center of the spiritual life of a modern Christian.

We all know how difficult it is to be silent while another man is speaking. It is even harder to be silent so that we may hear God's voice. Nonetheless, every day we should stop all activity for a while and look back over the events of the day as a whole. We should pick out a particular moment, or event, of that day, and ask ourselves questions like these about it: What does Jesus want to tell me by means of that event? What does Jesus expect of me in this situation, with those persons, in those circumstances? What response will I make to Jesus?

I do not mean that we should indulge ourselves in an elaborate reasoning process, but that we should withdraw into ourselves in an attitude of simple faith: "Jesus Christ is here, mysteriously present. I know it, because he has said that he will be with us always, even to the end of time. He is waiting for me, like a friend: 'I shall not call you servants any more . . . I call you friends.' With him, I can discover and realize the Father's plan of love: 'My food and drink is to do the will of my Father.'"

We must not be afraid of making mistakes. The Holy Spirit accompanies us and guides us in our daily pilgrimage to Christ, and we must ask him to do so. In the review of life, prayer and contemplation should play a greater part than the intellectual analysis of situations.

If we are faithful in our meetings with Christ in daily events, little by little he will enlighten us and we will see more clearly. For Christ is less hidden than we think. Our eyes are simply not accustomed to looking at him through the darkness of our senses. Jesus Christ calls us. He transforms us, and the suffering involved in that progressive purification certifies to the authenticity of our approach.

Those who, judging from externals, think that the review of life is an "easy way" are very much mistaken. After the exhilaration of the encounter, one learns very quickly that nothing is more demanding than obedience to Christ in daily life. In order to achieve union with him, we must gradually renounce our own plans and desires and replace them with the Father's plan which is realized in Jesus Christ. Initially, the two points of view are far from conforming to one another. But, after our death-to-ourselves there is the resurrection. And anyone who is willing to risk each day of his life for Christ—whatever that life may be—will enter into peace and joy.

Men with much experience say that "life is the best teacher." What they say is true; more true than they know. Jesus teaches us and transforms us in life and through life by bringing us to the concrete, historical realization of his mystery of love. We have only to respond freely to the Savior's daily invitation. The "exercise" which we call the review of one's personal life can help us. It can show us how to bind together ever more tightly the spiritual and the temporal. It can teach us how to live a life, and a Christian life, transfigured by love—that is, how to be simultaneously totally present to Jesus Christ, and totally present to life.

We think it is a mistake to believe that God is silent. He speaks. But often man does not answer. Nonetheless, man needs contact with God—which is to say that he needs prayer —because he was made by God and for God. Without that contact, man undergoes a sort of progressive spiritual asphyxiation. He is like a fish out of water. He becomes a spiritual orphan, and he begins to look around for compensations. The man who does not pray, or who no longer prays (if he once knew God), looks for, or invents, something outside of himself which he can make into an idol, a god-substitute, for him to enter into contact with. The worst thing that can happen is for man to choose himself as his own idol—his body, his emotions, his ideas. Then he has only himself to talk to. He is isolated. And that is what hell is.

There is another sort of tragedy that is not uncommon in today's world. It is the tragedy of men whose inability to go out of themselves, to relate to others and to an Other, is such that it constitutes a psychological disorder. It is a "mental illness." And the psychologists tell us that *all* mental illnesses are the result of difficulties in relating to others. Such men, of course, are not responsible, since they are ill. Nonetheless, they are no longer men. They have lost their human nature. And that is the tragedy of it all, not only for those affected but for all mankind. For all men are responsible. We have built a society that destroys its members. We have corrupted interpersonal relations at all levels by ridiculing and debasing love. And we have neglected to connect life and man to God. Outside of this latter, essential relationship, there can be no real relationship of love between men. Without it, no society, regardless of how "just" its structures may be, can better its members.

Unless we are very careful, we will atrophy man by cutting him off from his source. And this spiritual underdevelopment will not be the least of the collective sins of mankind at a time when man's growing awareness and his control over the world require rather a spiritual overdevelopment.

Unless we pray, and unless we pray more than did the men who preceded us, then we shall destroy ourselves.

It is not easy to pray. What seems to bother modern man about prayer is that praying is "talking in a vacuum." It is true that, in order to assert the transcendence of God, we have often placed him beyond and above life, in heaven. And then we asked man, when speaking to God, to detach himself from earth and to raise his eyes to heaven. Men tried to do it. And many men exhausted themselves trying. And then they gave it up, because they could not *see* the God to whom they were speaking, and because they could not hear his answer. Everything was dark and silent.

By disincarnating God we have disincarnated prayer. Here, again, we are acting as though Jesus Christ had never come. Certainly, we must pray "Our Father, who art in heaven"; but only, so to speak, after we have met Jesus Christ. For it is Jesus who reveals the Father to us and leads us to him. It is Jesus who teaches us to speak to the Father. And outside of Christ we will never find the road to God.

No one, as Jesus said, has ever seen the Father. But men have seen Jesus Christ, touched him, heard him speak. Like them, we can meet him, listen to him, and answer him.

Jesus Christ is alive among us. He speaks. He opens the dialogue. It is up to man to answer. And to pray is above all to answer God, who speaks to man through Christ, who lives today.

God speaks to us in the Bible, and especially in the Gospel. He also speaks to us in life, in events.* After what we have learned about reading the Gospel and about the review of one's personal life, it is easy to understand why those approaches should determine the two dimensions of our prayer.

In one section of France, when young people begin to court they are said to be "talking to one another." Once more, folk wisdom has gone to the heart of the matter. True love begins with mutual knowledge, and the latter can be the result of conversation. We must come to know Jesus of Nazareth by talking with him, and it is through the Gospel that we will succeed.

(I wonder why it is that when we talk about prayer, we almost immediately think about asking God for something. It is as though we want to get into God's good graces, just as we try to establish well-placed "contacts" in the world, so that our will may be done on earth.)

Love is freely given and freely taken. It is an exchange. Each of the lovers reveals himself to the other, and the two are thus united. After that, they can no longer refuse anything to one another. Similarly, Jesus makes himself known in the Gospel. He reveals the depths of his soul. Prayer is a response to that revelation, no more and no less. It is a conversation with Jesus, a request for explanations, an expression of admiration and gratitude. It is also an explanation of oneself by telling of one's own life and comparing it to that of Jesus.

When friends no longer speak to each other, their friendship weakens and dies. Sometimes one of them, still faithful, continues to speak to his friend, but without getting any answer. Then there is indifference, or a breaking off of relations: "I don't talk to him any more."

There are many Christians who don't talk to Jesus any

---

* I certainly do not intend here to deemphasize the real presence of Christ in the Eucharist. My intention here is to emphasize, for the sake of those who complain of "Jesus' silence," that Jesus speaks to us in the Gospel and in life, and that, moreover, he waits for our answer.

more, even though Jesus continues to talk to them through the Gospel. This is a senseless tragedy. If we have God for a friend, we should never let that friendship die.

Jesus Christ also speaks to us through events. We've already said that, except in the case of a special vocation, the ordinary meeting place between Christ and man is life. The second dimension of prayer, therefore, is man's dialogue with Christ in life.

Hopefully, it is now clear that not only does Christ take an interest in each instant of man's life, but he also participates in it. He must gather all things to himself in love, and he can do so only to the extent that we ourselves are present in and consent to that life and himself. Jesus Christ will not take our lives if we do not give them to him. And, from that point, we should be in continual dialogue with Christ. On the one hand, we must ask him to rectify and purify our lives; and, on the other, we must offer our lives to him so that he may permeate them and live them with us. All our lives, therefore, must become a prayer. And, for that, we must offer them in their totality. And we must also be faithful to our meetings with Christ at particular moments. The practice of reviewing our personal lives offers the opportunity to do this. Beginning from the event we choose, and scrutinizing that event in the light of faith under the guidance of the Holy Spirit, we are able to engage in conversation with Christ.

True friends feel the need from time to time to talk together. We too must stop occasionally and talk to Jesus. We must make the difficult offering of a part of our time.

Soon, however, we will discover that there are problems. We have said that, in order to hear God, we must be silent. But often it is psychologically impossible for modern man to be silent. Anyone who stops today for a moment of prayer is immediately overwhelmed by the "noise" of daily preoccupations, of his desires, failures, thoughts, and dreams. We must not lose heart. On the contrary, we should be glad, for through those difficulties Jesus teaches us what sort of prayer we must pray today.

I hope that I will be permitted to digress a moment here to mention the great, and unexpected, success of an earlier book of mine entitled *Prayer,* which has sold over a million and a half copies the world over. I mention it not out of vanity—which would be absurd—but to make a point. The book is a collection of very simple prayers drawn from life. And, for that reason, it answered a need felt, apparently, by an enormous number of Christians. These Christians wanted not only to present themselves to God without subtracting themselves from life, but also to integrate their lives totally into their prayers. The letters I received confirmed what I suspected, that people were torn between the deep desire to achieve that integration and the advice they had always received to the effect that they must "forget your worries, empty your mind," etc. This advice had been, in effect, to rid themselves of their bodies, of their human condition and vocation, and to behave like angels. Many readers were kind enough to write that they had been "liberated" from that mentality.

Why indeed should a man be asked to leave his life at the door when he prays? The noise within us when we try to spend a moment with God is the irruption of life into our field of consciousness. When we pray, all the thoughts that come, even the most apparently irrelevant ones, are not "distractions" designed to tear us away from God; they are invitations to put God into our lives and our lives into God. Prayer must never become a refuge into which we flee in order to escape from life. Every Christian, when he prays, is an ambassador from the whole world, and particularly of the people with whom he is associated and of the groups to which he belongs. He holds in his hands, so to speak, the record of his own life and of his brothers' lives in order to explain it to God. We should not try, therefore, to avoid "distractions." We should embrace them, for they are life, and offer them to God.

Naturally, it is difficult to remove from one's mind the things that are most important to us. And those things are precisely what we should offer to the Father through Jesus Christ—to ask his forgiveness, or to thank him, or to ask his help; but above all to ask that this person, this event, this particle of life not be diverted from its purpose but that it develop perfectly in Jesus Christ according to the will of the Father.

Let's not think for a moment that we are talking about a kind of prayer that consists in "giving up," a kind of prayer that is easy because it corresponds to the taste of modern man. Prayer is never easy, for it is always an attempt to go out of oneself in the presence of God. What we must do instead of constantly struggling to suppress things is to struggle constantly to offer things.

The Christian who is faithful to prayer should not expect to be freed from life's cares and tribulations—for that would be a failure. But, little by little, his various preoccupations will flow into a unified whole which, more and more spontaneously, will be directed toward God in Jesus Christ. The man who prays will never find any real vacuum or emptiness, nor will he find it necessary to resort to a kind of *idée fixe:* "I am trying to *fix* my mind on God"—which is a rather dangerous psychological game.† In the wake of life's tumult and disorder, there will eventually come a veritable procession of all of life—of persons whom he meets, of his milieu, of the world—on pilgrimage toward God in Jesus Christ. And Christ, with the loving collaboration of free man, will "bring everything together . . . everything in the heavens and everything on earth."

Later, much later, after a long period of perseverance and faithfulness which constitutes a necessary and preliminary stage, certain Christians will be able to appear before God in a state of profound interior silence. That state will not be the result of a suppression, or a surrender or a flight from life. Rather, it will be the just reward of those Christians who will have acquired the habit of leaving everything in Jesus' hands—of living all things in him as their lives unfold.

And then, like lovers who, after a day of constant sharing and communion, can spend a night in silence, without a sound, in tender companionship, these Christians, having forgotten nothing of life but having brought and given it all to Christ, will be able to give themselves—in silence.

† Human effort can do little to make us "concentrate" on God. We must depend on God to captivate us to the extent that all our faculties are unified and our perception is sharpened.

Contemplation, like prayer, is not the special property of a certain category of Christians, of spiritual aristocrats. It belongs to everyone. Anyone who truly loves can achieve contemplation.

True love, as it develops, achieves a certain economy of words and gestures. When one reaches the stage where a mere look suffices, then one has reached contemplation. To contemplate God is to look at him and love him. This attitude, however, simple as it is, is the end result of a process. To try to attain silence too quickly is dangerous, for silence, although it can serve to convey a fullness of love which no word or gesture can contain, can also serve to interrupt a conversation.

Some Christians are called by God to retire, partially or wholly, from the world in order to abandon themselves to contemplation. Modern man has a great deal of difficulty in understanding that kind of vocation; for men tend to think in terms of efficacity, while love operates at the level of generosity. A man, for example, on certain nights wants the company of his wife. "Leave your work," he says, "and come sit here next to me." He wants his wife close to him, *inactive* for his sake; for the essence of love is not to *do* something for the loved one, but to *be* there for him. Thus, some lives consist almost entirely in being in the presence of God, withdrawn from all other beings. And that is the summit of love.

Contemplation is a "gazing of the heart" in the light of faith. Every Christian, by virtue of his baptism, is able to contemplate God and to perceive his presence in life beyond sensible phenomena. We have already said that the Christian is a man who *sees*. He should make use of that ability to work toward the perfection of love. That is an obligation for the Christian; and it is an absolute necessity in the modern world. The more the world develops, the more will it have need of contemplatives in its midst. The more man becomes technologically oriented, the more he has a need to become a worshiper. It is difficult, and it will become more difficult, to recognize the "inner dimension" of creation as the universe passes progressively from the hands of God into those of man.

When I walk in the city, I notice there is hardly a single thing that man has not transformed in accordance with God's command. I see no earth; everything is covered with concrete. I see a few trees, rather spindly, standing humbly alongside the buildings that tower over them. If I look upward, I can see only a small slice of the sky. But I see a modern city, crowned by daring architecture; I see streets filled with men and automobiles, and buildings like beehives filled with busy people. I see factories, and I can sense the workers taking raw material, working with it, transforming it, making something of it by putting something of themselves into it. I see a world abuilding. I see man, the builder and the planner.

But nowhere do I see God.

It is true that God seems to be retiring, now that his children are grown. He is leaving them the initiative, the responsibility, and the work of construction. Some Christians are shocked. They think God is making a mistake in trusting man.

We cannot deny that secularization is taking place. It is a fact. Nonetheless, we must not look at it as sociologists, but as Christians. Man's power of creation is one of the most beautiful proofs of God's love for his creature. If man is taking over the universe, it is because God has willed it to be so. Now that man is about to succeed, now that he is beginning to live that "temporal autonomy" that he had so much trouble in conceiving, let us not call the realization of the Father's plan into question. But, by the same token, we must keep in mind the nature of that plan. It is very easy to confuse the autonomy of the temporal and spiritual orders with the separation of the two. It has been the whole purpose of this book to show that the spiritual order is not foreign to the temporal order, that it is not "alongside" it, but within it; distinct from it, but indissolubly bound to it by the will of God and by the ministry of the incarnate and redeeming Christ.

Many of the symbols of the past are, today, inappropriate to reveal the presence of the Living God in a secularized world. We must find new signs that will be intelligible to the men of our time. Man needs such signs. And the most accurate and effective sign will be that of the Christian who is committed to and involved in the construction of the world, and who is, at the same time, sustained by contemplation in the midst of life.

He will be the living symbol, and, as we have said, the prophet, of the Mystery of Jesus Christ.

To sum up, we may say that the Mystery of Christ covers the whole of the life of man, of mankind, and of the universe —yesterday, today, and tomorrow. It is the mystery of the Creation, the Incarnation, the Redemption, and the Resurrection. It is a story, or a history, of love; and there is nothing and no one who is not a part of it.

To be a Christian is not only to believe in Jesus Christ, but also to be *of* Christ, of the total Christ; that is, to belong to Christ who today is living the mystery of his love. It is to enter consciously into that mystery, to commit ourselves, personally and collectively, as a people and a Church, to the great advantage of creation, incarnation, redemption, and resurrection which is the realization of the Father's eternal plan. It is to work for the real development of man, mankind, and the universe.

To be thus committed is to commit one's life to and with the people who live around us, in our natural societies, in our social milieux, in our groups, structures, events, and history. It is to become inwardly involved, so that we may live the total reality of life and of what lies beyond life.

To become involved, however, one must love the world. No one can accomplish anything except by loving, and by loving passionately. God "so loved the world that he sent his Son." It is a look of love that is at the source of the redemptive Incarnation of Jesus Christ. It is a look of love which must be at the source of our commitment as Christians. Christians today must look at man, life, history, and the universe in the way that God looks at them.

If we love the world passionately, we will accept it as it is today, with its strengths and its weaknesses. We must not fear it, or be disappointed in it, or cry over it, but have confidence in it. Even if we can think of good reasons to be fearful, we should put those things out of our minds. We do not make a fire by stirring up ashes, but by finding the burning coal underneath and adding fuel to it. From that tiny beginning, a conflagration springs.

There is a fire at the heart of the world. Life is there, and it cannot die. That life is the life of the Risen Christ. Many men believe in God. Fewer believe in Christ. And fewer still believe in the Christ who is alive today. In order to be committed, we must indeed love the world. But we must also believe in Jesus Christ who is present in the world.

This attitude of faith is indispensable for Christians of our time. It is that attitude which enables us to understand, as we have explained, that there are not two times in life, a time when we live our human life as humans and look at God only indirectly; and a time when, on our knees, we offer to the Father our work, our leisure, our struggles, suffering, and joy. And it is that attitude which enables us also to understand that if the temporal and spiritual orders are different, they are nonetheless united in Jesus Christ and must be reunited by the mind, the heart, and the hands of Christians.

This attitude of faith will save modern man by giving a meaning to his life and his struggles, to man's painful upward climb, by finally freeing him from the necessity to fight or suffer or be happy for no purpose. Either our life has no meaning, goes nowhere, and is absurd in all of its parts; or else it is a unique moment in that great adventure of love which is the Mystery of Christ, and then it is sacred, and each of its moments carries within it the weight of eternity.

It is this attitude of faith, and the commitment which results from it, that will save the modern world. The Christian will no longer be absent from the world. He will not be content to stand aside and let it be built without him. He will be present, and he will join with Jesus to live, with him and in him, the demanding but exhilarating adventure of life—of that whole life which is the Christian life; that is, the life of Christ.

Man, life, and the world, daily permeated by the conquering love of Christ, taken by Christ and offered by him to the Father, will prosper. From this day, they will be transfigured. And tomorrow, they will be restored to life.